About the

Kate Hardy has been a bookw… When she isn't writing, Kate e… music, ballet and the gym. She … …sband, student children and their spaniel … …ich, England. You can contact her via her website: katehardy.com

Jessica Matthews grew up on a farm in western Kansas where reading was her favourite pastime. Eventually, romances and adventure stories gave way to science textbooks and research papers as she became a medical technologist, but her love for microscopes and test tubes didn't diminish her passion for storytelling. Having her first book accepted for publication was a dream come true, and now she has written thirty books for Mills & Boon.

Carol Marinelli recently filled in a form asking for her job title. Thrilled to be able to put down her answer, she put writer. Then it asked what Carol did for relaxation and she put down the truth – writing. The third question asked for her hobbies. Well, not wanting to look obsessed she crossed the fingers on her hand and answered swimming but, given that the chlorine in the pool does terrible things to her highlights – I'm sure you can guess the real answer.

The Surgeon Collection

The Surgeon's Heart

KATE HARDY

JESSICA MATTHEWS

CAROL MARINELLI

MILLS & BOON

First Published in Great Britain 2023
by Mills & Boon, an imprint of HarperCollins*Publishers* Ltd,
1 London Bridge Street, London, SE1 9GF

www.harpercollins.co.uk

HarperCollins*Publishers*
Macken House, 39/40 Mayor Street Upper,
Dublin 1, D01 C9W8, Ireland

The Surgeon's Heart © 2023 Harlequin Enterprises ULC.

Heart Surgeon, Prince...Husband! © 2019 Pamela Brooks
Unlocking the Surgeon's Heart © 2012 Jessica Matthews
Seduced by the Heart Surgeon © 2016 Harlequin Enterprises ULC.

Special thanks and acknowledgement are given to Carol Marinelli for her contribution to *The Hollywood Hills Clinic* series

ISBN: 978-0-263-31954-5

HEART SURGEON, PRINCE...HUSBAND!

KATE HARDY

To Sheila Crighton, a wonderful friend,
with love and thanks for the lightbulb.

CHAPTER ONE

'LUCIANO BIANCHI, THE new heart surgeon, is starting today,' Sanjay, the head of the cardiac unit, told Kelly. 'Can I ask you to look after him for me this morning—take him round the department, show him where the canteen is and introduce him to everyone? I'd do it myself, but I've got meetings with suits.' He rolled his eyes. 'All day.'

'Oh, the joy of budgets,' Kelly said, sympathising with her boss. 'Of course I'll show him around.'

'Wonderful. Thank you.' Sanjay patted her arm.

Rumours had already flown around the hospital. Luciano Bianchi wasn't just a cardiothoracic surgeon; he was a *prince*. His father was the King of Bordimiglia, a small Mediterranean country on the border between Italy and France. Apparently he'd trained in London and worked for some years at the Royal Hampstead Free Hospital; now one of the surgeons here was retiring, Luc was moving to Muswell Hill Memorial Hospital.

Everyone had looked him up on the Internet, of course; it was hard to reconcile the idea of an upper-class playboy who didn't take life too seriously with a man who'd spent years training to be a heart surgeon. So who was Luciano Bianchi—and would he be part of the team or would he be a royal pain in the backside?

From the photographs, he was definitely nice-looking enough to make all the women in the department sigh and speculate why he hadn't been snapped up years ago. Tall, with dark hair and dark eyes, Luciano looked more like a model for a high-end fragrance ad than a surgeon. But he didn't seem to date that much—or, at least, there weren't loads of paparazzi pictures of him with a princess or the daughter of some wealthy industrialist on his arm, on their way to some high society party or movie premiere. It looked as if he put his job before his position in society, which boded well for life at the hospital.

Kelly wasn't one for gossip, but one rumour that had caught her attention involved his work. He was allegedly going to set up a trial for a new surgical procedure to help patients suffering from hypertrophic cardiomyopathy— a condition where the muscular wall of the heart thickened and made the heart stiff, making it harder to pump blood around the body.

It was too late for a trial to help Simon; but it wasn't too late to help his younger brother Jake or Jake's daughter Summer.

Kelly would never forgive herself for the fact that she hadn't picked up on her late husband's heart condition. How could a trained cardiologist have missed something that massive? Since then, she knew she'd become a workaholic—but she was determined that nobody's symptoms would go unrecognised on her watch. She didn't want other families to have to go through what her family had been through. And getting Jake and Summer onto the trial might help to blunt the edges of her guilt. If she explained the situation to Luciano Bianchi, then maybe she could persuade him to at least consider Jake and Summer as candidates for his trial.

She kept an eye on the reception area from the office

where she was catching up with paperwork, and twenty minutes later Luciano Bianchi walked through the doors. She pushed her chair back and went out into the reception area to greet him. 'Mr Bianchi?'

He turned to look at her. 'Yes.'

Oh, help. Maybe she should have called him 'Your Highness'. But he was here in his capacity as a surgeon, not as a prince, so she'd used the convention that surgeons were called 'Mr' rather than 'Dr'. She summoned up her best smile. 'I'm Kelly Phillips, one of the cardiologists,' she introduced herself. 'Sanjay is stuck in meetings all day, so he's given me a reprieve from paperwork to show you round and introduce you to everyone. And, if you don't have any other plans, to take you to the canteen for lunch.'

Luc was used to people judging him first as a prince and secondly as a doctor, but maybe at last his reputation at work was starting to take precedence, because Kelly Phillips was definitely treating him as a surgeon and a colleague. He really liked the fact that she'd called him 'Mr Bianchi' rather than 'Prince Luciano'. And, OK, there was an unobtrusive bodyguard with him, because of who he was, but his security detail was discreet. Luc didn't want to be treated any differently from the other staff on the team. He was here to save lives, just like they were. A doctor first and a prince second: and he thought he could serve his country far better with his medical skills than by doing the job he'd been born to do but his older sister would do so much better.

'Thank you. That would be good,' he said, holding out his hand to shake hers. 'Nice to meet you, Kelly. I'm Luc.'

'Nice to meet you, too, Luc. Welcome to the department.'

She shook his hand, and it felt as if he'd been galvanised. He really hadn't expected to react so strongly to her, with his skin actually tingling at the contact with hers.

Then he shook himself.

Even if she wasn't already involved with someone, Luc had no intention of letting his relationship with Kelly Phillips become anything other than professional. Until the situation with his father was resolved, it wouldn't be fair to start dating anyone. He'd already learned the hard way that women who dated the prince didn't want to date the doctor, and vice versa. The two sides of his life sat uneasily together, and all his relationships seemed to fall through the fault line.

'Thanks for the warm welcome,' he said.

'It's a Muswell Hill Memorial Hospital tradition. First stop, staff kitchen,' she said. 'Though I'm afraid it's instant coffee and a kettle, here, rather than a posh coffee machine.'

Uh-oh. It sounded as if she was starting to see the prince rather than the surgeon. 'Which makes it much easier to add cold water so you can drink the lot down in one,' he said with a smile. 'Between the operating theatre, seeing my patients and drowning in paperwork, I'll take my caffeine any way I can get it. Instant's fine.'

She looked relieved at the reminder that he was just like any other doctor. 'And there's a treat shelf. Patients and their families are always bringing in biscuits or cake for us.'

'And then they wince and apologise for buying something so unhealthy, given that half of our patients have been given dietary advice to cut back on sugar and fat?' Luc asked with a smile.

'I suppose it's like taking a big tin of chocolates to a

gym at Christmas,' she said with a grin. 'Though we're just as grateful for the goodies as the personal trainers are.'

Because sometimes, after a rough shift, when you'd tried everything and it still wasn't enough to save your patient, cake and a team hug were the only things that could help stop you falling into a black hole. However much professional detachment you had, losing a patient was always grim. 'Yes,' he said softly.

'I assume you've already been given your computer login?' she asked. 'If not, I'll ask Mandy to chase it up for you. She's officially Sanjay's secretary, but she keeps an eye out for the rest of us. She knows everyone and everything, so she's the fount of all knowledge, and we keep her in flowers because she keeps us all sane.'

'I'll remember that,' he said. 'Yes, thanks, I've got my login, my staff ID and my lanyard.'

'Pick up your locker key from Mandy, and you're good to go.' She smiled at him again. And he was going to have to ignore the way his pulse rate kicked up a notch when she smiled.

The more he heard, the more he liked the sound of his new department. And all his new colleagues turned out to be as warm and friendly as Kelly, instantly accepting him as one of them rather than being slightly suspicious of Prince Luciano's motives For working in a hospital rather than a palace.

'I think we're both due in clinic now,' Kelly said when she'd finished introducing him to everyone, 'but I'll meet you back here in Reception at one for lunch. Patients permitting.'

'Of course,' he said. 'Thank you for showing me round.'

* * *

That handshake had thrown her.

Ever since Simon's death, Kelly had kept all her relationships strictly platonic, and she hadn't so much as looked at another man; she barely joined in with conversations in the staff kitchen about the latest gorgeous movie star. It was partly because she wasn't ready to move on; and partly because the whole idea of starting over again with someone, falling deeply in love with them and then risking losing them, was too much for her.

The sensible side of her knew that what had happened with Simon was rare—a life-threatening genetic condition that usually showed symptoms, but in his case it hadn't. The chances of dating another man with hypertrophic cardiomyopathy were small; the chances of dating another man with HCM who had absolutely no symptoms of chest pain, light-headedness or breathlessness were even smaller. So minuscule as to be absolutely unlikely.

But.

She could still remember the numbness and shock she'd felt when she'd taken that phone call, two years before. The way her life had imploded, as if in slow motion; she could see it happening but could do nothing to stop it. The sheer disbelief that her husband—the man who cycled to work every day, did a five-kilometre run every Sunday morning and loved playing ball with their nephews in the park—had collapsed and just died. They hadn't even had the chance to say goodbye; and it was her big regret that they'd waited to start trying for a family. Simon was a brilliant uncle and he would've been a great dad. He'd just never had the chance.

For the last six months, Kelly had been fending off well-intentioned matchmaking by her family and friends, urging her to go out on a date and have fun, because

Simon wouldn't have wanted her to be on her own for the rest of her life; he would have wanted her to be loved. She knew that; just as, if she'd been the one to die, she would have wanted Simon to find someone to share his life with and love him as much as she had.

But she just wasn't ready to move on. She couldn't forgive herself for not picking up on his HCM. She was a cardiologist; she'd treated quite a few people with Simon's condition and she knew all the symptoms. There must have been something she'd missed. Something she should have spotted. She'd let the love of her life down in the worst possible way. And she wasn't going to let any of her patients down.

She blew out a breath. And it was ridiculous to let Luciano Bianchi throw her. Absolutely nothing could happen between them. OK, so he seemed to be dedicated to his career; but even though he didn't have the lifestyle of a ruler-to-be, that was exactly what he was. The heir to the kingdom of Bordimiglia. No way would he be allowed to get involved with anyone who didn't have a single drop of blue blood in her veins. He'd end up marrying a princess for dynastic reasons. His relationship with her was strictly business. And that little throb of awareness when his skin had touched hers—well, she was just going to ignore it.

She managed to focus on her patients for that morning's clinic; and Luc's clinic clearly ran on time as he was waiting for her in the reception area at one o'clock.

'Hi. How was your first morning?' she asked brightly.

'Fine, thanks. We have a good team,' he said with a smile.

A smile that shouldn't have made her feel as if her heart had just done a backflip. She pulled herself back under control. Just.

'How was your morning?' he asked.

'Good, thanks,' she said. 'It was mainly follow-up appointments today, and it's always lovely to see your patients gaining in confidence, once they've had time to come to terms with their diagnosis and started to make the lifestyle changes that will help them.'

'I know what you mean.' He smiled. 'We held a yearly party for the heart transplant and bypass patients at the Royal Hampstead Free. It was great to see them all dancing and making the most of the time they didn't think they would get with their families.'

'That's such a nice idea,' she said. 'Maybe Sanjay will let us set up something like that here.' She walked with him to the canteen. 'It's your first day, so this is my shout—and don't argue, because it's a departmental tradition.'

'As long as I get to take the next new recruit under my wing and pay that forward,' he said.

'Deal.' She grinned. 'I think you're going to fit right into the team, Luc.'

He nodded, looking hopeful.

'The food is all pretty good here, and the coffee is decent,' she added.

They'd just sat down to eat their sandwiches when Kelly's phone pinged to signal an incoming text.

'Sorry to be rude,' she said, 'but do you mind if I check my messages? It's probably my sister Susie—she's due her twenty-week antenatal scan today.'

'And you should have been meeting her for lunch instead of babysitting me?' Luc asked.

She smiled. 'No, she's being seen in a different hospital. Even if we'd arranged to meet halfway, I would only have had time to say hello and give her a hug before I had to rush back here for clinic.'

'Then go ahead and read your message,' he said. 'You're not being rude. If it was one of my sisters in that situation, I'd want to know how the scan went, too.'

'It's probably just a round robin telling everyone it's fine, or she would have phoned instead of messaging me,' Kelly said. But she checked her phone anyway, then grinned. 'Yup. All's well, and she and Nick decided not to find out whether it's a boy or girl.'

'Is it her first baby?'

'Her third—she already has twin boys.'

'Twins run in your family, then?' he asked.

She shook her head. 'On Nick's side—her husband. Oscar and Jacob have just turned five, and I think she's hoping for a girl this time so she gets to do ballet as well as football. Do you mind if I just send her a quick reply?'

'Of course not.'

She tapped in Great news, love you. X—and then her phone pinged to signal another message from Susie. Kelly didn't bother reading beyond the first line because she knew exactly what her sister had in mind.

'Answer that as well, if you need to,' he said.

'It can wait.' Kelly grimaced. 'I love my sister dearly, but I swear since she's been pregnant...'

'Older sister bossing you about?' he guessed.

'Trying to.' She sighed. 'Actually, you might as well hear it from me, than from someone else in the department who means well. My husband died two years ago, at the age of thirty. He was cycling to work when he had a cardiac arrest. The paramedics couldn't save him, and the coroner's report said he had HCM. It was a complete shock because he'd had no symptoms whatsoever.'

'But, as a cardiologist, you think you must've missed something?' Luc guessed.

Kelly swallowed hard. 'I've been over and over it in

my head, trying to see what I missed, and he really *didn't* have any symptoms. His dad died young from a heart attack, but his dad had a high-stress job, plus he smoked and drank too much; everyone assumed his heart attack was because of all that and they didn't bother doing a post-mortem. I guess because of what happened to his dad, Simon was more aware of heart health than the average person, even before he met me. He didn't smoke, he drank in moderation, he ate sensibly, he cycled to work and exercised regularly. He did everything right.'

Yet still he'd died. And how she missed him. Why, why, why hadn't she joined the dots together and made him go for that all-important check-up that would've spotted his unusual heart rhythm? Why hadn't she made the connection about his father? Why hadn't she thought there might be more to his father's heart attack than his lifestyle?

'My sister, my mum and my friends have all decided that I've been on my own for long enough and they're forever trying to fix me up with a suitable potential partner,' she continued. 'That's why Susie's asking me to go over to dinner tonight. She says it's so she can show me the scan pictures, but I know she'll also have invited someone that she thinks is perfect for me.'

'And you're not ready?'

'I'm not ready,' she confirmed. 'I know they all mean well, but it drives me crazy and I can't seem to get them to back off. I loved Simon and I know he wouldn't have wanted me to be alone, but...' She sighed. 'Sorry. I didn't mean to dump all that on you. What I was really going to ask was if the rumours are true about you running a trial for HCM patients, and if so whether you were looking for people to join the trial?'

'Because you have a patient who might be suitable?'

She wrinkled her nose. 'Not my patient, but I do know two people. Simon's younger brother Jake, and his daughter Summer—she's four. After Simon's PM, I nagged Jake to get tested just in case there was a faulty gene involved, and unfortunately I was right. Which also makes me think they inherited the condition from their dad—except obviously there aren't any medical records to back that up.'

'And Summer has inherited the gene too?' Luc guessed.

'Yes. With a family history that spans at least two generations—and I'm pretty sure if you went back there would be more—they'll be good candidates. And you'll get a spread of age and gender.'

Even though Kelly was clearly devastated by her husband's loss, she was still thinking about his family and trying to help them, putting their needs before her own, Luc thought. He could certainly talk to their current medical practitioner and see if they would be suitable candidates for his trial.

But something else Kelly had said struck a chord with him. Maybe, just maybe, they could help each other out. He'd had a crazy scheme percolating in the back of his head for a while now, but he hadn't found the right person to help him. Maybe Kelly was the one; she was in a similar kind of position, so she might just understand his problem.

He was normally a good judge of character and he liked what he'd seen of Kelly Phillips so far; her colleagues had spoken highly of her, too. So maybe it was time to take a risk—after he'd had the chance to check out her background and got to know her a little more, because he wasn't reckless or stupid enough to ask her right at this very second. 'If you can ask their family doctor to contact me, we'll go through all the prelims and see if they fit the criteria,' he said.

'Thank you. I really appreciate that,' she said.

'It's not a promise that it will definitely happen, but it's a promise that I'll do my best to help,' he said.

'That's fair.' She smiled at him. 'So did you train at the Royal Hampstead Free?'

'Yes, and I loved working with the team there. But then this opportunity came up, so I applied for the role,' he said. 'How about you?'

'I trained here,' she said, 'and cardiology was my favourite rotation. I love the area, too, so I stayed. What made you become a cardiac surgeon?' she asked, sounding curious. Then she grimaced. 'Sorry. Ignore me; that was a bit rude and pushy. You really don't have to answer.'

'It goes with the territory. Given who my family is, most people expect me to be part of the family business rather than being a medic.' He shrugged. 'That's what probably would have happened—but my best friend, Giacomo, died when we were fifteen.' He winced slightly as he looked at her.

'From a heart condition?' she guessed.

He nodded. 'I'm sorry if this opens any scars, but yes—the same one as your husband.'

'HCM.' Three little letters that had blown her world apart.

'It wasn't genetic, in Giacomo's case. His family doctor thought the chest pains were just teenage anxiety because Giacomo was worrying about his exams.'

She blinked. 'Chest pains in a teenager and the doctor didn't send him for tests?'

'No. Knowing what I do now, I wish he had. His condition would've shown up on the ECG, and then medication or an ICD might've saved him. But hindsight is a wonderful thing.' He shrugged. 'Giacomo was playing football at school with me at lunchtime when he collapsed and died. The teachers tried to give him CPR but they couldn't get his heart started again.'

She reached across the table and squeezed his hand for a moment, conveying her sympathy. 'I'm sorry. That must've been hard for you.'

'It was. He was the brother I never had.' And it had shocked him profoundly to come face to face with his own mortality at the age of fifteen. Giacomo had been the first person he'd ever known to die, and the fact it had happened in front of him had affected him deeply. Not wanting to feel that way again, he'd put up a slight emotional wall between himself and everyone he loved. 'I'm reasonably close to both my sisters,' he added, 'but we don't talk in quite the same way, with Eleonora being two years older than I am and Giulia being five years younger.'

'So you wanted to save other families going through what your best friend's family went through?'

Just what he suspected she was trying to do, too. He nodded. 'Becoming a doctor pretty much helped me to come to terms with losing him. And I like my job— bringing people back from the brink and giving them a second chance to make the most of life.'

'Me, too,' she said.

When they'd finished lunch, they headed back to the cardiac ward together.

'Thank you for lunch,' Luc said.

'Pleasure. I might see you later today—if not, see you tomorrow and have a good afternoon,' Kelly said.

'You, too,' he replied with a smile.

And how bad was it that he was really looking forward to seeing her?

CHAPTER TWO

ON TUESDAY MORNING, Kelly was due in to the cath lab. Her first patient, Peter Jefferson, looked incredibly nervous, and his knuckles were white where he was gripping his wife's hand.

She introduced herself to them both. 'Come and sit down. I promise this looks much scarier than it is. I'm going to check your pulse and your blood pressure, Mr Jefferson, and then I'll put a little plastic tube called a cannula into your arm. Then all you have to do is lie on the couch for me, hold your breath and keep still for a few seconds, and the scanner will take 3D pictures of your heart so I can take a look at what's going on. Then we can talk about it and decide the best way to treat you to stop the chest pain. Is that OK?'

He nodded.

'I'm going to inject some special dye into your veins to help the scanner take the pictures. It'll make you feel a bit warm and you might notice a funny taste in your mouth, but that's completely normal and it'll only last for about thirty seconds,' she reassured him.

'And it's not going to hurt?' He was still gripping his wife's hand.

'It's not going to hurt,' she said. 'If you're worried about how you're feeling at any stage, just tell me. I might need to give you some medicine called a beta-blocker to slow your heart down very slightly, or some GTN spray under your tongue to make the arteries in your heart get a little bit wider—that will help me get better pictures of your heart. But it won't hurt,' she promised.

'It's just the chest pain has been so bad lately,' Mrs Jefferson said, 'and the medicine our family doctor gave him doesn't help.'

Angina that couldn't be helped by medication often meant that the arteries were seriously narrowed, and the treatment for that could mean anything from a simple stent through to bypass surgery under general anaesthetic. Hopefully a stent would be enough, but she wasn't going to worry him until she could review the scan pictures.

She gave them both a reassuring smile. 'Once we've gone through the tests, I should have a better idea how to help you. Can I just check that you've stayed off coffee, tea, fizzy drinks and chocolate yesterday and today, Mr Jefferson?'

He nodded.

'And he's been eating better lately and stopped smoking,' Mrs Jefferson added.

'Two of the best things you can do,' Kelly said. 'OK, Mr Jefferson. When you're ready, I'll check your blood pressure.'

As she'd expected, the first reading was really high; a lot of patients were so nervous about the tests that it sent their blood pressure sky-high. By the third reading, he was beginning to relax and Kelly was a little happier with the numbers.

Once she'd put the cannula in, she asked Mr Jefferson to lie on the scanner couch with his arms above his head. 'I'm going to put some wires on your chest now,' she explained, 'so I can monitor your heart rate during the scan, but again it's not going to hurt.'

But she really wasn't happy with what the scan showed her. His right coronary artery was severely narrowed, as were the two on the left. An angioplasty with a stent wasn't going to be enough to make any difference.

'I'm sure your family doctor has already explained why you're getting chest pain, Mr Jefferson, but I'd like to go through it with you again. Basically your heart pumps blood round your body, but sometimes deposits of fat and cholesterol—what you might hear called plaques—stick to the wall of your arteries and make them narrower. It's kind of like when you see the inside of a kettle in a hard water area and the pipes are furred up, except in this case the furred-up bits are inside the pipes rather than outside. This means not enough oxygen-rich blood gets through to your heart, and that's why it hurts.'

'But you can make my arteries wide again?' he asked.

'I was hoping I could do an angioplasty and put a stent in—that's basically a wire mesh that I can put inside your arteries to keep them open,' Kelly said. 'But in your case there's a lot of narrowing in three of your arteries, and I think your best option is surgery. I need to talk to one of my colleagues—the cardiothoracic surgeon—very quickly, so if you'll excuse me I'll be about five minutes. If you'd like to nip out to the waiting area to get a cup of water while I'm gone, please feel free.'

To Kelly's relief, Luc was in his office, dealing with paperwork.

'Can I have a quick word about one of my patients?' she asked.

'Sure.'

She drew up Peter Jefferson's scan results on the computer. 'My patient has angina, and the meds his family doctor prescribed aren't helping. I hoped that I might be able to do an angioplasty, but I'm really not happy with the scan results. I think he needs a CABG.'

'I agree. That narrowing is severe. I'd recommend a triple bypass,' Luc said as he reviewed the screen. 'Is he still with you?'

'Yes. He's in the cath lab with his wife. He knows I'm having a quick word with you.'

'Let me check my schedule.' He flicked into the diary system. 'Operating days for me are Wednesday and Friday.' He blinked. 'I've got a cancellation tomorrow, by the looks of it, so we can grab that slot now before someone else does. Do you want me to come and have a word?'

'Meeting you is going to reassure him more than anything I can say to him,' Kelly admitted. 'Would you mind?'

'No problem.' He smiled at her.

And her heart *would* have to feel as if it had done an anatomically impossible backflip because of that smile.

Kelly had got herself completely back under control by the time they went into the cath lab.

'Mr and Mrs Jefferson, this is Luciano Bianchi, one of our surgeons,' she said. 'We've had a quick discussion, and we both feel that the best way forward is surgery—a coronary artery bypass graft.'

'It means I'll take another blood vessel from your leg and attach it to your coronary artery on either side of the bit where it's blocked—that's the graft—so the blood supply is diverted down the grafted vessel.' Luc drew a swift diagram.

'I guess it's a bit like roadworks, when you get diverted down a slightly different road round the bit that's blocked. Your blood will flow through properly to your heart again and you won't get any pain,' Kelly said.

'Exactly,' Luc said with a smile.

'But what about the bit in his leg? Doesn't he need that vein?' Mrs Jefferson asked, clearly looking worried.

'It's one of the extra veins we all have close to the surface of the skin,' Luc said. 'The ones that return the blood back to the heart are deep inside your leg. The rest of the veins in your leg will manage perfectly well if I borrow a little bit for a graft, Mr Jefferson. I'll stitch it up and you'll have a little scar, but it's nothing to be worried about.'

'Heart surgery. Does that mean you have to cut through my chest?' Mr Jefferson asked.

'In your case, yes—unfortunately I can't do keyhole surgery for you because you need three grafts,' Luc said. 'It means you'll have a scar down your chest, but that'll fade with time. And once I'm happy with the grafts, I can re-join your breastbone with stainless steel wires and stitch up the opening.' He smiled. 'And I happen to have a slot free tomorrow morning, so I can fit you in then.'

'Tomorrow?' Mr Jefferson looked utterly shocked.

'Tomorrow,' Luc confirmed. 'Which gives you less time to worry about the operation.'

'Surgery.' Mr Jefferson blew out a breath. 'I wasn't expecting that.'

'I've done quite a few bypasses in my time,' Luc reassured him. 'You won't feel a thing, because you'll be under a general anaesthetic.'

'Isn't that the operation where you'll stop his heart beating?' Mrs Jefferson asked. 'I read up about that on the Internet.'

'It's one way of doing a bypass operation, using a

heart-lung machine to breathe and pump the blood round your body for you, but actually I prefer to do my surgery off-pump—where the heart's still beating while I operate,' Luc said.

Kelly hadn't expected that, and it intrigued her.

Mr Jefferson's eyes widened. 'But isn't that dangerous?'

'It's quicker, so you'll be under anaesthetic for less time, there's less chance of you bleeding during surgery, and you're also less likely to develop complications after the operation,' Luc said. 'So in my view it reduces the risks.'

'And after the surgery you'll be with us in the ward,' Kelly said. 'You'll be in Intensive Care at first, where we'll keep an eye on you to make sure everything's working as it should be. You'll still be asleep for the first couple of hours, but then we'll wake you up and your family will be able to see you.'

'You'll be well enough to get out of bed and sit in a chair, the next day,' Luc said. 'A couple of days later you'll be back on your feet, and a couple of days after that you'll be ready to tackle stairs again.'

'A whole week in hospital.' Mr Jefferson looked as if he couldn't take it in. 'My doctor said I'd be in here for half an hour, maybe a bit longer if you had to do a procedure like a stent. He didn't say I'd have to stay in for a week.'

'But if you need the operation, love,' Mrs Jefferson said, 'then you'll have to stay in.'

'I'm afraid you do need the operation, Mr Jefferson,' Luc said gently. 'Right now I know it feels very scary and a bit daunting. But it's the best way of preventing you having a heart attack.'

'But our daughter's having a baby next month,' Mr Jefferson said.

'Which is another reason to have the operation now. You'll be able to cuddle the baby without worrying that you'll start getting chest pains,' Kelly said. 'By the time the baby's crawling, you'll have made a full recovery and can really enjoy being a grandad.'

'And you won't be left to deal with everything on your own afterwards,' Luc added. 'Heart surgery is a big operation, and we'll help you recover on the ward.'

'You'll come back to us a few weeks after the operation to start a rehabilitation programme,' Kelly said, 'and that will help you get completely back on your feet. There are support groups, too, so we can put you in touch with other people who've already been through the same thing—they'll understand how you're feeling and can help you.'

'And it's really bad enough that I should have the operation tomorrow?' Mr Jefferson asked.

'Your arteries are severely narrowed,' Luc said. 'Right now that's causing the pains in your chest, and the medication isn't enough to stop the pain. But on top of that there's a risk that one of the plaques will split and cause a blood clot that will completely block the blood supply to your heart and give you a heart attack. That could do a lot of damage to your heart muscle.'

'And kill him?' Mrs Jefferson asked.

'We always try our best to save our patients but, yes, I have to tell you that's a possibility,' Luc said. 'I know it's a lot to take in, but we'd really like to keep you in overnight here and do the bypass tomorrow, Mr Jefferson.'

'So will the operation cure him completely?' Mrs Jefferson asked.

'It will stop the pain and lower the risk of having a heart attack,' Luc said.

'But because you have coronary heart disease you'll still need to look after your heart,' Kelly added. 'Your family doctor's probably already told you what you need to do. Stopping smoking and eating better are brilliant, so definitely keep that up, and maybe add in a bit more gentle exercise.'

Mr Jefferson still looked terrified. 'I hate needles. I can't even make myself give blood, even though I know I ought to. Coming here today for this was bad enough.'

Kelly held his hand. 'I know it's scary now, but in the long run you'll feel so much better. And your wife and daughter won't have to worry about you as much as they do now. Luc's really good at what he does, and so is the rest of our team. It's natural to feel worried, and you'll probably feel a bit wobbly at times after the operation—that's absolutely normal. But the operation is really going to help you. You're going to feel a lot better, and you're not going to worry that your chest pain or breathlessness is going to stop you playing with your grandchildren.'

'Are there risks?' Mrs Jefferson asked.

Luc and Kelly exchanged a glance.

'There are risks with all anaesthetic and surgical cases,' Luc said. 'But they're small, and we're experienced enough to know what to look out for and how to fix things. I know it all sounds really daunting, but there's a greater risk if we don't do the surgery.'

Mr Jefferson swallowed hard. 'All right. I'll do it.'

'Good man.' Luc rested his hand briefly on the older man's shoulder. 'We'll get you settled in to the ward, and I'll be doing rounds later if you have any questions. Dr Phillips will also be on hand if you need anything.'

'Or talk to any of the nurses,' Kelly added. 'That goes for both of you.'

'Thank you,' Mrs Jefferson said.

Once Mr Jefferson was settled on the ward and had been put on a nitrate drip, Kelly went back to the cath lab. The rest of her clinic was more straightforward, to her relief, and she managed to catch up with Luc afterwards.

'Thank you for talking to Mr Jefferson with me.' She'd liked Luc's warm, easy manner and the way he'd described things without being dramatic and terrifying their patient even more. He'd acknowledged Mr Jefferson's fears and reassured him.

'No problem,' he said.

'You actually do the surgery off-pump?'

He nodded. 'I'm assuming that's unusual for here, then?'

'Yes, it is. I haven't actually seen off-pump surgery done before.' And it was the first time in a long time that Kelly had been interested in seeing something different—that her old passion for her job had resurfaced instead of being buried by the fear that she might have missed something and let a patient down, the way she'd let Simon down.

'If you can spare the time, you're welcome to scrub in and observe as much of the operation as you like,' he offered.

'I'd love to. I won't be able to stay for the whole thing, but maybe I could come before or after my clinic tomorrow, if that's OK?'

'Whenever fits your schedule best,' he said.

'Thanks. I'm definitely taking you up on that.'

'Actually, you can spread the word that I'm always happy to have observers,' Luc said. 'The actual operation is only a part of caring for our patient. I'm a great believer in all areas of the team knowing exactly what happens in the other parts of a care plan, and the more we all understand what each other does, the more we can work together and help our patients.'

'That's very much Sanjay's approach as the head of the department,' Kelly said. 'Cross-fertilisation of ideas. And you're welcome in my cath lab any time, as are any of your students.'

'Thanks. I'll take you up on that.' He smiled. 'So is Mr Jefferson settled in?'

She nodded. 'His wife's just gone home to pick up his things. She had a bit of a chat with me beforehand. She's worrying about losing him.'

'Understandable, in the circumstances,' Luc said. 'But that must've brought back some tough memories for you.'

She shrugged. 'If anything, what happened to Simon has probably helped me empathise a bit more with my patients and their partners.' There had to be *some* good coming out of such a senseless death.

'You're still brave,' Luc said, patting her shoulder.

Again, his touch made her feel all flustered. Which was crazy. She hardly knew him and this wasn't supposed to happen. 'You have to get on with things,' she said.

As if realising that she desperately wanted him to change the subject, Luc said, 'So Mr Jefferson's on his own and he's got time to worry, then. I'll go and sit with him for a bit. Catch you later.'

Surgeons had a reputation for arrogance, Kelly thought, the next morning, but Luc Bianchi definitely wasn't one of them. Yesterday he'd deliberately taken time to sit with a nervous patient and reassure him. Today, he was courteous to the rest of the team in the operating theatre, asking them to do things rather than barking instructions at them, and even checking that they were OK with his choice of music to work to; and he'd made it clear that he was happy to explain anything he was doing and why.

She was fascinated by the glimpses she had of the off-pump bypass surgery where just the small area he was working on was kept still and the rest of the heart was visibly pumping. As a student, she'd been fascinated by cutting-edge treatments. Since Simon's death, she'd focused on keeping things safe and steady. Work hadn't been a chore, exactly, but she'd become hyper-focused. She managed to be there for the end of the op too, when Luc was closing up; his movements were deft and very sure.

'Thanks for letting me sit in,' she said before he went to scrub out. 'Can I buy you lunch and ask you a ton of questions about the op?'

'I'd be delighted to have lunch with you and answer anything I can,' he said, 'but I'm paying. I might have to rush back here if the team beeps me too.'

In other words, if Peter Jefferson developed any complications before he came round in the intensive care unit. 'Of course,' she said. 'Thank you. I'll see you when you've scrubbed out.'

The more time Luc spent with Kelly Phillips, the more he liked her. The kind, calm way she treated her patients; her inquisitive mind; the way she treated all her colleagues with respect.

'Was that really the first OPCABG you've seen?' he asked when he'd scrubbed out and joined her.

'Your predecessor preferred working on pump,' she said. 'So, yes, it was my first off-pump bypass graft. And it was fascinating.'

'And you have questions?'

'Absolutely. Let's get lunch, and I'll pick your brain,' she said with a smile.

She asked a lot of questions. All bright, thoughtful questions. Luc answered to the best of his ability, and finally she nodded.

'Thank you. I understand a lot more, now. But the most important thing is that you've made a real difference to Peter Jefferson's life.'

'We're not quite out of the woods yet,' he said. 'But I hope so.'

Over the next couple of days, Peter Jefferson moved from the intensive care area to the ward. But, when Kelly came to see him on Friday morning during her ward round, he started crying. 'This is so pathetic. I can't understand why I feel like this. I was a finance director, used to making decisions and dealing with huge sums of money, and now I'm crying all over the place and it's just not me. And I can barely even get out of bed without help.' He looked despairing. 'Now I'm just a shuffling old man.'

She sat on the bed next to him and held his hand. 'You've been through major surgery, Mr Jefferson. Lots and lots of people feel like this afterwards. You'll have good days and you'll have wobbly days. But the rehab programme will really help you, because you'll meet other people who are going through it too or are a couple of weeks further down the line than you are, and that will help you realise that what's happening to you and how you're feeling is all perfectly normal. It's going to take time to get you back on your feet and doing the same things you did before you had surgery, but you *will* get there. Just be kind to yourself.'

Luc walked onto the ward at that moment. 'Good

morning,' he said with a smile. 'I just popped in to say hello to you before I go into the operating theatre today.'

Mr Jefferson wiped his eyes. 'I'm sorry. I'm being so stupid.'

'You've had major surgery with a general anaesthetic. Of course you feel wobbly,' Luc said. 'Tell me, do you play chess?'

'I do.'

'Good. I'll get a board sorted out and I'm challenging you during my lunch break. I might be a bit late,' he said, 'depending on how the operation goes this morning, but I'll definitely be in to have a cup of tea and a chess match with you, OK?'

'But—you'll have been so busy this morning.'

'And a game of chess is the perfect way to relax,' Luc said. 'As long as you don't mind me eating a sandwich at the same time. I'm horrendously grumpy if I don't eat regularly.'

'Thank you, Dr Bianchi. That's—that's so kind of you.' Peter Jefferson wiped his eyes again.

'I'll see you soon,' Luc said, patting his hand.

'I need to see my next patient,' Kelly said, 'but I'll pop back later, too.' She walked out with Luc. 'That's really nice of you.'

'I just want my patients to be comfortable.' He shrugged. 'I don't suppose there's a chess board on the ward?'

'Probably not, but I might be able to borrow one from Paediatrics. I'll get that organised—and a sandwich for you. What would you like?'

'I eat anything, so the first thing you grab off the shelf will be fine,' Luc said. 'Thanks, and I'll settle up with you later.' He paused. 'Are you at the team thing tonight?'

'The ten-pin bowling? No, I'm working. Are you?'

'Yes. I thought it'd be a good way to get to know the team.'

'It is.' She smiled. 'Have a good time.'

'Thank you.'

To her relief, he didn't push to see if she was going to any of the other team events. She liked her colleagues very much—but going out was a strain. Too many people trying to push her into being sociable when she was really much happier here at work, making a difference to her patients' lives.

Luc spent the morning in Theatre fixing an aortic aneurysm on an elderly woman, his lunchtime with Peter Jefferson, and his afternoon in Theatre sorting out a narrowed aortic valve in a teenage boy suffering from severe breathlessness.

By the time he got to the bowling alley, he was glad of the chance to let off steam. Though he learned from his colleagues that Kelly hardly ever joined team events nowadays. Because she was still mourning her husband? He needed to tread carefully.

He didn't see her again until Monday morning. 'How was your chess match?' Kelly asked.

'It was fine,' he said. 'I think Peter was glad of the company. He was beating himself up a bit because he was shuffling, and just taking those few little steps exhausted him.'

'Two days before that, he was in Theatre, having major surgery. He's doing brilliantly,' she said.

'That's what I told him. I said that my patients always worry that it'll take ages to get fully back on their feet, and at the same time they're terrified of overdoing things in case it makes them have a relapse. How he's feeling is how all my patients feel.'

'I'll make sure I reassure him about the rehab sessions,' Kelly said.

'I assume it's the same as we did at the Royal Hampstead Free—an exercise programme tailored to the patient and graded so they can see their progress?'

She nodded. 'Plus there will be plenty of professionals there, he'll have a monitor attached during the exercises so we can keep an eye on his heart rate, his blood pressure and his pulse. The team will help each patient progress at the right pace for them, and their safety is paramount.'

'Good,' he said. 'Did you see your sister's scan photo, by the way?'

'Yes.' She took a photograph from her wallet and handed it to him. 'They're going to call the baby Reuben if he's a boy, and Emma if she's a girl.'

'Lovely.' His fingers accidentally touched hers, and again he felt that inappropriate zing. To stop himself thinking about it, he asked, 'So were you right and Susie had someone lined up to partner you at dinner?'

'Yes, and he was very sweet and very charming. He understood when I explained that it wasn't him, I just don't want to date.' She grimaced. 'My best friend's doing exactly the same thing this weekend. She's arranged pizza and tickets to a stand-up comedy thing for a group of us, and I know I'm going to end up sitting next to the eligible single man in the group. I know they love me and they mean well, but...' She shook her head. 'Sometimes I'm so tempted to invent a fake boyfriend, just to get them to back off.'

A fake boyfriend?

That wasn't so very far from the marriage of convenience he had in mind.

'Maybe you should,' Luc said carefully.

She wrinkled her nose. 'Except then they'd insist on

meeting him. And it's not really fair to ask someone to—well, be my fake boyfriend and lie to everyone for me.'

She could ask me, Luc thought—or maybe I can ask her. He wanted to get to know her a little better first, but he was beginning to think they really could help each other. 'If you explained the situation to someone suitable, I'm sure he'd be happy to help you out.'

'Really?'

For a second, he thought she was going to ask him, and his heart actually skipped a beat.

But then she spread her hands. 'I might think about that a bit more. But thank you for the male insight.'

If he nudged her to think about it a bit more, then hopefully she'd be receptive when he finally asked her a similar question...

CHAPTER THREE

OVER THE NEXT couple of weeks, Luc found himself working with Kelly on their patients' care between the cath lab and the operating theatre, where she needed to do the investigations and liaise with him about potential surgery. The more he got to know her, the more he liked her. The way she put everyone at ease, the way she told terrible jokes, the way she made the day feel brighter just because she was in it.

In other circumstances, he would've been so tempted to ask her out on a date. But she'd told him she wasn't ready to move on after losing her husband, and he had a political tightrope to walk in Bordimiglia. So he'd enjoy her friendship and he'd just have to start mentally naming every blood vessel in the body, from the internal carotid artery down to the dorsal digital artery, to stop himself thinking of anything else.

But on Sunday afternoon his eldest sister called him.

'Is everything OK, Elle?' he asked. He and Eleonora usually managed to grab a few words during the week, but there was something slightly antsy about her tone.

'Ye—es.'

'But?'

'Babbo wants to start taking things easier. He told me

yesterday that he's planning to step down at some point in the next year,' Eleonora said.

Meaning that King Umberto was expecting his wayward son to give up his job as a surgeon, come home and take his rightful place on the throne? So the clock he'd pretty much managed to ignore, thanks to its silence, had just started to tick. 'Is that Elle-speak for "come home right now"?' he asked wryly.

'No, I'm just putting you in the picture so you know what our father's thinking. He'll probably summon you home to talk about it at some time in the next month, though,' Eleonora warned.

Summon him home. Normal people of his age were happy to visit their parents; whereas Luc knew a visit home wouldn't be time to catch up with each other and enjoy each other's company. It would be another chance for his father to nag him about his future in the monarchy, and he'd end up having another argument with his father. He sighed. 'Elle, you and I both know you'd make a better ruler than I would. So does our father. And you're the oldest. It's ridiculous. This is the twenty-first century. It makes absolutely no sense that, even though I'm second-born, I should be the heir just because I have a Y chromosome.'

'It's how things are.'

He could hear the resignation in her voice. 'Well, things need to change. It's time our father modernised the monarchy.'

She sighed. 'I hate it when you fight.'

'Elle, I'm a cardiac surgeon. I've spent half my life either studying to become a doctor or practising medicine—and I'm good at what I do. I can make a real difference to my patients and their families, give people a second chance at life. That's such an amazing thing to be able to do. And I want to stay here for a couple more years, get experience in all the cutting-edge surgical developments. Then I can bring it home to Bordimiglia and set up a world-class cardiac centre.' And he'd name it after his best friend. So Giacomo would never be forgotten.

'Giacomo would be proud of you,' Eleonora said softly. 'His parents think you're wonderful.'

Whereas his own parents thought he was being stubborn and unreasonable. They'd given him the freedom to do what drove him, so far, but now it seemed the pressure was going to start in earnest: they'd want him to go back to being a prince instead of a surgeon. But that wasn't who he was. He could serve his country much better as a surgeon. Make a real difference to people's lives.

'I really hate all the fussiness of protocols and politics, Elle. If I become king, I'll make a dozen horrible gaffes in my first week, and we all know it. Whereas you're a born diplomat.' Though even Eleonora hadn't been able to talk their father into changing a certain tradition.

'Sometimes you have to pick your battles wisely. This isn't one we're going to win, Luc.'

Unless he did a little shaking up himself.

He'd talk to Kelly. Hopefully she'd agree with him that they could do each other a favour and his plan would work. 'Leave it with me,' he said.

'No fighting with Babbo,' Eleonora warned.

'I know. Mamma hates it when we fight, too, and so does Giu. And it's not that much fun for me, either. I'm not arguing for the sake of it. Don't worry, Elle.' He switched the conversation to how his niece and nephew were doing, and his sister sounded a lot less strained by the end of the call than she had at the beginning.

When he'd hung up, he went through the dossier on

Kelly that the palace PR team had quietly compiled for him. There was nothing the press could use to pillory her, so she'd be protected. There might be a bit of press intrusion, to start with, but it would soon die down because he knew that he was too quiet and serious and frankly *boring* to make good headlines.

He'd talk to her on Monday.

Luc spent Monday morning in clinic. His first patient, Maia Isley, had Marfan Syndrome—a genetic connective tissue disorder which caused abnormal production of the protein fibrillin, so parts of the body stretched more than they should when placed under stress. It was a condition which needed help from a variety of specialists, as the patient could develop scoliosis, have loose and painful joints, and suffer from eye problems. From a cardiac point of view, Marfan Syndrome could also cause problems with the aorta being enlarged, so patients needed regular check-ups and a yearly echocardiogram where the team could look at the structure of the heart and measure the size of the aorta.

Luc had already compared the new scan that Kelly had just performed to last year's, and he wasn't happy with the differences.

'How are you feeling, Mrs Isley?' he asked.

'Fine,' the young woman replied. 'But, from the look on your face, you're expecting me to feel worse than usual, right?'

Luc nodded. 'Obviously you've learned a lot about your condition, so you know there's a risk of your aorta— the biggest artery in your body, the one that starts at the top of the pumping chamber in your heart—getting wider, and that can make blood leak back into your heart so your heartbeat starts pounding and you get breathless.'

Maia shrugged. 'My heartbeat feels like it normally does.'

'And also there's a risk of the aorta tearing.'

'If it tears, I die, right?' Maia asked.

'There's a high chance, yes. Your aorta's grown wider since last year. We're at the point where we need to do surgery to make sure it doesn't tear,' Luc said. 'And we've got three options, depending on what you'd like to do. May I ask, were you thinking of having children?'

'I'd like to,' Maia said, 'but my partner's worried. Not so much the risks of the baby having Marfan's, because we can have IVF and with preimplantation genetic diagnosis so we can be sure the baby doesn't have the gene, but he read up that women with Marfan's were more at risk of aortic rupture, especially during pregnancy.'

'And he doesn't want to lose you,' Luc said softly. 'I understand that. Surgery now will take that risk away.' He drew three quick pictures. 'The first option is where we replace part of the aorta and its root, including the valve. The treatment's very safe and has a long track record, but you'll be at risk of developing a blood clot so you'll need blood-thinning medication for the rest of your life.'

'Which means I can't get pregnant, right?'

'Which means if you do want to try for a baby, your doctor will switch your blood-thinning meds to one that's injected under the skin and doesn't cross the placenta,' Luc said. 'Or we can do a different sort of surgery where we replace part of the aorta but keep your valve—it's called a valve sparing root replacement or VSRR for short. Because we're keeping your valve, you won't need the blood-thinning medication, but there's a one in four chance we'll have to redo the operation within the next twenty years.'

Maia looked thoughtful. 'What's the third?'

'It's a very new treatment where we make a special sleeve to go round your aorta, called a personalised external aortic root support or PEARS.'

'So it wraps round and acts like a support, say like when my knee's playing up and I have to strap it up?' Maia asked.

'Yes. The idea is that it'll keep your aorta at the size it is now, so it won't get any wider in the future—and that reduces the risk of a tear or the valve leaking. The procedure's not as invasive as replacing the root or the valve-sparing surgery, though I'll still need to open your chest under a general anaesthetic. And it means it'll be more appropriate if you do want to have a baby, because it'll keep your aorta at this size and reduce the risks during pregnancy. But it's still a very new procedure,' Luc warned, 'so not that many have been done.'

'So how do you do it? Wrap it round?'

'We give you a CT scan and we make a 3D computer model of your aorta from the scan, print it, and we use that to make a fabric mesh support tailored exactly to your aorta,' Luc explained.

'3D printing? That sounds cool,' Maia said. 'I know you said it's new, but have you done many?'

'You'll be my second patient—and the first at this hospital,' Luc said. 'Though, if you decide to go for that option, I'll ask one of my former colleagues to come over and assist, because he's got more experience than I have. Or it might be that we end up doing the operation at my old hospital.'

'Can I talk the options over with my husband?' Maia asked.

'Of course,' Luc said. 'I'll want to see you again anyway, and maybe he can come with you if he has any questions. Though I'll give you some leaflets to take away with you—it's a lot to remember and it's always good to have things written down so you can refer back.'

'Thank you,' Maia said. 'I know there are risks, but I'm leaning towards that 3D support thing. I like the sound of that much more.'

'Let's book you in my clinic for next week,' Luc said, 'and you can talk it over with your husband in the meantime and bring all your questions with you to clinic.'

After clinic, he managed to catch Kelly. 'Are you free for lunch? I could do with your opinion on something.'

'Sure.' She smiled at him.

'Maybe we could grab a sandwich and head over to the park,' he suggested. Where it would be quieter and more private than the hospital canteen and he could sound her out.

'That sounds good,' she said.

'Thanks for doing that echo on Maia Isley for me,' he said when they'd found a quiet bench in the park.

'Her aorta's quite a bit bigger than last time. Are you planning surgery?' she asked.

'She's talking it over with her husband, but there's a fairly big chance she'll opt for PEARS.'

'Aortal support?' Her eyes gleamed. 'If she does, I'd love to sit in on the op. I've heard about it but not seen it done.'

'Given that you're her cardiologist,' he said, 'if she takes that option then you'll be involved in the CT scans and you can definitely sit in on the op. We might need to print the 3D model of her heart elsewhere, but I'm sure Sanjay will be happy for you to be involved, and maybe do a presentation to the rest of the team. I need to talk to one of my old colleagues as well as Sanjay, so we might end up doing the actual op at the Royal Hampstead Free instead of here, or it might be that my colleague comes here to help out.'

'I am so up for that,' she said. 'I've never done anything like that before.'

He smiled. 'That's important to you, isn't it? Being able to make a difference.'

'Yes. And I'm pretty sure it's the same for you.'

'It is.' Should he ask her now? He'd been thinking about it ever since Elle had called him. He took a deep breath and said carefully, 'I think you and I could make a difference for each other.'

'Job enrichment? Absolutely,' she agreed. 'We've got a new F1 doctor starting next week. I'm responsible for her training, and it'd be great if she could do some observation or even some work in the operating theatre as well as in the cath lab. And your trainee surgeon might enjoy doing some stent work with us.'

'That's fine, but actually I was thinking on a more personal level.' He paused. 'What you were saying the other week about inventing a boyfriend.'

She frowned. 'What about it?'

'I need to get married. So if you married me, it would solve a problem for both of us.'

Her green eyes widened in apparent shock. 'What? That's crazy!'

He winced. He'd been thinking about this for a while; for her, this was completely out of the blue. 'Sorry. I could have put that better. I'm not hitting on you, Kelly. I mean a marriage in name only.'

'You're the heir to the kingdom of Bordimiglia,' she said. 'Surely you've got to marry someone of royal blood? And why do you need to get married? And why me?'

It was a fair list of questions. 'This is in confidence, yes?'

'It's a little late to be asking that now,' she said. 'I might be the heart of the hospital gossip machine.'

'I'm pretty sure you're not,' he said, 'though you have a point.'

'OK. In confidence.'

'Trust you, you're a doctor?' he asked wryly.

'You started this,' she reminded him. 'And you haven't given me any answers yet.'

'From the top—my parents expect me to get married to someone who'd be suitable as a queen. So, yes, you're probably right about the royal bloodline. The problem is, someone who wants to be queen doesn't want to be married to a cardiac surgeon.' He knew that from bitter experience. 'A cardiac surgeon is who I am and who I want to be.'

She frowned. 'But you're a prince. Don't you have to take over from your dad?'

'Technically, yes. But he's the king and he can change the rules of succession if he wants to,' Luc explained. 'I told you I have two sisters, Eleonora and Giulia. Elle's the oldest and she'd make an absolutely brilliant queen. Apart from the fact that she's good with people and everyone loves her, she's astute—she's got a real business mind, and she'd do a lot for our country.'

'Would she actually want the job, though?' Kelly asked.

'We've talked about it, and she agrees that she'd make a better ruler than I would. She already does a lot of royal duties and she advises our father on ecology issues. I don't believe I should get the job just because I'm the son. And I'm a much better doctor than I am a politician. I know I've had a really privileged life and I appreciate that. I'm not shirking my duty—I want to serve my country in a different way, to make it a leading research centre for cardiac health. In a couple of years' time, I want to go back to Bordimiglia with everything I've learned here and set up a new cardiac centre. All our father has to do is change the rules of succession, so then his oldest child instead of his son will take over when he decides to step down. Elle deserves her chance to change our bit of the world. All I'm suggesting is pushing a little bit harder to give her that chance.'

'So getting married to someone who doesn't have royal blood will make you ineligible to rule?' Kelly asked.

'Technically, no, but getting married to a fellow doctor would give my parents a very clear signal that I'm committed to my life as a cardiac surgeon.' Given that she was a workaholic—and he knew exactly why—maybe there was something else he could offer to sweeten the deal. 'I'm going to need good staff when I set up that cardiac centre, including someone who could help to train the cardiologists of the future.' He paused. 'I'd like to headhunt you.'

'Me.' She looked thoughtful.

'I want to change people's lives for the better,' Luc said.

'As a surgeon, you do that on a one-to-one basis. As a king, you could do that for a lot more people, all at the same time,' she pointed out.

'Except I don't actually want to be a king,' he said. 'I love my job and I don't want to give it up. As I said, I'm not shirking my duty—Elle would make a better ruler than I ever could. It's in everyone's best interests for her to be the next ruler.'

'I'm not sure getting married will convince your parents of anything,' she said. 'And I really don't get why you're asking me.'

'Because you're a fellow doctor. You understand my working hours and you don't have any false expectations about my life as a surgeon,' he said. 'And it will help you out, because if you're married then your family and friends won't need to keep trying to find you a suitable partner.'

Kelly stared at Luc.

He seemed perfectly serious.

She couldn't quite get her head round this. The heir to the throne of Bordimiglia had just suggested that they get married—offering her a marriage of convenience that would stop everyone trying to find her a new partner and make his parents realise that he wanted to keep his career as a surgeon. It was the last thing she'd expected. OK, so she'd said to him that she'd been tempted to invent a boyfriend to get her family and friends to back off from the matchmaking: but there was a huge difference between an imaginary boyfriend and a marriage of convenience.

'We've known each other for less than a month,' she said. 'I admit, I looked you up on the Internet before you started here so I know a lot about you—but you know next to nothing about me. For all you know, I could be an axe-murderer.'

To his credit, he blushed slightly. 'You're not.'

Then she realised what he must've done. 'You had me checked out?'

'Yes,' he admitted, 'though I was pretty sure before that. You wouldn't have spent all these years training as a cardiologist if you were an axe-murderer. Plus I've worked with you. Anyone who works with you will know exactly who you are—you're caring, you're bright and you're very good at your job.'

It wasn't often Kelly was lost for words, but she'd never had a near-stranger propose marriage to her before. And this was so out of the blue. Getting married was a huge thing. How could he sound so casual about it?

'The way I see it,' he continued, 'we're in a similar situation and we can help each other.'

'We're not at all in a similar situation,' she countered.

'But the same solution would work for both of us,' he said.

'I—we—I can't get married to you, Luc,' she said. 'What about love?'

'We don't need it. This would be a marriage in name only. We're giving each other a breathing space from other people who want us to do things we don't want to do.'

'What if one of us falls in love with someone?'

'Then we'll have a quiet divorce,' he said.

A really nasty thought struck her. 'Is that your price for putting Jake and Summer on your trial?'

'No, that's totally separate and it depends on whether or not their doctor approves. I'm still waiting to hear back. If their doctor says no, I'll still do whatever I can to help them, but I'll need to see their medical history before I can make any kind of suggestions.'

Which was fair enough. You had to know the facts about your patient before you could suggest a course of treatment. 'Marriage.' She shook her head. 'I married Simon because I loved him. Getting married to you, when we barely know each other, and for such a cynical reason—that seems wrong.'

'Don't say no just yet,' he said. 'Take some time to think about it. What I'm suggesting is a marriage in name only. I'll make no demands on you. And we can give it a time limit—six months. That should give you enough time for your family and friends to back off and let you move on when you're ready, and for me to convince my father to do the right thing and make Elle his official heir.'

'Six months,' she repeated. 'And then what?'

'A quiet separation and eventual divorce,' he said. 'Though if you want to come back with me to Bordimiglia and help to train the cardiologists, then we can stay married for longer. Whatever suits you best.'

Being involved in a cutting-edge cardiac facility and training the cardiologists of the future... In a different country. A brand-new opportunity to save lives and a complete change in her own life.

Maybe this was what she needed to help her finally move on from the past. A new start.

'So what exactly would this marriage entail?' she asked.

'You'd need to live with me, to make it look convincing,' he said. 'But my place is big enough for you to have your own room. Your own suite, if that's what you'd prefer.'

She couldn't quite get her head round this offer.

'Please, just think about it,' he said, clearly thinking that she was going to refuse. 'I need your help, and in return I can help you. Talk it over with someone you trust.'

'Won't you have to vet them, first?'

'If you trust them, that's good enough for me,' he said softly. 'Talk it over. Then you and I can revisit it—say a week today.'

She was pretty sure her answer would still be the

same in a week's time. But he'd asked for her help, and it felt mean to refuse without even thinking about it. That wasn't who she was. Talking it over with her sister would be impossible; if she was going to convince Susie to stop trying to fix her up with someone, telling her about Luc's marriage of convenience idea would make Susie even more worried. But maybe her best friend would be a good sounding board—and Angela was super-sensible. She might come up with a better solution to both their problems.

Kelly saw a lot of Luc over the next couple of days. She ended up having lunch with him on Friday, but he didn't push her to give him an early answer. Instead, he made her laugh, telling her tales from his student days, and about one of his uncles who'd told him and his sisters spooky stories and then hidden inside a suit of armour in the castle and scared them all by making them think the suit of armour was a ghost walking.

The more time she spent with him, the more she found herself having fun—something she hadn't really done since Simon's death. Maybe Luc was the one who could help her move on. She could help him and he could help her.

Though she had a feeling that he hadn't told her the whole story. He'd made that comment about her being a fellow doctor who could understand the hours he worked. Had his parents expected him to date someone with the right background but who hadn't appreciated that Luc was dedicated to his career—someone who had hurt him, perhaps?

She'd have to think of a tactful way to ask him.

And in the meantime she'd planned to see her best friend for dinner.

She made Angela's favourite, sweet potato and black bean curry for dinner on Saturday night. But Angela almost choked on it when Kelly told her about Luc's suggestion.

'Have you lost your mind?' Angela asked. 'The hospital clinic thing, yes—that'd probably do you a lot of good, giving you a fresh start. But marrying someone you barely know? Of all the insane schemes…'

'I'd been thinking about inventing a boyfriend so everyone would back off. And this would do the same thing. If I was married, Susie would stop trying to find me a partner, so would Mum and so would y—' Kelly stopped. 'Um.'

'So would I?' Angela frowned. 'It's been two years, Kel. Simon loved you and he wouldn't—'

'—have wanted me to be alone,' Kelly finished. 'I know. Ange, we've been through all this. I haven't met anyone who's made me feel in the slightest bit how I felt about Simon.' She ignored her growing awareness of Luc. That wasn't the same thing at all.

'You weren't madly in love with Simon from the very first second you met him. Your feelings for each other developed as you got to know each other. So you're not comparing apples with apples, are you?' Angela asked. 'You have to give someone a chance to grow on you.'

'Actually, Simon and I knew pretty early on. And I'm really, *really* tired of being paraded in front of suitable men,' Kelly said.

'Technically, I think the men are being paraded in front of you,' Angela pointed out.

'You know what I mean. Getting married would stop the matchmaking.'

'But why did he ask *you*?'

'Because we're in a similar situation.' She gave her

best friend a wry smile. 'Funny, he said that to me, and I disagreed—but the more I've thought about it, the more I realise that he's right. Getting married would solve both our problems.'

'You can't get married to someone you don't love and who doesn't love you. And he's a *prince*, Kel. You'll have the media on your back for the rest of your life.'

'I haven't got a wild past,' Kelly said. 'So it's not an issue. I'm boring.'

'Of course you're not boring.'

'In terms of front-page news, I am.'

Angela frowned. 'OK. Just supposing you do go along with this, what about his family?'

'He thinks this will convince his parents that his older sister—who actually wants to do the job—would be a better ruler than he is.'

'Hmm.' Angela didn't look convinced. 'I foresee lots of arguing, and because they're who they are it'll all be in public. Tell him he's crazy.' Her eyes narrowed. 'Or is there something you're not telling me? Are you already dating him?'

'I work with him. He's nice with junior staff, he's brilliant with patients and watching him work is amazing. I'm getting the chance to do cutting edge stuff.'

Angela looked thoughtful. 'You haven't denied that you're dating him.'

'He's my colleague.'

Angela scoffed. 'You marrying a stranger—'

'Marrying a colleague, in name only,' Kelly corrected.

'But someone you've known for just a few short weeks.'

'Almost a month,' Kelly pointed out.

'That's the definition of a stranger in anyone's books. Nobody's going to believe it.'

Kelly frowned. 'So people will think I'm a gold-digger?'

'Anyone who knows you will know that's not true,' Angela said. 'No, I mean nobody will believe you're marrying someone you barely know. You loved Simon. No way will you settle for anything less than love.'

'It could be a whirlwind romance,' Kelly said thoughtfully.

Angela blinked. 'So *that's* what you're not telling me. You like him. And I don't mean just as a colleague.'

Kelly felt the colour rise in her face. 'That isn't the deal. It's a marriage in name only.'

'So you *do* like him.'

Kelly squirmed. 'It feels wrong. It feels disloyal to Simon. And, anyway, Luc doesn't feel like that about me.'

'But he asked you to marry him.'

'To solve a problem for both of us and give us both breathing space.'

'If he wanted to convince his parents that he's unsuitable for the job, surely he should marry someone completely unsuitable—say the modern equivalent of a Wallis Simpson?' Angela suggested.

'He's trying to convince them that he wants to keep doing what he's already spent his life either training for or actually doing. Marrying a fellow doctor kind of underlines that.'

Angela groaned. 'You're talking yourself into this.'

Kelly shook her head. 'Right now, I'm asking your advice.'

'That's easy. Don't get married,' Angela said promptly. 'Surely dating him will be enough?'

'For me, it would,' Kelly said. 'But not for him.'

'Kel, you got married to Simon because you loved

him. How can you even think about getting married for any other reason this time?'

'We're helping each other out.'

'It's insane.'

'You could,' Kelly suggested, 'meet him for yourself and see what you think.'

'It sounds as if you've already made your mind up,' Angela said.

'He's not pushing me for an immediate answer. He said I should talk it over with someone I trust. Which is you.'

'I love you, Kel,' Angela said. 'You've been my best friend since we met on the first day of sixth form. But I worry that if you do this you're going to get hurt. You've already been through enough, losing Simon.'

'Did I say Luc's doing a trial for HCM patients? There's a possibility that Jake and Summer could be on it.'

Angela's eyes widened. 'I hope that this marriage thing isn't a condition for them being on the trial.'

'Of course it isn't. I don't think it's a condition of the job offer and I'd love the chance to be involved in training the cardiologists of the future. What I'm trying to say is that he's not going to hurt me,' Kelly explained. 'He's one of the good guys. We're just doing each other a favour.'

'An insane favour,' Angela said, and hugged her. 'Think about it a bit more. Do yourself a list of pros and cons so you can make a really informed decision. But, whatever you do, don't rush into it. Because I think this could go very wrong, very quickly.'

CHAPTER FOUR

KELLY THOUGHT ABOUT it all weekend. Was Angela right and it would all end in tears? Or would it work the way Luc thought it would, and buy them both some time?

On Monday, she was still undecided.

'Can we talk over lunch?' Luc asked when he saw her in the staff kitchen before their shift started.

'How about over dinner tonight?' she suggested. 'My place? It'll be more private than the hospital canteen.'

'That'd be good. What time?' he asked.

'Half past seven?'

'OK. Let me know the address,' he said.

'I'll text you,' she promised. 'Let me know if there's anything you don't eat or you have any allergies.'

'No allergies and I eat anything,' he said. 'I'll bring the wine—red or white?'

'You really don't need to.'

'Red or white?' he repeated.

She smiled. 'White. Thank you.'

Offering to cook dinner for a prince. Was she crazy? He must be used to eating meals cooked by Michelin-starred chefs. Then again, she knew he saw himself as a surgeon rather than a prince, so maybe this was more like cooking dinner for a colleague. A friend. *A potential husband in name only...*

She pushed the thought out of her mind and concentrated on her clinic and her ward round. After her shift was over, she headed for the supermarket and bought salmon, Puy lentils, Chantenay carrots, spinach, fresh ginger and a lime. She knew she already had mixed berries and Greek yoghurt in her fridge; she bought a box of shortbread thins to go with them, then headed back to her flat to marinade the salmon.

At half past seven precisely, her doorbell rang. Luc stood on the doorstep, carrying a beautiful bouquet of flowers and a bottle of wine.

'Thank you. They're lovely, but you really didn't have to,' she said, accepting the flowers and the wine.

'I wanted to,' he said.

'And this wine is from Bordimiglia?' she asked, looking at the label.

'It's a white Pinot Noir—and it's very drinkable,' he said with a smile. 'It's from one of the vineyards on our estate.'

But his parents didn't just own a vineyard. They ruled the country.

'Do you need a temporary parking permit for your car, or did you get a taxi?' she asked.

'A permit would be great—my driver's staying with the car.'

Driver? Of course. He'd need to have someone on security detail. She had to remind herself that Luc was a prince first and a doctor second, even if he saw himself as being the other way round. 'I'm so sorry. I didn't think to make dinner for your driver. I can add a few more veg and make it stretch a bit.'

'It's fine. He's got a sandwich and a bottle of water.'

'Even so, if he'd like to join us, he's more than welcome. Ask him when you take the permit out.' She took a permit from the kitchen drawer, scratched off the date and time and handed it to Luc.

When Luc came back, he said, 'Gino says thank you for the offer, but he's happy with his sandwich.'

But she still felt like a terrible hostess. 'At the very least I can make the poor man a cup of coffee.'

'He won't say no to that. Black, no sugar,' Luc said. 'And yes, I do make coffee for my security team. I don't expect them to wait on me.'

But they were always there. Even though they were discreet, they were always there. He never had time on his own. 'It must be hard, living your life in public all the time.'

Luc shrugged. 'I was born into it, so I've never known anything different. I guess it'd be harder if you don't come from that kind of background.'

'Is that what happened?' she asked gently. 'You met someone, but they couldn't cope with being in a gold-fish bowl?'

'Something like that.' For a second, he looked really sad. 'There are two sides to my life—Luc Bianchi, the cardiac surgeon, and Prince Luciano, heir to the king-dom of Bordimiglia. I'm pretty much stuck in the middle. Women who embrace Prince Luciano's lifestyle don't like the other side of me, or the hours I work; and women who date Luc the surgeon don't tend to like the Bordimiglia side.' He spread his hands. 'Until everything is resolved with my father, I can't really be clear about who I am and what my partner can expect from life—and it's unfair to get involved with someone who wants one side of me and might well end up with the other instead.'

'Hence your insa—' She bit back the word, and in-stead said, 'idea of getting married.' She made coffee and opened the box of shortbread thins. 'Take some of these to Gino to go with the coffee.'

'I will.' He smiled at her. 'You're a kind woman, Kelly.'

She brushed aside the compliment. 'It's what any normal person would do.'

His expression said otherwise, but he took the coffee and biscuits out to Gino. 'Something smells good,' he said when he came back.

'Baked salmon marinated in ginger and lime, on a bed of Puy lentils, with steamed Chantenay carrots and spinach,' she told him.

He grinned. 'I don't think you can get any more heart-healthy than that. Then again, given that you're a cardiologist...'

'Oh, I practise what I preach,' she said, smiling. 'I'm not telling my patients to eat a Mediterranean diet while I tuck into masses of high-fat, low-fibre junk. But I also don't think that eating healthily has to be boring.'

'Agreed.' He paused. 'Can I do anything?'

'Open the wine, if you like. I'm about to serve up.'

He did so, and they sat at the small bistro table next to the French doors that overlooked her patio.

'This is lovely,' he said after his first mouthful.

She smiled. 'Pleasure.'

'It's a nice flat,' he said.

'Thanks. It's within walking distance of the hospital, too.'

'Did you live here with your husband?'

She shook her head. 'I moved here a year ago. I had a lot of happy memories in our old flat, but it made me sad to go home. I stuck it out for a year—people say it's not a good idea to make big changes until a year after the funeral—and then I found this place.'

'I can see why you like it.' He gestured to the garden. 'And you get the sun here in the evening. That's always nice.'

But he wasn't here to make small talk. She took a gulp of the wine to give her courage. 'Oh. That's very nice.' She took a deep breath. 'I guess we need to discuss your, um, proposal.'

'Did you talk to anyone about it?'

She nodded. 'My best friend, Angela. She's an accountant and she's very sensible.'

'And?'

'She thinks it's…' She paused, thinking of a tactful way to say it. 'She thinks the job in the new clinic would be good for me, but the marriage bit isn't workable.'

'Why?'

'Because I married Simon for love, and she thinks I wouldn't settle for anything less, second time round. You're practically a stranger.'

'Fair point,' he said.

'So I was thinking. My original idea was to have a fake boyfriend. Maybe I can be your fake girlfriend instead,' she suggested.

'Fake dating would work for your situation,' he said, 'but it wouldn't be enough to convince my parents that I'm a surgeon rather than a prince.'

'A fake engagement, then,' Kelly said.

He shook his head. 'Engagements can be broken off. It's got to be marriage.'

'It's not plausible, Luc,' she said. 'We've known each other for a little less than a month. Yes, we get on well at work and as part of the team outside work, and I think we're well on the way to becoming friends—I like you and I think you like me.'

'Agreed.'

She ignored the little shiver of desire that rippled down

her spine. That wasn't appropriate. They were talking about liking each other, not attraction. 'But you're a prince. You can't get married just like that.' She snapped her fingers. 'I mean no offence and I'm certainly not saying you're unlovable, but nobody is going to believe that I'd get married to you. Work with you, yes, and come and help you set up the clinic—but not married.'

'What if,' he said, 'we had a whirlwind romance?'

'That's what I said to Angela.' She wrinkled her nose. 'OK. Supposing we pretend to start dating and get everyone to believe we've fallen madly in love with each other within the space of a couple of weeks. That's just about plausible. But I still don't think anyone would believe that either of us would rush into marriage. I'm thirty-two and you're...?'

'Thirty-five,' he confirmed.

'Exactly. We're not impulsive teenagers, Luc. We're old enough to be sensible. We both have responsible jobs—positions that take years of training and experience. We're not going to get married in a rush.'

'Maybe we've had this whirlwind romance, I whisked you off to New York for a mini break and we got so carried away by the romance of the city that we applied for a wedding licence while we were out there,' he suggested.

She frowned. 'Surely you have to apply for a wedding licence weeks in advance?'

'In New York, you can get married twenty-four hours after you get the permit,' he said.

She looked at him. 'You've researched it, haven't you?'

'Yes,' he admitted. 'And it would work. We could fly to New York for a midweek break. We'd apply for our licence on our first day there, have dinner somewhere fancy and catch a show on Broadway maybe, then get married the second day.'

'You mean we'd elope?' But her family and friends would be so hurt if she got married again without any of them being there. Though if she told them the truth, that it was a marriage of convenience to help Luc, that would make the whole thing pointless regarding her own situation.

'Eloping stops all the complications,' he said.

Not in her eyes. 'Won't your family and friends be hurt that you didn't want to share your special day with them?' she asked.

'They'd understand that you, as a widow, would want this to be low-key.' He wrinkled his nose. 'The alternative would be a full-blown State wedding in Bordimiglia.'

That was definitely out of the question. 'Sorry. I can't stand in a church and make promises, not when I've...' The words stuck in her throat. Not when she'd done it before. For love.

He reached across the table and squeezed her hand briefly. 'I'm sorry. I'm being selfish and asking too much. It's something I've been thinking about for a while, and what pushed me into asking you is that my sister Elle rang me last weekend. She told me that our father wants to retire within the next year. Which means I'm running out of options. I need to act now.'

'I still don't see how getting married will make your parents think that you're not fit to be king,' Kelly said.

'Not that I'm unfit to be king,' he corrected, 'but that I'm committed to a life in medicine. Getting married to a doctor in a related specialty could do that.'

'Can't you just talk to your parents?' she asked.

'I've tried, believe me. I've brought it up time and time again. But my father's stubborn,' he said wryly.

'Getting married won't change things,' she said. 'Why

don't we brainstorm other ways to help you stay as a surgeon?'

He spread his hands. 'I'm all ears.'

She thought about it. And thought some more. 'I've drawn a blank,' she was forced to admit in the end. 'I know if I told my parents what I wanted to do, they'd tell me to follow my dreams and they would support me. But I think it's different for you. There are expectations.'

'Exactly. But I understand why it's not an option for you.'

Just for a moment, his expression was so bleak and lonely. Her heart went out to him. She'd been there; she knew how it felt, with loneliness like a black hole sucking you in. This time, she was the one to reach across the table and squeeze his hand. 'I can't believe nobody's fallen in love with you before—or that you haven't fallen for someone.'

'Things don't always work out the way you plan,' he said.

'What happened?' Then she grimaced. 'Sorry, that was unspeakably nosy of me. Ignore that. You don't have to answer.'

'No. I've dragged you in this far. You deserve the truth. I did fall in love with someone, when I was in my last year as a medical student. I thought Rachel loved me.' He blew out a breath. 'I met her family and we got on well. So then I took her back to Bordimiglia to meet mine. They liked her. She seemed to like them, too.'

So what had been the problem? Kelly wondered.

'But she was really quiet on the way back to London. And she didn't ask me to stay over at her place, that night, the way she usually did.' He looked away. 'She wasn't in lectures, the next day, and she didn't answer her phone. I was worried about her, so I called round. And that's when she broke up with me. She said she loved me, but she couldn't handle the public side of my life—seeing speculation in the news about her, having her dad's speeding fine dragged up and her sister's divorce spread across the gossip pages. She'd been doorstepped that morning by a couple of paps—it must've been a slow news week and they'd picked up on me taking her to meet my family, then dug up every single bit of dirt they could while we were away. I'd gone straight into lectures so I hadn't seen the papers.' He sighed. 'If I'd been just a normal medical student, it would have been fine. Rachel and I would have been married by now, maybe with a couple of children if we were lucky.'

'But you're a prince,' she said softly.

He nodded. 'The same thing happened with the next two women I dated who weren't from the same kind of background as me. They were fine with me working the stupid hours of a junior doctor, because they did it themselves. But they hated the protocol and politics of the other side of my life—not to mention the press intrusion.'

'What about dating someone from your background?'

He shrugged. 'I tried that, too. They were fine with the protocols and the formality and the dressing up.'

'But they weren't so keen on dating a doctor?' Kelly guessed.

'Not when they missed a film premiere because I was stuck in the operating theatre, or I got called away from a dinner party because a patient had developed complications and I needed to be there. I mean—did they seriously expect me to walk away from my patient in the middle of an op and tell the head of department to find someone else to finish the operation because I had to go to a *party*?' For a moment, he looked disgusted. 'I guess the answer is for me to give up my job and do what my father wants.'

'But you'd be miserable and all the experience you have would be wasted. You're bringing new procedures to our department, things that will make a real difference,' she said. 'You're helping to train the surgeons of the future.'

'Which would be the whole point of my clinic in Bordimiglia. Cutting-edge stuff.'

'That's not the same as being a whiny, over-indulged brat who's rebelling against what his parents want just for the sake of it,' she said.

'Thank you for understanding.' He looked sad. 'I can't see a way out. If I stay as I am, it's going to upset my parents—they'll feel I'm rejecting them. If I give up my career as a surgeon, I feel as if I'm throwing away all the help I've been given from my tutors and my colleagues over the years, not to mention letting my patients down. And yes, sure, as the king I could still set up a new hospital—but I wouldn't be the one working there and making a difference and passing on my skills to younger surgeons. And what's the point if I'm not going to be involved with patients? I want my skills to make a difference, not my finance.' He shrugged. 'Whatever I do, I lose.'

'Whereas if it's your father's idea to change the rules of succession...'

'Then that would make me fourth in line for the throne, behind Elle and my nephew Alessio and niece Anna. Which is perfect.'

She bit her lip. 'I'd like to help you. But getting married—that's a huge step.'

'I know I'm asking a lot, And we don't know each

other very well. And, really, what do you get out of marrying me? A massive disruption to your life.'

'According to my family and friends, I don't have a life—just work,' she said.

'I'd be the same, in your shoes,' he said. 'I'd want to double-check everything so no patient ever went undiagnosed again. Which isn't possible, because if someone doesn't show any symptoms they wouldn't have any reason to get themselves checked out, and you wouldn't get the chance to diagnose them.'

'I know. My head agrees with you,' she said.

'But your heart doesn't?'

'No,' she admitted. 'And I think that's partly why I can't move on. Because I still think I should've noticed something.'

'Nobody could've noticed it,' he said. 'But you got his brother and his niece checked out.'

'It doesn't feel like enough,' she said. She blew out a breath. 'I can't fix my situation, but I guess I could help you fix yours.'

'Which isn't a fair exchange. It feels as if I'm using you,' he said, 'and that's not who I am.'

'You're not using me, because you're not making any false promises. You're offering me an opportunity with the job, a chance to make a real difference and have a fresh start. Something to look forward to instead of backwards. And you have a point that everyone will stop nagging me to date if I'm married.' She looked at him. 'I love my family and friends, and they'd expect to be invited to my wedding.'

'Which means mine would need to be there, and then it'd be a complete circus.'

Kelly noticed that Luc hadn't said anything about loving his family. Or maybe it was different, in royal circles, and duty took precedence over love.

'It's possible to arrange a quick State wedding,' he said, 'but then the media would be all over it, speculating that you were pregnant, and...' He grimaced. 'It'd be easier if we eloped.'

'I can't do that. It'd hurt everyone and make them feel pushed away, and they've all been so supportive. I can't get married in a rush to someone they've never even met.'

'What if it was a whirlwind romance and I swept you off your feet?'

'Prince Charming?' she asked wryly.

He narrowed his eyes at her. 'Not funny.'

'Sorry.'

He wrinkled his nose. 'Actually, I should be the one apologising for the sense of humour failure. If it wasn't so close to home, it would actually be funny.'

'Apology accepted,' she said.

'I know I'm asking a lot,' he said. 'But I could make it worth—'

'Don't you dare insult me by offering me any kind of payment,' she warned, before he could offer.

'How about I make a donation to a charity of your choice?' he suggested, and named a substantial amount of money.

She felt her eyes widen. 'Luc, that's a small fortune.'

'It's worth it to me,' he said softly. 'It means I can follow my dreams and I'm free to be who I really am.'

'I want to help you, Luc. But marriage is huge.'

'I know.' He paused. 'Don't say no just yet. Let's spend a few days getting to know each other better. And then, if you feel we can go ahead, I can maybe meet your family and convince them I'm sweeping you off your feet.' He gave her a wry smile. 'Though this feels a bit like that film my sisters loved, the one with the woman who's about to be deported so she proposes to her secretary.'

'Oh, the one with Sandra Bullock and Ryan Reynolds? I loved that.' She smiled. 'Or the Gerard Depardieu one, where he and Andie MacDowell made that whole fake photo album so he could get his green card, and he got deported.'

'Except we're going to carry this off and not get found out.'

'Problem is, I've already talked to my best friend about it. Not that Ange would say anything if I ask her not to. She's just worried that I'm going to get hurt.'

'I promise you're not going to get hurt, and I can make exactly the same promise to her,' Luc said. 'I keep my promises.'

'That's good to know.'

'And your dad doesn't have a speeding conviction and your sister's happily married, so there will be no nasty headlines about anyone in your family.'

She winced. 'So you know about my whole family from your dossier on me?'

'It's not that big a dossier. Just enough to establish the basics, and confirm that the press won't be able to drag up anything to pillory you with,' he said. 'But you're right. We need to get to know each other. So. You always wanted to be a doctor?'

'When I was really little, I wanted to be a ballerina, like in the Angelina stories. Except I was truly hopeless at classes and always fell over my feet. And then I thought I might like to be a gardener, like my grandad, and grow beautiful flowers. And then one of my teachers suggested being a doctor, and I liked the thought of being able to make a difference. So I did the three sciences for my A-Levels, got into uni and ended up training here.'

She smiled at him. 'I know you said you wanted to become a doctor after your best friend died.'

'Specifically a cardiologist. Except when I worked in the cardiac department I discovered that I liked surgery. Though I did flirt a bit with being in a rock band,' he confessed. 'I was the rhythm guitarist and did the backing vocals in a band called Prince of Hearts when I was a student.'

She laughed. 'That's such a perfect name. Did you write your own stuff?'

He smiled back. 'No. And if I'm honest we weren't much good. It was fun, though.'

'There's a band in the hospital—Maybe Baby,' she said. 'Half of them are in the maternity ward and half in paediatrics. They play all the hospital functions. You never know—you could join them.'

'I'm *really* not that good,' he said. 'And I can prove that to you if you'd like to have dinner at my place on Wednesday.'

'You're on.' She looked at him. 'So do you do the cooking, or do you have staff?'

He winced. 'A mix of the two. It's not because I'm too spoiled to cook.'

'You're a cardiac surgeon. You work long hours. If you lived on your own, it'd be takeaways or microwave meals.'

'Is that what you do?' he asked.

'No. But I like cooking.' She paused. 'I'm assuming your security staff live in, so your place is a lot bigger than this.'

'Yes,' he said. 'But I will cook for you myself on Wednesday. Is there anything you hate, or are allergic to?'

'I don't eat red meat, but other than that I'm easy to cook for,' she said with a smile.

'I'd also like to take you out tomorrow night, if you're free?' he asked. 'To a restaurant,' he clarified, 'then I can have all my focus on you and not on burning your dinner.'

She laughed and nodded. 'That would be lovely.'

He lifted his glass. 'Here's to getting to know each other better.'

Kelly echoed the toast. But part of her was wondering just what she'd let herself in for.

CHAPTER FIVE

ON TUESDAY, KELLY and Luc were both busy with patients and Kelly's morning overran when she was called down to the emergency department to see a six-year-old girl who'd had a cardiac arrest. Jordan's mum had died from Long QT Syndrome, a condition that caused an electrical disturbance to the heart which could lead to a dangerous heart rhythm. The condition could be inherited—like Simon's hypertrophic cardiomyopathy—and, according to the notes, Jordan had had a previous cardiac arrest on the way home from school, two years before. Thankfully Jordan's grandmother had learned emergency life skills at work and had been able to resuscitate her.

'So the doctors didn't suggest fitting an ICD, last time?' Kelly asked Mrs Martin, Jordan's grandmother, out of earshot of the little girl while Jordan's grandfather stayed by her bedside.

Mrs Martin shook her head. 'They said the medication would be enough.'

Medication was the first-line treatment for the condition, but Kelly would've scheduled in frequent cardio tests if the girl had been her patient. 'OK. Did they explain Long QT Syndrome to you?'

'Not really.' Mrs Martin grimaced. 'I read up about it and, when we moved to London, I asked our family doctor if he thought Jordan might need an operation. He said the medication was working so leave it for now.'

'As you've read up about the condition, you know that Jordan's at risk of having more cardiac arrests.'

'And she could die suddenly, like Savannah did.'

'Yes,' Kelly admitted. 'It's brave of you to say it out loud.'

'I don't feel very brave,' Mrs Martin admitted. 'I'm terrified we're going to lose her.'

'There is an option that will help,' Kelly said. 'You might have read about it. It's an ICD—that stands for "implantable cardiac defibrillator"—and it's a little device about the size of a matchbox. If Jordan's heart rhythm suddenly becomes abnormal, the ICD will give her heart a tiny electric shock and that will make her heart go back into the right rhythm.'

'So it means an operation?'

'Yes. I can do it here in the cath lab. For adults, I'd do it under a local anaesthetic with sedation, so they'd be too sleepy to remember anything. But, because Jordan's so young, I'd rather do this under a general anaesthetic. You can be with her all the time until she's asleep,' Kelly reassured her, 'and then we'll ask you to wait outside while we do the op, to help us prevent any infection.'

'How long does it take?' Mrs Martin asked.

'A couple of hours,' Kelly said. 'What I'll do is make a small cut here—' she indicated a place below her own collarbone '—to make a little pocket for the ICD. Then I'll connect the electrode to her heart, through a vein, connect the other end of the ICD, test it to make sure it's working, then sew up the cut I made. The stitches will dissolve, so you don't have to worry about them being removed.' She smiled. 'Then we'll wake her up, and you can join her in the recovery area. When she's properly awake, we'll take her back to the children's ward, and she can go home in a couple of days.'

'I...' Mrs Martin swallowed. 'It was hard enough, losing her mum. I can't lose her as well.'

Kelly took her hand. 'The ICD is going to make things a lot less stressful for both of you. If her heart goes into an abnormal rhythm, the ICD will act like a pacemaker and give her a small electrical signal to make her heart go back to beating normally. If that isn't quite enough, then it will give her a small electric shock and that'll do the trick.'

'And you'll do the operation yourself? We won't have to see another doctor?'

'If there's a complication, I might need to get one of the cardiac surgeons in to give me a hand to fit a slightly different sort of ICD,' Kelly said, 'but in any case I'll be there. Let's go and see Jordan and her grandad, and I'll explain to her what's going to happen and answer any questions you all might have.'

'I just don't want to lose her.' A tear slid down Mrs Martin's cheek. 'It'd be like losing Savannah all over again.'

'Fitting the ICD will give her a much better chance,' Kelly promised. 'While you go and see Jordan and your husband, I'll grab a computer and check the schedule so I can give you a date.'

By the time she'd finished explaining the operation and reassuring Jordan and her grandparents, Kelly had just enough time to grab a sandwich and gulp down a mug of coffee deliberately made half with cold water before her next clinic started. She didn't even bump into Luc on the ward rounds, but he'd left her a text. Pick you up at quarter to seven.

OK, she texted back. Dress code?

Smartish came the answer.

Was she going out with the Prince or with the heart surgeon?

He hadn't said she needed to wear anything as formal as a ballgown, so she hoped that her little black dress would be smart enough, teamed with heels she could also walk in. As it was a nice evening, a walk after dinner would be lovely.

At quarter to seven precisely, he rang her doorbell.

She'd never seen him wear a formal suit before; it looked good on him, and her mouth went dry.

Then she remembered that this wasn't a real date. It was a getting-to-know-you thing to help her decide if she could go ahead with the marriage of convenience. They weren't really going to have a whirlwind courtship. She needed to squash the inappropriate feelings right now.

'You look lovely,' he said.

'Thank you. So do you,' Kelly said, feeling slightly awkward and shy,

He introduced her to Gino, his driver and security detail, and then Gino drove them to a seriously plush hotel overlooking Kensington Park Gardens. 'I thought maybe we could walk through the Italian gardens here, and then along the bank of the Serpentine,' Luc said.

'That sounds perfect,' she said. 'Am I dressed up quite enough for this place, though?'

'You're fine,' he said with a smile.

The menu was amazing. 'It's really hard to choose,' she said.

'The food's good here,' he said. 'I think anything you choose will be excellent.'

And it was also expensive enough not to have prices on the menu.

'We're going halves on the bill,' she said.

'No. My idea, my bill,' he said. 'Don't argue.'

'Provided I can treat you to dinner another time.' She narrowed her eyes at him. 'Assuming I'm fake-dating a heart surgeon.'

His smile was slightly weary. 'You are. And thank you.'

Once they'd chosen their meals, Luc said, 'So tell me about you.'

'I thought you had a dossier on me?'

'Which isn't the same thing at all,' he said. 'It's bare bones.'

'OK. I'm the youngest of two girls. My sister Susie is a lawyer and had twin boys, my dad Robin works in financial services, and so does my mum Caroline. I trained as a doctor in London and I love my job.' She looked at him. 'You?'

'I thought you said you'd looked me up on the Internet?'

'And it's a good rule of thumb not to believe everything you see there,' she pointed out.

He inclined his head. 'Well as I mentioned, I'm the middle of three—my older sister Elle has a girl and a boy, and my younger sister Giulia is married but doesn't have children yet,' he said. 'You know who my parents are. They all work in the family business. I trained in London and stayed because I like the city and I love my job.'

'OK. That's background done,' she said. 'We already know how each other ended up in cardiac medicine. How about music?' she suggested. 'I know you were in a band, so what do you listen to?'

'I operate to Bach because it's regular and calming, but it's nineties indie bands all the way in the gym and when I'm driving,' he said. 'You?'

'My guilty pleasure is eighties pop—the sort of thing

I grew up with my mum playing in the kitchen,' she said. 'And I love the Proms. Anything Mozart.' She looked at him. 'Are you actually allowed to go to a gig or a concert?'

He laughed. 'My life isn't *quite* that restricted. Yes. So we can go to some, if you like.'

'That sounds good.' She smiled. 'Movies?'

'Sci-fi and action all the way,' he said.

'How clichéd.' She rolled her eyes. 'Blokey stuff. And there was me hoping that you liked obscure French films.'

'I think that's a double bluff and what you really like seeing are rom-coms—the soppier, the better,' he said.

She laughed. 'Busted. Anything with Ryan Gosling or Tom Hanks is just fine by me. I normally go with Susie or Ange. And I read practically everything.'

'Anything set in Ancient Rome, for me,' he said.

Funny, this was so easy, Kelly thought. Luc was good company, and they had a fair amount in common. This was starting to feel like a proper date, getting to know each other—which was weird and yet nice at the same time. 'So you were saying about music at the gym. I take it you have a personal trainer come to you?'

'I have a gym at home,' he said, 'and a pool. Not just for me—my team use it as well. And sometimes we train together. How about you?

'Dance aerobics a couple of times a week, and taking the boys to the park with Susie at weekends. On wet days, we've taken them to the trampoline park to burn off some energy. They've got this amazing obstacle course that adults can go on, too.'

'That sounds like fun.' He looked slightly wistful.

She was about to ask him if he was allowed to do that sort of thing, then remembered what he'd said about going to concerts and decided not to remind him about the restrictions in his life. Instead, she said, 'So are you a lark or an owl?'

'Owl,' he said. 'I'm all about sitting watching the stars.'

'In London?'

'You'd be surprised. There are a few sites in London where you can see the Milky Way at night,' he said. 'Maybe we can do that together some time.'

'I'd like that. I've always wanted to see the Northern Lights. Simon and I went to Iceland, but it rained for the whole week we were there and we weren't lucky enough to see them.'

'That's on my bucket list, too,' he said. 'Along with seeing Old Faithful in Yellowstone.'

'Good choice,' she said. 'We saw the Strokkur geyser in Iceland, and it was amazing, despite the rain.'

He smiled. 'So are you a lark or an owl?'

'Lark,' she said. 'I'm all about the sunrise. With the hours I work, it wouldn't be fair to have a dog—but if I did I'd take him for walks half an hour before sunrise, when the world is quiet and full of birdsong.'

By the time they'd finished their meal, Kelly felt she knew Luc a lot better. And, in other circumstances, she would have been tempted to forget all this fake stuff and date him properly. She *liked* the man she was getting to know; and he was definitely attractive, with those huge dark eyes and that killer smile. It shocked her, because she hadn't expected to have any feelings like this again. She'd been so caught up in work that she'd forgotten to have fun.

So maybe Luc was the one who could help her move on with her life.

But she knew that for him this was just a means to an end—persuading his parents to let him live the life he chose and continue making a difference to his patients. It wasn't a prelude to really dating each other. Today was simply letting them get to know each other so their stories would be straight if anyone asked awkward questions.

Luc pretty much underlined it when he said softly, 'Tell me about Simon.'

'We met at a party—a friend of a friend. He was an architect. He saw me home and we ended up spending the whole night talking. We started dating, but we pretty much knew each other was The One right from the beginning. We moved in together after six months and got married six months after that. He loved his job and he was really good at it.' She smiled. 'He used to run in the park every weekend and he cycled everywhere.'

'Did you join him?'

'No to the cycling, and I prefer to walk rather than run. But I was always happy to do long walks through London with him, looking at the buildings. And some of them are amazing—all you have to do is look up and you see things you never even knew existed.' She gave him a wry smile. 'We'd planned to extend our house and start a family. He'd drawn up all the plans, and the planning permission came through on the day he died.'

Luc reached across the table and squeezed her hand. 'I'm sorry.'

'It is as it is,' she said. 'I don't have any regrets about our life together. We were happy. I just wish we'd had more time—or that I'd had some idea about his heart condition so he'd had treatment for it. The only things I regret are the things we didn't get the chance to do.'

'I'm glad you were happy,' he said.

'Now I just want Jake and Summer to get the treatment they need. Jake followed Simon in a lot of things—he's an architect, too. But he and Millie started their family earlier than we planned to.'

'I'm still waiting to hear from their doctor,' Luc said. 'But I'll push again tomorrow.'

'Thank you.'

When they'd finished their coffee, Luc suggested walking through the water gardens.

'It's so pretty here,' Kelly said. 'As it's an Italian garden, does it remind you of home?'

'A bit—and I have to admit my own garden is an Italian one, with a fountain and topiary to give layers and height,' he said. He caught her fingers in his, startling her. 'If this is going to be a whirlwind romance,' he said as her eyes widened, 'people will expect me to hold your hand at the very least, and if you flinch every time we touch then everyone will know we're faking it.'

'Good point.' But this was the first time she'd held hands with a man since Simon, and it felt strange.

Clearly her feelings showed on her face, because he let her hand go and asked, 'Would you rather we stop this whole thing right now?'

She shook her head. 'I said I'd think about it. It's just...'

'I'm not Simon,' he said. 'And I'm taking this too fast for you.'

She winced. 'I'm sorry. I'm making a mess of this.'

'You're absolutely not,' he said. 'Let's keep walking.'

Kelly could understand why his girlfriends from a different background would find it hard to deal with the intrusiveness and all the protocols; but she didn't understand why someone from Luc's world couldn't relate to the other side of him, the doctor who needed to make a difference to the world for his best friend's sake. Her heart ached for him.

Would it be so hard for her to agree to help him? Just for a few short months? Or, if she agreed to help him with the clinic as well, would it get too complicated?

To distract herself, she said, 'I'm fitting an ICD to a six-year-old girl with Long QT Syndrome on Thursday. Are you around if there are complications?'

'I'm teaching,' he said, 'but if you need me I can be there.'

'I'll ask my patient's grandmother if your students can observe.'

'Thanks.' He looked at her. 'Given that you mentioned her grandmother, I presume there's a familial link?'

She nodded. 'Her mum. Who died.'

'That must be hard for you.'

'Dealing with a genetic cardiac condition that can be fatal? No, actually, it gives me hope that I can help people,' she said. 'Just… OK, I admit I get too involved. I want to save everyone, even though I know I can't.'

He took her hand and squeezed it. 'I know how that feels. But we do our best and that has to be enough.'

When Gino pulled up outside her flat, Kelly said to Luc, 'You and Gino are very welcome to come in for coffee.'

'Thanks, but I need to get back. See you tomorrow at work,' he said. 'And I'll see you at my place tomorrow night for dinner. Anything except red meat, right?'

'Right,' she said with a smile. 'Thanks for a lovely evening.'

'You're welcome. I've enjoyed getting to know you better.'

So had she. And that was worrying.

Luc spent the entire Wednesday working on a tricky coronary artery bypass graft, and didn't get a chance to see

Kelly once he'd left the operating theatre. He texted her swiftly. I'll send Gino to pick you up.

It's fine. I'll get the Tube, she replied. Text me the address.

He did so, admiring her independent streak. And he'd really enjoyed her company last night. In other circumstances, he would've been tempted to ask her out properly. But he knew she wasn't ready to move on; the way she'd been so startled by him holding her hand was proof of that, and he could've kicked himself for being so insensitive. She hadn't agreed to marry him yet, and although they'd talked about making it look like a whirlwind courtship he'd taken things too fast. He needed to be patient. Even though he knew the clock was ticking for him.

And today would show her more of the other side of his life. Would it make her back away, the way Rachel had?

Luc was a prince. Of *course* he'd live in a mansion on the edge of Hampstead Heath, Kelly thought as she reached his address. And of course it would be a gated community where she'd have to check in with the concierge before she could even walk down his road.

The house was amazing—a new build, and yet with a nod to past architectural styles at the same time. Simon would've loved the Georgian symmetry of the three-storey facade, the shape of the roof, the dormer windows and the curved roof above the portico by the front door. There was a sweeping carriage drive in front of the house, and the garden was planted immaculately. Kelly felt a little like Cinderella; she definitely wasn't dressed up enough for this place.

But when Gino answered the front door to her, he was dressed in jeans.

And so was Luc, when she walked inside.

'Thank you for coming,' Luc said. 'Can I get you a drink?'

'A glass of water would be lovely.' And please don't let him put it into some fragile, priceless crystal that she'd end up dropping, she begged silently. 'And these are for you.' She handed him a bag. 'I forgot to ask if you'd prefer red or white, so I played it safe.'

'I love Sauvignon Blanc,' he said with a smile when he looked at the contents. 'And these are seriously good chocolates. Thank you very much.'

'It didn't feel quite right, bringing you flowers. Given your front garden, I think I made the right choice.'

'Maria—my housekeeper—had a hand in the planting. I admit, I don't really notice the flowers in the house, but she likes them. If my team's happy, then I'm happy.' He smiled at her. 'Would you like a guided tour before dinner?'

'Yes, please. I'd love to see this Italian garden you told me about yesterday.'

The interior of the house was even grander than the outside. The large living room had French doors, enormous sofas, a huge cream rug on the maple floors, and small occasional tables that held lamps and the largest vase of lilies she'd ever seen. And to think that if she agreed to his marriage of convenience she would be living here for a few months. She'd be terrified of breakages and spills whenever Susie and the twins came to visit.

Though she loved the large oil painting of a seascape on the living room wall. 'That's beautiful.'

'It's the view over the harbour from the castle in the Old Town in Bordimiglia,' he said.

The dining room was equally large, with a table big enough to seat twelve, and again it overlooked the garden. In the centre of the table was a huge vase of red tulips. 'They're gorgeous,' she said.

'Maria's favourites,' he said with a smile. 'And my mother's.'

'Mine, too.'

The kitchen was bigger than her entire flat, and everything was glossy white and gleaming chrome. The sort that would show every single fingerprint, she thought; this was definitely a high-maintenance house. There was a smaller table at one end of the kitchen, set for two.

'I thought we'd eat in here tonight—it's a bit cosier than the dining room,' Luc said. 'I tend to eat in here if it's just me.'

'Something smells very nice,' she said.

'My speciality,' he said.

There were a couple more sitting rooms, then a study lined with books and with a state-of-the-art computer on an otherwise clear desk, a comfy chair that was clearly his reading spot, and a small coffee table next to it stacked with medical journals. Next to that was a music room containing a baby grand piano, a couple of electric guitars on stands, and an amplifier.

'I'm expecting a demo,' she said.

'After dinner,' he promised. 'Though remember I warned you I'm not professional standard, and that wasn't false modesty.'

The hallway was massive, with marble flooring and a beautiful curving wrought-iron staircase. 'Bedrooms,' he said, 'all with en-suite bathrooms. The staff quarters are through here, on three floors.' He gestured to a corridor. 'The gym and pool are that way.' He led her down a different corridor. 'This is the garden room, for days when it's too wet to be outside.' The room was even bigger than the kitchen, with marble floors and comfortable chairs and what looked like orange trees in huge terracotta pots.

And from there he led her out into the garden. There was a huge stone terrace with a table and chairs, and massive pots containing bay trees and box hedges clipped into massive globes. Next to it was an English country garden full of colourful shrubs and late spring bulbs; beyond that lay a formal Italian garden complete with more neatly clipped topiary, marble statues and a fountain with stone dolphins.

'That's stunning,' she said.

He looked pleased. 'I love it out here.'

'And the Heath's just over there?'

'Behind the cypress trees,' he said.

'It's lovely, Luc.' And surprisingly homely, given the sheer scale of the place. She should've felt intimidated; she couldn't even begin to imagine how much the mortgage would be on a property like this. And yet the place was welcoming and full of warmth.

'I'm not going to rush you, but have a think about whether you could live here for a few months,' he said.

'I will,' she promised.

'Good. Come and have dinner,' he said, catching her fingers between his.

His speciality turned out to be macaroni cheese and greens, which he served with a heritage tomato salad and ciabatta bread.

'I'm impressed,' she said after her first taste. It was creamy without being sickly, and the cheese had a nice sharp bite to it. 'Tell me you made the bread as well.'

He wrinkled his nose. 'I'm not going to lie. That was Maria. But I did make the macaroni. Admittedly using dried pasta, but the sauce isn't from a jar.'

She smiled. 'Simon was a terrible cook. I always used

to tease him that he could burn water. He could design the most gorgeous buildings, and if he did a quick scribbled sketch it looked like a flawless piece of art. But he always got too distracted to follow a recipe. The deal was that I cooked and he washed up.'

'Sounds fair, as long as you like cooking.'

'I do—it relaxes me,' she said.

'I have to admit I cheated and bought chocolate ganache pots for pudding,' he said.

'Considering how many hours you spent in Theatre today, you could've ordered in a takeaway or bought a meal from the supermarket and that would've been fine,' she said.

'No. I promised you I'd cook for you, and I keep my word,' he said.

'It's appreciated,' she said.

After dinner, they headed for the music room.

'So do you play the piano or anything?' he asked.

'No. Susie, Mum and I will sing our heads off to the radio or if we're watching a musical together. But none of us ever tried playing a musical instrument—well, except the recorder and the triangle at infant school, but that doesn't count.'

Luc sat down at the piano and patted the wide bench next to him. 'Give it a go. Let's try something.'

When she sat down, he lifted the lid and played four notes. 'Can you do that? Start at middle C,' he said, and pointed to the key in front of the keyhole.

Dubiously, she did so. Then she looked at him. 'I recognise that.'

'You said you were a Tom Hanks fan, so I hope you would.' He grinned. 'You're going to play that half and I'll do the melody. You repeat it four times—down two keys, down two keys, up one key, then back to the beginning.'

She did a couple of practice runs, getting it horribly wrong, but he got her to persevere. And then, when she was more confident, he joined in with the melody of 'Heart and Soul'.

'See? You can play,' he said.

'Barely. Play me something,' she urged.

He played a Mozart sonata she recognised, and some Bach. Then he looked at her. 'Eighties pop and nineties indie. I'll play, but you have to sing. Deal?'

'Deal.'

To her surprise, he played 'Come on Eileen'.

She laughed. 'That always gets Mum up on the dance floor.' She sang along with him, realising just how good his voice was.

'Your turn to choose,' he said.

'Eighties pop. So it's got to be Rick Astley or Wham!' she said with a grin.

'As you wish.'

She looked at him, wondering if he was teasing her with a reference to one of her favourite movies, but his face was deadpan. Maybe that was because he was a prince and had been taught to mask everything. She wasn't going to overthink it.

He played 'Never Gonna Give You Up', followed by 'Wake Me Up Before You Go-Go'. Between them, they sang nearly a dozen hits from the eighties and nineties, with Luc hamming it up and making Kelly laugh until her stomach ached.

He finished with Oasis's 'Wonderwall', and she let him sing it solo. When he played the last note, he turned to her. His eyes were dark and looked huge. And then he leaned forward and brushed his mouth lightly against hers. Not demanding, just gentle and so sweet that it made her heart feel as if someone had just squeezed it. At the same time, her mouth was tingling where his lips had touched her skin.

He'd said he would give her time and not rush her into a decision. And she knew he meant it, because he looked as shocked as she felt. Clearly this had been an impulse.

She could back away. Or she could kiss him back. And right at that moment she really wanted to kiss him. Would it be so bad if she gave in to the urge? She rested her palm against his cheek. 'Luc,' she said, and her voice sounded strangely rusty to her own ears.

He twisted his head so he could drop a kiss into her palm, and her stomach swooped.

It was the first time she'd wanted to kiss a man since Simon's death. The first time she'd wanted a man to kiss her. And this was a man who'd asked her to marry him in name only.

This shouldn't be happening.

As if her doubts showed on her face, he said softly, 'It's getting late. I'll drive you home.'

'Are you allowed?'

'Gino will drive, then. But I'll see you home.'

'Thank you.' She let her hand drop back into her lap. 'And for this evening. It's been fun.'

'I can't remember when I last enjoyed myself so much,' he said. 'You're good company, Kelly.'

'Even though I'm terrible at playing the piano?'

'Your singing makes up for it,' he said with a smile. 'So. Tomorrow's whirlwind date. How about the cinema? You pick the film, and I'll arrange tickets.'

'Even if it's a soppy rom-com instead of an action movie?' she tested.

'OK. Theatre, then. Let's do a musical.'

'You're on. I'll organise tickets.'

'Actually, Gino will need to organise tickets.' He grimaced slightly.

Of course. His security detail would need to vet everything. 'OK. I don't mind what we see. Any music is a treat. But I'll pay for the tickets,' she said.

'I'll pay for the tickets,' he corrected. 'But you can buy me dinner, if it makes you feel better.'

'It does.'

This time, when Gino drove them home, Luc held Kelly's hand all the way. Again, he waited until she was indoors before they drove off. And Kelly felt as if the dried-up edges of her life were starting to soften again. Sitting at the piano with him that evening, singing and laughing together... She'd felt happier than she had in a long, long time.

And for a second she could almost feel Simon's arms round her, giving her a hug. Hear him whisper, 'Be happy.'

She shook herself. How fanciful. She didn't believe in ghosts.

Besides, Luc wasn't the one to make her love again. This was a temporary favour to buy time for both of them, and she really mustn't get carried away and forget it.

CHAPTER SIX

On Thursday night, Luc took Kelly for dinner at a small Italian restaurant after work.

'As you didn't call me, I'm assuming your ICD went well?' he asked.

'Very. How was your teaching day?' she asked.

'Good. Oh, and I have some news for you. Obviously I can't discuss confidential medical information, but you might want to check in with Jake and Summer and ask them if they have some news for you.'

Her eyes widened. 'Are you telling me they're on the trial?'

'As I said, I can't discuss confidential medical information,' he repeated. 'But Jake isn't under the same constraints as I am. He can tell you all the details that I can't.'

'Thank you. You have no idea how much this means.'

'The judgement was made purely on a clinical basis,' he said. 'As a surgeon, I have to be impartial and keep emotions out of it.'

'I know. But you could've refused even to consider them. And I feel a lot better knowing that they're both going to get more check-ups than usual.'

'With proper treatment and follow-up, most patients with HCM live a normal life,' he reminded her gently. 'I'm sorry that Simon was unlucky.'

'Yes.' She blew out a breath. 'I'm not going mopey on you.'

'I know, but that news was bound to make you feel emotional. I probably should've handled it better,' he admitted.

'You're a good man, Luc,' she said, and reached across the table to squeeze his hand.

He was going to have to be careful. Their relationship was a total fake. He really couldn't allow himself to react to her touch like this. Growing up as a prince, he'd learned to keep his feelings private and wear a public mask of smiles. Whatever was happening in your private life, you just got on with your duty. This was the same thing. If Kelly agreed to it—and he really hoped she would—there would be a time limit. After that, they'd have a quiet divorce and they'd be strictly friends and colleagues. Letting himself fall in love with her wasn't part of the deal.

'Les Mis!' she said as they reached the theatre. 'This is always a treat.' She beamed at him. 'Thank you so much, Luc. Though I hope you brought tissues. I always cry. Especially at "On My Own" and "I Dreamed a Dream".'

'You've seen it more than once, then?'

'Susie and Ange love musicals as much as I do. So does Mum, so I've seen it with all three of them—separately and together. And I organised a team night out to see it, about five years ago.'

He winced. 'Sorry. I should've guessed that you'd already seen it, or at least checked with you first.'

'I would've still said yes, because I absolutely love this show,' she said, and reached up to kiss his cheek.

How easy it would be to turn and face her properly, and to change that kiss on the cheek into something more sensual.

Luc kept himself firmly in check, and ushered her into the theatre.

'We've got a box?' she asked, looking surprised when he led her up the stairs.

He shrugged. 'It keeps Gino happy.'

'Got it.' She squeezed his hand. 'We have amazing legroom and a fantastic view—we're looking down so we can see the patterns of the choreography as well.'

Typical Kelly, looking on the bright side instead of being disappointed that she wasn't among the crowd like everyone else. He appreciated that.

As she'd predicted, Kelly cried during the sad songs, and he had to borrow a handkerchief from Gino to help her mop them up. And this time, after Gino had driven them back to her place, Luc accepted her offer to come in for coffee. Gino, too, accepted, but insisted on sitting at the kitchen table rather than with them in the living room.

'It feels rude, leaving you out here on your own, Gino. You're my guest,' Kelly said.

'I'm working,' Gino said gently. 'But thank you for looking after me so well.' He gestured to the tin she'd brought out of the cupboard. 'I love cannoli wafers. And your coffee's good.' He patted her arm. 'Go and chat to Luc, *bella*. You both know where I am if you need me.'

Luc followed Kelly into the living room. The walls were painted a bright sunny yellow; there was a bookcase stuffed with a mix of medical textbooks and novels, a comfortable sofa with a coffee table next to it and a small television. There were a lot of framed photographs on the mantelpiece. 'May I?' he asked, gesturing to them.

'Of course.' She came to stand beside him and talked him through them. 'That's my sister Susie, on her wedding day to Nick, both of them with the twins just before last Christmas because they always do a family portrait, Mum and Dad with me on my graduation day, and Simon and me on our wedding day.'

They looked so happy together. Luc's heart ached for her. He'd felt bad enough when Rachel had broken off their relationship but they hadn't even got to the engagement stage. How much worse it must have been for Kelly to marry the love of her life and then lose him before they could start their longed-for family—and it was an extra twist of the knife that Simon had died from an undiagnosed cardiac condition, when Kelly was a cardiologist.

It was clear to him that she hadn't moved on from loving Simon. That she might never be ready to move on. Which meant he felt a lot less guilty about asking her to help him; she wasn't going to be taking a risk with her heart because it still belonged to Simon. No way was she going to fall for him and get hurt.

'They're lovely photos,' he said. 'Who's this with you?'

'Angela—my best friend. We met on the first day of sixth form. That's us at our prom.' She smiled. 'We look so young there.'

'And beautiful.'

'I wasn't fishing,' she said.

'I know.' The words had slipped out before he could stop them. He really needed to get a grip. 'What would you like to do tomorrow?'

'I'm working, and I think you might be co-opted onto the team pub quiz,' she said. 'But I was thinking—on Saturday, my parents are having a barbecue.' She looked at him. 'And I was wondering if you'd like to meet my family.'

He went very still. Did that mean she was going to

agree to help him? Or was this kind of the last test—if her family liked him, then she'd agree to the marriage of convenience?

'I'd like that,' he said carefully.

'Good.' She smiled. 'My family's nice, Luc. They'll ask you a gazillion questions, but it'll be relatively easy to deflect them if we keep the story as close to the truth as possible. We met just over a month ago when Sanjay asked me to show you round on your first day, and we liked each other. We've been on a couple of dates.'

He sucked in a breath. 'So, the whirlwind courtship?'

'Yes. I'll help you,' she said.

'Thank you. I know it's a big ask.'

'I still have my doubts,' she admitted. 'But you're helping me. I'm not *quite* as much of a workaholic as I was even a month ago, and the new procedures you've brought into the department have reinvigorated my love of medicine—I'm doing my job because I love it, not because I'm scared of losing someone. So I want to help you, too. And that includes your new clinic. It's the fresh start I think I need.'

'That's fantastic news. Thank you. I really appreciate it.' He paused. 'So what can I bring to the barbecue?'

'Just yourself.'

He shook his head. 'That's not how I was brought up. Wine, flowers, chocolates?'

'Dad's just been diagnosed as diabetic, so not chocolate,' she said. 'Flowers and wine would be very nice. Not too—' She grimaced and cut off the words. 'Sorry. That was about to sound really ungrateful and I don't mean it that way.'

'Not too showy-offy,' he guessed. 'Noted. And you weren't ungrateful.'

'Just... My family's very ordinary.'

'Actually,' he said, 'behind the image, so's mine. You'd get on well with my sisters. My parents would like you, too.'

Once he'd finished his coffee, he turned to her. 'I'd better get going.'

'Thank you again for this evening, Luc. I really enjoyed it.'

'Me, too,' he said. He leaned forward and kissed her very lightly on the lips. 'Good night.'

'Good night.'

Her pupils looked huge, and he wondered whether she was feeling that same unexpected spark as he was. But he wasn't going to make things difficult by asking.

He was still thinking about it when Gino drove him home.

'All right, boss?' Gino asked. He'd been with Luc for ten years, long enough to know him well and comfortable enough in his position to ask awkward questions.

'Yes,' Luc fibbed.

'I like her,' Gino said.

'She's a good colleague. A friend,' Luc said.

'You don't look at each other as if you're just friends,' Gino pointed out.

That was a good thing. It meant they'd be able to convince her family at the weekend and he'd uphold his half of the deal. But on the other hand it was a bad thing. It wasn't supposed to be more than friendship, and he couldn't afford to let things get out of hand. The last thing he wanted was for Kelly to get hurt. 'Maybe,' Luc said casually.

Thankfully Gino didn't push it any further. And everything between himself and Kelly felt totally as usual at work the next day.

On Saturday, it was raining.

Luc rang Kelly. 'Given the weather, do I assume the barbecue is cancelled?'

'Absolutely not. Dad's been known to sit in pouring rain, holding a massive golf umbrella over himself and the barbecue—on more than one occasion. If it was snowing in the middle of June, he'd still insist on having a barbecue.' She laughed. 'The twins will be there. I hope you don't mind children.'

'I like children just fine,' he said. 'I'm an uncle to two, remember. Which means I have an amazing line of bad jokes.'

'That's good. I'll see you in a couple of hours, then.'

This was ridiculous, being nervous, Kelly told herself sharply. Luc wasn't the first man she'd taken home to meet her family.

But he was the first man she'd taken home since Simon's death.

And she needed to make this convincing, because she was about to tell her family an enormous white lie. Not to hurt them, but to give her a breathing space from the nagging and to stop them worrying about her.

She was still jittery by the time Luc rang her doorbell.

He frowned. 'What's wrong?'

'I feel guilty,' she said. 'About what we're doing.'

'You're not doing anything wrong. You're doing me a massive favour,' he reminded her.

'I know.' She bit her lip.

'You're taking me to meet your family, so they can see for themselves that I'm not going to make you unhappy.' He smiled at her. 'If we turn up with you looking anxious, that's pretty much going to wreck our cover story.'

'I guess.'

'I could tell you terrible jokes all the way to your parents' house.'

'I think I'll manage,' she said.

'Good. Let's go.'

'Let me get everything out of the fridge.' She'd made salads earlier and put them into storage boxes.

Luc helped her into the car. 'I brought half a case of wine and some flowers for your parents. I hope that's acceptable.'

She looked at the bouquet of peonies and pink gypsophilia. 'Mum will *love* those.'

'Not too showy-offy?' he checked.

She winced. 'Sorry. It's hard for you. I imagine people expect the Prince to turn up with things gift-wrapped in pure gold. But it's the cardiac surgeon my family's meeting.'

'It's a strange line to walk,' he agreed. 'Thank you, Kelly. For making me feel real.'

Right at that moment, the uncertainty in his eyes made her want to lean forward and kiss him, reassure him that everything was going to be just fine.

And, even though she felt nervous about it, she didn't want him to feel bad. So she leaned forward and brushed her mouth against his. 'You'll do.'

Her mouth tingled, flustering her slightly; but she could see the same thing in his expression.

This was strange. A fake relationship that needed to look real—yet, at the same time, was starting to feel real.

Could this really be the start of something they both weren't expecting?

She pushed the thoughts aside. It wasn't going to work out that way.

As she'd half expected, her family was gathered in

the large farmhouse kitchen that also doubled as the dining room.

'Mum, Dad, I'd like you to meet Luc Bianchi. Luc, my parents, Caroline and Robin, my sister Susie and her husband Nick, and the twins, Oscar and Jacob,' she introduced them swiftly.

'Delighted to meet you all,' he said, and handed Caroline the bouquet and the box of wine to Robin.

'How gorgeous! Thank you,' Caroline said, and gave him a hug. 'Nice to meet you, Luc.'

'Yes, good to meet you. And thank you for the wine.' Robin shook his hand.

'Wait a second—aren't you...?' Susie asked, looking shocked.

'Yes,' Luc said. 'Prince Luciano of Bordimiglia. Otherwise known as Luc Bianchi, cardiac surgeon.'

'So do we call you "Your Highness"?' Nick asked as he shook hands with Luc.

He smiled. 'No. Luc's fine. Um, I do have my driver with me outside, if I could perhaps have a parking permit for the car?'

'You're very welcome to a parking permit,' Caroline said, 'but your driver is most certainly not waiting outside. There's plenty of room here and plenty of food, so I'd be happier if he joined us.' She winced. 'Oh—is that allowed?'

'It is. And thank you,' Luc said.

'Come with me, and we'll sort out the parking,' Robin said. 'Actually, then I'm going to put you to work doing barbecue stuff with me and Nick.'

Luc grinned. 'I've already heard the story about the barbecues in the rain under the golf umbrella.'

'They always make me come inside if it starts thundering,' Robin said, looking disgusted. 'We're all going to take turns doing the manly jobs. Barbecuing, umbrella-holding and twin-wrangling.'

'Count me in. Oscar and Jacob, I have a question for you,' Luc said. 'Why did the cake visit the doctor?'

'I don't know,' the twins chorused shyly.

'Because it was feeling crummy,' Luc said.

Kelly winked at Luc to show her approval: it was about the best thing he could have done. The boys and her father all loved corny jokes.

Robin clapped him on the back. 'I must remember that for the office on Monday. I think you and I are going to get on famously, Luc.'

'You,' Susie said to Kelly as soon as Luc was out of earshot, 'have some explaining to do.'

'Luc's a cardiothoracic surgeon,' Kelly said. 'He started at the hospital about five weeks ago. Sanjay asked me to show him round the department and take him to lunch, the first day, because he was in meetings.' So far, all so true.

'And you're dating him?' Caroline said. 'But...'

'But nothing. The pair of you are constantly throwing eligible men at me. Shouldn't you be pleased that I'm dating someone?'

'He's a *prince*,' Susie said.

'A very low-key one who sees himself as a surgeon first,' Kelly pointed out.

'But what about when he has to take over from his father?' Caroline asked.

'He doesn't want to be King. He's trying to persuade his father to change the succession laws so his oldest sister can take over. And I have to say he's a brilliant surgeon. I've sat in on a couple of his ops. And,' Kelly added, 'he's doing a trial of new treatment for HCM. Jake called me the other day to tell me that he and Summer are going to be on it.'

'Oh, darling. That's great news.' Caroline hugged her. 'I take it Luc knows about Simon?'

'Yes. Actually, HCM is why he became a doctor. His best friend died from it when they were fifteen. So he understands why I wanted Jake and Summer on the trial—though that's strictly because they met the trial guidelines and not because I asked him.'

Susie hugged her, too. 'OK. But even though he's a doctor, Kel, he's still a prince.'

'A doctor first,' Kelly said. 'He plans to go back to Bordimiglia in two years' time and set up a state-of-the-art cardiac clinic.'

'So where does that leave you, if he's not staying here?' Susie asked.

'It's early days,' Kelly said. 'Though he's going to need a good cardiologist.'

Caroline looked shocked. 'You mean you'd go with him?'

'It's a good opportunity, and maybe that's what I need to help me move on,' Kelly said. 'A change of scene. No memories.'

'It's a long way away,' Caroline said.

'I know. But nothing's set in stone,' Kelly said.

'Obviously the paparazzi haven't got wind of you dating him, yet,' Susie said.

'No, but it'll be fine,' Kelly reassured her.

'But he's a *prince*, Kel.' Susie looked worried.

'A surgeon,' Kelly said firmly. 'Give him a chance. You might like him. Mum, where do you want me to put these salads?'

Luc was touched by how easily Kelly's family made him feel at home. They were clearly treating him as a surgeon rather than a prince, and he appreciated that. He was kept busy alternately manning the barbecue, holding the golf umbrella over whoever was manning the barbecue next, ferrying cooked food indoors and keeping the twins out of mischief, working as a team with Robin and Nick.

And how good it felt to be treated as a normal person, as part of a normal family. Though, at the same time, it made him feel guilty. He'd pretty much pushed his own family away in an attempt to be his own person; although he was close to his sisters, his relationship with his parents was much trickier, and he knew they all hid behind the excuse of his parents' royal schedule. He needed to make more of an effort to find a compromise. The kind of relationship Kelly had with her family was exactly what he wanted. Just he didn't quite know how to make that work.

The rain stopped, and while he was manning the barbecue Kelly came over with a plate of salad and a glass of wine.

'I've been despatched to make sure the cook's OK,' she said with a smile.

'Very OK.' On impulse, he stole a kiss. 'Thank you for inviting me.'

She went slightly pink. 'Pleasure.'

'Your family's lovely,' he said softly. 'I appreciate the fact they're seeing me for myself and not my position.'

'Expect to be grilled later,' she warned. 'But they like you.'

'Good.' He stole another kiss. Because that was what a new boyfriend would do, wasn't it? The fact that he actually wanted to kiss Kelly was completely beside the point.

And it was good to eat a normal family meal in a normal family environment. When Oscar fell over and scraped his knee, Luc was the nearest and scooped him up to deal with it and talked to him about knights in armour to distract him from the sting of the antiseptic.

And, just as Kelly had warned, Susie insisted that they should do the washing up together after the meal while everyone sat out in the garden, now the rain had lifted. Grilling time, he thought. 'You're Kelly's big sister. Mine would be the same and want to be sure whoever I brought home had good intentions,' he said. 'So what do you want to know?'

'You're dating my little sister,' Susie said.

'I am,' he agreed. It wasn't the whole truth, but enough to count.

'And you know about her past.'

'I know how much she loved Simon and how devastated she was at losing him. So I understand why you're all worried about her. I'll be careful with her,' he said. He smiled. 'Just to reassure you, I think a lot of your sister. I respect her professionally and personally.'

Susie looked wary. 'But your world is very different from ours, Luc.'

'I'm a heart surgeon,' he said softly. 'So, actually, my world is pretty much the same as Kelly's. We work in the same department. Sometimes she sits in when I operate on her patients, and sometimes I ask her to run tests on mine.'

'Except she's an ordinary woman and you also happen to be a prince. Can I be honest?' At his nod, she said, 'The newspapers can be unkind. That worries me.'

'The media can be vile,' he agreed, 'but there's nothing about your family they can use to hurt her.'

'You checked us out?'

This was where he needed to reassure her properly. 'Yes—for Kelly's sake. As you say, the newspapers can be unkind. I've been there before and it ended badly,' he said softly. 'I mean to take care of Kelly and make sure the press can't hurt her—or, by extension, any of your family and close friends. I admit, there probably will be some press intrusion, and I apologise in advance for that. But our press team will be there to support you. Anything you need, you'll have it. I'll make sure you, Nick and your parents have all the relevant phone numbers before I leave today. They'll be available to you twenty-four-seven.'

Susie still looked worried. 'Gino's a nice man, but he's your bodyguard.'

'Which I know is a strange thing if you didn't grow up with it, but I'm used to it. He's part of my team. And my team's protection will extend to Kelly,' he said.

'You're the first man she's actually brought home since Simon, so it's obvious that you matter to her,' Susie said.

Guilt lanced through him. Kelly's family was nice, and they really loved her. They were close. Whereas his own family was nice, and he'd distanced himself from them. It made him feel selfish and horrible. 'She wanted me to meet you.'

'Because you matter,' Susie repeated.

'Because she loves you all, and she doesn't want you to worry about her.' That much was true. He wanted to stick to the truth as much as he could. 'And of course you'll worry,' he added gently. 'But I promise you I won't hurt her.'

'OK.' Susie took a deep breath. 'And this clinic you want to set up?'

So Kelly had mentioned it to her family, then. 'My best friend died from HCM when we were fifteen. It's why I became a cardiac specialist—I saw what his family went through and I wanted to save other people from that, I guess, and to save other fifteen-year-olds losing their best friends, the way I did,' he added wryly. 'I want to set up a cutting-edge cardiac clinic in Bordimiglia.' He paused. What he needed to give Kelly's family was some reassurance that he wasn't going to whisk her off with him right this very second. 'I asked Kelly if she would consider coming back with me and training the next generation of cardiologists. But it's still a couple of years away—I wouldn't leave Muswell Hill Memorial Hospital in the lurch by accepting this post and then disappearing in a couple of weeks to set up my new clinic. I plan to spend a couple of years in my current role, getting more experience, and give them plenty of time to replace me.'

'That's fair,' she said. 'But Bordimiglia's a long way from England.'

'A couple of hours on a plane,' he said. 'Which is just as quick as if, say, she'd moved to Manchester and you took the train to see her.'

Susie nodded. 'And I guess she has a point. Working in a place where there are no memories might help her move on. And that's all we want—for her to be happy again.'

'I understand,' he said softly.

'I apologise for the grilling.'

'No apology needed. It's good that her family looks out for her. My sisters will probably grill her in the same way at some point.' He smiled. 'But actually as soon as they meet her they'll see her for who she is and they'll love her.'

When Susie and Luc reappeared from the kitchen, to Kelly's relief they both looked relaxed rather than awkward. And Luc was fine about the idea of taking the twins to the park to play football. It made her heart squeeze sharply—Simon had been a fantastic uncle and had loved going to the park with the boys—but she appreciated that Luc was making the effort to fit in with her family.

Susie hugged Kelly as they stood on the sidelines, watching the men play football with the twins. 'I really like him. He's a lot more down to earth than I would have expected from someone in his position. Nick and Dad like him, too.'

'And Mum?' Kelly checked.

'She's as worried as I am,' Susie admitted, 'but he pretty much reassured me—'

'—when you grilled him in the kitchen,' Kelly finished.

'A man who doesn't complain about helping with the washing up or being grilled by a bossy older sister is one to keep hold of,' Susie said. 'We all just want to see you happy.'

'I am,' Kelly promised.

In a weird way, this thing with Luc was helping her to move on. She'd never forget Simon and she'd always love him, but she was starting to think that she could move on and find happiness again.

On the Wednesday, Luc's patient Maia Isley was scheduled to have the new personalised external aortic root support treatment. Kelly had already been involved in the scans where they'd made a 3D computer model of Maia's heart, and Luc was happy with the tailored mesh support that he was going to wrap round her aorta. His colleague from his old department had come over to lend a hand with the operation, and Sanjay joined Kelly to watch the operation.

'So today we're making history,' Sanjay said.

'It's wonderful to be part of new developments,' Kelly agreed.

And it was wonderful to watch Luc operating. She noticed how deft his hands were and how his confidence and clear direction made the rest of the team relax. Maia had agreed to let them film the operation to use for training in the department, for their colleagues who couldn't be there to see it.

'It's amazing how far we've come since I was your age,' Sanjay said.

She grinned. 'You're not that old, Sanj.'

'Sometimes I feel it,' he said. 'I'm glad Luc's joined us. I did worry that we might have a problem with press intrusion, but his PR team has been excellent.'

She'd remember to tell that to her parents and Susie later, to help ease any worries they might have. And what she and Luc were planning might still have an effect on the hospital; but hopefully Luc's team could spin it positively.

'Are you OK?' Sanjay asked.

'Sure. Just a bit overwhelmed by what we're doing here today,' she said. Which was true... Just not the whole truth.

'You and Luc seem to be getting on really well,' Sanjay said.

'He's a good man. I like him a lot.'

'Agreed,' Sanjay said.

And if her boss had noticed that they were getting on well... Then hopefully they'd manage to convince everyone at work that their marriage was real.

CHAPTER SEVEN

THE FOLLOWING WEEKEND, Kelly sorted out the final arrangements for New York with Luc.

'Do you want me to pack hand luggage only?' she asked.

'No. Bring whatever you like,' he said.

'Are you sure? Packing luggage for the hold means we'll have to wait around for the plane to unload.'

'Not quite,' he said.

She frowned. 'How come?'

'We're using a private jet,' he explained.

She felt her eyes widen. 'You own a plane?'

'No. I'm chartering a flight.' He shrugged, as if it wasn't a big deal. 'It makes life a lot easier for Gino and the team.'

Security. Of course. She should've thought of that.

'So we're going to New York tomorrow—just you and me?' she checked.

'And three of my security team. You haven't met Federico and Vincenzo yet,' he said, 'but they're nice.'

'Right.'

'They've known me for years and they're as discreet as Gino. You'll hardly know they're there,' he reassured her.

But it brought home to her just how unusual his life

was. How odd hers was going to be, once she'd married him. 'OK,' she said, the doubts flooding through her.

'Are you OK with flying?' he asked.

'I've never been in a private jet,' she said, 'but I'm assuming it's super-safe or Gino wouldn't let you set foot on it.'

He smiled. 'Exactly.'

The enormity of what they were about to do filled her head. 'You're not having second thoughts about all this?'

'No,' he said, sounding perfectly serene and confident. Then he looked at her. 'Are you?'

'Yes,' she admitted. She'd told her parents that Luc was taking her away for a few days, but had told a white lie in saying that she didn't know where.

'Your family have met me, and it went just fine,' he reminded her. 'I understand that they'll be upset at not being included in the wedding, but I'll take the blame for whisking you off your feet. If they want some kind of celebration when we get back, I can organise that,' he added. 'And I'll buy you a dress when we're out there.'

'Are you sure this isn't going to land you in a huge amount of trouble?' she asked.

'There will probably be a bit of a row,' he said, 'but nothing I can't handle. Sometimes you just have to step out of a box to help other people think outside of that same box.' He kissed her lightly. 'Don't worry. It's going to be fine. And I really appreciate what you're doing for me.'

On Monday morning, Kelly was packed and waiting when Luc rang her doorbell at six a.m.

'Ready?' he asked.

'Ready,' she fibbed, and locked the door to her old life behind her.

Luc insisted on carrying her case to the car. 'Gino you already know; this is Federico and Vincenzo,' he introduced her swiftly.

'Good morning,' she said shyly.

Travelling with Luc's entourage was nothing like anything she'd experienced before. At the airport, there was no queueing to drop off baggage, or for security and passport control, not even for boarding. Everything was smooth and efficient.

The plane itself was amazing: wide, comfortable seats with plenty of legroom, work tables, a large galley and washroom, and access to all their baggage.

Now she understood why he'd said that luggage wouldn't be a problem. And she could also understand how the ordinary women Luc had dated had felt overwhelmed by this side of his life, because she was feeling pretty much that way, too.

'OK?' he asked.

'Right now, I'm feeling a tiny bit out of my depth,' she admitted.

'I'm sorry. It's not meant to be that way.'

'I know.' She squeezed his hand. 'You're not trying to be showy-offy. This is just how your world is.'

'Thank you for understanding.' Though his dark eyes were filled with concern.

'It's all right, Luc. I know what I'm doing. Ish,' she said. 'I'm not going to let you down.' On impulse, she kissed his cheek, and his pupils were huge as he looked at her.

'If there's anything at all I can do to make this easier, just say.'

Short of flying her entire family over to be there for the wedding—and then it would be massively unfair to leave his family out, plus this was going to be a marriage in name only rather than a real one—there was nothing he could do. Though she appreciated the offer. 'It's fine,' she said.

'OK. Our flight lasts for eight hours and we leave at seven, so we'll arrive in New York at three p.m. our time—that's ten a.m. US time,' he told her.

'Got it,' she said.

The flight was the most comfortable Kelly had ever experienced. The captain came to introduce himself and his cabin staff, and then they served the most amazing breakfast: freshly squeezed orange juice, exotic fruit, smoked salmon and scrambled egg on rye bagels, and truly excellent coffee.

They all watched a movie, played several board games—and Kelly really liked the fact that Gino, Federico and Vincenzo all played competitively rather than letting Luc win—and then finally they landed in New York and were whisked through security.

She sent a text to her parents, Susie and Angela to tell them she'd arrived safely.

New York! How lovely. Have a wonderful time, darling, was her mum's response.

Amazing! Have fun in the Big Apple and fingers crossed you get to see a Broadway show, was Susie's.

But Angela's reply made Kelly bite her lip. Are you sure about all this? Not too late to change your mind xx.

Oh, but it was. She'd promised to help Luc. Backing out now would be mean. And he was right—they weren't hurting anyone. She hadn't introduced him to Angela yet. Her friend clearly didn't approve of their plan and she didn't want to cause any unnecessary friction.

There was a limo waiting outside, which took them to a gorgeous white stone building on Fifth Avenue, twenty storeys stretching up into the blue sky.

She blinked. 'I recognise this building.'

He smiled at her. 'As a Tom Hanks fan, of course you would.'

'*Sleepless in Seattle*,' she said. 'Luc, this is—'

He pressed one finger to her lip. 'I know. And I can afford it, so don't worry. If we're going to elope, I thought we should do it in style.'

And how, she thought, in one of the poshest hotels in New York, right on Central Park. 'OK. And thank you.'

A bellboy in a black uniform and wearing a black brimless cap shaped like a drum took their luggage up to their room. Again, it was a million miles away from the small and ordinary hotel room Kelly would normally have booked. They actually had a suite, with two bedrooms, two bathrooms and a sitting room overlooking Central Park.

'Gino, Vincenzo and Federico also have rooms on our floor, and they'll need to check out our suite first whenever we come back to it,' Luc said. 'I'm sorry for the intrusiveness.'

'Don't apologise. It's necessary,' she said. 'But it must be hard for you, always having to be aware of security.'

'I grew up with it, so I don't know any different,' he said. 'Pick whichever room you'd like.'

'Are you sure?'

'Very sure,' he said with a smile.

'Thank you.'

The bedrooms were both gorgeous, but Kelly chose the one with the view of the park. There was a separate bathroom with a mosaic floor and walls; as well as a king-sized bed, the bedroom contained a sofa and a desk with a gilded Louis XIV chair. The decor was white and grey and navy, with accents of gold; though the overall effect was stylish rather than overpowering.

'This is amazing,' she said.

'I'm glad you like it. I'll give you time to freshen up,' he said, 'and then we can go and finalise the paperwork to get our wedding licence. Then we'll have the rest of the day to explore.'

'OK.' Kelly discovered that the shower in her bathroom had jets of water coming out of the wall, as well as a massive shower-head that worked as a spray or as a waterfall. How her mum, sister and best friend would love this.

Mindful of the time, she was quick to shower and change, and she was grateful when Gino handed her a takeaway cup of coffee in the limo. 'To keep you going, *bella*,' he said with a smile.

'Grazie,' she said, smiling back.

The limo took them to the Manhattan City Clerk's Office Marriage Bureau. Luc had already completed most of the paperwork online to save them some time. Their passports acted as their photo ID, and Kelly had brought along the original copies of her marriage certificate to Simon and his death certificate. Taking them out of the folder made her catch her breath.

Luc looked at Kelly, and it suddenly registered with him what she was holding. Her marriage certificate and Simon's death certificate.

Of course this was going to be hard for her. Guilt flooded through him. So much for his good intentions. This was hurting her anyway.

He took her hand. 'Kelly. I'm sorry. I didn't mean for this to be hard for you.'

'It's all right.'

But her eyes were a little bit too bright.

'You don't have to do this,' he said. 'We can call it off right now.'

She gave him a wry smile. 'Considering how much planning's gone into this—not to mention that we've flown thousands of miles to get here, and how much money this has cost—it'd be a bit daft for me to back out now.'

'Money isn't important. You are.' It shocked him to realise how important she'd become to him, but he shoved the thought aside. Not now. 'We can call it off.'

'I said I'd help you.'

'But it's not meant to be at a personal cost to you.'

'It's fine. Just…' She swallowed hard. 'I guess this is one way to make myself move on.'

'Not if you're not ready,' he said firmly. 'I won't do that to you.'

And it was a lesson to him, too, not to get carried away. Not to want what she wasn't ready to give anyone. He'd really have to keep a lid on the pull of attraction he felt towards her. It would make everything much too complicated.

'I'm fine.' She nodded. 'Really. I made a promise and I'm going to keep it.' She gave him a small smile.

Finally, the licence was processed and Luc tucked it safely away in his wallet. 'Time for some shopping,' he said.

'Not all women love shopping, you know,' she pointed out. 'Though I do need to get some souvenirs for Mum, Dad, Susie, Nick, the twins, Ange and Rod.'

'I have your mum, Susie and Angela covered,' he said, 'and we can find things for everyone else when we do the touristy stuff.'

'What do you mean, Mum, Susie and Angela are covered?' she asked.

He wrinkled his nose. 'I can't tell you without spoiling a surprise for you. But trust me on this.'

Kelly realised that she *did* trust him. She knew the surgeon and it looked as if she was going to get to know the prince.

'We'll do just two shops today,' he said. 'We need wedding rings and your dress.'

How different it was going to be from her last wedding, when her mum and her sister and her best friend had gone dress-shopping with her and they'd made a day of it, including lunch and afternoon tea. Again, the memory put a lump in her throat. But this wasn't a real marriage, she reminded herself. She and Luc didn't love each other the way she and Simon had. They were friends, and they were just helping each other to solve a problem. None of this was real; the marriage would be in name only.

She wasn't that surprised when the limo took them to Fifth Avenue. On the corner was a store she'd seen in plenty of photographs, with the words 'Tiffany & Co.' carved into the door's lintel, and an iconic statue of Atlas holding a clock above that. Inside was a massive sales floor and a huge sweeping staircase.

'It's the first time I've ever been here,' she said. 'It's incredible. Just how I imagined it. No wonder Holly Golightly was so entranced by this place.'

He smiled and took her hand. 'Let's get what we need.'

With the help of the sales girl, they both chose very plain platinum wedding bands.

'You should have an engagement ring, too,' Luc said thoughtfully.

'There's no need. We're not actually getting engaged,' she reminded him.

'This is meant to be a whirlwind romance, so you need

an engagement ring.' He smiled. 'There's a cafe here now, so maybe we should've come here first and had breakfast at Tiffany's—apart from the fact that we've already had breakfast, and our day started in the middle of the night here.'

She smiled. 'That film always makes me sob buckets.'

'The bit with the cat. It's the same with my sisters,' he said.

Would she ever meet his family? Or would they cast him out for marrying someone well below his social status? Her doubts came flooding back again. 'What if your parents disown you?'

'They won't disown me. I love them and they love me—there's just this one sticking point, which we're sorting out.'

And if he'd misjudged this and they did disown him, she thought, then she'd ask for an audience—or whatever you did with royalty—and tell his parents that he was a good man and a brilliant surgeon, and he deserved better from them.

He chose a heart-shaped diamond on a plain platinum shank to go with her wedding band. 'Given our jobs,' he said softly, 'this is appropriate—and I want you to keep it afterwards.'

'But...' There hadn't been a price on it, so she hated to think how much it had cost.

'No buts. You're giving me the chance to do what I love, and this is the very least I can do,' he said firmly. 'Think of it as a token of my esteem.'

'Normal people don't buy their friends super-expensive jewellery. Even if they are a hot-shot heart surgeon.'

'You're getting both sides of me for the time being,' he reminded her. 'And now, I think, lunch.'

They ended up grabbing a snack in the cafe at Tiffany's, and then the whirlwind stuff started in earnest.

'Romantic touristy things are the order of the day,' Luc insisted, and the result was a horse and carriage ride through Central Park.

Kelly thoroughly enjoyed the carriage ride, and she didn't have to fake her smile when Luc took a selfie of them with his arm round her shoulders. Right at that moment, she couldn't think of anyone she would rather have shared it with. Then Luc asked the driver to stop by the entrance to one of the gardens. 'Let's go for a little stroll here,' he said, and helped Kelly out of the carriage. 'It's the Shakespeare garden, so all the plants are inspired by his plays. There used to be a white mulberry tree here, that was apparently from his garden.'

It was stunning, with trees covered in pink and white blossom and beds full of late spring flowers. Luc paused by a bed full of bright red tulips. 'I think,' he said, 'this is the place.' Then he took the duck-egg-blue box out of his pocket. 'Where better to get engaged than here?'

To Kelly's surprise, he actually dropped down on one knee.

'Dr Phillips, would you do me the honour of becoming my wife tomorrow?' he asked softly.

For a crazy moment, this whole wedding thing actually felt real. As if Luc was asking her to share his life properly, rather than in name only for the short time they agreed to.

'I...' Her mouth went dry. 'Yes.'

He smiled up at her, and it felt as if her heart had done an anatomically impossible backflip. Then he rose to his feet again and slipped the heart-shaped diamond onto her ring finger.

And then he kissed her.

Slow and sweet and heady, and her head was spinning slightly when he broke the kiss. She didn't think it was the jet lag, either: it was all Luc. Those sensual dark eyes, that beautiful mouth...

She was lost for words, and something about his expression made her think that it was the same for him, too.

It felt odd to have a ring sitting on her finger again. Odd, but strangely comforting.

They walked hand in hand through the gardens. Their first stroll as an engaged couple. And tomorrow they'd be married.

She pushed the nerves away. 'I love tulips,' she said. 'Especially those gorgeous red ones.'

'I know.' He smiled. 'You said so the night I cooked for you.'

She was surprised but delighted that he'd remembered.

'That reminds me, I haven't organised your bouquet,' he said. 'Would you like tulips?'

'Are we allowed to have a bouquet in the Clerk's Office?'

'Of course,' he said.

'Then red tulips would be nice,' she agreed.

'I'll arrange it. And I guess we ought to go and find your dress.' He paused. 'I do have an official photographer arranged for tomorrow. I hope you don't mind.'

'And they're the photos we're going to use to tell everyone?' she asked.

'Sort of. When we get back to London, I thought we could tell your family in person and mine by video call.'

'OK.' She took a deep breath.

'It's going to be fine.' He stroked her cheek. 'Actually, I couldn't have found anyone nicer to be married to.'

Did that mean he wanted to make the marriage real? Or were they both getting carried away by the romance of their 'elopement'? Because here in middle of Central Park, an oasis of calm in one of the busiest cities in the world, it was starting to feel like a fairy tale.

The horse-drawn carriage took them back to the limo, and Luc asked the limo driver to take them to the best bridal shop on Fifth Avenue.

'It's unusual for a guy to come shopping with his bride for a dress,' the shop assistant said once she'd greeted them and they'd explained what they wanted.

'It's not a traditional wedding—we're eloping,' Luc explained. 'We came here for a few days and I guess the place swept us both a bit off our feet. We got a marriage licence this morning, and we're getting married tomorrow in Manhattan.'

'How romantic!' The sales assistant smiled. 'And your accent tells me you're from England.'

'London,' Kelly said swiftly, not wanting to complicate things. 'We're doctors.'

'What sort of doctors?' the assistant asked.

'Heart surgeon and cardiologist,' Luc said.

The assistant clapped her hands together. 'Two heart doctors—well, isn't that cute? So do you have any idea what sort of dress you'd like?'

'Not a traditional long wedding dress,' Kelly said. 'Something pretty and summery. No veil.'

'OK. I can do that. What's your bouquet like?'

'Very simple—an armful of glossy red tulips,' Luc said. 'Which I'm going to order right now while Kelly tries on dresses.'

'I can give you the number of a good florist,' the assistant said. 'And if you'll allow me to suggest a few ideas, Kelly...'

'I'm completely in your hands,' Kelly said with a smile.

Half an hour—and six dresses—later, Kelly was wearing a white silk knee-length shift dress with a sweetheart neckline and a lace overlay; the sleeves were pure lace. Thanks to some very quick and deft manoeuvring by the assistant, Kelly's hair was up in a simple chignon, and she was wearing red, strappy high-heeled shoes to match the tulips that would be in her bouquet.

'You look amazing,' the assistant said with a smile.

Kelly barely recognised the sophisticated woman in the mirror as herself.

In that dress and shoes, and with her hair like that, she looked exactly like a suitable bride for Prince Luciano.

Or would Luc Bianchi think she'd gone too far?

'Thank you so much for your help,' Kelly said.

'My pleasure, sweetheart. I love dressing brides.' The assistant grinned. 'Especially ones with cute accents.'

'I'd better check that Luc likes the dress before I say yes.'

The assistant shook her head. 'It's bad luck for him to see the dress beforehand. And besides, I think he'll love it. He clearly adores you. I think it's so romantic that you came out here for a romantic time together and now you're actually getting married, just the two of you.'

And Luc's security team, who just happened to be browsing in the store, but Kelly didn't say that.

She changed back into her normal clothes and joined Luc outside.

'Everything OK?' he asked.

'Fine, thanks,' Kelly said with a smile. 'I have the perfect outfit.'

'And you, sir—I assume you have a suit?' the assistant asked when she'd boxed up Kelly's dress and shoes.

'I do,' Luc confirmed. 'It's a formal dark grey lounge suit.'

'With an ordinary shirt and tie? You know,' the assistant said thoughtfully, 'since this isn't a traditional wedding, you could get away with wearing something a little less traditional. Like losing the suit jacket, wearing a waistcoat instead, and adding a bow tie to match the bride's bouquet and shoes. It'd look amazing in photographs. Especially if your photographer shoots everything in black and white and then colours in just the red.'

Kelly and Luc looked at each other.

'Less traditional and less formal—I'm in,' he said with a grin. 'And you have an excellent eye for detail. Thank you.'

The assistant grinned back and found him a wing-tip white shirt, a red silk bow tie and a waistcoat that was grey silk at the back and red silk at the front. 'Have a wonderful time in New York. Happy wedding day for tomorrow—and every happiness for your future.' She hugged them both.

'Thank you,' Kelly said, hugging her back.

When they were back outside the shop, Luc looked at her. 'I think we should send her flowers.'

'Great idea,' Kelly said.

He smiled at her. 'We have the rings, the dress, the licence, and the bouquet is ordered—I think we have everything we need. What about your hair and make-up?'

She lifted one shoulder in a half-shrug. 'I can do all that myself.'

'I know it's not a traditional wedding,' Luc said, 'but that doesn't mean you should miss out on having a fuss made of you. I'll talk to the hotel and organise hair and make-up. And please don't argue; I'd like to do something nice for you.'

'Then thank you. That would be lovely.' She stifled a yawn. 'Sorry. I'm starting to flag a bit.'

Luc glanced at his watch. 'It'd be eleven at night, our time, and we had an early start; plus long-haul flights are tiring. How about we have an early dinner at the hotel and an early night tonight?'

'That sounds really good,' Kelly said gratefully.

She was almost too tired to enjoy the spectacle of the hotel's dining room, full of palm trees and pillars and with an amazing stained-glass dome, and she knew she wasn't appreciating how good the food was.

Luc kissed her goodnight in their parlour. 'I'm going to stay up for a bit, but I'll be quiet so I don't disturb you.'

'I can stay up a bit later with you,' she said.

He stroked her cheek. 'You look tired. Go to bed. I'll see you tomorrow. And prepare to be pampered in the morning.' He paused. 'Just out of interest—what's the neckline of your dress?'

'Sweetheart,' she said. 'I guess, since it's not a traditional wedding, you could see it now.'

'No. We'll stick with that particular tradition. I'm not going to see you now until the wedding. I'm going to have my breakfast with the guys tomorrow, and I'll have yours delivered by room service. The limo will take you to the Clerk's Office—I'll meet you there.'

And then, she thought with a shiver that was a mixture of excitement and nervousness, they'd get married...

CHAPTER EIGHT

THE NEXT MORNING, Kelly woke to find herself alone in the suite. Luc had left her two packages with a note propped up against them.

> *Another tradition—something 'old and borrowed',*
> *and something blue. See you at the Clerk's Office*
> *at two. L xx*

She remembered the old rhyme. The new was obviously her dress and shoes. The 'blue' turned out to be a Tiffany box containing an exquisite pair of sapphire stud earrings.

But the 'old and borrowed' really made her catch her breath: a beautiful and clearly antique string of pearls. Another note from Luc said,

> *These were my grandmother's, if you'd like to wear*
> *them today.*

Meaning that he'd like her to wear them?

OK. She could do that. And he'd made it clear that they would be borrowed, which was fine by her.

By the time she'd showered and dressed, room service arrived with her breakfast. And then she had an appointment at the beauty salon: a massage to relax her followed by having her hair and nails done. She had a sandwich and fruit for lunch—beautifully presented and making her feel very spoiled—and finally the beautician did her make-up. Just as they finished, the Reception called to say that her flowers had arrived.

The bouquet was gorgeous: a simple posy of glossy red tulips that matched her shoes and Luc's tie and waist-coat, with matching red silk ribbon tied round the stems to make them easy to carry.

Back in her room, she changed into her dress and stared at herself in the mirror.

In less than an hour's time, she'd be Luc's wife. For a few months.

Nerves fluttered in her stomach. But Luc was a good man, and she trusted him. Her family liked him. And what they were doing meant that Luc would be able to carry on with his career, making a real difference to the world, instead of being forced into a job that he'd hate. They were doing the right thing.

She brushed one finger along the pearls. 'Luc didn't tell me about you,' she said, 'but I'm guessing you were special to him, if he wants me to wear your pearls. I hope you know that I'll support your grandson through this whole thing.' She dragged in a breath. 'And, Simon. I'll always love you. This isn't to disparage our wedding at all. I'm helping a friend, and he's helping me. And then we're going to move on with our lives. I won't forget you, but I'm also not going to live in seclusion, because I know you'd hate me to shut myself away from the world. I just want to wait until I'm ready.'

The Reception called to tell Kelly that the limo was ready whenever she needed it. She headed downstairs, and sat in the back looking out at the city as the driver took her through the streets of Manhattan. Towards Luc. Towards their wedding. Towards whatever the future held.

Luc took a deep breath as he waited outside the Clerk's Office in Manhattan. Five minutes until Kelly was due to arrive.

He knew she'd keep her word and turn up for their marriage of convenience, but he felt as nervous as any real groom might feel.

'Are you sure about this, boss?' Gino asked.

'Yes. It will send a very clear message to my father.' Luc looked at Gino. 'So I don't expect you to risk your position by being the witness. I can ask the photographer to do that.'

'Ask someone you barely know? Are you kidding?' Gino frowned and shook his head. 'It will be my privilege to be your witness. Besides, I'm already an accessory.'

Luc clapped his hand on Gino's shoulder. 'True. And thank you. I assure you there won't be any consequences.'

'I don't care if there are,' Gino said. 'I like Kelly. A lot. And you've been much happier since she's been around.'

'We're friends. The marriage is in name only,' Luc reminded him.

'She likes you. And I think you like her, too.'

He did. He was aware that his feelings towards Kelly had grown and changed over the last few weeks. That he was starting to fall for her. But he didn't want to put any pressure on her. He knew she needed time to get over losing Simon. It wasn't fair to ask her for something she couldn't give, and besides any real emotional involvement would make their simple marriage of convenience way too complicated. 'The limo's here,' he said, more to distract himself than Gino.

And he caught his breath as the driver helped Kelly out of the car. She looked absolutely stunning. The dress was gorgeous, the flowers and her shoes were the perfect pop of colour, and she was wearing his grandmother's pearls.

'Hi,' he said when she walked towards him. And how odd that his voice had gone all croaky, his palms were sweaty and his heart rate was galloping. Kelly was his friend. This was going to be a marriage in name only. So why did this feel right now as if it was for real?

'Hi.' Her voice was all breathless and shy, too.

'You look lovely.' And he couldn't resist leaning forward and kissing her lightly.

She blushed. 'You look pretty good, too. And thank you for the loan of these.' She touched the pearls with a fingertip.

'Pleasure.' He smiled. 'My grandmother would have liked you very much.'

'Were you close to her?' Kelly asked.

He nodded. 'She was the one who persuaded my father to let me train as a doctor in the first place.'

'These,' she said, 'feel like a symbol of approval.'

'They are,' he said softly. 'Ready?'

'Ready,' she confirmed.

They walked into the Clerk's Office together and collected their number so they could wait to be called into one of the two chapels. Luc took a snap of them on his phone. 'For posterity,' he said.

'You look beautiful, Kelly,' Gino said.

'Thank you.' She smiled at him.

'This is Patty, our photographer,' Luc said when a woman came over to them. 'Patty, thank you for coming. This is Kelly.'

'Pleased to meet you, honey,' Patty said. 'Your dress

is beautiful. And the colour coordination between you—
that's good.'

'We were thinking,' Luc said, 'or, rather, the wonderful sales assistant at the bridal shop suggested, maybe you could process some of the photos in black and white—'

'—and pick out the accents in red?' Patty finished. 'Great idea.'

Patty took a few shots of them together, and then their number was called.

'This is it,' Luc said, feeling incredibly nervous. There was no going back now. And this was the right thing to do, he was sure.

The chapel was painted apricot and peach, with a pink striped abstract painting next to the lectern. The officiant announced them, and they stood at the lectern in front of the clerk.

'Welcome, Luc and Kelly,' the officiant said. 'If there is anybody present who knows of any reason why these two people should not get married, please speak now.'

There was silence.

'Do you, Luc, solemnly declare to take Kelly as your lawful wedded wife?'

'Yes, I do,' Luc said.

'Do you promise to honour and cherish her for as long as you both shall live?'

'I do,' Luc agreed.

'As a symbol of your promise, please place the ring on her finger,' the officiant directed.

Luc did so, smiling at Kelly. Nothing about this part was fake. He'd honour her always.

'Do you, Kelly, solemnly declare to take Luc as your lawful wedded husband?' the officiant asked.

'Yes, I do.' Her voice was firm and clear.

'Do you promise to honour and cherish him for as long as you both shall live?'

'I do,' she affirmed.

'As a symbol of your promise, please place the ring on his finger.'

She slid the matching ring onto his finger. Luc caught her gaze, and he could see how enormous her pupils were. So did she feel this strange, unsettling, meant-to-be feeling, too?

'And as much as you both have consented to be united together in matrimony and have exchanged your wedding vows in front of us all here today, by the power vested in me by the laws of the great state of New York, I now pronounce you husband and wife,' the officiant said.

And that was it.

They were married.

'Mr and Mrs Bianchi, congratulations on behalf of the state.' The officiant smiled at both of them, signed a piece of paper with a flourish, waited for them both to sign it along with Gino as the witness, and then gave them their official marriage registration.

'So this is it,' Luc whispered.

'We're married,' she whispered back.

'You may kiss the bride,' the officiant said.

Luc did so, intending it to be light and easy, but somehow he couldn't quite pull away from her. He was aware of everything about her: the sweetness of her scent, the warmth of her skin, the feel of her mouth against his.

When he finally broke the kiss, he felt thoroughly flustered. And she looked as if she felt exactly the same way.

Patty took a couple of photographs, and then Luc held Kelly's hand as they headed outside. Patty posed them outside the doorway, with the words 'New York State' above their heads. She took a shot of them smiling, another with them showing off their wedding rings, another of them kissing—and then she took the bouquet and gave it to Gino for safe keeping. 'A little prop,' she said with a grin, and gave them a banner which proclaimed 'just married' in capital letters, with a heart separating the words.

Luc laughed. 'Just about perfect for two cardiac doctors.'

They held up the banner and Patty took a shot, then another of them on the steps under the words 'Office of the City Clerk'.

'Iconic pictures,' she said thoughtfully when she collected the banner and returned the bouquet to Kelly. 'I know just the place.'

At her direction, the limo driver took them to Brooklyn Bridge Park. She took a few shots of Luc and Kelly by the river with the iconic skyline and Brooklyn Bridge behind them, and then she shepherded them towards the carousel. 'It's a hundred years old,' she said with a smile. 'I think this is perfect for you two.'

She posed them both on the horses and in one of the chariots, taking photographs of them as they whirled round on the carousel.

'And that's a wrap,' she said with a smile. 'Thank you for being patient. I'll deliver the final photographs at your hotel before breakfast tomorrow morning, and email you the link to the downloads so your family and friends can see them when you get home and order any prints they choose.'

'Thank you.' Luc shook her hand warmly, and Kelly hugged her.

'So now the photographs are over,' Luc said when Patty had left, 'that means dinner and dancing. I have things booked, if that's all right with you?'

'It all sounds wonderful,' she said. 'It's my first time

in New York, so everything is new for me and I've had an amazing time already. I loved the carousel.'

'Me, too,' he said. 'Can you walk in these shoes?'

'Yes.'

'Then let's take a stroll,' he said.

And somehow it felt natural to walk with his arm around her shoulders, talking and enjoying the views and taking snaps on their phone for her to send home. As if they really were married and enjoying their honeymoon.

The limo took them back to Manhattan for a swish meal in a Michelin-starred restaurant. And it was an incredible space, with pale walls and classical architecture that reminded Luc of the ancient palazzos in Bordimiglia. The tables and chairs were all made of dark polished wood, the starched damask tablecloths were white, and in the middle of each table was a bowl of tulips—some red, some yellow, some pink and some a dramatic deep purple. The whole thing looked beautifully stylish.

'Tulips! Our wedding flowers. Did you ask for them especially?' Kelly asked.

'No,' he admitted. 'It's pure serendipity. But I did ask if they would swap the red meat options on the tasting menu for something else of your choice, and they agreed.'

'Thank you.'

The meal was exquisitely cooked and exquisitely plated, and each course was served with the perfect matched wine. After coffee, and the nicest petits fours Luc had ever eaten, the limo took them to a small, intimate jazz club.

'Would you dance with me...?' He paused. 'Are you still Dr Phillips, or will you be known as Dr Bianchi?' It was the one detail they hadn't discussed—and it was an important one.

'If I kept my name,' she said, 'it might look suspicious, so I guess I'll be changing my name to yours.'

'Then will you dance with me, Dr Bianchi?'

'With pleasure, Mr Bianchi,' she said.

Kelly loved the little basement space, with the jazz trio playing old love songs and the singer crooning into an old-fashioned radio-type microphone.

'The perfect evening for an elopement,' she said. Even if it wasn't a real one.

As she'd pretty much expected, Luc was an excellent dancer with a good sense of rhythm, and he guided her expertly through the steps of the dances she didn't know, whisking her through foxtrots and quicksteps and a cha-cha-cha.

And then everything slowed right down and he held her really, really close for an old-fashioned rumba. Kelly found herself holding Luc just as tightly, their movements so tiny and slow that it was as if they were swaying, rather than moving across the dance floor.

She looked up at him and there was a slash of colour across his cheeks. His eyes were huge and his mouth was slightly parted. And she couldn't help reaching up and stealing a kiss.

'Kelly,' he whispered, and kissed her back.

The whole world melted away.

She had no idea how long they kissed, what was playing, who was near them. All she was aware of was Luc—the warmth of his body, the scent of his skin, the feel of his mouth against hers.

When he broke the kiss, they were both shaking.

'This isn't supposed to be happening,' he said.

'I know,' she said. It was a marriage in name only. The rules were simple. And yet things were changing.

This whole thing felt like a fairy tale—a dream. 'It's our wedding day,' she whispered.

'Yes.' He kissed her again. 'My beautiful bride.'

In name only. Except right now that wasn't what she wanted. She wanted *him*.

The sensible side of her knew that this would be complicating things. That if she followed her heart right now, tomorrow would be awkward and full of difficult questions. But she'd spent the last two years hiding away, burying herself in work. Since Luc had come into her life, things had started to change. She'd enjoyed their dates and getting to know each other. He'd reminded her that life could still be fun—that you could be a serious doctor and dedicated to your work, but at the same time you could enjoy a show or sit on a merry-go-round or dance to the kind of music that heated your blood.

Life was short. You couldn't predict what was going to happen.

Tonight, would it be so bad to give in to the desire that pulsed through her veins?

'Kiss me,' she whispered.

And he did.

It's our wedding day.

This was supposed to be in name only.

He really shouldn't have brought her to the jazz club, where the music oozed sensuality and the dance steps made him aware of every move she made. He should take a step back right now. He should definitely not be kissing her.

Yet he couldn't resist her.

Not when her green eyes were huge, when her lips were parted, when her voice was all soft and she was asking him to kiss her.

They both regret this tomorrow. It was so far away from their deal.

But he couldn't stop himself.

He kissed her. Danced with her, hardly aware of the beat of the music because the beat of his blood was thrumming in his veins. Held her close. Wanting her.

Being with her made him feel different. Made him want things he'd trained himself not to want, because it wouldn't be fair to start a relationship and then change all the rules.

Yet that was what was happening right now. Here, on the dimly lit dance floor. On their wedding day. *Their wedding night.*

'Kelly,' he whispered. 'It's our wedding night.'

She stroked his face. 'I don't want to dance any more.'

He needed to do the right thing. 'I'll take you back to the hotel.'

'And stay with me?'

His heart skipped a beat—and another. 'Kelly...'

'As you said, it's our wedding night.'

And they were both sober. It wasn't alcohol making him dizzy, it was desire. Desire he could see matched in her eyes—or was he just seeing what he wanted to see?

'Kelly...' He was lost for words. Tongue-tied. At sixes and sevens.

'Luc.' She reached up and kissed him, and he was lost.

He took her hand and led her out of the club to the limo. They didn't talk on the way back to the hotel, but it wasn't an awkward silence. When they arrived at the hotel, Luc's fingers tightened around hers and he helped her out of the car. Federico shadowed them to the lift, and then it was just the two of them.

Kelly looked suddenly nervous. And Luc could guess exactly why. It was their wedding night. They were alone.

And her doubts and common sense were clearly creeping back in.

He kissed her lightly. 'If you've changed your mind, I won't pressure you.'

'I've not changed my mind. Just… It scares me a bit,' she admitted.

'I know. This kind of scares me, too,' he said softly, and kissed her again.

That strange, dizzying feeling was back, and she made no protest when he picked her up and carried her across the threshold of the suite.

'Tradition?' she asked, her voice husky.

He set her back on her feet. 'Tradition.' And he wanted that feeling back, the way things had been at the club. Romantic and sensual, just the two of them in a bubble and tomorrow could take care of itself. 'Dance with me again.'

She nodded, and he flicked into the Internet on his phone to find some soft, slow music. When he opened his arms, she walked into them and swayed with him to the music. When he kissed her, she kissed him all the way back. And when he picked her up and carried her to his room, she made no protest…

The next morning, Kelly woke in Luc's arms. In Luc's bed.

Memories of the previous night came rushing back, and her cheeks flooded with colour. She couldn't even blame last night on drinking too much, because they hadn't. They'd drunk wine with their meal, but not massive amounts.

Last night had been because they'd both wanted it.

But would things be different today?

'Good morning,' he said.

'Good morning.' What was the etiquette in this sort of situation—when you woke up in the bed of the man you'd married in name only? She didn't have a clue. Right now she was going to take her lead from Luc.

'I know we didn't plan last night,' he said.

He could say that again. 'No.'

'And we're going to have to decide what happens now.'

'We could pretend it didn't happen,' she said.

'If that's what you want.' He paused. 'Or maybe we could look at this another way. We're here for a couple more days. Maybe we could have this as a kind of time out. Make this a real honeymoon.'

And did that mean the start of a real marriage? She hadn't let herself think of that possibility. It wasn't part of their agreement. But she really liked the man she was getting to know. The physical attraction was there, too. Did he feel the same?

She wasn't a coward, so she asked, 'And when we get back to London?'

He looked at her. 'It could get complicated. In London, it would be sensible to stick to Plan A.'

'A marriage in name only.'

'A marriage in name only,' he agreed.

The sensible side of her knew he was right. If they let themselves get emotionally involved, it would start to get messy when they had their quiet divorce in a few months' time. Besides, while they were out here they needed to take some convincing photographs to make their families believe that they were in love and had got married in a rush—and being intimate with each other was the best way to make it look convincing. So they needed to keep the here and now separate from the future.

'A real honeymoon here,' she said, 'and Plan A when we're back in London. That works for me.'

He stroked her face. 'Thank you.'

Kelly still felt a little shy with him, but at the same time she was starting to be more confident. Room service brought them coffee and the photographs that Patty had dropped off.

'She's done a fantastic job,' Luc said. 'And our sales assistant was right about the monochrome photos with an accent.'

'They're perfect. We should send her one of these with the flowers,' Kelly said.

'Agreed.' He kissed her lightly. 'Give me five minutes to sort it out, and we can go down for breakfast.'

'OK.'

Funny, this time round she hadn't married for love. But the way she and Luc were looking at each other in the photographs was very, very convincing. Either Patty was a genius photographer, or she'd spotted something that Kelly and Luc hadn't quite admitted to themselves was there...

She shook herself. This wasn't a good idea. She couldn't fall for him. They didn't have a future.

'It's all arranged,' Luc said. 'Patty's going to courier a photograph over to the florist, and everything will be there this morning.'

'Perfect,' Kelly said with a smile.

After breakfast, the limo took them to the Met. They spent the morning wandering around, enjoying the art, and then headed for the Cloisters which housed the Met's medieval art collection.

'This is gorgeous,' she said. 'Those arches make this feel like being in the middle of medieval Italy.'

'It reminds me of the old parts of Bordimiglia,' Luc agreed.

They wandered through the gardens hand in hand,

and visited the famous Unicorn Tapestries. Then Luc glanced at his watch. 'We need an early dinner. Is Times Square OK with you?'

She smiled. 'I'm happy to go wherever you like.'

He'd booked a table at a small place where they served the nicest pizza she'd eaten outside of Italy.

'Ready for this?' he asked, looking pleased with himself.

'Ready for what?'

'A couple of minutes and you'll see for yourself,' he said, shepherding her down Broadway. He stopped outside a theatre.

She looked up to read the sign and blinked. 'No way. No *way* have you got tickets for *Hamilton*. It's booked up years in advance!'

'There are certain advantages,' he said, 'to the other side of my life.'

She shook her head. 'I can't believe this.'

'Believe it. Here's the proof.' He produced tickets from his pocket and smiled at her. 'I think we need a selfie.'

She threw her arms around him. 'Luc, you're amazing. I've wanted to see this show so much—and, even though Susie calls me the Ticket Whisperer, I couldn't get tickets for us. Now I'm seeing it. On Broadway. With you. It's a real dream come true.'

She posed for a selfie with him, making sure to get the tickets and the theatre's sign in the shot. Then she looked at the picture and noticed the time. 'Oh, it'll be gone midnight back home. I'll send this tomorrow so I don't wake anyone up.'

Just as he'd done with *Les Misérables*, Luc had organised a box. 'Better get the programmes,' he said. 'We need four.'

'Four?' Kelly was mystified.

'You'll find out why later.'

'Why can't you tell me now?'

'Because I'm annoying,' he said with a grin, refusing to enlighten her.

The musical was every bit as good as she'd hoped, and she loved every second of it. And then, after the show, he shepherded her down to a restricted area where they got to meet the cast. At that point, she realised why he wanted four programmes: because the cast signed one each for her mother, Susie and Angela as well as one for her.

'That was so nice of you, tonight,' she said when they were finally back at their hotel. 'You really didn't have to organise that.'

He shrugged. 'I thought you'd enjoy it—and that your mum, Susie and Angela would appreciate a souvenir you definitely wouldn't get elsewhere. And if you can let me know some appropriate dates, my press team will organise tickets for you all to go together in London.'

She smiled. 'That would be amazing. Thank you so much.'

The next morning, before breakfast, Kelly sent the photographs to her mum, sister and Angela.

All three texted straight back with messages along the lines of How awesome is that? Can't believe how lucky you are.

Not just me. Luc says he can organise tickets for us all in London, she texted back. Just let me know dates.

Five minutes later, she looked at her new husband. 'According to the barrage of texts I've just received, you're now officially the new hero of three women in London.'

He laughed. 'Let me know the dates and I'll organise it.'

They went sightseeing again, taking the ferry out to

Ellis Island and went to see the Statue of Liberty; Kelly bought paperweights for her dad, her brother-in-law and Angela's husband. They spent the afternoon in the Museum of Natural History seeing the dinosaurs and got models for the twins, and Luc's nephew and niece. Finally they watched the sunset from the Empire State Building before heading out to dinner.

But better than all the sights was being with Luc. Something seemed to have shifted in their relationship, and she was seeing him differently. As a lover, not just as a colleague.

This was a dangerous game. Kelly knew they were going back to Plan A once they were back in England. But, for now, it was fun to dream.

On their last morning in New York, they headed back to the Clerk's Office to sort out the paperwork to authenticate their American wedding certificate in Europe with an Apostille. And then it was time to go back to London.

'Time to tell everyone,' she said.

At the airport in New York, Kelly texted her parents.

About to catch flight. Can we come and see you tonight when we get back? Ask Susie, Nick and the boys, too, please.

Luc put his arms round her. 'Don't look so worried. Everything's going to be just fine.'

She hoped so. She really, really hoped so.

CHAPTER NINE

'So DID YOU have a wonderful time in New York?' Caroline asked, hugging Kelly and Luc in turn.

'We did, Mum,' Kelly said. 'And we brought presents.'

'Dinosaurs!' Jacob and Oscar chorused in delight when they opened their parcels, and they disappeared to play some complicated game about pterodactyls and a T-Rex.

'Dad, Nick, we hope you like these,' Kelly said.

The men duly exclaimed over their Statues of Liberty.

'Mum and Susie...' Kelly handed over the parcels with a grin.

'Oh, wow!' Susie hugged them both when she saw the signed programmes. 'That's amazing.'

'And the tickets are booked for next month, in London,' Luc added.

'That's so kind of you.' Susie and Caroline were all smiles.

Kelly's pulse felt as if it had doubled. 'Um, we also have some news.' She swallowed. 'While we were away...' Her throat dried, and so did the words.

'It was all my fault,' Luc said. 'I kind of got swept away by the romance of New York.'

'You got engaged?' Caroline asked.

'Um—not quite.' Kelly held out her left hand.

'Hang on. There are two rings on your finger. Are you trying to tell us you got *married*?' Susie demanded.

'It's my fault,' Luc said again. 'And I apologise. And we'll have a proper celebration with you now we're back in London.'

'You got married.' Caroline's voice was flat, and Kelly realised just how her mother was feeling. Hurt and pushed out—because Kelly hadn't confided in her. Because Kelly had resisted all the suitable men paraded in front of her, and then got married to someone her family had only met once.

'Mum, we never meant to hurt anyone,' she said.

'If the other side of my life got involved, everything would be stuffy and formal, and I didn't want to put Kelly under that sort of stress,' Luc said. 'We really didn't do it to leave anyone out or hurt anyone.'

'We just wanted to keep it low-key,' Kelly said.

Luc put his arm round Kelly. 'I know it's fast and we've only known each other for a couple of months. But I have a huge amount of respect for Kelly. She's a brilliant doctor and one of the nicest people I know.'

'What about love?' Robin asked softly. 'You haven't said anything about love.'

Kelly went very still. Was Luc going to lie?

He'd really miscalculated this. Kelly had warned him that her family would be hurt, but Luc had been so focused on proving a point to his father that he'd brushed her worries aside. He'd thought of how his own family would react, with coolness and all emotions buried. Which wasn't how Kelly's family was at all.

And now he had to fix this. The last thing he wanted to do was to cause a rift between Kelly and her family.

He knew what Robin wanted him to say. That yes, Luc loved his daughter.

But he and Kelly hadn't talked about their feelings. He was pretty sure Kelly wasn't in love with him. She liked him, yes, and the physical attraction between them had been obvious in New York. But love? They hadn't said the words. And it felt wrong to say them now.

What did he do?

If he said no, he'd hurt her family. If he said yes, he'd probably freak Kelly out. It was a tough line to walk; but he was used to having to juggle the two sides of his life. Used to diplomacy, even though he wasn't as good at it as his sisters were.

He chose his words carefully. 'As you can imagine, I grew up in a rather different world. One where you pretty much keep your emotions private. Love isn't something I'm comfortable talking about.'

'It's a simple enough question,' Caroline said, her voice very neutral—but Luc could see the worry in her eyes. 'Do you love Kelly or don't you?'

He could feel the tension in Kelly's frame. To make this convincing as a whirlwind relationship, he knew what he had to say. Yet, if he said it, would Kelly think he was an accomplished liar, someone she couldn't trust?

It all depended on how you defined love.

Friendship plus physical attraction: under that definition, he loved Kelly. And he'd kept his emotions in check for so long that he wasn't sure he knew what love felt like any more.

'Yes,' he said softly. And he increased the pressure of his arm very slightly round Kelly so she'd know that it was a yes he could explain, and *would* explain later.

Either he was lying to her family or he'd been lying to her—and she didn't think Luciano Bianchi was a liar.

They'd never talked about love. If he loved her, surely

he would've said the words to her in private, not blurted them out in front of her family?

Then again, her parents had pretty much forced the issue. Whatever he said would be difficult. If he said no and admitted it was a marriage of convenience, all hell would break loose. He chose to say yes. So was this a white lie to make a family feel better about their elopement? Or did Luc actually mean it?

And what did that little squeeze of his arm actually mean? Was it his way of saying they'd talk later, or was he saying sorry he hadn't said the words before, or was he saying he was stuck and he didn't want to hurt anyone and he wasn't putting any pressure on her?

She didn't have a clue. And it left her own feelings in a complete tangle. How did she feel about him? It wasn't the same kind of relationship she'd had with Simon—but was this love?

She couldn't think straight. Could hardly breathe. Couldn't meet her family's eyes.

Had she just made the biggest mistake of her life?

'If you really love my sister,' Susie said, 'then I'm happy. I get why you wanted to keep it low-key.'

Because Kelly had had the big wedding, last time round.

'And all we want is to see you happy. To see you living again instead of just existing for nothing except work. And I've seen the change Luc's made in you. Those photos you sent us from New York, with the two of you on Broadway—you looked so happy. Happier than I've seen you in two years,' Susie continued.

'So you're not angry with us?' Kelly asked.

'I think,' Robin said, 'we're sad we didn't get the chance to share it with you and throw confetti and drink champagne and dance very, very badly to the terrible music you girls all love.'

'But if you're happy, that means the world to us,' Caroline said.

'I'm sorry again,' Luc said. 'Maybe we can have a private celebration.'

'Just the family? That would be nice,' Nick said.

'A barbecue,' Robin said.

'Done. My place,' Luc said.

'Which I assume is where you're going to be living, now, Kelly?' Robin asked.

She nodded. 'Maybe we can do the celebration stuff next weekend.'

'Perfect,' Susie said. 'And please tell us you have *some* photographs from the wedding, even if they're selfies on your phone.'

'You have to wait for twenty-four hours between getting your licence and getting married,' Luc said, 'so I managed to book a photographer. I can give you the download link if you'd like to see them.'

'If?' Susie said, raising her eyebrows at him. 'Of course we want to see them.

'And, um, I have champagne in the car. Maybe we can have a toast while we look at the photographs. And obviously I'll order any prints you'd like,' he added. 'I know it doesn't make up for you not being there, but we really did want it to be low-key.'

'Champagne is an excellent idea,' Caroline said.

Luc fetched it swiftly, and Robin led the toast. 'To Kelly and Luc. Wishing you every happiness.'

'Every happiness,' the others echoed.

Everyone seemed to enjoy the wedding photographs. 'I love this one on the carousel,' Susie said softly. 'You look happy. It's so good to see the light back in your eyes.'

'I wish you'd been there,' Kelly said, hugging her. 'But if we'd both had our families there...'

'It wouldn't have been low-key any more,' Susie finished. 'Just as long as you're happy.'

'Have you told your own family yet, Luc?' Robin asked.

'No.'

'As the heir to the throne, you've deprived your country as well as your family of your wedding,' Caroline said quietly.

'They've already had my sisters' weddings,' he said. 'And Kelly's right—my life is complicated. I see myself as a doctor, not a king. I'm not the oldest child, and I think my older sister—who would make a fantastic queen and a much better ruler than I would—should be the one to take over from my father. It's utterly ridiculous that one chromosome should make so much difference, in this day and age,' he added, his words heartfelt.

'I agree with that,' Susie said. 'Though I think your family might be upset.'

His parents certainly wouldn't react with the warmth and openness of Kelly's parents, Luc thought. Maybe he could learn from Kelly how to make that particular relationship a little easier and less formal.

'So are you a princess now, Kelly?' Robin asked.

'No. As with your royal family, only someone of royal blood can be called a prince or princess after marrying into the royal family,' Luc answered. 'My father does have the right to bestow a title, if he chooses.'

'But that's not why I married Luc. I'm still Dr Kelly, the way I always was,' Kelly said. 'Although I'm Dr Bianchi now.'

'Still our Kelly,' Caroline said. She looked at Luc. 'Welcome to the family.'

'Thank you.' Awkwardly, Luc took his arm from round Kelly's shoulders and went to shake Caroline's hand.

She hugged him. So did Robin, Nick and Susie. 'Welcome to the family.'

Back in the car, Luc sighed. 'I'm sorry for hurting your family, Kelly.'

'They've forgiven us—now they're over the initial shock, they just want us to be happy,' she said. 'But I think your family will give you a harder time than mine.'

'We'll cross that bridge when we come to it.' He raised her hand to his mouth and kissed it.

'You told my family that you loved me.'

He knew she'd bring that up. 'If you define love as friendship plus physical attraction, then yes, I love you. I wasn't lying.'

'That's a very clinical way of putting it.'

Especially when those three little words had been said to her by her previous husband, and he'd meant that she was the love of his life. Guilt flooded through him. 'Most of the time, I have to keep my emotions under wraps. I'm expected to behave with quiet dignity,' he pointed out.

'Eloping to New York is hardly quiet dignity.'

'I know. But it was my idea, so I'm taking the blame.'

'It wasn't just you. I could have said no.'

'Thank you,' he said, 'for saying yes. And for being so supportive.'

'I said I'd help you.'

'But it's caused a row with your family—or as near a row as I guess you get to, given how nice they all are—and I really am sorry for that.'

'They'll come round,' Kelly said. 'Your family, on the other hand, might disown you for what we've done.'

He shrugged. 'Isn't there a famous quote, "never trouble trouble till trouble troubles you"?'

'Yes,' she said wryly, 'but I have a nasty feeling you might have troubled trouble.'

Back at Luc's house, they went into his study together.

'Here goes,' he said. He switched on his laptop and video-called his parents.

There was a quick exchange in Italian that Kelly couldn't follow, and then Luc said, 'Can we speak English, please, Mamma?'

'English?'

'I'd like you to meet someone,' he said. 'Kelly, this is my mother, Vittoria. Mamma, this is Kelly.'

'Pleased to meet you, Your Majesty,' Kelly said, wishing she'd thought to ask Luc about etiquette before he'd called home.

'And you, my dear,' Vittoria said.

'Is Babbo around?' Luc asked.

'He's in Rome on business. Why?'

Luc coughed. 'I have some news. Kelly and I work together. She's a cardiologist. And we went to New York this week together.'

'I see,' Vittoria said.

Kelly didn't have a clue what Luc's mother was feeling. Now she understood what he meant about keeping his emotion under wraps. Quiet dignity definitely summed up his mother. Quiet *enigmatic* dignity.

'While we were there, we got married,' Luc said.

'Married.' Again, that quiet, measured, completely inscrutable tone. 'I see. And you want me to tell your father?'

'No—I'll do that. But I wanted you to be the first to know.'

'I see.'

Her own family had been upset at first. Kelly didn't have the faintest idea how his mother was feeling, right now. Horrified? Disapproving? Angry? Hurt? Without a clue how the other woman was feeling, she had no way of reassuring her or making things better. But she wanted to say something to support Luc. 'Luc's a good man. An excellent surgeon.'

'Indeed. He's also the heir to the throne of Bordimiglia,' Vittoria said.

'You know how I feel about that, Mamma,' he said.

'Indeed. You know how your father feels, too.' Vittoria paused. 'Did it not occur to you to introduce us before you got engaged, let alone married? It's very discourteous to your wife.'

Kelly really hadn't expected that, and it made her feel even more guilty. 'It was discourteous to *you*, too, and I apologise for that.'

'I think I know whose idea it was to get married in a rush, child,' Vittoria said. 'We will speak later, Luciano.' And the screen went black.

Luc blew out a breath. 'That went relatively well.'

Was he kidding? She stared at him in disbelief. His mother had just hung up on him! How on earth could he think it had gone well? She'd be devastated if her mum had hung up on her.

'Babbo's on business, so I can't just call him. I'm going to leave him a voicemail asking him to call me before he speaks to Mamma.' He sighed. 'Things might get a little sticky over the next day or two.'

'Even though I didn't make any vows about for better or worse,' Kelly said, 'I'm your wife and I'll stand by you.'

'Thank you.' He closed his eyes for a moment. 'I kind of wish we were back in New York.'

'Rewinding time so we didn't get married in the first place?'

'No. I wish we were still on honeymoon. You and me, enjoying the sights of New York with the rest of the world a million miles away.'

On impulse, she wrapped her arms around him. 'We'll weather the storm.'

'Eventually.' He dropped a kiss on the top of her head. 'I shouldn't ask you this, but you haven't chosen your room yet. Would you stay with me tonight?'

Hold him until they both fell asleep? Common sense dictated that she should find an excuse; they'd both agreed that London would mean a return to Plan A rather than the closeness they'd shared in New York. But she wasn't going to push him away when he needed her. And right now she needed the comfort of his arms around her, too. 'We've had a long day. Yes.'

He kissed her lightly. 'I'll call my father. I guess I'd better talk to my sisters, too. If Mamma hasn't already done that.'

'I'll be here. Even if my Italian is currently limited to yes, no, hello, goodbye, please and thank you, I can at least be polite.'

'You,' he said softly, 'are an amazing woman.'

He left a swift message on his father's voicemail, and called his sisters. When he'd finished explaining the situation to them, his mobile phone rang.

'It's my father,' he said as he looked at the screen. 'I'd better take this.' Again, the entire conversation was conducted in rapid Italian, and Kelly felt very much surplus to requirements. She had absolutely no idea from Luc's expression how the conversation was going. But eventually he hung up.

'How did they take the news?' she asked.

'My father said we'll talk after he gets back from Rome. My sisters both say I'm an idiot but they'd like to meet you—sooner, rather than later.'

'Did you tell them it's a marriage of convenience?'

'No. They need to think it's real.'

'I'll do my best,' Kelly said. 'But I'm a cardiologist, not an actress.'

'And all this is well above and beyond the call of what I asked you to do. I really didn't expect it to get this complicated,' he said.

'Me, neither. But it's done now. We'll make the best of it.'

He held her close. 'I'm not sure I'd be quite as understanding if our positions were reversed.'

'Actually, I think you would,' she said.

She curled into his arms that night, and his lovemaking was so sweet and tender that it brought tears to her eyes. The next morning, they headed to her flat and packed all her belongings ready for the removal van. But when they returned to Luc's house, visitors were waiting for them.

Even before Luc spoke, Kelly could see the family resemblance and knew exactly who they were.

'Elle! Giu! I didn't expect to see you,' he said, sounding shocked.

His older sister rolled her eyes, hugged him and cuffed his arm. 'You are in *so* much trouble.'

'Getting married without your family. It's mean to leave us out,' his younger sister agreed.

He blew out a breath. 'That wasn't the intention. Did Mamma send you?'

'No. It was my idea,' Elle said. 'And we haven't seen you for ages.'

He winced. 'I'm sorry. That's my fault. I do love you all.'

'But you're focused on being a doctor,' Giulia said. 'We know.'

'Nice to meet you, Kelly,' Eleonora said. 'Now, Luc, go and do something while Giu and I get to know our new sister-in-law.'

'I'm not leaving her alone with you for you to grill her,' Luc said.

'Something to hide, brother dearest?' Giulia asked sweetly.

'No,' Kelly and Luc said simultaneously.

Eleonora and Giulia raised their eyebrows at each other.

'That's too swift a denial. They're definitely hiding something,' Elle agreed.

'We're not. We fell in love and we couldn't wait to get married. I sent you the wedding photographs,' Luc said. 'So you can see for yourself.'

His sisters shook their heads. 'You're almost Pinocchio, Luc. Your nose twitches when you lie,' Giulia said.

'It does not.'

'Oh, but it does. We have a theory,' Elle said casually, 'that you might have got married to someone unsuitable just to prove to our parents that you're unsuited to be King and Babbo should disinherit you.'

Luc's hand tightened round Kelly's, warning her not to react.

'Except we saw the press office report, Kelly,' Giulia said. 'And there's nothing remotely unsuitable about you. If you'd been a party girl who'd been in rehab a couple of times, or you had a brother who was in and out of jail, or something else that would make a lot of work for the palace PR team, Luc might have got away with it. But you're not quite what we expected.'

'We're in love,' Luc insisted.

'Also not true, because you would've told us and got us on your side to help talk Babbo round to the idea of you marrying someone who wasn't royal. So, basically, you're busted and you might as well tell us the truth,' Elle said.

'You're right,' Kelly said to Luc. 'She'd be a brilliant ruler. She's scary.'

'That comes from having two children under the age of five,' Giulia said. 'It makes you develop the scary mum radar. So are you going to tell us the truth?'

Luc raked a hand through his hair. 'I'm the heir. I'm pulling rank.'

Elle scoffed. 'No. You're going to make coffee, because we gave Maria the rest of the day off.'

'Better idea. I'll make the coffee and some choc-chip cookies to go with it,' Kelly said.

'Better idea still,' Giulia said. 'We'll come with you and make cookies, and Luc can go and do blokey stuff.'

'Bu—'

'We're going to have a girly chat. It might involve the menstrual cycle,' Giulia said.

Luc laughed. 'I'm a doctor. I don't get embarrassed that easily. You can talk about menstruation. I might even be able to give you some good advice.'

'Luc, just go and do something useful,' Elle said. 'We want to talk to Kelly.'

'No interrogation,' Luc warned.

Elle rolled her eyes. 'As if we'd interrogate someone who's just promised to make us cookies.'

'Susie grilled you. I'd expect nothing less,' Kelly said.

But she also knew she'd have to be really careful about what she said.

'Cookies first,' Giulia said.

'In *my* kitchen,' Luc said plaintively.

'*Ciao*, Lukey. You don't have enough X chromosomes to join us,' Elle said, and together she and Giulia swept Kelly into the kitchen.

Luc's sisters kept everything light until the cookies were out of the oven. Then Eleonora made a pot of coffee.

'Right. We already worked out why he married you— you're a cardiologist, and marrying you shows Babbo how committed Luc is to his job, because he's chosen a partner in the same line of work.' She looked at Kelly. 'But what do you get out of marrying him? It's clear you're not a gold-digger.'

Kelly remembered how Luc had defined love, last night: physical attraction plus friendship. That worked for her, too. 'I love him,' she said.

Eleonora looked at her. 'You've known each other for how long?'

'Nearly two months. We met when he first came to work at the Muswell Hill Memorial Hospital,' Kelly said. 'Sanjay—our boss—asked me to show him round. And then we kind of fell for each other.' Sticking to the truth as much as possible would mean less chance of slipping up.

'You're a widow,' Giulia said.

Clearly she'd read the files on Kelly. Kelly nodded.

'I'm sorry you lost your husband.'

'Thank you.'

'You must have loved him very much,' Elle said.

'I did.'

'Two years. It's a long time to be alone,' Giulia said.

'My friends and family felt it was time for me to move on.'

'What about you?' Elle asked. 'How did you feel about it?'

'Not ready,' Kelly admitted. 'But then I met Luc.' And that was true. Since their 'honeymoon', they'd grown closer. A lot closer. To the point where they hadn't quite gone back to being sensible.

'So has your family met Luc? Or are you keeping this secret from them?' Giulia asked.

'They've met him,' Kelly said. 'They liked him. But we didn't tell them about the wedding until last night, when we came back from New York.'

'How upset were they?' Elle asked.

'They were upset at first,' Kelly admitted. 'And we both feel bad about that. But they understood why we wanted to keep everything low-key. I'm sorry if we've upset everyone in your family. That wasn't the intention.'

'Luc's idea, was it?' Giulia asked.

'It was the least complicated option,' Kelly said. 'Except now I'm wondering if we should have told everyone first.'

'Mamma is doing her Serene Swan bit and Babbo is frothing at the mouth,' Giulia said.

'I'm sorry,' Kelly said again. 'But I know how much Luc loves his job. And he's really good at what he does. I sat in on some of his operations and he's amazing to watch. He's already made a difference to our department—he's brought in new ideas and new training. He's wonderful with patients and he even gives up his breaks to sit and reassure nervous patients. And he's great with junior staff. He's helping to train the surgeons of the future. That's really important. And he wants to open a state-of-the-art cardiac unit in Bordimiglia in a couple of years' time.'

'But all his life he's known that he was born to take over from my father,' Elle said gently.

'And he's protested about it,' Kelly said. 'I believe your grandmother persuaded your father to let Luc go to medical school.'

'She did,' Giulia said.

'And you, Elle, are already doing some of your father's job—and Luc says you're excellent. That you would make a much better ruler than he would. I trust his clinical judgement absolutely and I trust his judgement outside work.'

'Even the elopement?' Giulia asked.

Kelly winced. 'We thought we were doing the right thing.' She looked Elle in the eyes. 'Do you think he'd make a better job than you would of running the country?'

'No,' Elle said.

'So,' Kelly said, 'we agree on that. Giulia, do you think Elle would be a better ruler than Luc?'

'Yes,' Giulia said.

'Then the way forward is obvious. I want to help Luc to follow his dreams and set up that cardiac centre,' Kelly said. 'I believe in him.'

'So do we,' Elle said.

'I'm assuming your parents sent you to check me out,' Kelly said. 'So what are you going to tell them?'

'That you're a doctor,' Elle said. 'That you're nice. That you believe in Luc.' She paused. 'But I do think Luc rushed into this—and that's probably my fault, for telling him that Babbo has been talking about stepping down next year. It panicked Luc into making a rash decision.'

'So you think he shouldn't have married me?'

'Not this quickly,' Elle said. 'He hasn't given you a chance to see the other side of his world. You might find it too much to deal with.'

'Like Rachel?' Kelly asked.

Giulia looked surprised. 'He told you about that?'

Kelly nodded. 'I know he's been hurt before. And I would never hurt him.'

'I believe you,' Elle said.

'So will you support Luc?' Kelly asked.

Elle spread her hands. 'Right now I could happily punch him for being so impetuous and causing a row with our parents, but we all know his heart lies in medicine. Taking him away from that would be like ripping his soul out. He'd do his duty if he had to, I know. But I wouldn't force him to do that.'

'So where do we go from here? And what can I do to help?' Kelly asked.

'I think, just be yourself,' Giulia said. 'Our parents will calm down—as I'm sure your family will, too. We'll get to know each other.'

'But I'm satisfied that you care about my brother,' Elle said. 'You're fighting his corner. And that's what I want for Lukey. Someone who'll back him but who'll also see when you need to compromise and talk him round from being stubborn.'

'Thank you.' Kelly hugged them both. 'Luc loves you. He talks about you with a great deal of affection and respect.'

'We love him, too,' Elle said. 'So we'll work on Babbo and make him think about the situation.'

'Hopefully he'll think it's his idea to change things the way Luc wants. The way we all want it, really,' Giulia said.

Elle smiled. 'Welcome to the family.'

CHAPTER TEN

EARLY ON SUNDAY MORNING, Kelly's mobile shrilled. She checked the screen, then answered swiftly. 'Susie? What's wrong?' she asked. 'Are the boys OK? Mum and Dad? Nick?'

'It's not us,' Susie said. 'It's the news. Someone sent your wedding photo to the press.'

'Luc's family knows. His sisters are staying with us right now,' Kelly said.

'It's not that, either. Kel, you need to talk to his press people. It's what they're saying about you.' Susie gulped. 'About Simon. How he died from heart disease and you're a cardiologist.'

Kelly felt sick. The very thing she wasn't able to forgive herself for. They'd homed straight in on it. And it wasn't just her who'd be hurt by this—it would be her family and Simon's family, too. 'Do Mum and Dad know?'

'Not yet. I'll tell them,' Susie said. 'But you need Luc's PR team to jump on it now. There's no way you're to blame for Simon's death, and you know it.'

Kelly dragged in a breath. 'I'd better call Jake, too. And I'll call you back to let you know what's going on.'

She flicked into the Internet on her phone, and the sick feeling increased. According to the news, 'Dr Death'—

meaning Kelly—married Prince Luciano in secret. And there was the picture of them outside the Clerk's Office in Manhattan. Looking into each other's eyes and laughing. How on earth had the press got hold of this? And where did they even begin to untangle this mess?

She knew Luc would be in the gym, where he worked out every morning with his security team. She showered and dressed swiftly, then went in search of him.

'What's wrong?' Luc asked, putting down the barbell he'd been working with.

She opened her mouth to tell him, and to her horror all that came out were racking sobs.

'Kelly?'

She held her phone out to him.

He read the story and wrapped his arms around her. 'I'm so, so sorry. I never thought they'd stoop this low. I'll get in touch with the PR team and get them to ask for a retraction.'

'They're calling me "Dr Death".' And how that description hurt.

'That's rubbish, and you know it. Think how many lives you've saved.'

'My patients—if they see this, they'll worry I'm not treating them properly, and the stress could trigger a full-blown CV event.'

'Anyone who's been treated by you will know how thorough you are and that this is utter rubbish,' he reassured her. 'I'll sort this. Go and grab some coffee, and I'll talk to my press team, Sanjay and the hospital press team.'

'I need to ring Simon's family. I never told them I got married to you.'

'Call them, and if they want to talk to me that's fine.'

He held her close. 'Don't worry. We'll fix this. I'll get Elle and Giu.'

'Your family is going to hate me.'

'No, they're not. Elle and Giu will know immediately that this is all rubbish. So will my parents.' He hugged her again. 'We'll fix this. Call Jake and make a coffee.'

It was one of the most horrible conversations she'd ever had. Jake reassured her that he and the rest of his family knew she wasn't to blame for his brother's death—and she was the one who had made him and Summer get checked out. But she still hated herself.

'Congratulations on the wedding, Kelly. I hope you'll be happy,' Jake said. 'Simon wouldn't have wanted you to be alone.'

'Thank you,' she said, feeling guilty about lying to someone else. 'And I'm sorry. I should've told you that I was seeing someone instead of letting you hear about it in the press.'

'We're not on his trial because of you, are we?' he asked.

'No. I asked him if he'd consider you, yes, but you met the requirements or you wouldn't have been accepted,' she said.

She called Simon's parents next, feeling the same flood of guilt about not forewarning them. By the time she finished, Eleonora and Giulia had joined her in the kitchen.

'Toast. Eat,' Giulia demanded, putting a plate in front of her.

'I can't.'

'You can and you will. The press can be vile. But none of this is your fault,' Giulia said.

'I'm so sorry,' Kelly whispered. 'It's made trouble for your family.'

'That doesn't matter. We're used to the press. You're not,' Eleonora said. 'We'll remind them of the laws of defamation and get your name cleared.'

'How did they even know we'd got married?' Kelly asked.

'You sent the picture to the woman who sorted out your wedding dress. One of her colleagues saw it and recognised Luc—she's a big fan of European royal families—and she leaked the news to the press,' Eleonora said. 'And they started digging for information about you. Unfortunately they decided to spin it a nasty way.'

'That's so unfair to Simon's family,' Kelly said.

'And it's grossly unfair to you, sweetie. Give it an hour and they'll be singing a different tune,' Giulia said.

Luc walked back into the kitchen. 'The castle press team is already on it—they picked it up earlier but I didn't see their messages. I've given a statement. Sanjay sends his best and says not to worry, Kelly—we're all behind you on this. Though you and I are in a tiny bit of trouble with the department for sneaking off and getting married without telling them. We need to turn up with cake tomorrow.'

'We can make cake,' Eleonora said. 'And you need to talk to our parents.'

'I've already done that,' Luc said. 'Mamma was very definite about this being another good reason to get married properly instead of eloping. And that I don't have the sense I was born with. And that I need to look after my wife more carefully.'

'She doesn't hate me for dragging your family's name through the mud?' Kelly asked.

'You haven't. It's not your fault. It's probably a slow news week,' Giulia said. 'Mamma doesn't hate you. She's not happy about the secret wedding, but she's looking forward to meeting you.'

'We need to make sure your family is protected, too,' Eleonora said. 'We should have everything cleared up today, but maybe they'd like to come and spend the day here, just in case anyone decides to doorstep them.'

'I'll arrange it,' Luc said. 'Elle, Kelly has two nephews around the same age as Alessio and Anna.'

'I'll call Riccardo and get him to bring them over. The flight's only a couple of hours.' She frowned. 'Babbo's meant to be in Paris. We might be able to get him and Mamma over. But if they can't make it then the others will be here. And what better way to show the press that our families are united than to have a family party?'

Before Kelly knew quite what was going on, it was all arranged. As Eleonora had said, King Umberto and Queen Vittoria were due in Paris and couldn't move their schedule, but Eleonora's husband and children and Giulia's husband would be there.

Luc was smiling as he told them, 'Kelly, your dad is dying to practise his barbecue skills. I suggested everyone should bring their swimming things, so between us we can keep all the children amused. And you and I are going to take cake and bubbles to the paps.'

'We're facing them down?' Kelly almost squeaked.

'We're charming them into seeing the truth.' Luc looked at Eleonora. 'I don't suppose you can tell Ric to bring your best tiara?'

'No,' Eleonora said, rolling her eyes at him. 'But yes to playing nice with the paps. Kelly, your father and I can join you as our family representatives, if you wish. And I'm sorry you've had such a baptism of fire.' She patted Kelly's shoulder. 'Now, we have cake to make.'

This was surreal, Kelly thought, making cake in the

kitchen with two princesses. But Eleonora and Giulia were down-to-earth, and by the time her family arrived she was a lot more relaxed. She introduced them all swiftly, and the women all bonded over making desserts and salads, while the men played with the children in the garden and sorted out the barbecue.

'Do we call you "Your Highness" or "Your Majesty"?' Susie asked Eleonora.

'Neither. You're family, so we stick with first names,' Eleonora said. 'Call me Elle.'

When Eleonora's children arrived, it took all of five minutes for the children to become firm friends. Kelly's new brothers-in-law were relaxed and charming.

'You learn to grow a thick skin with the press,' Eduardo said. 'You can't please everyone, and everyone on social media has an opinion. Unless you really *are* behaving badly and deserve what they say about you, take what they say with a pinch of salt.'

'Though in this case they're being unfair,' Riccardo said. 'So the press team will jump on them and put them straight. You'll get an apology tomorrow.'

'Today would be better,' Luc said. 'And I think Kelly and I have a delivery to make.'

The photographers and journalists hanging round the far side of the gate on Luc's road all seemed shocked at having cake, champagne and chilled sparkling water served to them by a prince.

'Kelly's family and mine are celebrating our good news,' Luc said, 'and we thought you might like some refreshments.'

'That's nice of you,' one of the photographers said.

'We eloped to try to get out of the speeches and hours of photographs,' Luc said. 'Which kind of backfired. But my wife is an excellent cardiologist. I'm sure you'll all agree that if you're not experiencing any symptoms, you won't think there's anything wrong with you or that there's any need to see a doctor. And if it's the sort of condition that only gets picked up by having electrodes attached to your chest and being hooked up to a monitor, it can't possibly be diagnosed. There wasn't anything for Kelly to miss. Just so you're aware, the head of our cardiac unit has given a public statement saying exactly that.'

One or two of the journalists shuffled, looking guilty. 'Sorry.'

'I just hate to think that any of my patients have read the news and started getting worried about their own treatment. Stress isn't a good combination with a heart condition,' Kelly said.

'I don't think any of us thought about them,' one of the photographers admitted.

'You're all trying to sell newspapers and make a living,' Luc said. 'I get that. But a lot of people have been hurt needlessly by the story. Yes, we eloped, and it hasn't turned out to be the easy solution we thought it was going to be. But haven't any of you been swept away in the heat of the moment?'

'We all make mistakes,' one of the journalists said.

'Exactly. So enjoy cake and bubbles on us,' Luc said.

'Thank you, Your Highness. And we hope you're very happy together,' one of the other journalists said.

'Give us a kiss?' one of the photographers asked, holding up his camera.

Luc grinned. 'We're in the middle of a family party. We've been playing in the pool with all the kids and we're not exactly dressed up for an official photograph.'

'Just like any other family on an early summer Sunday afternoon when it's not raining,' the photographer said. 'Actually, our readers would love to know you're just like us.'

Luc and Kelly exchanged a glance, and did as they were asked, to a barrage of camera flashes and clicks.

And by the time they'd finished the barbecue, the photographs of that kiss were all over the news sites. Except this time the headlines said *The Surgeon To Mend Her Broken Heart*.

At the end of the afternoon, everyone crowded round Luc's piano while he played. He deliberately chose the kind of songs that Kelly, her mum and her sister loved; and Kelly was thrilled that her new sisters-in-law joined in.

The only sticky moment was when Oscar spilled blackcurrant juice all over the white carpet. But Luc was completely unfazed. 'I've spilled coffee on this carpet before now. It will be fine. Stop worrying,' he said.

'It's absolutely true,' Giulia said. 'If anyone spilled things when we were growing up, it was always Luc. Don't worry.'

Eleonora was already in the kitchen, and returned with kitchen towel.

Between Eleonora, Kelly and Susie, they managed to get the stain out of the carpet. And while they were doing that, Giulia and Caroline made tea. 'The English solution to everything,' Giulia said. 'And it's definitely better here than it is anywhere else in the world...'

Later that night after everyone had gone home, Kelly curled in Luc's arms.

'I know that look,' he said. 'What are you thinking?'

'That today started horribly but the end was really nice. Our families get on.'

'Four children splashing around in the pool will make

anyone laugh and get on,' he said. 'But you're right. Today was nice. Even though you panicked a bit too much over spills.'

Kelly paused. 'How today was—is that the kind of family thing you had, growing up?'

'My generation is a little less formal, as adults,' he said.

Which told her that his childhood had been much more restricted.

'It is how it is,' he said softly, as if guessing what she was thinking. 'I like this side of my life. The private side, where I'm a doctor rather than a prince.'

She just hoped that he'd get the chance to keep it that way.

'I've been in touch with Elle and Giu a little more often recently than I have been for a couple of years,' he said. 'And that's all thanks to you. Seeing you with your family has reminded me of what I'm missing.'

'I'm glad you're getting closer to them,' she said. 'I wouldn't be without my family.'

'And I wouldn't be without mine. Though I wish my father wasn't so stubborn.'

She stroked his face. 'And you don't think you might be a chip off the old block?'

'Probably.' He kissed her. 'But thank you. You're making my world a better place.'

'Good.' She kissed him back. 'Being a doctor doesn't mean you can't be close to your family. And maybe if you let your dad a bit closer, he might start to understand why you feel the way you do. And then you might be able to reach some sort of compromise.'

'I'm beginning to think,' Luc said, 'that women are much more diplomatic than men.'

'I don't know about that. The way you were with the

press—I wouldn't have had a clue how to get them on my side. You made things better again.'

'Though if you'd never met me, you wouldn't have been in the press in the first place,' he pointed out.

'But you fixed it. That's the main thing.'

'My press team fixed it.'

'To your brief.' She paused. 'You might be a better king than you think you'd be.'

'Are you on my dad's side, now?'

'No. I'm just saying that maybe you need to look at things through his eyes. Work out a compromise together. Maybe there's a way you can work at your clinic but also carry out some royal duties as well—have the best of both worlds.'

'Maybe,' he said. 'Maybe.'

At work on Monday, Luc and Kelly went to see the head of the cardiac department before the start of their shift.

'I'm glad the papers have got the story right now,' Sanjay said. 'Are you all right, Kelly?'

She nodded. 'I'm just so sorry the hospital got dragged into this.'

'The press team are rushed off their feet giving tips and writing articles on heart health,' Sanjay said, 'so it's working out in the right way now.' He looked at them. 'Though you *are* in trouble about the wedding.'

'We brought cake,' Luc said, indicating the box he was carrying.

'Not good enough. I thought something might be going on, but I don't like rumours so I didn't ask.'

Kelly winced. 'Sorry.'

'Your private life is your affair—but you really can't get married without a proper cardiac department cele-bration,' Sanjay said.

'He's right. Dancing and toasting you in champagne. That's the very least you're getting away with,' Mandy, Sanjay's secretary said, coming in. 'I can't believe you two kept something like that quiet.'

Kelly and Luc exchanged a glance.

'I guess we kind of made everyone miss out on the wedding, so I'll get a reception organised,' Luc said. 'I'll ask my team to make the arrangements. Maybe we can do it instead of the next team night out?'

'A week on Friday. Good idea,' Sanjay said. 'Apart from all that stuff in the papers, I imagine your families aren't wonderfully happy about you eloping.'

'We didn't do it to hurt people,' Kelly said.

'You did it to avoid the fuss and the media circus. I understand that—though you rather got the media circus anyway,' Sanjay said. 'But we still want to celebrate your wedding with you. It's great news. Congratulations.'

The rest of their colleagues reacted in the same way, shocked by the way the news had broken and furious with the press on Kelly's behalf, a little hurt that they'd been kept in the dark about the wedding, but pleased for both of them.

Over the next week, they were rushed off their feet at the hospital. Luc worked on a rare domino transplant with two other surgical teams—a new heart and lungs for a patient who had cystic fibrosis, and then her healthy heart was transplanted to a patient with right ventricular dysplasia, a genetic disorder that caused a dangerously abnormal heart rhythm. After the operation, Luc was physically drained but mentally invigorated.

'I love the fact we can do this and give someone such great quality of life,' he said. 'It's only the second time I've worked on a domino transplant. The first team re- moved the heart-lung from the deceased donor, I transplanted them to my patient and removed her heart, and the third team implanted her heart into their patient.' He wrapped his arms around her. 'Normally, patients don't know anything about the donors or their families; but as they're being looked after in adjacent rooms I think there's a good chance they'll meet.'

'And your cystic fibrosis patient could hear her heart beating in someone else's body.' She paused. 'Something like this doesn't happen often. It'll be in the news.'

'I think the journalists will be a bit more sympathetic, this time round,' he said. 'Though the most important thing is that our patients are going to be able to walk down the corridor without having to stop and rest. As cystic fibrosis is a genetic condition, she'll still need treatment for it, but at least her new lungs will be working and not displacing her heart any more,' he added. 'She'll still need a lot of care, and there are the usual risks of organ rejection, infection and complications, but she'll have fewer symptoms and a better quality of life.' He looked at Kelly. 'I wish Babbo could understand how this feels. To be able to make a real difference to someone's life.'

'Maybe you should show him. Ask your patients if they'd mind doing a video interview with you so your father can see for himself,' she suggested. 'Explain it won't be shown to anyone else, and you'll delete it once your father's seen it.'

'That,' he said, 'is a brilliant idea.' He hugged her. 'And we have our wedding reception on Friday.'

'It's so good of Maria to make us an official wedding cake.'

'She's loving the fact that I put her in complete charge of the reception and gave her free rein to choose whatever she thought appropriate,' Luc said. He smiled. 'I hope everyone doesn't mind swapping the team bowling night out for dancing, a buffet and bubbles.'

'Given that we're inviting partners and children as well, everyone's happy,' she said. 'Though maybe we should have waited a little bit longer so your family could make it as well as mine.'

'We promised work we'd do it—besides, it's less complicated this way,' he said.

On Friday night, Gino drove them through Hampstead to a nearby stately home. Maria had arranged taxis for all the guests, and Luc and Kelly were the last to arrive.

They walked through a marble-floored hall with Venetian glass chandeliers hanging from the ceiling and massive paintings in gilt frames hanging on the wall.

'I feel a bit of a fraud,' Kelly whispered.

Luc's fingers tightened round hers. 'We're just giving everyone what they want to see—and a party. It's fine.' He smiled at her. 'And you look amazing, by the way.'

'So do you.' They'd decided to wear the same outfits they'd worn for the actual wedding, to make everyone feel that they were part of the day.

When they walked into the main hall, they could see the band set up at one end of the room, a generously laid out buffet table, and plenty of seating round the edges for guests. Music was playing through the sound system, but it stopped as soon as Luc and Kelly were in the room. Everyone turned to look at them, and then there was an eruption of party poppers and confetti.

'Speech,' someone called.

'And that,' Luc said with a grin, his voice booming over the crowd, 'is one of the best reasons ever for eloping. No long speeches to send everyone to sleep. I'll just say thank you all for coming, a special thank you to

Maria for organising everything and making us a wonderful cake, and thank you to Maybe Baby for agreeing to be our band for the night. Enjoy yourselves, everyone.'

The party was in full swing and Luc and Kelly were dancing when a couple walked up to them.

'I think,' the man said, 'the next dance with the bride should be mine, given that she's my new daughter-in-law.'

'Babbo!' Luc hugged his father. 'I thought you and Mamma were on a state visit somewhere?'

'We explained that our wayward son was having a belated wedding reception,' his mother said. 'Since we were deprived of the wedding itself, we weren't going to miss the reception.' She smiled at Kelly to soften the edge of her words. 'I know whose idea it was to elope. Hopefully you can teach my son better manners than I did.'

'I—um—Your Majesties—' Kelly, completely flustered, was about to dip into a curtsy, when King Umberto took her hand. 'No formalities, child. This is my son's wedding party, so we will conduct it how he likes it—with no pomp or ceremony. But I would like this dance.'

'Yes, Your M—'

'Babbo will do,' the King cut in with a smile. 'And I look forward to meeting your family. Eleonora has told me all about them.'

'I—um—thank you,' Kelly said.

Once she'd danced with the King, she and Luc introduced his parents to her family. Although Umberto and Vittoria were more formal than their children, they did seem to be genuinely pleased to meet Kelly's family, and the introductions were easy.

'I had no idea they were going to be here,' Luc said.

'You're not the only one who can spring surprises, little brother,' a voice informed them.

'Elle!' He hugged his sister. 'I should have guessed you'd have something to do with it.'

'I've been looking forward to your second wedding reception—even though, being you, you gave us practically no notice.' Elle hugged Kelly. 'Cake, dancing and spending time with my favourite sister-in-law. What could be better?'

'I assume you're staying with us?' Luc asked.

Elle shook her head. 'Babbo arranged a hotel. But we'll be round to see you in force tomorrow for a proper family dinner party.'

'I was going to give Maria the weekend off.'

Elle grinned. 'Too late. She's already planned the menu and has everything ordered for delivery first thing tomorrow. And your family will be there too, Kelly.'

'They know about it?' Kelly asked.

'They know. Actually, Mamma had a long video call with Caroline earlier this week. Thankfully your mother is a little better with technology than mine.' Elle patted Kelly's shoulder. 'Just so you know, she thinks my brother made a good choice. Even if he went about it in an unconventional way.'

'I'm glad you're all here,' Luc said. 'I do love you all. Even if you think I'm an ungrateful brat.'

'Not a brat, and not exactly ungrateful. You just don't march to the same drum as Babbo,' Elle said.

The rest of the evening passed in a blur.

And then Keely, the paediatrician singer from the band, spoke up. 'We have a special guest tonight—you might not know he plays rhythm guitar as well as being a heart surgeon, but he does. Please give a round of applause for Luciano Bianchi.'

'How...?' Luc asked.

Elle gave an overdramatic shrug and spread her hands. 'No idea.'

'Of course you don't,' Luc said, rolling his eyes, and went onto the stage to join the band. Anton, the lead guitarist from the maternity department, handed him a guitar, and Luc joined the band for a couple of songs.

'I have it on good authority that he sings as well,' Keely said. 'And I think he should sing something for his new bride.'

Anton swapped Luc's guitar for an electro-acoustic, and Luc stared at Kelly.

Singing to his bride in public.

The woman he'd married in name only—except it wasn't quite turning out that way. She still hadn't moved into her own room at his house, and waking up with her in his arms was turning out to be the best part of his day. Despite their agreement, he was definitely falling in love with her. Everything about her, from her kindness to the way she sang in the shower to her infectious giggle.

But did she feel the same way about him? Was he just her transition partner, the one who would help her to move on from losing the love of her life? Or was this thing between them changing for her, too?

He was aware that everyone was waiting for him to play. And there was only one song he could think of. The one he'd sung to her, the first night she'd come to his house and they'd sat together at his piano.

The room felt huge; yet, at the same time, it felt so small that he could hardly breathe. This was telling the world how he felt about her, singing a romantic song they'd expect to hear and yet not putting pressure on Kelly. Would she know that he was singing this for real—

for her—or would she think that it was all part of their fake marriage?

His hands were shaking and he made a real mess of the introduction to the song. How could he mess up four simple chords like that? 'I can assure you I'm a better surgeon than I am a musician,' he said, making everyone laugh—including Kelly and his parents. And then he began the song again, holding Kelly's gaze and hoping that she knew what he was trying to tell her.

Everyone cheered when he'd finished. And then thankfully he was able to hand the guitar back to Anton and dance with his bride again.

'That was a beautiful song,' she said. 'The one you sang to me, that first night at your house.'

'Yes.' Pleased that she'd remembered, he stole a kiss.

At the end of the evening, Luc and Kelly said their goodbyes and headed back to his house.

'I guess,' he said, 'as that was our official wedding reception, I should do official groom stuff.' He picked her up and carried her over the threshold.

She kissed him before he set her back on her feet, so he carried her upstairs to their bed. And tonight felt the same as New York: just the two of them, and the rest of the world was a million miles away.

'Kelly,' he whispered.

'What?'

He was going to tell her he loved her—but then he chickened out. If he told her now, and she wasn't ready to hear it, he'd blow his chances of making their marriage a real one. 'Thank you for tonight,' he said instead. 'For being so great with my parents.'

'I liked them,' she said, and kissed him. 'I'm glad they came. It was good to meet them. And I have the feeling that Elle might just talk your father round...'

CHAPTER ELEVEN

THREE WEEKS LATER, Kelly had a half day. She'd been too busy to notice during the morning, but she felt odd. Queasy.

Probably low blood sugar, she told herself. She was meeting her sister for lunch, so it would be at least another half an hour until they ate. She went to the kiosk by the staff canteen to buy a cereal bar to tide her over, but the scent of the coffee made her feel even more queasy.

It wasn't until she was on the Tube and the cereal bar had done nothing to settle her stomach that the likely reason hit her.

No.

Ridiculous.

Of course she couldn't be pregnant. She and Luc had used protection whenever they'd made love.

But contraception wasn't always one hundred per cent effective.

She swallowed hard. Her period was late, but that was probably due to all the stress she'd been under lately— wasn't it?

Though the idea wouldn't leave her. Especially because the scents in the cafe where she met Susie made her feel even queasier than she'd felt in the hospital.

'Are you all right, Kel?' Susie asked.

'Course I am,' Kelly fibbed. This wasn't something she was ready to discuss with anyone. Not until she'd re-assured herself that she was being ridiculous. She managed to keep the conversation light until Susie left to pick the boys up from school, and then she headed for a nearby supermarket and bought a pregnancy test. Not wanting to wait until she got home, she went to the toilet in the supermarket. Thankfully, the cubicles were all empty, so she didn't feel guilty about taking her time. She took a deep breath. This would reassure her that everything was fine and she was panicking over nothing.

She did the test, and watched the screen. A little square box appeared at the left hand side of the screen to show her that the test was working. Another appeared; another; and then the final one to say that the test was over.

Was she or wasn't she?

Time slowed down, and every second felt like a minute. But finally the word flashed up on the screen. Absolutely definite.

Pregnant.

Oh, help.

What did she do now?

This wasn't part of the deal. Her marriage to Luc was supposed to be in name only—something that wasn't real. Except over the last few weeks they'd moved towards a rather different relationship. Friendship plus physical attraction. Did that really equal love?

But this pregnancy was a real game-changer. They couldn't pretend anything, any more. They had to face the reality.

She had absolutely no idea how Luc would react.

Would he insist on making their marriage permanent, for the sake of the baby? Would he expect to be part of the baby's life if they stuck to their original plan and had a quick divorce after a few months? Would he ask her to have a termination?

Kelly didn't think he'd choose the last option. She didn't want that, either. But as for their future… She had absolutely no idea what she really wanted, either. Her head was too much in panic mode now she knew she was pregnant.

She and Simon had planned to start trying for a baby—a much-wanted addition to their family who would be so very deeply loved. But she and Luc weren't in that position. His parents had been surprisingly kind and accepting, but she was pretty sure that Eleonora had had to talk them round to the idea; her first conversation with Vittoria, on Luc's laptop, had been awkward in the extreme. Would the baby change things? Would the news make things better, or would it be an extra complication?

And if the baby was a boy and the King didn't change the succession rules, that meant the baby she was carrying would be second in line to the throne. She and Luc would both be trapped; they'd both have to give up the careers they'd worked so hard to build. And no way would he be able to follow his dream of setting up his cardiac clinic.

She stared at the test stick. Given that it was digital, there was absolutely no way she'd misread it.

Pregnant.

All the way back to Luc's house, her mind was in a whirl.

'Are you all right, *bella*?' Maria asked when she walked in.

'Fine,' Kelly fibbed. 'Just a bit tired.' And she had no idea how to tell Luc.

She picked at her food that night, and he noticed.

'What's wrong? I know you met your sister for lunch. Susie and the baby are all right, aren't they?'

'Yes.' It wasn't Susie's baby who was the issue. It was theirs.

He frowned. 'Whatever's upset you, is it something I can help with?'

She blew out a breath. 'Luc, we need to talk. In private.'

'Now you're worrying me.'

He was going to be a lot more worried when she told him the news, she thought.

When she didn't answer, he said, 'OK. Let's go for a drive.'

'No.' This was going to be a shock to him, and driving wouldn't be sensible. 'Let's go for a walk in the garden.'

'If that's what you want, sure.'

Right at the bottom of the garden was a fountain; next to it was a wrought-iron bench. They sat down, and Luc waited patiently until Kelly was ready to talk.

She took a deep breath. 'There isn't an easy way to say this. I know we didn't plan it and we took precautions—but I'm pregnant.'

His expression was utterly inscrutable. 'How pregnant?'

'I'm a couple of weeks late.'

'And your cycle's regular?'

She nodded. 'Every twenty-eight days. Practically to the hour. We've both been busy since we came back from New York so I didn't notice I was late. It didn't even occur to me until today, when I felt a bit off-colour and then the smells in the cafe made me feel a bit sick. I thought I was being ridiculous, and then I realised my period was late.'

'Have you told anyone else?'

She shook her head. 'I didn't even tell Susie of my

suspicions. I did a test on the way home—and I thought you ought to be the first to know.'

He was going to be a father.

The world spun for an instant.

He really hadn't expected Kelly to tell him this. And he had no clue about whether she was shocked or pleased or *anything*. They hadn't even discussed children. Their marriage was supposed to be in name only—except he'd changed the terms when he'd made love to her on their wedding night.

'Thank you for telling me first.' He paused. 'If my calculations are right, this is a honeymoon baby.'

'That's what I thought, too. Conceived in New York.' She swallowed hard. 'So, what now?'

'We're married,' he said. 'Our baby is legitimate. And, as he or she is my child, the baby will be a prince or princess.' And that changed everything. The baby would need his protection. He needed to make things right. He looked at her. 'So perhaps we should forget the few months we originally planned.'

'You mean, wait until after the baby arrives before we have our quiet divorce?'

'I mean, forget the divorce altogether. We're going to be parents, Kelly.'

'And what happens when your father finds out about the baby? If Elle has been trying to persuade him to change his mind about the succession rules, this baby...' Her voice tailed off and she stared at him.

'As things stand right now, then the baby will be second in line to the throne. If Babbo does decide to change the rules, the baby will still be fifth in line—it will be Elle, Alessio, Anna, me and then our baby, and then Giu.'

She raked a hand through her hair. 'Which means

we're both trapped. We can't continue working here at Muswell Hill Memorial Hospital.'

'Not necessarily,' he said. He'd already disrupted her life so much. He needed to do the right thing and let her choose what she wanted to do. 'What do *you* want?'

'I...' She shook her head. 'I don't know. I hadn't even considered this might happen.'

'But you'd planned to have children with Simon.'

She looked away. 'Simon isn't here any more.'

Had she reached the stage where she was ready to move on and make a new life for herself? Or was she still in mourning? Luc had no idea. But now his head was clearing from the shock of the news and he knew exactly what he wanted from his life. He wanted Kelly and he wanted their baby.

'I need time to think about this,' she said. She looked him straight in the eye. 'What do *you* want?'

Crunch point.

If he told her that his feelings towards her had changed, would she be relieved or would she back away?

'I think we should stay married,' he said.

'For the baby's sake.'

Her tone was flat and he couldn't read her expression. He could pussyfoot around the situation; then again, he'd always hated the intricacies of diplomacy. He preferred to tell it like it was. Telling her the truth couldn't make things any worse. 'Your life as my queen would be very different,' he said. 'And it wouldn't be what you'd signed up for. I know that. But, baby or no baby, I still don't want to be king. I want to be a cardiac surgeon. And I happen to like being married to you.'

'Because I'm safe?'

Did she really have no idea how he felt about her?

'Remember the song I sang at our wedding reception? I meant every word,' he said. 'I don't want to stay married to you for the baby's sake—I want to stay married to you for mine. I've fallen in love with you over the last couple of months, Kel. I thought I'd forgotten what love feels like, but being with you and waking up with you in my arms every morning makes the world feel like a much better place. And I know why. It's because I love you.'

She looked utterly shocked.

Did that mean that she hadn't guessed? Or did it mean that she didn't feel the same way about him and was horrified to think that he loved her?

He pressed on. 'I know you'll always love Simon, and I don't intend to supplant him, but love stretches, Kelly. I hope you can learn to love me, too, to make our marriage a real one and make a family with me. But I'm not going to put pressure on you. I know I come with complications.' His royal lifestyle was the reason why Rachel had left him. Would it be the same for Kelly? The press had been horrible to her on the news of their marriage; although they'd weathered that particular storm, had it made her wary about how her life would be with him in the future?

'I'll give you as much time as you need to think, and I'll support whatever decision you make. But, even if you don't want me to be part of your life, I want to be part of the baby's life and give you all the support I can.'

She said nothing, and Luc felt sick. Maybe he shouldn't have declared himself after all. Maybe the past was just about to repeat itself.

'I'll give you time to think about what you want,' he said again, rising to his feet. 'Or to talk to someone you trust. Your mum, your sister, your best friend. No pressure.'

* * *

To make their marriage a real one and make a family with him.

And he hoped she'd learn to love him.

But was that how he really felt, or was he only saying that because of the baby—because the baby would be a royal heir?

Kelly hadn't thought herself ready to move on, yet. And there was only one place she could go right now: only one person she could speak to.

'I need to go out,' she said.

'I'll get Gino to drive you.'

She could see that he was holding himself in check and trying not to smother her. 'Thank you, Luc. For giving me time,' she said, and reached out to squeeze his hand.

It didn't take long to drive to the church where Simon was buried. She'd had Gino stop to buy flowers on the way; and she knelt on the ground in front of the gravestone while she arranged them in the vase.

'I miss you,' she said. 'And I wish we could've had the chance to grow old together. But it wasn't to be.' She sat down properly and wrapped her arms around her knees. 'If I'd been the one to die, I would've wanted you to find someone else. Not to replace me, but to share your life and love you, the way you deserve to be loved, because I wouldn't have wanted you to be lonely. And I'm pretty sure that's the way you feel—felt—about me.' She dragged in a breath. 'I've met someone. We liked each other right from the start. We became friends. And we got married to solve a problem for both of us—to show his dad that he was committed to a life in medicine, being a heart surgeon; and to stop everyone trying to find me a new partner. Except it didn't quite work like that.'

Over the weeks of their marriage, it had changed.

'It didn't stay being a marriage in name only. He says he loves me, Simon, and I believe him. And I... I think I love him.' Now she'd said it out loud, it felt real. 'We're having a baby. It wasn't planned—but he's going to be as good a dad as you would've been. He's got a niece and nephew who adore him, and he's great with Jacob and Oscar. There's a bit of me that's scared he only loves me because I'm carrying his heir, but it's time for me to take a risk. To stop grieving and live again.'

Finally she could give herself permission to move on.

'I'll always love you and you'll always be part of me. But I want to make a life with Luc. Be his partner, be a cardiologist, and be the best mum I can be to our baby.' She smiled and stood up again. 'I guess I need to have a serious talk with Luc now. I won't ever forget you, and I'll always stay in touch with your family. That won't change.' She pressed her hand on the top of the gravestone. 'Wish me luck. We're still going to have to persuade Luc's dad that he's a heart surgeon rather than a future king. And I'm definitely not a queen. But we'll get there.'

Gino drove her back to Luc's house. When she walked through the front door, she could hear that he was playing the piano. Bach, the same kind of music he operated to: which gave her a clue that he was trying to think, to work out a solution to their situation. She tapped on the door of his office and went inside; he stopped playing as soon as she walked in.

'That sounded great,' she said. 'You don't have to stop.'

'Are you OK? Do you need anything?' he asked.

'Yes—and yes,' she said.

He looked faintly nervous. 'What do you need?'

'I need you to be honest with me.' She walked over to him and nudged him to budge over on the piano stool. 'I went to Simon's grave.'

'Uh-huh.' She could tell he was doing his best to keep his voice neutral, but it was obvious that he was on tenterhooks.

'What you said about loving me. Did you mean it, or are you saying that because of the baby?'

'I meant it,' he said. 'It isn't just about the baby. Remember you said I needed to see things from my dad's side? Knowing that I'm going to be a father makes me realise that I want our child to grow up being loved and valued for their own sake, not because they'll be my heir. And that's how I feel about my wife. I want her to know I love her and value her for herself, not because she's pregnant with the potential second in line to the throne.' He took her hand. 'I love you, Kelly. For who you are, not what you represent.' He dropped a kiss into her palm and closed her fingers over it.

'You love me.'

'I love you for you. While you were gone, I took a hard look at my life. I know what I want. But I also know I need to be fair and give you the choice, not pressure you into doing what you think you ought to do.'

She nodded. 'What you said about love stretching. You're right. I'm finally ready to move on. And what I need is you.' She swallowed hard. 'Because somewhere along the way I fell in love with you, too. Waking up to every new day in your arms sounds just about perfect to me. I want to share my life with you and our baby—to make a family.'

'Married for real,' he said.

'Married for real,' she echoed. 'It's early days, but I think our family needs to know about the baby. We kept them in the dark about getting married and that was a huge mistake. We need to prove to them that we won't do that again, so we'll trust them with the news. And I think we need to go to Bordimiglia and have a very frank conversation with your dad.'

'Sort it out once and for all.' Luc looked at her. 'What if my father says he won't change the succession rules?'

'Then you get to be King. But if that happens, then when you're King, *you* can change the rules,' she said. 'Maybe you can work out a compromise where you share the royal duties with Elle and Giu, and get time to do some part-time work as a cardiac surgeon as well. You can have the best of both worlds.'

'Compromise.' He looked at her thoughtfully. 'And you're prepared for the media circus when we officially announce your pregnancy?'

'Yes—because I know you'll be by my side and I can handle anything with your help.'

'You're sure about this?' he checked.

'I'm sure about this. I love you,' she said simply.

'I love you, too,' he said. 'And we'll go to Bordimiglia on our next days off. Be open with my parents. And then face whatever happens next—together.'

'Together,' she agreed.

EPILOGUE

Ten months later

'YOU HAVE EVERYTHING you need, *bella*?' Umberto asked.

'We do, Babbo. *Grazie,*' Kelly said, and hugged him.

'I'm glad you're having Giacomo christened here in Bordimiglia. Of course, we would have come to London if you'd wanted us to,' Umberto said.

'But we're following the tradition and having him christened in the same place as his father, his grandfather, and every great-grandfather as far back as you can trace your family,' Kelly said with a smile.

'Tradition is good,' Umberto said to his son.

'Agreed. But I'm glad you've modernised the monarchy and Eleonora is taking over from you at the end of the summer,' Luc said. He cradled his son tenderly, talking directly to him. 'Girl power is good. You tell your *nonno.*'

Obligingly, Giacomo gurgled.

'That's our boy.' With a grin, Luc handed his son over to Umberto.

Umberto smiled. 'My beautiful grandson. I wonder if he'll grow up to be as challenging as you, Luc?'

'He'll grow up to be himself,' Luc said. 'And I expect we'll fight like mad when he's a teenager. But I will teach him that family and love are the two most important things, and everything else is about negotiating a good compromise.'

'Compromise.' Umberto smiled. 'Your mother can't wait for you to come back to Bordimiglia next year to set up the new cardiac hospital, when your trial has finished. And it's going well?'

'It is.' Luc smiled at Kelly. 'Obviously I can't talk about any of my patients.'

'But I can,' Kelly said. 'My brother-in-law and niece are on the trial, and they're doing well. Thanks to Luc, I'm a lot less worried about their future.'

'I'm glad. And now I understand what you do in an operating theatre,' Umberto said. 'Seeing that video diary of your patient, how that poor man was breathless and could barely walk across the room, and then after you operated on him he was training to run a marathon—that is truly amazing.'

'It's good to be able to give someone a second chance at making the most of their life,' Luc said. 'And thank you for letting me do that instead of making me give it up to take over from you.'

'Your sister will be a better queen than you would have been a king. And it's right that she should get the chance to do that,' Umberto said. 'And your family will always be welcome to stay with us here, Kelly. They won't have to rely on video calls.'

'Grazie.' Kelly smiled at him.

'And now, duchessa, I think we're ready for church,' Luc said. As he'd predicted, Kelly wasn't officially a princess, but his father had bestowed the title of Duchess upon her.

'Back to your mamma, little one—though all your grandparents, aunts and uncles are going to be demanding cuddles later,' Umberto said, and handed the baby back to Kelly. Luc put his arm round Kelly's shoulder, and together they walked from the castle to the chapel and posed in the doorway for the media before walking down the aisle and sitting in the pew, waiting for the christening ceremony to begin.

'Old traditions and a new family,' Luc said softly.

'Old traditions and a new family,' Kelly echoed.

* * * * *

UNLOCKING THE SURGEON'S HEART

JESSICA MATTHEWS

This book is dedicated to cancer survivors everywhere – especially my friend Carla Maneth, who so graciously shared her experiences and insights – and to the memory of those who fought hard but didn't win the battle – especially my mother and my father-in-law.

CHAPTER ONE

IT WAS a shame, really. A man as handsome as Lincoln Maguire should have a personality to match, shouldn't he? The good doctor—and he was more than good, he was *exceptional* when it came to his surgical expertise—was so completely focused on his work that he wouldn't recognize a light-hearted moment if one landed in the middle of his operating field.

Christy Michaels peered sideways at the man in question. His long, lean fingers danced across the keyboard as he clearly ignored the hospital staff's ideas and opinions regarding Mercy Memorial's part in Levitt Springs' upcoming Community Harvest Festival. Apparently, talk of craft booths, food vendors, and a golf tournament to benefit the cancer center and the local Relay for Life chapter didn't interest him enough to join in the conversation.

It wasn't the first time he'd distanced himself from the conversations swirling around him; he was the sort who came in, saw his patients, and left, usually with few people being the wiser. Today, though, his distant demeanor—as if these details were too unimportant for his notice—coupled with her own special interest in the center and the treatment it provided, irritated her.

"I have an idea," she blurted out, well aware that she didn't but it hadn't been for lack of trying. She'd been considering options—and discarding them—for weeks, because none had given her that inner assurance that "this was the one".

Yet as voices stilled and all eyes focused on her—except for one midnight-blue pair—she had to come up with something unusual, something noteworthy enough to shock Dr Maguire into paying attention. With luck, he might even come out of his own little world and get involved.

"Make it snappy, Michaels," Denise Danton, her shift manager, said as she glanced at her watch. "The festival committee meets in five minutes and it takes at least that long to walk to the conference room."

Acknowledging Denise with a brief nod, she began, "It's something we haven't done before."

One of the nurses groaned. "If you're going to suggest a bachelor auction, it's already been mentioned. Personally, I think we need a newer idea."

Darn it, but that *had* been her suggestion. Rather than admit defeat, she thought fast. "We could create our own version of *Dancing with the Stars*. Only we would call it *Dancing with the Doctors*."

Instantly, his hands slowed, and she was immensely pleased. And yet he didn't look away from the digital pages in front of him, so maybe he was only thinking about Mrs Halliday's chest tube and her antibiotic regimen.

"How would that work?" someone asked her.

She ad-libbed. "We'd sell tickets for the public to watch the doctors and their partners perform. People could vote for their favorite pair—making a donation for the privilege, of course—and at the end, one lucky team is crowned the winner and all proceeds benefit the hospital."

Denise looked thoughtful. "Oh, I like that. We'd have to strong-arm enough physicians to participate, though."

"I'm sure any of them would jump at the opportunity to

raise money for a good cause. Right, Dr Maguire?" she asked innocently.

If she hadn't taken that moment to glance directly at the side of his face, she might have missed the weary set to his mouth as well as the barely imperceptible shadow on his skin that suggested his day had begun far earlier than hers. The wisps of walnut-brown hair appearing out from under his green cap were damp, and perspiration dotted the bridge of his chiseled nose. His scrub suit was wrinkled and his breast pocket had a frayed edge at the seam.

Funny thing, but she hadn't noticed he'd looked quite so frazzled when he'd sat in the chair.

Instantly, Christy felt guilty for distracting him. In hindsight, she realized it wasn't his scheduled surgery day, which meant he was obviously filling in for one of his partners. It also meant he was rushing to finish the paperwork so he could see his private patients. From the volume of cases he brought to the hospital, his waiting room was probably packed and growing more so by the minute.

"Sure, why not," he answered without any real emotion, his attention still focused on his computer screen.

"Okay, then," she said brightly, ready to leave him to his work. "Denise, you can mention this at your meeting—"

"Dr Maguire," the other woman said boldly, "you wouldn't mind participating, would you?"

This time, his hands froze. To Christy's surprise and dismay, his dark blue gaze met hers instead of Denise's and she was sure she saw exasperation in those depths. He clearly held her responsible, not only for being interrupted but also for having to field Denise's request.

However, when he addressed Denise, his tone was as pleasant and even-tempered as ever. "I'll forego the spot to make room for someone who's more capable."

"Ability has nothing to do with it," Denise retorted. "This is all for fun and as Christy said, it's for a good cause."

"But—" he began.

"If you sign up, I just *know* more of the medical staff will be willing to join in," Denise coaxed. "And with you on the program, we'll sell tons of tickets. Just think how much we'll earn for the cancer center."

Christy groaned inwardly. He *would* be a big draw because she couldn't imagine anyone who wouldn't be willing to fork out money to see the straitlaced, cool, and collected Lincoln Maguire cut loose on the dance floor. More importantly, because it was a known fact that he didn't date, everyone would want to speculate about the lucky woman he'd chosen to be his partner.

His thoughts obviously ran along the same track because he shot a warning glare in her direction before he spoke to Denise. "You're giving me far too much credit—"

"Nonsense." She clapped her hands softly in her excitement. "This is going to be great. The committee will love this idea. I can't wait to tell them—"

"Stop right there," he ordered in his most authoritative voice.

No one moved. Christy didn't even breathe because she suddenly had a feeling of impending doom as he pinned her with his gaze.

"If you're penciling me on the list," he said firmly, "I have a couple of conditions. One, if you have more volunteers than you can accommodate, my name will be the first to be removed."

Denise frowned, but, apparently recognizing his tone brooked no argument, she nodded. "Okay. Not a problem."

"Second, in the event that doesn't happen—and I suspect someone will make sure that it doesn't," he added dryly, "Christy must agree to be my partner."

Everyone's heads turned toward her in a perfectly choreo-graphed motion. Expressions ranged from surprise to curios-ity and a few were also speculative.

"You want...what?" Christy asked hoarsely. He might be her best friend's brother-in-law, but that wasn't a solid con-nection to warrant such a request. After all, they'd only been at Gail and Tyler's house together on two occasions and they'd hardly spoken to each other.

"To be my partner."

This wasn't supposed to happen. "Why me?" she asked.

He raised an eyebrow. "This was your idea," he reminded her. "It's only fair that you participate, too."

He had a point, although if she had her choice, she'd pick someone who complemented her, not someone who was vin-egar to her oil. While in the hospital they'd dealt with each other amicably over the past two years—he gave orders and she carried them out—but in the private atmosphere of Gail's home their differences had been highlighted. As a man who prided himself on control and self-restraint, she'd seen how he didn't appreciate her outspoken and sometimes impulsive nature.

Neither would she delude herself into believing he'd set his condition with romantic motives in mind. According to Gail, her brother-in-law had mapped out his life so carefully that he wasn't allowing for a wife until he was forty, and as he still had two or three years until then, his work was his mistress.

"Unless, of course, you object," he added smoothly, if not a trifle smugly, as if he *expected* her to refuse so she could provide his get-out-of-jail-free card.

She didn't blame him for thinking that. It was no secret she wasn't interested in a romance any more than he was, but while his excuse was because his work consumed his life, her reasons were entirely different.

However, he'd issued a challenge and she was living proof that she didn't back down from one. If dusting off her dancing shoes and practicing her two-step meant the workaholic, type A personality Dr Maguire would participate in a night of fun and frivolity, then she'd do it.

She shrugged. "Okay, fine with me."

"Good," Denise said. "It's settled."

"I don't know how settled this is." He sounded doubtful and hopeful at the same time. "Won't the committee, as a whole, have to approve the idea first?"

"Trust me, they're going to love the concept," the older woman assured him. "I can already think of fifty ways to promote the event and guarantee a brilliant turnout. Now, I'm off. Hold the fort while I'm gone, people, so that means everyone back to work!"

The crowd dispersed, but Christy hardly noticed. Dr Maguire—Linc, as Gail affectionately called him—sat in his chair, arms crossed, as he drilled her with his gaze.

A weaker woman would have quaked under his piercing stare, but she'd stared death in the face and Linc Maguire wasn't nearly as intimidating. Still, she felt a little uncomfortable as she waited for him to speak. From the way he worked his jaw and frowned periodically, he obviously had trouble verbalizing his thoughts.

"*Dancing with the Doctors*?" he finally asked, his expression so incredulous she wanted to laugh, but knew she shouldn't. "Was that the best you could do?"

She shrugged, relieved that he seemed more stunned than angry, at least at this point. "On short notice, yes. However, from everyone's response, the idea was a hit."

"It was something all right," he grumbled. "If I were you, I'd pray the committee thinks it's ridiculous and dreams up another plan."

"I don't think *Dancing with the Docs* is so bad," she protested. "You have to admit the concept is unusual. We've never done anything like this before."

"We haven't had an old-fashioned box supper or a kissing booth either," he pointed out. "It doesn't mean we should start now."

Unbidden, her gaze landed on his mouth. To her, it was perfect with the bottom lip just a little wider than the top. No doubt there was a host of other women who'd agree.

Oddly enough, it only seemed natural for her gaze to travel lower, down his neck to a sculpted chest that even the shapeless scrub top and white undershirt didn't disguise. His skin was tan, and dark hair covered his muscular arms, indicating that somewhere in his busy schedule he found time to work out on a regular basis.

Oh, my. And she was going to be in his arms, pressed against that chest, in front of hundreds of people? Maybe she *should* start praying the committee wouldn't be interested in her idea. Better yet, she could pray for enough physicians to volunteer so the team of Maguire and Michaels would be excused from the lineup.

She swallowed hard. "It's for a good cause," she said lamely.

"Tell yourself that when you're nursing a few broken toes," he mumbled darkly.

His expression reminded her more of a sullen little boy than a confident surgeon and it made her chuckle. "You don't dance?"

He shook his head. "Other than a slow shuffle? No."

She wasn't surprised. In her view, Lincoln Maguire was too controlled and tightly wound to ever do anything as uninhibited as gliding around a dance floor in step to the music. However, she was curious about his reasons.

"You surely practiced a few steps for your senior prom, didn't you?"

He blinked once, as if she'd caught him off guard. "I didn't go. The girl I'd asked turned me down."

Remorse hit her again. She hadn't intended to embarrass him, or trigger bad memories. "I'm sorry."

"I'm not," he said, matter-of-factly. "We were just good friends and she was waiting for a buddy of mine to dredge up the courage to ask her himself. As soon as I knew her feelings leaned in his direction, I told him and the rest, as they say, is history. In fact, they celebrated their twelve-year anniversary this year."

"Talk about being versatile," she teased. "You're a surgeon *and* a matchmaker."

He grinned. "Don't be too impressed. They were the first and only couple I pushed together."

She was too caught up by the transformation his smile had caused to be embarrassed by her remark. He looked younger than his thirty-seven years and appeared far more approachable. His chiseled-from-granite features softened and he seemed more hot-blooded male than cold-hearted surgeon.

His smile was also too infectious for her not to return it in full measure. However, if she told anyone he had actually softened enough to smile, they'd never believe her.

Neither would anyone believe her if she told them they'd actually discussed something *personal* instead of a patient. As far as she knew, it was the first time such a thing had happened in the history of the hospital.

"I hate to break this to you," she said, "but a slow shuffle won't cut it when it comes to a competition."

"Only if your *Dancing with the Doctors* idea takes hold," he pointed out. "With luck, it won't and we'll both be off the hook."

She heard the hopeful note in his voice. "Trust me, the committee will love it. You may as well accept the fact you're going to dance before hundreds of people."

He frowned for several seconds before he let out a heavy sigh of resignation. "I suppose."

"And that means you're going to have to learn a few steps. A waltz, maybe even a tango or a foxtrot."

"Surely not." His face looked as pained as his voice.

"Surely so," she assured him. "It'll be fun."

He shot her a you've-got-to-be-kidding look before his Adam's apple bobbed. He'd clearly, and quite literally, found her comment hard to swallow.

"Tripping over one's feet in front of an audience isn't fun," he pointed out.

"That's why one learns," she said sweetly. "So we don't trip over our feet, or our partner's. Besides, I know you're the type who can master any skill that's important to you. Look at how well you can keyboard. Most docs are still on the hunt-and-peck method but you're in the same league as a transcriptionist."

"I'm a surgeon. I'm *supposed* to be good with my hands," he said, clearly dismissing her praise. Unbidden, her gaze dropped to the body part in question. For an instant she imagined what it would be like to enjoy this man's touch. Would he make love with the same single-minded approach he gave everything else in his life that he deemed important?

Sadly, she'd never know. She couldn't risk the rejection again. However, it had been a long time since she'd been in a relationship and he was handsome enough to make any girl dream of possibilities....

"Hands, feet, they all follow the brain's commands. 'Where there's a will there's a way'," she quoted.

He rubbed the back of his neck as he grimaced. "Are you always full of helpful advice, Nurse Pollyanna?" he complained.

Oh, my, but she'd just experienced another first—the most taciturn physician on staff had actually *teased* her. She was going to have to look outside for snow, which never fell in the Midwest in August.

"I try." In the distance, she heard the tell-tale alarm that signaled someone's IV bag had emptied. As if the noise had suddenly reminded him of time and place, he straightened, pulled on his totally professional demeanor like a well-worn lab coat, and pointed to the monitor.

"Keep an eye on Mrs Hollings's chest tube. Call me if you notice any change."

She was strangely disappointed to see the congenial Lincoln Maguire had been replaced by his coolly polite counterpart. "Will do."

Without giving him a backward glance, she rushed to take care of John Carter's IV. He'd had a rough night after his knee-replacement surgery and now that they'd finally got his pain under control, he was catching up on his sleep. She quickly silenced the alarm, hung a fresh bag of fluid, then left the darkened room and returned to the nurses' station. To her surprise, Linc hadn't budged from his spot. He was simply sitting there...as if waiting. For her, maybe? Impossible. Yet it was a heady thought.

"One more thing," he said without preamble.

"What's that?" she asked, intending to head to the supply cabinet on his other side in order to replenish the supply of alcohol wipes she kept in her cargo pants pocket.

He rose, effectively blocking her path. "I'll pick you up tonight."

Flustered by his statement, she made the mistake of meeting his blue-black gaze, which at her five-eight required some effort because he was at least six-three. It was a gaze that exuded confidence and lingered a few seconds too long.

"Pick me up?" she said. "What for?"

"You're going to Gail and Ty's for dinner, aren't you?"

"Yes," she began cautiously, "but how did you know?"

"Because they invited me, too."

Great. The first time Gail had hosted a dinner to include both of them, it had turned into a miserable evening. It had been obvious from the way Gail had steered the conversation that she'd been trying to push them together and her efforts had backfired. Lincoln had sat through the next hour wearing the most pained expression in between checking his watch every five minutes. To make matters worse, his attitude had made her nervous, so she'd chattered nonstop until he'd finally left with clear relief on his face. After that, Gail had promised never to put either of them through the misery of a private dinner again.

While the past few minutes had been pleasant, she wasn't going to believe that *this* dinner would end differently. Given his unhappiness over the fundraising idea, the results would be the same. It was inevitable.

"How nice," she said inanely.

"So I'll swing by and get you."

She bristled under his commanding tone. He might be able to expect his orders to be obeyed at the hospital, but this was *her* private life and she made her own decisions.

"Thanks, but don't go to the trouble. I'll drive myself."

"It's not inconvenient at all. Your house is on my way."

She stared at him, incredulous. She'd always believed he barely knew who she was, but he knew where she lived? How was that possible?

"Don't look so horrified," he said impatiently, as if offended by her surprise. "Gail gave me the address and suggested we come together."

Good old Gail. Her friend simply wouldn't stop in her effort to convince her to get back in the dating game, but to use her own brother-in-law when their previous encounter had turned into such a disaster? It only showed how determined—and desperate—her happily married buddy was.

"That's sweet, but I'd rather—"

"I'll pick you up at six," he said, before he strode away, leaving her to sputter at his high-handedness.

For an instant, she debated the merits of making him wait, then decided against it. Given their differing personalities, they'd clash soon enough without any effort on her part. There was no sense in starting off on a sour note. Besides, Gail had set dinner for six-thirty, which meant she'd timed her meal to be ready minutes later. If Christy flexed her proverbial muscles to teach Linc a lesson, she'd also make four people unhappy.

In a way, though, having him fetch her for dinner had that date-night feel to it. Although, she was quick to remind herself, just because it seemed like one on the surface— especially to anyone watching—it didn't mean it was *real*.

Wryly, she glanced down at her own chest, well aware of how deceiving appearances could be.

Linc strode up the walk to Christy's apartment, wondering if the evening would be as full of surprises as the day had been. He'd gone to the hospital as he did every morning, but today he'd been swept into the fundraising tide before he'd realized it. He couldn't say what had prompted him to force Christy into being his dance partner, but if she was going to drag him into her little schemes then it only seemed fair for her to pay the piper, too.

Of course, being her partner didn't pose any great hardship. She was sociable, attractive, and his thoughts toward her weren't always professional. He might even have allowed his sister-in-law to matchmake if Christy didn't have what he considered were several key flaws.

The woman was always haring off on some adventure or getting involved in every cause that came down the pike. While he'd been known to participate in a few adventures himself and had gotten involved in a cause or two of his own, he practiced restraint. Christy, on the other hand, seemed happiest when she flitted from one activity to another. She was like a rolling stone, intent on moving fast and often so she wouldn't gather moss.

His parents, especially his mother, had been like that. He, being the eldest, had always been left to pick up the pieces and he'd vowed he'd never put his children in a similar position.

No, Christy wasn't the one for him, even if she'd captivated him with her looks and her charm. He simply needed a way to get her out of his system and the *Dancing with the Docs* idea seemed tailor-made to do just that. They'd spend time practicing and he'd learn just how unsuitable they were together. Then, and only then, he could forget about her and begin looking for the steady, dependable, down-to-earth woman he really wanted.

Your ideal woman sounds boring, his little voice dared to say.

Maybe so, he admitted, but there was nothing wrong with "boring". Perhaps if his parents had relegated their dream of becoming a superstar country music duo to the past where it had belonged, they wouldn't have driven that lonely stretch of highway halfway between here and Nashville at four a.m. They'd have been safe in bed, living long enough to see their children grow to adulthood.

As for tonight, he hadn't been able to coax the reason for their gathering from his sister-in-law or his brother, but it had to be important. After the last dinner-party fiasco between the four of them, only a compelling reason would have convinced Gail to repeat the experience.

Gail had been immensely disappointed that he and Christy hadn't clicked together like two cogs, but, as he'd later told her, Christy was everything he wasn't looking for in a romantic partnership. After all the upheavals in his life—his parents' deaths, school, work, college studies, raising siblings—he wanted someone who wasn't in search of the next spine-tingling, hair-raising adventure; someone stable, calm, and content. While it wasn't a bad thing that Christy's friendliness and sunny disposition attracted people like sugar called to ants, he wasn't interested in being one of a crowd of admirers.

Tonight he'd sit through dinner, learn what scheme Gail was up to now, spend the rest of the evening in Ty's den watching whatever sports event was currently televised, then drive Christy home. Dinner with Ty's family wasn't a red-letter occasion, but hanging with them was better than spending time alone.

He leaned on Christy's doorbell, but before the melodic chime barely began, he heard a deep-throated woof followed by thundering paws. Gail had never mentioned her friend owned a dog, so it was entirely possible he'd come to the wrong apartment.

His sister-in-law had told him apartment 4619, but given that the nine was missing from the house number above the porch light, he may have made an error in guessing his prize lay behind this particular door. However, the whimsical fairy stake poked into the pot of impatiens seemed to be the sort of yard ornament Christy would own.

As the footsteps—both human and canine—grew louder, he was already framing an apology for the intrusion when Christy flung open the door with one hand tucked under the black rhinestone-studded collar of a beautiful cream-colored Labrador.

He'd definitely come to the right place.

"Hi," he said inanely, aware he was out of practice when it came to picking up a date.

"Hi, yourself." Christy tugged the dog out of the way. "Come in, please."

He stepped inside and wasn't quite sure if he should look at her or the dog. He wasn't worried about Christy biting a hole in his thigh, though, so he focused on the animal and held out his hand for sniffing purposes. "Who is this lovely lady?"

"Her name is Ria," she said. "She's very protective of me, but she's really a sweetheart."

As expected, Ria sniffed his hand, then licked it, making Linc feel as if he'd passed doggy muster. "I can see that," he said.

She eyed her pet as Ria nudged Linc with her nose. "It appears you two are friends already."

"Dogs usually like me," he said. "Why, I'm not sure." His fondest memories involved pets, but after their family's golden retriever had died of old age when Linc had been sixteen, they'd never replaced him. As it had turned out, a few years later, his hands had been full trying to raising his younger siblings and attend college, without adding the responsibility of a canine.

"Animals are a far better judge of character than we are," she said. "However, Ria doesn't usually give her seal of approval so soon after meeting someone."

"Then I'm flattered." Then, because time was marching on, he asked, "Shall we go?"

Pink suddenly tinged her face. "I'm sorry, but I need a few more minutes."

He couldn't imagine why. She wore a red and white polka-dotted sundress with a matching short-sleeved jacket. Her bare legs were long and tanned and her toenails were painted a matching shade of red and one little toe had a silver ring encircling it.

Wisps of her short reddish-blonde hair framed her face

most attractively and seemed to highlight her fine bone structure. From the freckles dancing across the bridge of her nose, she either didn't need makeup to create that warm glow or she only wore just enough to enhance her natural skin tone. He also caught a delightful whiff of citrus and spice that tempted him to lean into her neck and inhale deeply.

Certain she sensed his intense, and appreciative perusal, he met her gaze, hardly able to believe the non-hospital version of the dark-eyed Christy Michaels was so...gorgeous. As far as he was concerned, a few more minutes couldn't improve on the vision in front of him. The idea that he would spend his evening seated across from such delightful eye candy instead of poking inside someone's abdomen suddenly made him anticipate the hours ahead.

"You look great to me," he commented.

Apparently hearing the appreciation in his voice, she smiled. "Thanks, but Ria has carried off my sandals. She does that when she doesn't want me to leave, and now I'm trying to locate where she's stashed them. Would you mind checking around the living room while I go through my bedroom again?"

Ever practical and conscious of the time, he suggested, "You could wear a different pair."

"No can do," she said, plainly impervious to his suggestion. "They match this dress perfectly and nothing else I own will look quite right."

He wanted to argue that it was just the four of them and no one would notice much less care if her sandals coordinated with her dress, but she'd already disappeared down the hallway, leaving him to obey.

"Okay, Ria," he said to the Lab, "where's your favorite hiding place?"

Ria stared at him with a dopey grin on her face.

"No help from you, I see." Linc raised his voice. "Where does she normally hide her treasures?"

"Under the furniture," she called back, "or in her toy box."

Linc glanced around the great room and decided that Christy lived a relatively spartan existence. She didn't own a lot of furniture and other than a few silk flower arrangements scattered around, the surfaces were free of what he called dust-collectors, although none would pass the white-glove treatment.

Spartan or not, however, the room had that cluttered, lived-in feel. Decorative pillows were thrown haphazardly, a fuzzy Southwestern print afghan was tossed carelessly over one armchair, and women's magazines were gathered in untidy heaps on the floor.

Dutifully, he peeked under the floral-print sofa and found a few mismatched but brightly colored socks. Some were knee-length and others were just footies, but each one sported varying sizes of chew holes. Next, he moved to the matching side chair where he unearthed two pairs of silk panties—one black and one fire-engine-red—that couldn't claim more than a dollar's worth of fabric between them.

After adding the lingerie to his pile, he pinched the bridge of his nose and told himself to forget what he'd just seen and touched. Knowing her tastes ran along those kinds of lines, when he saw her on duty again, he'd have a difficult time keeping his mind off what might be underneath her scrub suit.

Shoot, why wait until then? His imagination was already running wild over what color underwear she was wearing under her sundress.

He carefully glanced around the room in search of something resembling a doggie toy box and found a wicker basket tucked on the bottom shelf of the bookcase in the corner filled with playthings that a canine would love. Resting on his haunches, he rummaged through a pile of half-chewed dog bones, several balls and Frisbees, a short rope, and an assortment of stuffed animals before he struck bottom.

"No shoes in here," he called out as he rose.

"Thanks for checking," she answered back.

His watch chimed the quarter-hour. "We really should be going."

"Just a few more minutes. I promise."

Because he had so little time for leisure reading, the books on her shelves drew his gaze next, and he took a few minutes to glance at the titles. Most of her paperbacks were romances with a few adventure novels sprinkled among them. He also ran across several cookbooks and a few exercise DVDs, but tucked among them were a few books that piqued his curiosity.

Chicken Soup for the Survivor's Soul. Life after Cancer. Foods that Fight. Staying Fit after Chemo.

Before he could wonder what had caused her interest in such topics, she returned to the living room, wearing a pair of strappy red high-heeled sandals that emphasized her shapely legs. "Sorry about the wait," she said breathlessly. "I found them in my laundry basket."

"Great. By the way, I ran across a few things you might have lost." He plucked his pile of treasures off the coffee table and handed them to her.

Her face turned a lovely shade of pink as she eyed the scraps on top. "I wondered where those had gone," she said, her chuckle quite pleasing to his ears. "I've blamed the washing machine all this time. Ria, you've been a bad girl."

Ria sank onto her belly and placed her head on her front paws.

"But I love you anyway," she said as she crouched down to scratch behind the dog's ears. "Now, behave while we're gone."

As she rubbed, Ria responded with a contented sigh and a blissful doggy smile before rolling over onto her back for a tummy rub. Obviously Christy had The Touch, and immediately he wanted to feel her fingers working their magic on *his* sore spots.

He tore his gaze from the sight, reminding himself that Christy wasn't his type even if she could engender all sorts of unrealistic thoughts. She was too perky, too lively, and too *everything*. Women like her weren't content with the mundane aspects of living. They wanted the constant stimulation of social activities, four-star shopping and exotic vacations. Staying home for popcorn and a movie would be considered slumming.

"Are we ready now?" he asked, conscious of his peevish tone when all he wanted to do was shake these wicked mental pictures out of his head.

She straightened. "Of course. Sorry to keep you waiting."

To his regret, the warm note in her voice had disappeared and he wondered what it would take to bring it back. If he walked into his brother's house with icicles hanging in the air, his sister-in-law would read him the Riot Act. He didn't know why Gail was so protective of Christy, but she was.

Minutes later, Linc found himself on the sidewalk, accompanying her to his car. He couldn't explain why he found the need to rest his hand on the small of her back—it wasn't as if the sidewalk was icy and he intended to keep her from falling—but he did.

That small, politely ingrained action made him wonder if his plan to concentrate on his career should be revised. He was thirty-seven now and he had to admit that at times he grew weary of his own company. To make matters worse, lately, being around Gail and Ty made him realize just how much he was missing.

Now was one of those moments. Especially when he caught

a glimpse of a well-formed knee and a trim ankle as he helped her into the passenger seat.

He might be physically attracted to Christy Michaels, but their temperaments made them polar opposites. He had enough drama in his life and when he came home at night, he wanted someone to share his quiet and peaceable existence, not someone who thrived on being the life of a party.

Opposites or not, though, he wasn't going to pass the drive in chilly silence. Given how much she obviously loved Ria, he knew exactly how to break the ice.

"After seeing your dog, I'm wondering if I should get one," he commented as he slid behind the wheel.

"They're a lot of work, but the companionship is worth every minute," she said. "Did you have a breed in mind?"

"No, but I'd lean toward a collie or a retriever. We had one when I was a kid. Skipper died of old age, but we didn't replace him."

She nodded. "I can understand that. Bringing a new pet home can make you feel guilty—like you're replacing them as easily as you replace a worn-out pair of socks—when in actuality, you aren't replacing them because they'll always be a part of you, no matter what."

Spoken like a true dog lover, he thought, impressed by her insight.

"Why don't you have a dog now?" she asked.

"Isn't it obvious? A pet doesn't fit into my lifestyle."

"Oh." He heard a wealth of emotion—mainly disappointment—in the way she uttered that one word. It was almost as if she found him lacking when she should have been impressed by his thoughtfulness. After all, the poor mutt would be the one suffering from inattention.

"You're probably right," she added politely. "They do have a habit of ruining the best-laid plans."

The conversation flagged, and he hated that the relaxed

mood between them had become strained once again. Wasn't there anything they could discuss without venturing into rocky territory? If he didn't do something to lighten the tension, they'd face an uncomfortable evening ahead of them. He'd already promised Gail he'd be on his best behavior, so he had to repair the damage before they arrived.

Recalling another subject in which she'd seemed quite passionate, he asked, "Any word on the festival fundraiser idea?"

"According to Denise, it's a go." To his relief, the lilt in her voice had returned, although her revelation wasn't the news he'd wanted to hear.

"I was afraid of that."

"Still worried about dancing in front of people?"

"Not worried," he corrected. "Uncomfortable."

"As a surgeon, you should be used to being in the spotlight."

"Yes, but it isn't the same spotlight," he insisted. In the OR, he actually knew what he was doing and was at ease in his own skin. Sailing around a dance floor didn't compare.

"The problem is, my schedule for the next month is a killer and lessons are out of the question," he explained. "My partners are going on vacation and—"

"No one said you had to take lessons," she pointed out.

The motto he'd lived by was simple. *Anything worth doing was worth doing well.* If he was going to participate in this dancing thing, then he'd put forth his best effort.

"Whatever we do at the time of the competition will be fine with me," she added. "If you just want to stand and sway to the music, I'll be happy."

"You told me this morning it wouldn't be good enough," he accused.

She shrugged. "I changed my mind. I'm not participating to win a prize."

He didn't think the possibility of taking first place was her motive. She was simply one of those people who threw her-self into whatever project caught her fancy, which was also why he disagreed with her remark about being happy. Christy had too much vim and vigor to be content with a lackluster performance. Even *he* wasn't satisfied and he was far less outgoing than she was.

All of which meant that he was going to have to carve out time in his schedule for lessons—lessons that involved hold-ing this woman with her citrusy scent and skimpy underwear in his arms.

Merely picturing those moments was enough to send his blood tumbling through his body at a fast and furious rate. The things a man had to do for charity...

Christy had known her evening was off to a bad start when Ria hid her shoes. She'd hoped to find them before Linc ar-rived but, as luck would have it, she hadn't. Although he'd been polite about it, clearly the delay had taxed his patience and his perfectly timed schedule.

Yet she'd enjoyed the little courtesies he'd shown her. Being in the close confines of his vehicle, she'd been painfully aware of his fresh, clean scent to the point her throat went dry.

Of all the men in her circle of friends and acquaintances, why did *he* have to be the one who oozed sex appeal? After feeling his hand at her waist, she honestly didn't know how she'd survive an evening as his dance partner.

To make matters worse, Gail had seated her next to him at the dinner table and his arm had brushed against hers on several occasions as they'd passed the food.

Maybe she needed to call an escort service in order to calm those suddenly raging hormones, but her fear of rejection was too strong to risk it. If a man who'd supposedly loved her hadn't been able to handle her diagnosis and resultant treat-ment, who else could?

No, better that she hurry home after dinner, take Ria for a long run at the dog park until they were both too tired to do more than curl up on the sofa with a carton of frozen chocolate yogurt, a handful of dog treats, and a sappy movie on the TV screen.

Linc's voice forced her to focus on her surroundings. "Okay, you two. What's up? And don't tell me 'Nothing' because I know you both too well to believe otherwise."

Gail and Ty looked at each other with such an expression of love between them that Christy was half-jealous. Made a little uncomfortable by their silent exchange, she glanced at Linc and immediately noticed the similarities between the brothers.

They had the same bone structure, the same complexion, and the same shade of brown hair. Both Maguire males were handsome but, to her, Linc's features were far more interesting—probably because life had left its imprint on them. According to Gail, as the oldest brother, Linc had stepped into his parents' role after their deaths in a car accident when he was nineteen and he'd guided his younger siblings through their rocky teenage years. It was only logical that the sudden responsibility had formed him into the driven, purposeful man he was today.

Christy glanced at her dark-haired friend and saw the gentle smile on her face. "You're pregnant again?" she guessed.

Gail patted her husband's hand as she shook her head. "No. But maybe we can announce that when we get back."

"Get back? Where are you going?"

Ty answered his brother's question. "Paris."

Christy was stunned…and envious. It was one of the cities she'd put on the bucket list she'd created during her chemotherapy sessions. "Oh, how fun. I've always wanted to go there."

Linc didn't seem to share her excitement. "Paris? As in France? Or Paris, as in Texas?"

"France," Ty told him. "My company is opening an overseas branch and they want a computer consultant to be on site. They chose me."

Linc reached across the table to shake his brother's hand. "Congratulations. You've worked hard for this. I'm proud of you. How long will you be gone?"

Ty exchanged a glance with Gail. "Two months, give or take a few weeks, depending on how well the project progresses. Because Gail knows the secretarial ropes of our firm, my boss has offered to send her as my assistant."

Theirs had been an office romance and after Derek had arrived, Gail had cut her work status to part time.

"And the kids?" Christy thought of six-year-old Emma and eight-year-old Derek, who'd already been excused from the table to play outside with their friends. "What about them?"

Gail's expression turned hopeful. "That's why you're both here tonight. We wanted to ask a favor."

"Anything," she promptly replied.

"Would you and Linc be their guardians and take care of them while we're gone?"

CHAPTER TWO

CHRISTY was overwhelmed by their request but in her mind she didn't have any doubts as to her answer. She loved the Maguire children and she couldn't wait to step into a temporary mom role. Because of her diagnosis and the resultant treatment, she'd already resigned herself to the possibility that Ria might be the closest thing to ever having a child of her own, so the idea of acting as a fill-in mother was exciting.

She was also quite aware that Gail had chosen *her* out of all their friends and family to take on this responsibility. Okay, so they'd asked Linc, too, but he didn't really count. His work was his life and by his own admission his schedule for the next few weeks was packed. For all intents and purposes, she'd be on her own.

It was a heady thought.

It was also quite daunting.

She started to speak, but Gail forestalled her. "Christy, I know you'll immediately agree because it's in your nature to help out a friend. And, Linc, I know you'll accept because you're family, but before either of you commit yourselves, I want you to know *exactly* what you'd be letting yourselves in for. And if either of you have second thoughts, we won't be hurt or upset."

"Okay," Christy said, certain she wouldn't change her mind no matter what Gail and Ty told them. "We're listening."

"First, we'd expect you to live here because it will be best if Derek and Emma stick with the familiar."

Christy hadn't considered that, but Gail's plan made perfect sense. Living in their home wouldn't pose any hardship whatsoever. What it would require, though, was coordination between her schedule and Linc's to be sure they covered every hour of every day, and she was curious how Gail had ironed that small but important detail. No doubt, she'd learn the answer shortly.

"What about Ria?" she asked. "I'd hate to board her for that length of time."

"She's welcome, too," Ty answered. "In fact, I know the kids would be thrilled. They've been asking for a dog for some time, and looking after Ria will give them a taste of what pet ownership is about."

Satisfied by how easily that potential problem had been averted, Christy relaxed. She imagined her Labrador and the kids playing Frisbee in the large Maguire back yard and could hear the children's laughter interspersed with Ria's excited woofs. They'd have a great time.

"Second," Gail continued, "the fall term starts next week so the kids will already be in a routine before we leave the week after that. On the days Christy doesn't work, you'll have to take them to school and pick them up at four, which shouldn't pose a problem.

"The days you both work are little trickier as there's a two-hour window when Linc would be on his own. One of the neighborhood high-school girls—Heather—can come by around six-thirty to fix breakfast and take them to school. She'll come sooner to cover that window if Linc's on call, but you'll have to let her know the night before.

"Then, at the end of the day, the kids can walk across the street to the church's after-school daycare until Christy's shift ends at five. The daycare is open until seven, so that works out well." She smiled. "Repeat as necessary."

"It sounds as if you've thought of everything," Christy said.

"We tried," Gail answered.

"Do Emma and Derek know you're asking me?" As Linc stiffened beside her, she corrected herself. "I mean *us*?"

"It was the only way they'd agree to being left behind," Gail admitted ruefully. "I suspect they think you'll cater to their every whim. I know what a pushover you are, Christy..." she softened her statement with a smile "...so I'm counting on you to be firm."

"Be firm," she repeated. "Got it."

"Don't kid yourself," Ty warned. "They'll push you to the max. You can't be the benevolent aunt and uncle. This isn't a weekend vacation."

"In other words, you expect us to give them a healthy breakfast, send them to bed on time, and eat dinner before dessert," Linc said.

His sidelong glance made Christy wonder if he'd mentioned those things purely for her benefit. Didn't he think she had an ounce of common sense? He obviously suspected she'd offer cookies and cake for breakfast, lunch, and dinner, and let them stay up as late as they pleased. While she didn't consider herself a rule-breaker, she also knew that every moment should be lived to its fullest. If a few rules had to be broken on occasion, then so be it.

Now that she'd raised the question in her mind, she took it a step further. Did he have the same lack of faith in her nursing skills as he obviously did in her parenting abilities? There hadn't been a single incident when he'd questioned her patient care, but she'd ask him when they were alone.

"We're asking a lot from both of you," Ty added, "but you were first on our list."

"I appreciate the vote of confidence," Christy said. "Count me in."

"Me, too," Linc added. "We only need to choose which days are yours and which are mine."

She nodded, although she would have preferred having Linc suggest that she be their sole caretaker while he filled in when his schedule allowed. Clearly, he wanted equal, or as near equal, time as possible.

Darn the man!

"Actually, we want you both to stay here," Gail said. "Together."

Christy met Linc's startled gaze and guessed that her own surprise mirrored his. "At the same time?" she asked redundantly.

Gail nodded. "That way, if Linc gets called out for a patient in the middle of the night, he won't have to worry about the kids because you're just down the hall. You two won't have to rearrange and juggle your own schedules, so it'll be less disruptive for everyone."

They wanted her to stay here, in their house, with Linc? Christy had a difficult time wrapping her brain around that concept. While they were amicable enough to each other at the hospital, being together twenty-four seven meant they'd drive each other crazy within a week, and then where would the kids be? Most likely in the middle of a war zone.

What concerned her even more, though, was the simple question of how would she handle being in such close proximity to a guy she found so attractive? If seeing him in a scrub suit and interacting with him on a purely professional basis made her nervous and sent her imagination soaring, how would she manage if she saw that handsome smile, those broad shoulders on a regular, casual basis?

"This is how we want it," Gail said, as if she sensed Christy's reservations. "The kids will handle our absence better if they stay in their normal surroundings. That's not to say they can't spend a night or two elsewhere, but we'd feel better knowing they're in familiar territory and in the same homey, two-parent environment."

"We know it won't be easy for either of you because you're both so fiercely independent, so if it's a problem, we can ask someone else," Ty said.

Miss the opportunity to pamper Gail's kids? Not a chance. Yes, Linc would probably drive her crazy with his rigid, no-time-to-stop-and-smell-the-roses attitude, but she was an adult. She could handle the inevitable clashes.

On the other hand, Linc went to work early and stayed late. Chances were they wouldn't see each other until the kids went to bed. Afterward, they could each slink into their separate corners.

It was a workable plan, she decided. If it wasn't, she'd dream up a Plan B. Emma and Derek's well-being was what mattered, not her personal preferences.

"If you can handle the arrangements we've outlined—"

"Piece of cake," Christy said, although the idea of living under the same roof as Linc gave her some pause.

"Not a problem," Linc added. "We can learn to live with each other for a few weeks."

"Good. Then it's settled." Gail beamed. "You don't know what a relief this is for us."

As Christy glanced around the table, Gail was the only one who seemed remotely satisfied with the arrangement. She saw a combination of speculation and caution in Ty's eyes as he studied his brother. Linc's squared jaw and the chiseled lines around his mouth reflected resignation rather than enthusiasm. No doubt her reservations were clear on her face as well.

Living under the same roof was only a two-month gig or less, she consoled herself, and those six or eight weeks were nothing more than a single pebble along life's riverbed. She could endure *anything* for that length of time, because the benefits of being with Emma and Derek overshadowed the potential problems. If she could survive breast cancer, she could handle Lincoln Maguire's idiosyncrasies.

"I know what you're going to say." Ty held up his hands to forestall Linc's comments the moment the two of them were alone on the shaded back-yard patio, "but before you unload, hear me out."

Linc took a swig from his bottle of cold root beer. "I'm listening."

"You're upset we asked Christy to help you, but honestly our decision is no reflection on your parenting abilities. You've had the kids before and they came back raving about the great time they had. They love you and I know you love them."

He did. No matter how busy he was, he'd move heaven and earth for his niece and nephew. They were his family, and even if he wasn't in any hurry to have one of his own, those bonds were still important to him.

"I can't imagine a single scenario you can't handle by yourself with your eyes closed and one hand tied behind your back," Ty added loyally.

"Thanks for the vote of confidence."

"After all," Ty continued, "you kept us on the straight and narrow when you were hardly out of your teenage years yourself. Joanie and I weren't angels either, if I recall. I'm sure there were times when you wanted to tear out your hair, and ours, too, but you didn't. When you finally decide to focus on your personal life instead of your professional one, you're going to be a great dad."

Linc recognized Ty's strategy. "You can stop heaping on

the praise, pip-squeak," he affectionately told his brother. "In the middle of all that, I know there's a 'but'."

Ty grinned sheepishly. "I never could fool you for long, could I? The thing is, we're talking two months. You don't have the usual nine-to-five job, and we had to think of a contingency plan for the times you work late, go in early, or get called out in the wee hours, because we don't expect you to put your doctor business on hold for us."

Linc shifted in his chair, suddenly uncomfortable at hearing how lonely his life sounded, even if the description was uncannily accurate.

"I'll confess that sharing the responsibility with another person bothered me," he admitted soberly, "but your way is best for the kids' well-being. I even see your point about asking us to stay here *together.*"

He saw the logic behind their request, but he didn't like it, especially now that he'd seen those small scraps of silk Christy called underwear. How was he supposed to focus on the youngsters when a picture of her wearing a pair of those and just a smile kept popping into his head at the most inopportune times?

He might not find fault with her nursing skills, but taking care of patients wasn't the same as maintaining a home and looking after the needs of two children on a round-the-clock basis.

Did she even know how to boil water? If the stories circulating about her were to be believed—and he didn't dispute them because he'd heard her share some of them herself— she rarely sat still long enough for such mundane things. Canoeing down the Amazon, skydiving in California, whitewater rafting in Colorado, cross-country motorcycle trips and a few laps around the Daytona 500 speedway were only part of her repertoire of experiences.

Lessons from Martha Stewart or Rachel Ray weren't on the list.

Her culinary skills aside, he hoped she had more redeeming qualities than being Gail's friend who was the life of every party and who owned a dog that Emma and Derek loved. As far as he was concerned, they could have handled the nights he was on call on a case-by-case basis, but if this was how his brother wanted it, then he would suffer in silence.

"I'm glad you're being a good sport about this," Ty said. "And when you feel your control slipping over the edge, think of your circumstances as some of the medicine you forced down our throats as kids." He grinned. "It tastes terrible going down, but in the end it cures what ails you."

Two weeks later, Christy made a point to hang around the nurses' station to lie in wait for Linc. Ever since their dinner with Gail and Ty, he'd slipped in and out of their unit like a wraith. She knew he was extra-busy right now, with one of his partners on vacation, but she wasn't completely convinced that he wasn't avoiding her as well.

As of tonight they'd more or less be living together and she had a few issues she wanted to iron out before they actually became roomies, but those would have to wait. Her patient, Jose Lopez, a recent ruptured appendix case, concerned her.

Her patience paid off. Linc strode in shortly before eight looking more handsome than a man who had spent his day with sick people had a right to. His yellow polo shirt stretched across his shoulders and his hair had a damp curl as if he'd just got out of the shower.

He didn't walk with a cocky swagger but carried himself with a quiet confidence that suggested no problem was too big for him to solve. She certainly hoped so because today she had one.

She immediately cornered him before he could disappear into a patient room.

"I don't like the way Jose, Mr Lopez, looks," she said without preamble.

"Okay," he said with equanimity. "What's his complaint?"

"He doesn't have one, as such."

He lifted one eyebrow. "You aren't giving me much to go on. A diagnosis of 'He doesn't look right' isn't strong enough to justify a battery of tests."

Her face warmed under his rebuke. Other physicians would have attributed her impression as that proverbial gut feeling no one could afford to ignore, but clearly Lincoln Maguire didn't believe in intuition. He only wanted cold, hard evidence. As far as she was concerned, he'd answered her private question about what he thought of her nursing savvy.

"I realize that," she said stiffly, her spine straight, "which is why I've been watching him. He doesn't complain about pain as such, but he finally admitted he has a few twinges because I've caught him rubbing his chest. According to the nursing notes, he received an antacid for heartburn several times during the night."

"You don't think heartburn is a possibility?" he asked.

"No," she said bluntly, "but only because I think his skin color is off."

He retrieved the chart on the computer and began perusing the notes. "How are his oxygen sats?"

"On the low end of normal."

"Shortness of breath?"

She shook her head. "He said his chest sometimes feels a little tight, but that's all."

He stared thoughtfully at the computer before meeting her gaze. "It could be anything and it could be nothing."

"I know, which is why I wanted to ask you to check him thoroughly."

He hesitated for a fraction of a second before he shrugged. "Okay. Duly noted. I'll see what I can find."

She'd been half-afraid he'd dismiss her concerns, so she was grateful to hear of his intentions to follow through. And because she was relieved to pass the burden onto his shoulders, she chose to make small talk as they strode toward the room. "Are you ready for tonight?"

"I am," he said. "Do you need help taking anything over to Ty's house?"

"Not now," she said. "I'm only moving some clothes and a few books. What I don't bring now, I can always get later."

"Fair enough." He strode into Lopez's room and the subject was closed.

Christy watched and listened as Linc checked his patient, seeming much more congenial with Jose than with her, but, then, a lot of the nurses had said he was far more personable with his patients than with the staff. She took some comfort in that because she'd begun to wonder if he was only uncomfortable around her.

"I hear you're having a few chest twinges," Linc mentioned as he pulled out his stethoscope and listened to Jose's heart and lung sounds.

"Some. It's happening more often than it did yesterday, though. Sometimes I cough for no reason," the forty-year-old replied. Jose was of average height, but between his wife's reportedly fantastic cooking and his years as a stonemason, he was built like the bricks he laid for a living. "Do you think it's the hospital food? Maybe it's giving me the heartburn." His tanned, leathery face broke into a smile.

Linc laughed. "If you're hinting that you want me to give Francesca permission to bring you some of her famous enchiladas, you'll be disappointed."

"It was worth a try, Doc."

Christy watched the friendly exchange, stunned by how

Linc's smile made him seem so...*normal.* Clearly, the man did have moments when he wasn't completely focused on his work, but she'd gone on countless rounds with him over the past year and had never heard such a heartfelt sound. She would have remembered if she had. Somehow, she sensed the two of them had more than a simple doctor-patient relationship, which only made her curious as to what connection a blue-collar worker like Jose had with the highly successful general surgeon.

He flung the stethoscope around his neck. "A few more days and you can eat her cooking to your heart's content. Meanwhile, though, I want to check out these little twinges and the cough you're having. We're going to run a few tests so be prepared for everything from X-rays and EKGs to blood work."

Jose's expression sobered. "You think it's my heart?"

"Not necessarily. If your chest feels tight and you're noticing a cough, pneumonia is a concern," he said, "so I'm going to try and discover what's going on. As you said, you may only have heartburn but, to be thorough, we're going to check out everything. Okay?"

His confidence was reassuring because Jose's face relaxed. It was obvious why Linc's patients loved him, and why he was so very busy.

"Are you having any pain in your legs?" Linc asked.

Jose wrinkled his face in thought. "I had a charley horse earlier in my right calf, but it's gone now."

Linc immediately flung back the sheet and checked his legs. "We'll look into that, too," he said, sounding unconcerned, "and as soon as I get those results, we'll let you know what we've found. Okay?" He patted Jose's shoulder before he left.

Outside Lopez's room, Christy immediately pounced. "Then I was right. You found something."

"Not really," he admitted.

"Oh." Her good spirits deflated.

"Are you sure his condition has changed in the last twenty-four hours?"

She knew what her intuition was telling her and she wasn't going to back down. "He said himself he has a cough and his chest feels tight," she reminded him. "Now he has a muscle spasm in his leg. Those are new symptoms."

He looked thoughtful for a moment. "Okay," he said decisively. "I want a chest X-ray, a Doppler exam on his legs, and blood drawn for a blood count, a cardiac panel and a D-dimer test."

She recognized the latter as one used to diagnose the presence of a blood clot. "Do you suspect a PE?" She used the shorthand for pulmonary embolism.

"I suspect a lot of things, but in the interest of ruling out as much as we can we'll add that to the list of possibilities. I also want a CT scan of his lungs and if the results are inconclusive, I want a VQ scan."

The CT scan was a quick way to detect a blood clot, but not every clot was detected using this procedure, which meant the next step was the VQ scan. The two-part ventilation-perfusion procedure used both injected and aerosolized radioactive material to show the amount of blood and air flowing through the lungs. Naturally, if the patterns were abnormal, intervention was required.

"I'll get right on it," she said.

"And call me ASAP with those results," he ordered in the brisk tone she knew so well.

As Christy placed the various orders into the computer system, she was hoping the tests would show something to support her nagging intuition, although she hoped it would be something relatively uncomplicated.

Several hours later the results were in. Shortly after Christy phoned him with the radiologist's report, Linc appeared on the unit. Asking for her to join him, he marched directly into his patient's room.

"Jose," he said briskly, "I have news on your tests."

Jose nodded his salt-and-pepper head. "I had a feeling something was wrong when they stuck me in that fancy X-ray machine," he said. "How bad is it?"

"You have a very small blood clot in your leg and a small one in your lung, which isn't good," Linc said bluntly.

"But you can fix it. Right?"

Christy recognized the hope and the uncertainty on the man's face. She knew exactly how he felt.

"This is where I give you the good news," Linc said kindly. "I'm going to start you on a variety of blood thinners and other drugs that will work to dissolve the clots so they don't break off and plug a major vessel. It'll take time—you won't be cured overnight—but eventually you should be fine."

Jose leaned head back against the pillows in obvious relief.

"The other good news is that you had a nurse who was on the ball so we could catch the problem early," Linc said as he eyed Christy. "A lot of patients aren't that fortunate."

"And I should be fine?" Jose repeated, clearly wanting reassurance that the final outcome would be positive.

"Yes."

After a few more minutes of discussing Jose's treatment plan, they left. Outside the room Linc pulled her aside. "Increase his oxygen and keep a close eye on him. I want to know if there's a change, no matter how slight."

"Okay."

"Tomorrow, we'll—" he began.

"It's Saturday," she reminded him. "I'm off duty. Emma and Derek, remember?"

He looked surprised, as if for a minute he'd forgotten what day it was. "Then I'll see you tonight," he said.

"Before or after dinner?"

"Before, I suppose. Why?"

She was flying high on her success, so she couldn't hold back from teasing him. "Just checking to see if I can serve dessert as the appetizer or not."

His eyes narrowed ever so slightly. "You're kidding, aren't you?"

"Of course I am," she responded pertly. "Contrary to what you might think, I can exercise self-control and I do use the gray matter between my ears from time to time."

His eyes suddenly gleamed with humor. "I stand corrected. Either way, though, I'll be at the house in time to take Gail and Ty to the airport."

She received the distinct impression that he would move heaven and earth to do so. It also occurred to her that he might be as reluctant to see his brother leave as his niece and nephew were.

"Okay, we'll save you a piece of cake."

"Do that. By the way, good work with Lopez today."

His unexpected praise only added to her high spirits. "Thanks."

"See you tonight," he said, before he turned on one heel and left.

She stared at his backside until he rounded the corner, startled by how *husbandly* he'd sounded. Suddenly she realized that not only would she see him tonight, she'd see him *every* night thereafter, too.

It also meant that every night he'd drop the trappings of his profession and she wouldn't have the barrier of the doctor-nurse relationship to keep her wicked imagination in check. He'd appear as a normal guy—one who mowed the grass, took out the trash, left dirty dishes in the sink, and woke up every morning with his hair mussed and a whiskery shadow on his face.

Anticipation shivered down her spine.

She was being completely unreasonable.

Linc walked into the kitchen of Gail and Ty's house with his small entourage and fought to keep his voice even-tempered. It had been a long day in his practice and seeing off his younger brother to another country for two months—*Paris*, no less—had been far more emotionally draining than he'd expected. He'd left his twenties behind ages ago and was a highly respected surgeon, yet he felt as lost as he had when he'd moved Ty into his first apartment.

Ty might not need him in that big-brother-knows-best role, but it was still hard to accept whenever the fact hit him between the eyes. No, he wanted to veg out with nothing more mentally or emotionally taxing than a game of checkers with Derek or a tea party with Emma, but if Christy had her way, it wouldn't happen.

"Going out to dinner when Gail has a refrigerator full of food waiting for us is unnecessary," he pointed out. "Need I also remind you it's Friday night?" Which meant every restaurant was packed and would be for quite a while.

"I know it's Friday and I agree that eating out isn't *necessary*," she said with a hint of steel underneath her sweet tone, "but it would be *fun*."

He rubbed his face. *Fun* was going to become a four-letter word if every activity had to be measured against that standard. "We have all weekend for fun."

She rubbed the back of her neck in a frustrated gesture and drew a deep breath. "I realize that," she finally said, "but look at those two. Don't you think they need something as a pick-me-up *now*, rather than tomorrow?"

He glanced at Derek and noticed his slumped posture in

the straight-backed chair, his ball cap pulled low as he rested his chin on his propped arm. Emma sat beside him and occasionally wiped her eyes and sniffled as her thin shoulders shook. Christy's Lab stood between the two, gazing at one then the other, as if trying to decide which one needed her comfort more.

They made a dejected picture, which was only understandable. They'd just driven home from the airport after saying goodbye to their parents and the reality of the situation had hit them hard.

"I agree they're down in the dumps, but a fast-food hamburger won't make them feel better."

"You might be surprised." She clapped her hands. "Hey, kids, how does a picnic sound? Ria needs a spin around the dog park and while she's running around with her buddies, we'll enjoy our dinner in the great outdoors."

A picnic, at seven o'clock at night, with dark clouds rolling in and rain in the forecast, wasn't Linc's idea of fun. While the kids didn't seem overly enthusiastic with her suggestion, interest flickered in Derek's eyes and Emma's shoulders stopped shaking as she gazed expectantly at Christy. Apparently Ria recognized the word *park* because her ears suddenly perked and her tail wagged.

"Then it's settled," she declared, although as far as Linc was concerned she'd simply made an executive decision. Because he knew they had to do something drastic or the entire evening would remain miserable for everyone, he let it stand. "Everyone can make his or her own sandwich and then we're off."

Before Linc could wonder where the dog park actually was, Christy had emptied the refrigerator and created an assembly line of fixings. "Who wants to be first?" she asked.

The two children rushed to her side and began assembling their sandwiches with her help. Linc hovered in the background, ready to kill the idea if the kids gave him the slightest bit of encouragement.

They didn't. In fact, he would never have thought the idea of a picnic would have turned the mood around so quickly. Ordinary sandwiches suddenly became gourmet delights under Christy's tutelage. Every now and then a tasty nugget would fall and an ever-vigilant Ria would snap up the evidence.

He noticed Derek had made himself a man-sized meal while Emma's dinner was a dainty mix of meat, cheese, and pickles sliced into four perfect triangles. Christy, he'd noticed, used a special roll and included lots of lettuce and tomato as well as thinly sliced cucumbers, avocado, and black olives on a thin layer of slivered turkey.

She glanced at him with a raised eyebrow. "You'd better start assembling or you'll end up without."

"Yours looks so good, maybe you can make an extra," he said hopefully.

"Sorry. Dinner tonight is self-service." She slid the package of rolls in his direction. "He who doesn't fix his own doesn't eat."

"Yeah, Unca Linc," Emma said as she speared olives onto her fingers and began eating them. "You have to get in the spirit. Ria and I are gonna play catch with her Frisbee. Wanna play with us?"

"We'll see," he said as he opened a roll and piled on his ingredients. Just before he was ready to position the top part of the bun, Christy held up a shaker.

"What's that?" he asked.

"A little extra flavor," she said. "Garlic, onion, and few other spices. Want to try some?"

Three people's gazes rested on him and each one reflected open curiosity, as if they were expecting him to refuse. Was he that predictable?

"Sure, why not?" he said. "Tonight's a night to throw caution to the wind and have fun. Who cares about bad breath? Right, kids?"

"Right," they echoed.

Yet as he watched Christy pop a slice of avocado into her kissable mouth, he realized there was an advantage to having garlic breath. He wouldn't be tempted to do something immensely stupid on their first night together.

Soon they were on their way with food and bottled drinks in the ice chest, a few blankets, Ria's toys and water bowl. By the time they'd arrived at the dog park, Christy had led them in a noisy rendition of "B-I-N-G-O" that made his ears hurt.

"Aren't you going to sing?" Christy asked him when the group stopped momentarily for breath.

He couldn't stop a smile, neither did he want to because the excitement had become infectious. "First you roped me into dancing, and now you expect me to become a vocalist? A man has to draw the line somewhere," he said, pretending affront.

"Spoilsport." She obviously didn't take offense because she chuckled, then immediately led them in the next stanza.

As he looked into the back seat in the rearview mirror, hearing Emma and Derek's laughter was far better than seeing them with sad faces, so he didn't have the heart to tell them to tone down the noise level.

He also didn't have the heart to scold them for eating only half of their food because they were in such a rush to play with Ria before the rain fell.

"They're going to be starving later," he said as Christy wrapped up their sandwiches.

"Probably," she agreed, "but their sandwiches will keep. How's your dinner?"

He polished off his last bite before grabbing a bunch of red grapes. "Delicious."

"Then we should do this more often."

"Maybe," he said, unwilling to commit.

"Food always tastes better eaten outside."

He glanced around the park, noting that several other families had taken advantage of the picnic tables. "Oh, I don't know," he mused, thinking of ants and flies and a host of other associated nuisances, not to mention spilled drinks and sticky hands. "It isn't always a great experience."

She chuckled. "Let me guess. Your idea of eating outside is gobbling down a bagel or a burger while you're stuck in traffic."

It was uncanny how accurately she could read him and they'd hardly spent any time together. How much of his soul would she see by the end of two months? "Yeah," he admitted.

"That doesn't count. You have to soak up the ambience of your surroundings. Allow nature's scents of pine and honeysuckle and lavender to mingle with the aroma of the food." She inhaled. "That's what dining outdoors is all about."

As she closed her eyes, he had the strangest urge to trace the line of her jaw with his fingertips and kiss away the fleck of avocado on the corner of her mouth. He also wanted to see if her strawberry-blonde hair was as soft as it looked, discover if she'd fit against his body as perfectly as he imagined.

Giving in to temptation wasn't a wise thing to do. He simply had to deny that sudden attraction because if he didn't, it would only create more problems in the long run. They were only two people who shared the responsibility of two kids for a few weeks. Nothing more, nothing less.

And yet her soft skin beckoned and his fingers itched to explore...

A sudden crack of thunder told him the storm would arrive soon. Immediately, he rose. "Come on, kids. Time to load up and head for home."

As the children scampered back to their picnic table, with Ria keeping pace, he was once again grateful to see smiles on their faces.

"They really needed this, didn't they?" he mused as he helped Christy pack up the ice chest.

"Of course they did. Otherwise they would have moped all evening."

"Bedtime still could be rocky," he warned.

"Probably," she admitted, "but why do you think I wanted them to chase Ria? I predict they'll be too tired to think much about their parents being gone."

"And if they do?"

"Then we give them something to look forward to tomorrow. Before they know it, one day will slide into another and the weeks will fly by."

She was right. His whole life had been about staying busy and the years had blended together. Other than a few milestones to mark the passage of time, including his birthday, one month wasn't any different than the next.

"I hope you're right. In any case, your picnic idea was brilliant."

She laughed. "Oh, my. Two compliments in one day. You aren't feverish, are you?"

As she placed her palm on his forehead, his heart immediately pounded to a double-time beat. He was hot all right, but it had nothing to do a virus and everything to do with her.

CHAPTER THREE

"TELL me the story of the princess again, Unca Linc," Emma demanded.

"We read Penelope's tale already," he told her.

"Not hers. I want to hear the one you have in your head."

Christy smiled at the sight of the six-year-old, wearing her frilly pink nightgown, snuggled under Linc's left arm, while Derek, clad in camouflage pj's, lounged on the chair's opposite arm.

What struck her most with the scene was how comfortable Linc appeared. His smiles were wide and his touch gentle as he tousled Derek's damp hair and tickled Emma's ear.

How had she ever thought him cold and unfeeling?

"Aw, Emma, not again," Derek moaned. "I want to hear the knight story and how he killed the dragon and slept under the stars with his trusty steed, Thunder."

"Trusty steed?" Christy chimed in as she perched on the edge of the sofa. "Oh, I want to hear about him, too."

Linc cast an exasperated glance at her. "It's late and you know the rule, one make-believe story per night. Which story did I tell last time?"

"Emma's," Derek said.

"Mine," Emma reluctantly admitted.

"Then it's Derek's turn." He gave Emma a hug meant to console her. "I'll tell the princess story tomorrow."

"Okay," she said in a long-suffering tone. "I'll wait until then."

"That's my girl," he praised. "Let's see, how does it start again?"

"Once upon a time," Derek prompted.

"Ah, yes. Once upon a time there was a young knight who was left in charge of his parents' castle while they went to visit the king. It would be a long journey so to help the knight, the baron and his wife left behind two trusty advisors to guide the young man in case problems should arise."

Christy listened to the story unfold, finding herself as riveted as the children. He'd just reached the part about the baron's son finding a wounded doe when his cell phone jangled.

His warm tone disappeared as he took the call and his professional persona became fully evident. She hoped the reason for the interruption was minor, but when he clicked off his phone, she sensed their family interlude had ended.

"I have to go, kiddos," he apologized affectionately. "So I'll finish the story with 'To be continued'."

Apparently this wasn't the first time a story had been cut short under similar circumstances because the children didn't argue. They simply flung their arms around his neck and kissed him. "'Night, Uncle Linc," they chimed in unison before they slid off his lap. "See you in the morning."

As soon as the two disappeared down the hall, Christy asked, "Problems, I take it?"

He nodded. "Jose is having severe pain in his other leg. I don't know how long I'll be."

That wasn't good news. In spite of being heavily dosed on blood thinners, Jose could still be developing blood clots.

"I didn't realize you were on call."

"I'm not, but Jose asked for me."

Which meant he wouldn't refuse to go to the hospital, she realized. "I hope everything goes okay for him."

His eyes seemed uncommonly tired as he paused in his path to the door. "Me, too."

Christy hated that his already long day had just been extended. She made a mental note to keep the children as quiet as mice tomorrow morning so he could sleep late. In any case, who would have thought Gail's scenario would have played out so soon? As much as she would have liked to split the parenting duties, sharing them was turning out to be for the best.

As she'd predicted earlier, both Derek and Emma had fallen asleep almost immediately after she'd tucked them in and kissed them goodnight.

She was ready for bed herself, but she and Linc hadn't discussed their sleeping arrangements. Commandeering the master bedroom on her own seemed presumptuous on her part. Although the luxury of Gail and Ty's king-sized bed was enticing, her sense of fair play dictated that Linc deserved the perk. His tall frame would fit so much better there than on the daybed in the guest bedroom. His late and/or early comings and goings would disrupt the household less if he had immediate access to a private bathroom.

Christy turned down her bed, unpacked her clothes, lined her bottles of pills and vitamins on the top of her dresser next to her doctors' appointments cards, tidied the kitchen and let Ria out for her last toilet break of the evening. An hour had passed and Linc still hadn't returned.

She patted on her weekly facial mask, took a long, leisurely shower, slipped on her pink breast cancer awareness Minnie Mouse sleep shirt, then slathered on body moisturizer while Ria watched from her spot on the floor.

Still no Linc.

Afraid that poor Jose was in serious shape, she decided to

wait for news. She convinced Ria to lie on her pallet in the living room, then curled up in the easy chair Linc had vacated earlier with one of the paperback books she'd brought from her personal library.

She didn't realize she'd begun dozing until Ria's low grumble startled her awake. As soon as the back door opened, her pet bolted upright and dashed into the kitchen like an enthusiastic puppy rather than a fierce protector.

Clearly, Linc was home.

She padded after her to find Linc rummaging in freezer for ice. Stifling her yawn, she asked, "How did things go?"

"Good." He filled his plastic tumbler with water and took a long swig of his drink.

"What happened?"

"Jose developed a DVT in his other leg."

She translated his shorthand into "deep vein thrombosis", which shouldn't have happened given all the medication they'd given him earlier in the day. "And?"

"I called in Howard Manning and he inserted a Greenfield filter into his vena cava to stop the clot from entering his lung."

"How's he doing?"

"Fine for now. He'll be monitored closely for a while."

Christy noted the lines of exhaustion on his face and his weary-looking gaze when he glanced at her. While her shirt was perfectly modest and covered as much of her body as regular clothing, she was quite aware they were still only pajamas.

"You should be asleep," he said as he finished off the drink.

"I think I was."

"You didn't have to stay up."

"I wanted to hear about Jose. I also didn't want Ria to think you were a burglar and sound the alarm, but she obviously knew who you were because she didn't."

As if aware of the hour and disappointed by the lack of attention his humans were paying her, the dog gave a wide, noisy yawn, then turned around and headed for her rug.

"I also couldn't go to bed because we hadn't worked out our sleeping arrangements. I was afraid you'd either stumble around and wake everyone or spend the night in a chair."

"Right now, a chair sounds like heaven."

"Well, there's a bed waiting for you." Aware of how suggestive her comment sounded, she hurried to explain. "I took the spare room. The master bedroom is all yours."

He rubbed his eyes as he nodded. "I should be chivalrous and argue, but maybe tomorrow when I'm not beat."

"Argue all you want, but I've already unpacked my stuff. Do you have to go in early or can you sleep late?"

His smile was small and lopsided. "It's my weekend off, so I don't need an alarm clock."

"Then I'll keep the kids extra-quiet while we eat breakfast."

"It's not necessary. A few hours and I'll be good as new. Wake me in time to help."

"Okay," she said, only because she didn't want to argue with him at two a.m. At some point they would have to discuss job duties and meal planning, but not now. "Will you go to the hospital this weekend to check on Jose?"

He nodded. "I'll drop by late morning or early afternoon."

She knew he wasn't on call this weekend, which made her curious about his plans. "Do you give all of your patients the royal treatment? I don't think any of them would fault you for taking a night or a weekend off and passing their care off to one of your partners."

He refilled his tumbler and drank deeply again. "Probably not, but Jose isn't just a patient. I've known him and his wife for about five years."

"As a patient?"

He shook his head. "I met him when I hired him to build an outdoor fireplace. Because he was eager for the job, he'd work on evenings and weekends when I was at home, and his wife sent along some of her cooking." He grinned. "I think she used me to clean out her leftovers, but I didn't mind. Everything was delicious. Eventually, I got to know their family and when the oldest son expressed an interest in medicine, Jose asked if Emilio could job-shadow me for a week before he started college."

"And you did," she guessed.

He chuckled. "Yeah. Now he's in his final year of medical school." A note of pride filled his voice.

She was half-surprised by his story, and yet, after seeing him interact with his niece and nephew, she wasn't. Obviously he was a completely different person around the people who'd been lucky enough to enter his charmed circle of friends and family. Oddly enough, she realized that she wanted to be included.

Not because she had any romantic designs on him, she hastened to tell herself. Even if her ex, Jon, hadn't blasted the stars out of her eyes, getting that close to a guy wouldn't happen before she got the all-clear on her five-year check-up. It would take someone special to deal with the baggage she carried and she honestly didn't think there was a man alive who could.

"Does he know about his father?"

"I called him this evening. Francesca was too rattled to make sense and I knew Emilio would have a lot of questions." Suddenly he yawned. "Sorry about that."

Immediately, she felt guilty for keeping him from his well-deserved and much-needed sleep. "I'm the one who's sorry. If I hadn't stayed up to ask about Jose, you'd already be in bed asleep. So, go on." She made a shooing motion. "I'll get the lights and lock up."

"Okay, but in the morning you and I need to sort out a few details," he began.

"I'll be here," she promised. Then, looking around, she asked, "Where's your suitcase?"

He snapped his fingers. "I left my duffel bag in the car."

"I'll get it while you hop in the shower."

She expected him to argue, but he simply nodded. "Thanks. It's on the back seat."

When she returned with his bag in hand, she was surprised to hear dead silence. She knocked softly on the master bedroom's door and when she didn't hear an answer, she assumed it was safe to enter.

However, as she peeked inside, she found him lying fully clothed on top of the king-sized bed.

She wanted to wake him so he could change into something more comfortable than his dress clothes and crawl under the covers, but the lines of exhaustion on his face stopped her. The medical residents she'd encountered during her nursing career had learned to fall asleep as soon as they were horizontal, regardless of what they were wearing, and Linc obviously hadn't given up those old habits.

Knowing she couldn't leave him as he was, she tugged off his shoes and placed them side by side on the floor beside his bag. Determined to protect his rest as much as she could, she reassured herself the curtains were tightly pulled and the alarm clock was turned off. By the time she tiptoed to the door and flicked off the overhead light, an occasional soft snore punctuated the silence.

She smiled. Until now, she would have sworn that a man as tightly in control as Linc was wouldn't allow his body to do anything as ordinary as snore. It would be interesting to see how many of her other preconceived opinions he'd disprove over the coming weeks, although she hoped he wouldn't.

Learning that Lincoln Maguire was a great guy underneath his staid exterior would only lead to heartbreak.

Linc woke to the most delicious aroma—coffee. He sniffed the air again, trying to catalog the other scent that mingled with his beloved caffeinated breakfast blend. It reminded him of...

Waffles. His eyes popped open and it took him a few seconds to realize he wasn't in his own bed. Memories of last night crashed down and he immediately checked the bedside alarm clock.

Eleven-thirty. No wonder the sun was peeking around the edges of the heavy drapes. He couldn't remember the last time he'd slept that late, although he vaguely remembered waking at one point to use the bathroom and shed his clothes before he crawled between cool, fresh-smelling sheets.

He also didn't recall the last time he'd awakened to the aroma of a delicious meal. Although he didn't expect her to prepare his breakfast, he hoped she'd prepared extra for him this morning. As he swung his bare legs over the bed's edge, his stomach rumbled in agreement.

Raking a hand through his hair, he rose, stepped into his previously discarded pants, and followed his nose.

Derek and Emma were seated at the kitchen table and Christy stood in front of the stove, clad in a pair of above-the-knee light blue plaid cotton shorts that showed off her delightfully long legs and a matching blue button-down shirt. Both children had powdered sugar dusting their faces, syrup smeared around their mouths and milk mustaches.

Emma saw him and her eyes lit up. "Christy?" she asked in a loud whisper. "Can we use our regular voices now?"

"Not until you're uncle is awake," she whispered back.

"But he is," she declared in a normal tone. "Morning, Unca Linc."

Christy turned, spatula in hand, and her eyes widened before a big smile crossed her face. "Good morning," she said as her gaze pointedly remained above his neck. "The coffee's ready if you are."

He nearly smiled at her discomfiture, then decided it wouldn't win him any brownie points. "You read my mind. Thanks. Can I pour you a cup, too?"

She shook her head. "I'm not a coffee drinker."

"Really?" he asked as he poured his own mug. "I thought everyone who worked in the medical profession mainlined the stuff."

"I used to, but I switched to herbal tea. It's better for you."

"Probably, but you can't beat a bracing cup of coffee to jump-start the day." He watched her flip a perfectly made waffle out of the iron and dust it with powdered sugar. "That smells good."

She chuckled. "Are you hinting you'd like one?"

He was practically drooling, but he was too conscious of his morning scruffiness to agree. His face itched, he needed a shave and a shower, and his teeth felt furry. He definitely wasn't presentable for the dining table.

"I should clean up first."

"Probably," she agreed, "but this waffle is ready and the griddle's still hot if you'd like seconds." Her gaze traveled up and down his full length, making him even more aware of his half-dressed appearance. "Judging from the way you look, the kitchen will be closed before you come back, so I suggest you eat first and shower later."

He got the sneaking impression that once she unplugged the waffle iron she wouldn't plug it in again. How had he ever thought her easygoing and malleable? She had a steely spine that he'd never seen and certainly hadn't expected.

"I should put on a shirt," he began.

Once again, she avoided his gaze. "Suit yourself, but, whatever you do, I promise to sit downwind."

"Mom never lets Dad eat at the table without a shirt," Derek said, "but if Uncle Linc can, can I?"

This time Christy looked at him helplessly, her gaze sliding from his pectorals to his face and back again. "Well," she began, "these are extenuating circumstances—"

"If those are your mom's rules, then they'll be ours, too," Linc said firmly. "I'll be right back."

The lure of the waffle was too great and the slices of ham too appetizing to do more than grab yesterday's wrinkled shirt and slip it on. He'd only buttoned the middle two buttons before he was back in the kitchen and sliding into an empty chair.

If Christy noticed his speedy return, she didn't comment. Instead, she simply set his plate in front of him, passed the meat platter and returned to the stove.

Linc dug in. He was hungry enough to be grateful for the hospital's bland cafeteria food, but he was pleasantly surprised to discover Christy's meal actually melted in his mouth. When she delivered a second waffle as perfect as the first one, he could only utter a long sigh of appreciation.

"These are delicious," he said as he drenched it with maple syrup.

"Surprised?" She took the chair beside him and began sectioning her grapefruit.

"A little," he admitted. "Where did you learn to cook like this?"

"My mom. She owns an exclusive little gourmet restaurant in Seattle and she sends recipes for me to try before she adds them to her menu."

"Then that explains all the fancy food in the fridge."

Confusion spread across her face. "Fancy food?"

"You know. The organic milk, the fruit and vegetables I can't identify."

She smiled. "I don't consider organic food as being fancy. As for the unidentifiable stuff, I try new things to see if I'll like them." She motioned to his plate. "Speaking of new things, how would you rate this recipe?"

"It's a keeper." The cuckoo suddenly popped out of his door and chirped twelve times. "I didn't realize it was noon. Did you guys sleep late, too?" he asked.

"We've been up for *hours*." Derek drained his milk glass and wiped his mouth with his forearm until Christy cleared her throat and he sheepishly swiped at it with his napkin.

"Hours and *hours*," Emma added. "Christy said we had to be quiet, so we ate our breakfast on the patio."

"Isn't this breakfast?" he asked.

"This is lunch," Christy corrected. "Breakfast was at eight and consisted of cold cereal, fresh strawberries, pineapple, and toast."

"Whole wheat," Derek mumbled with disgust.

She chuckled and Linc was entranced by the sound. "With all the jelly you slathered on, you couldn't taste or see that I didn't use white bread."

Emma obviously didn't care because she continued her play-by-play account of the morning. "Then we took Ria for a walk around the block so he could get 'quainted with the dog smells in the neighborhood. After that, we watered Mama's flowers and weeded and before we knew it, Christy said it was time to eat again. I think she's almost as good a cook as Mama is, don't you?"

He'd been put on the spot by a mere six-year-old. No matter how he answered, he was going to have one female in the household unhappy. Christy obviously saw his dilemma because her eyes twinkled with humor. He wouldn't receive any help from that quarter....

"Almost," he agreed loyally, as he exchanged a smile with Christy that said otherwise.

"We'll wait for you in the cafeteria," Christy told Linc a few hours later as he parked in the physicians' parking lot. They'd decided to spend the afternoon running errands, including driving to his house to pick up a few of what he referred to as "necessities", but on the way he'd wanted to run in and check on Jose.

"I won't be long, I promise."

"Yeah, right," she said, unable to hide her skepticism.

"You don't believe I can get away in a reasonable amount of time?"

"Only if you went incognito," she said.

"I thought I was," he said. "No one will expect to see me looking like this."

"Like this" meant dressed in a polo shirt, cargo shorts, and a pair of sandals. It wasn't his usual garb, so he'd cause quite a stir when the staff saw him. She spoke from experience because she still couldn't believe this was the same man who'd sat at the kitchen table a few hours ago looking scruffy and bleary-eyed.

A little water and a shave could do amazing things.

As great as he looked now, though, her first image of him was indelibly etched in her brain. His muscles had flexed and rippled under his skin just from the simple act of pouring his own cup of coffee. As much as she'd enjoyed seeing those wide shoulders as nature intended, it was a good thing Derek had piped up when he had. She might have done something really stupid, like set off the smoke alarm or drool in her grapefruit.

Nope, if more women saw the sight she'd been privileged to see, cardiology offices would be standing room only.

"They won't, but if you're going to be longer than thirty minutes, give me a call, will you?"

"Okay, but, whatever you do, don't load them up with a bunch of sugar and junk food."

She paused, momentarily hurt by his remark. "Do you honestly think I'll turn them loose at the candy machine?"

He shifted uncomfortably in the seat. "I think you'd spoil them if you had the chance," he began slowly.

"And you wouldn't, I suppose."

"Once in a while, I do," he admitted, "but—"

Aware of two sets of little ears in the back seat, she lowered her voice and clenched her fingers into a tight fist as she interrupted, "But you think I'll do it all the time."

"Maybe not all—"

"Why else would you remind me?"

He shut off the engine, then gripped the steering wheel with both hands. "I only meant—"

She cut him off once again. "I know what you meant." She didn't know why his lack of faith bothered her, but it did. Yes, they'd only been joint parents for less than twenty-four hours, but where had he gotten the idea she'd let Emma and Derek run amok, nutrition-wise? And if he thought she'd turn a blind eye to their eating habits, what did he think she'd do when making other decisions?

"All I can say is, if you're that worried, you'd better finish your business as quickly as possible so you can supervise what they choose for a snack," she said stiffly.

"I am *not* worried," he said.

"You are, so you may as well admit it." As she turned to face the children, she pasted on a smile and injected a lighter note into her voice. "Okay, gang. Let's go!"

While the two scrambled out of their seat belts, he grabbed her arm. "I'm not worried," he repeated.

"Of course not," she said politely. "My mistake." Then, shaking free, she hopped out of the car and herded her two charges into the hospital like an overprotective mother hen.

When she directed them to the stairwell, Derek complained, "Can't we take the elevator? Uncle Linc is."

"We'll take it on the way up," she prevaricated, unwilling to see for herself or admit that sharing such close confines at the moment was more than she could handle.

With luck, an hour or so of mindlessly watching the fish swim around the aquarium would restore her good mood.

Linc had major damage control facing him. For a man who was normally efficient at stating his thoughts, he'd missed the mark today. He'd hurt Christy with his thoughtless remark—that had been evident and he deeply regretted doing so.

To make matters worse, in trying to explain, he'd practically told her that she was a pushover when it came to Derek and Emma and he knew she wasn't. Christy's mere glance this morning had convinced Derek to use his napkin instead of his sleeve and if she could do that, she'd be immune to any cajolery they might try.

He checked Jose's chart and slipped into his room to visit for about fifteen minutes. Satisfied by his progress, he strode toward the bank of elevators, ready to leave. As he punched the "Down" button, he wondered if he should kill time elsewhere in the hospital. If he arrived in the cafeteria too soon, Christy would assume he'd hurried to check on her.

The point was he *was* in a hurry, but not for that particular reason. If anyone saw him, he could easily get embroiled in a patient case and he had too many other things to do this afternoon—*family* things—that wouldn't allow it. His objective also included getting to know Gail's best friend because there seemed to be more to her than had previously met his eye.

On the other hand, Christy seemed like a forgiving sort, so perhaps during their time apart she'd decided to cut him some slack.

He strode into the near-empty cafeteria and saw Emma and Derek peering into the giant aquarium in the far corner of the dining hall.

"Hi, guys. Are you enjoying the fish?" he asked.

"I like the spotted ones," Emma declared as she pointed to one. "Do you know what kind of fish he is?"

Linc referred to the chart posted above the aquarium. "A Dalmation Molly."

Emma giggled. "She looks like a fire-truck dog, doesn't she?"

"She does," he agreed, then asked, "Where's Christy?"

"She's over there with that guy." Derek inclined his head in her direction.

Linc glanced at the corner in question and saw her with a fellow he recognized as one of the physical therapists. From their wide smiles and the laughter drifting across the room, both appeared entirely too comfortable with each other for Linc's taste.

"He's got the hots for her," Derek said with a typical eight-year-old boy's disgust.

Linc had arrived at the same conclusion and was instantly envious. His reaction was completely illogical, but when he saw the guy scoot his chair closer and fling his arm over her shoulder to draw her close enough to whisper in her ear, he felt an envy he hadn't noticed before.

"See?" Derek said with satisfaction. "Maybe we should warn Christy that he wants to get in her—"

Derek's blunt description finally registered and Linc cut

off the boy's sentence. "Whoa there, buddy. Does your mother know you're a teenager in an eight-year-old body?"

A blush crept across Derek's face, which suggested his mother probably didn't know the extent of her son's education. "I watch TV," he defended.

"Really?" Linc raised an eyebrow. "Before I ask what sort of programs you're viewing and if your mother knows you are, we aren't going to say a word to Christy. We don't want to embarrass her."

He, on the other hand, was jealous.

The boy shrugged. "If you say so, but it's still true. He held out her chair for her, got her a refill, and keeps putting his arm around the back of her chair and leaning in close. I think he might be her boyfriend."

A boyfriend. Linc hadn't considered the possibility that Christy might have her own reasons for not wanting to share the house with him. Living under someone else's roof with another guy, no matter how innocent it might be, could certainly strain a relationship.

On the other hand, although he didn't socialize with the staff, he'd picked up enough tidbits from conversations around him to know the gossip currently circulating on the grapevine. He'd never heard her name linked to anyone else's. If he had, he would have remembered.

On the other hand, her relationship might be new enough that it hadn't become the latest news yet. Or, as Derek had said, this Masterson fellow might still be trying—

"He isn't," Emma interrupted with childlike certainty.

Linc's mind was too focused on Derek's report of Masterson's activities to follow Emma's train of thought. "He isn't what?"

"Her boyfriend. I heard Mama telling her that she needs to get one, but Christy only laughed and said she'd think about it after her next pet. Do you think she's going to get another dog? I hope she finds a little one next time. One you can carry in your purse."

Linc was totally confused. A boyfriend was contingent on Christy's new pet? Emma had obviously missed a few important details.

"How long ago did you hear your Mom and Christy talking?" he asked. If their conversation had taken place months ago, Christy could easily have found someone since then to play that role, new pet or not.

"A few days before Mama and Daddy left. Oh, look." Once again, she pointed to the tank. "Those two fish are *kissing*." She giggled.

He glanced at the tank and saw two fish with their mouths pressed together. The fish clearly didn't spend their days swimming aimlessly around their environment. Once again, he referred to the posted list of names and photos.

"They're called Kissing Gourami," he reported.

"Do you think they like each other, Unca Linc?" Emma asked.

"Don't be silly." Derek rolled his eyes. "Fish don't like each other like people do."

"How do you know?" Emma's eyes flashed. "You don't know everything just 'cause you're older than me. If it's a boy fish and a girl fish, they could, *too*, like each other—"

"Enough," Linc said firmly. "We aren't going to argue here. We'll research the subject on the internet when we get home."

To his surprise and delight, Christy joined them at the tank. "Actually, those two aren't getting along right now," she said.

"They aren't? But they're acting like they do," Emma protested.

"They're a peaceful species, but the males fight over their territory like other animals. When they do, they press their mouths together."

The little girl frowned as if trying to puzzle over how such a move could be a sign of aggression. "They don't have much room to fight over," she remarked, her attention riveted to the pair in question.

"I don't know how large they consider their territories," Christy replied. "Maybe one raced the other to the food and he was a sore loser. Or maybe one cut in front of the other while they were swimming."

"I get it," Linc said, humored by her story. "They're having the aquatic equivalent of road rage. And I thought I had an active imagination."

Emma tugged on his shorts pocket. "What's road rage?"

"It's when one driver gets angry with another driver and they get into an argument."

"Oh."

"The point is, Em," Christy interrupted, "it doesn't take much for guys of any species to find a reason to flex their muscles."

He had a feeling she'd directed her last comment to him.

"Yeah, but they fight by kissing?" Derek shuddered. "Yuck."

Christy grinned. "You don't like the idea of locking lips with the guy you want to punch?"

"No way."

While Derek and Christy discussed the more acceptable forms of dealing with conflict, Linc realized that her former companion had disappeared. "Is Masterson's coffee break over?"

"Dan had only stopped in for his usual afternoon soda and ran into us. He's on the *Dancing with the Docs* committee and was trying to convince me to volunteer."

"Did he? Convince you, that is?"

She shook her head. "I told him my days were full enough as it is with being a participant, but I'd save him a dance."

Linc felt an unreasonable desire to remind her that she would be busy dancing with *him*, but he didn't. He did, however, make a mental note to carve out time for lessons the week after next. By then, his partners would have returned from their respective vacations and he could implement a less hectic schedule in the weeks ahead.

"As enjoyable as it is to stay and chat about the fish or the upcoming festival, we have plenty to see and do today," she said.

"You're right. We should leave," he agreed. After tossing the empty cracker wrappers and milk cartons into a bin, Linc ushered the group to the elevator. As they were making their ascent, curiosity drove him to ask, "Emma said you might be getting another dog?"

She smiled. "Afraid not. Ria is all I can handle for now." She touched her finger to the tip of the little girl's nose. "Whatever gave you that idea, Em?"

"We were wondering if that guy you were with was your boyfriend. I said he wasn't 'cause you told Mama you'd get one after your next pet and you still just have Ria."

Linc had expected her to laugh in her usual melodic way— the way that made him smile whenever he heard the sound. He wasn't prepared to see her face turn pale and her hand shake as she touched her throat.

Something had driven the color out of her face. He didn't understand what, but he intended to find out.

CHAPTER FOUR

CHRISTY tried to remember the details of her conversation with Gail and wondered how much Emma had heard. She opted to pretend ignorance. "Trust me. I don't intend to replace Ria or give her a doggy brother or sister. Okay?"

"Then you won't ever have a boyfriend?"

Emma had no idea how painful her innocent question was. "Someday. If I find the right guy," Christy answered lightly, although she had her doubts. In her experience, the good ones were already taken.

Suddenly aware of Linc's speculative gaze, she wondered why the elevator suddenly slowed to a crawl. "I'm too busy for a fella right now anyway." She brushed a lock of unruly hair off Emma's forehead. "I'm looking after my favorite kids, remember?"

Fortunately, they'd arrived on the main floor at that particular moment. As soon as the stainless-steel doors opened, she edged her way through the space so fast she was the first one out.

"What's next on our agenda?" she asked, hoping Linc hadn't noticed her too-bright tone. A quick glance showed an impassive expression so she relaxed, certain she'd successfully dodged that uncomfortable situation.

"My place," he said.

It came as no surprise that Linc lived in an upper-middle-class neighborhood. His sprawling, ranch-style house stood in the middle of a well-manicured lawn. Hostas and other shade-loving perennials circled the large maple trees and a mixture of petunias, marigolds, and other annuals she didn't recognize filled the flower bed next to the front entrance.

"When do you find the time to work outdoors?" she asked as they walked inside.

"I have a yard service," he confessed. "I also have a house-keeper who drops in every three weeks, although there isn't much for her to do."

She didn't expect there would be. The man spent most of his life at the hospital.

"Can we go to the back yard and play, Uncle Linc?" Derek asked.

"Sure," he told them, "but don't get too involved because we won't be staying long."

"Okay." The children scampered through the house and a few seconds later an unseen door slammed.

"What are we getting?" Christy asked, trying not to be awed by his house and failing. The home was built with an open floor plan similar to hers, but his living room also had a gorgeous red-brick fireplace in one corner. His décor included a lot of woodwork and deep accent colors in blues, greens, and browns, which gave a very relaxing atmosphere.

"My single-cup coffeemaker," he said as he skirted the island on his way to the end of the counter where the appliance in question was located. "You don't drink coffee, so it seems a waste to make an entire pot for the one cup I drink on my way to the office."

"True." She glanced around again. "This is absolutely lovely."

"You like it?" he asked.

"Very much. If I lived here, I'd have a tough time leaving to go to work."

She heard childish laughter and screams of delight, so she moved to the French doors that opened onto the patio. There, she looked outside into the most beautiful back yard she could imagine.

An outdoor fireplace and a bricked-in grill formed the wall on the west side of the patio and protected the table and chairs from the setting sun. On the east side, a couple of cushioned lounge chairs were grouped together with a small end table in between.

Beyond that, a pair of large oak trees stood like sentinels in the fenced yard. A tree house was nestled in one and a tire swing hung from a huge branch in the other. A gym with a climbing rope and a slide stood off to one side and both Emma and Derek were crawling over it like agile monkeys.

"This is fantastic!" she exclaimed. "Did you or a previous owner create all this?"

He joined her at the door, his smile wide with well-deserved pride. "Ty and Jose did most of the physical labor, but I helped."

"It's amazing," she remarked, awed by his thoughtfulness for his niece and nephew. She was also extremely aware of his proximity as she could almost feel the heat radiating off his body and the most delightful masculine scent surrounded her. "I suppose you don't call this 'spoiling' your niece and nephew?"

He shook his head. "I call it self-preservation. Gail and Ty always designate one night a month as their date night, so I began hosting sleepovers at my place. Sometimes they stretched into a full weekend. After one visit of hearing 'We're bored, Unca Linc,' and 'Can we go to the park and play on the swings' every five minutes, I decided it would be easier on all of us if they had something special to play on here. So I commissioned everything you see."

"I'm very impressed." And she was. He might be single-minded about his work, but he didn't completely ignore his family, as she'd first thought.

"Impressed enough to forgive me for my comment this afternoon?"

She had to think a minute to remember. "Oh, that. I'd already forgotten."

"Really?" he asked. "You were rather upset."

She shrugged. "At the time I was. As a general rule, I try to look at what happened in terms of the big picture and usually nothing is so bad that it's worth making a fuss about. Although it takes me a bit longer to reach that point when my feelings are hurt, eventually I get there."

"That's a very healthy attitude to have."

Facing one's mortality had a tendency to change one's perspective. "Thanks."

"I didn't mean to hurt your feelings."

She fell silent. "I accept your apology, but the question is do you trust me to exercise good judgment with Derek and Emma? If you don't, I'd like to know now."

"I don't *distrust* you," he said slowly. "Old habits simply die hard and as the responsible person in my family, it seemed like I was always reminding my siblings to do one thing or another. My parents left me in charge a lot, and by the time they died, it had become second nature. 'Don't forget your lunch money. Pick up a loaf of bread on your way home from school. Start the laundry when you get home.'"

"Ah, the controlling type."

"If by controlling you mean trying to keep everything organized and running smoothly, then yes."

"I'm surprised you took on that responsibility by yourself."

He grinned. "I did, and I didn't. My grandmother was still alive and she wanted Ty and Joanie to move in with her, but Gram was already showing signs of senile dementia and had a heart problem. Taking care of two teenagers would have completely done her in. The three of us voted to move her in with us. She felt useful and we unobtrusively kept an eye on her."

"That's amazing."

He shrugged. "It was the best solution at the time and in hindsight I'm glad we made that decision because a year later she died in her sleep."

"I'm sorry," she murmured.

"She was a great gal. She tended to deliver last-minute instructions every time anyone left the house—young or old, it didn't matter—and I suppose I picked up that habit early on."

"How did Ty and your sister handle those *little reminders*?"

"We had our moments, but they listened." His grin was a beautiful sight to see. "Or at least they pretended to listen."

"So is that what I should do?" she teased. "Pretend to hang on your every word until your ego can't fit through doorways?"

"It's a pleasant thought, but I'd rather have honesty."

"Honesty I can do."

As they exchanged a smile, she felt as if they'd reached a milestone. Sharing the responsibility of the children didn't seem quite as frustrating as she'd once thought. Maybe, just maybe, they could get through the next two months without feeling as if she were tiptoeing through a minefield.

Oh, they were certain to clash; it was inevitable because he was the type of man who grabbed the horns of leadership. He was used to being the guy with the answers and had been for most of his life. Becoming a surgeon had only reinforced his independence. To him, decisions weren't by group consensus and consequently he expected people to follow his directives without question.

She, on the other hand, believed in hearing both sides and

weighing all the pros and cons before arriving at a solution. To her, flexibility and family relationships were far more important than schedules and to-do lists. Life was simply too precarious not to enjoy it to the fullest.

"I'll try to be more sparing with my reminders," he added, "but in case I forget, don't take them personally."

"Okay, as long as you understand I don't handle 'control' very easily."

He chuckled. "I suspected as much. Now that we've cleared the air, we should discuss our free time."

"Free time?"

"Yeah. If you ever want to go out with Masterson—"

"I don't," she said firmly. "He's a great guy, but..." she wasn't ready to bare her soul, so she relied on her standby excuse "...the sparks aren't there."

"Are you sure? He certainly has them."

"Were you *spying* on me?"

He held up his hands. "I'm only repeating what Derek said."

The knowledge that an eight-year-old boy saw the very fire she'd been trying to extinguish was disconcerting.

"The point is, whether you want to go out with him or anyone else, I'm sure Gail and Ty don't expect either of us to forego dating for the next two months. We need to create a schedule."

Another schedule. How in the world did the man keep track of them all? She pictured his daily calendar and imagined a block of time designated as 'Christy's date', and inwardly smiled.

She didn't know if he was fishing or being kind, but admitting she didn't have a romantic interest and only went out with her girlfriends or colleagues for an occasional beer at the end of a long week made her seem...sad and pathetic. She'd endured enough of people's well-meant sympathy over the past four-plus years and she especially didn't want any from Lincoln Maguire.

"Your suggestion is noted," she said instead. "I'll give you plenty of notice when I have plans. What about you? Is there a lady friend in your life that I should work around?"

"Not really. I have met someone, though. No, I take that back. We've been passing acquaintances for a while, but lately I'm seeing her a little differently."

The idea that another woman had attracted his attention was unsettling, which was a completely illogical response. Just because her pulse did that stupid skittery thing when he was around and just because they were living together under the most innocent of terms for the sake of two minors didn't mean she had a right to be possessive. A man who thrived on control and preferred having everything in its place wouldn't be interested in a woman who walked a tightrope between being cured of cancer and having a relapse.

"Anyone I know?" she asked, realizing her off-handed question was as painful as poking herself in the eye.

"I'd rather not name names at this point."

She didn't know what was worse—knowing the woman's identity or being left to speculate. "Okay, but if you ever ask her out—"

"You'll be the first to know."

His promise brought little comfort because the green-eyed monster had perched on her shoulder.

Linc had hoped Christy would be more forthcoming about her personal life when he'd mentioned creating a date-night schedule, but she hadn't. Hearing she didn't feel the sparks with Masterson had come as some relief, but Masterson wasn't the only guy sniffing around her. She attracted single fellows like grape jelly attracted orioles, although, as far as he could tell, she didn't encourage them.

No doubt they responded to her ready smile and open friendliness, which he completely understood. He lingered longer on her nursing unit than he did elsewhere in the hospital because lately, even if he only spent a few minutes with her and they never discussed anything except patient care, being with her seemed to rejuvenate him.

It was an odd observation. She was unconventional and impulsive—two traits he hadn't been looking for in his ideal significant other because he wasn't about to have *his* children live through the same upheaval and uncertainty he had—but apparently, like the other eligible males in the hospital, he was drawn to her because of them.

For the first time he began to wonder if steady and dependable was really what he wanted. After all, he'd met a multitude of steady, dependable women and yet he hadn't bothered to get to know any of them. Was it possible that deep down, in spite of his avowal otherwise, he wanted the excitement that his parents had enjoyed as they'd pursued their dream together?

Maybe he did, but he'd certainly go about achieving it in a different way, and he certainly wouldn't do so by placing an unreasonable burden on his children. Surely there was a happy medium? He simply had to find it.

In the meantime, though, he'd solve the riddle of the "pet" comment Emma had overheard because his instincts said there was more to that particular story than Christy had divulged.

To his surprise, the pieces which hadn't fit suddenly slid into place later that evening.

"Unca Linc, I need you."

Emma's loud whisper pulled his attention away from his latest *Lancet* journal as he sat in the recliner with his feet raised. "What's up, Em?" he asked in a normal voice.

"Shh," she whispered, holding a finger to her lips. "I don't want Christy to hear. I need you. *Now*." She motioned frantically for him to join her.

The worry on her elfin features convinced him to follow. As soon as he reached her side, she pulled him into the hallway that led to the bedrooms.

"What's up?" he whispered back.

"I'm in a bit of a pickle," she admitted, "but I can't 'splain yet. Christy will hear."

He smiled at her turn of a phrase because it sounded like something his sister-in-law frequently said. "She's outside."

Emma's shoulders heaved. "Oh, good."

"So what's this pickle you're in?" he asked, trying to not smile when Emma was clearly distressed.

She stopped outside Christy's room and the story poured out of her. "I know we're not s'posed to go into rooms when we're not invited, but Ria and I were playing and Ria ran in here and I came after her. She was jumping and I was trying to stay out of her way but we both bumped into the dresser and Christy's stuff rolled off and some of the bottles fell off the back and I can't get them out!" Her voice rose. "Now Christy's going to be mad at us and she won't let me play with Ria or talk to Mama and Daddy when they call tonight and I just gotta talk to them! Please, Unca Linc. You hafta help me."

With that, she burst into tears.

Linc's mouth twitched with a smile, but laughing at Emma's worries wouldn't allay his niece's fears. Instead, he crouched down and hugged her.

"None of this is as bad as you think," he consoled, wiping away her tears with his thumbs. "We'll get the bottles and set them back on top of the dresser. No harm done."

Emma sniffled.

"Were they big bottles or little ones?" he asked.

"Little. Mama gets the same ones when she's sick."

She must have knocked over prescription bottles. "Okay. Give me two minutes and everything will be just like it was."

"But she'll know I came into her room without her permission," she hiccupped, "and then I'll be punished. So will Ria."

The Labrador sat on her haunches next to the bed, her usual doggy smile absent, as if she recognized the gravity of the situation.

"You may get scolded, but Christy wouldn't stop you from talking to your mom and dad."

"You don't think so?" Her watery blue-gray eyes stared into his. "What we did was wrong."

"Yes, it was, but not allowing you to talk to your mom and dad would be mean, and deep down you know she isn't mean." He paused. "Am I right?"

She nodded and the worried wrinkle between her eyes lessened.

"I'll move the dresser, we'll find her things and put them back the way they were. Now, don't cry. Okay?"

She swiped her nose and nodded. "Okay."

Linc pivoted the dresser far enough to locate the missing prescription containers. After retrieving them, he moved the furniture so the legs matched the same carpet depressions as they had previously. Satisfied he'd hidden the evidence of the mishap, he placed the two he'd rescued at the end of the row of her other medications and neatly stacked the appointment cards.

Noticing that she'd positioned each bottle so the labels faced outward, he lined his in the same manner, half-surprised that someone as young and obviously healthy as Christy required so much medication. As he turned away, he caught one drug name out of the corner of his eye and his blood immediately ran cold.

Tamoxifen.

Although he didn't prescribe it for his patients, he knew exactly what it was used for—the treatment of certain types of breast cancer.

The books on her shelf now made sense, as did the row of pill bottles and vitamins, her organic hormone-free milk, and the refrigerator full of fresh vegetables and low-fat dairy products.

It also made her guiding philosophy of life understandable. After battling cancer, there weren't many other problems too big to face and definitely not many worth getting upset over.

But, oh, how he hated to think of what she'd gone through, both physically and emotionally.

"Unca Linc." Emma tugged on his pants. "Are you done? We should go."

"You're right, we should." He ushered her out of the room and closed the door firmly behind him, wishing he could block off his new-found knowledge as easily.

"There you two are," Christy said with relief as she and Derek met Linc and Emma in the living room. "It's almost time for Gail and Ty to call. Linc, can you power up the laptop?"

While he obeyed, she addressed the children. "Let me look at you and make sure you're both presentable."

She stood them side by side and cast a critical eye on them. The clean clothes they'd changed into an hour ago were still clean. Emma's hair was neatly combed, but Derek's definitely needed a bit of straightening. She couldn't do it properly so she simply smoothed the unruly locks with her fingers.

"Gail and Ty aren't expecting them to look their Sunday best," Linc teased her. "They know these two. If they're too neat, Gail will accuse us of replacing her kids with some-one else's."

"I don't want them to think we're neglecting—"

"Trust me, they won't. As long as they're not bleeding, a

little dirt and stray hair won't faze Gail and Ty." He pushed a few keys, then set the laptop on the coffee table in front of the youngest Maguires, who were bouncing with excitement on the sofa. "Here we go."

At seven o'clock on the dot, thanks to a wireless internet connection and a webcam, Gail and Ty appeared on the computer screen and the conversation began.

Christy moved into the background and listened as the children talked about their recent activities and Gail mentioned a few of the sights they'd seen. She and Linc gave a short statement about how well things were going and eventually, after a promise for a follow-up call on Thursday and a tearful goodbye, he closed the connection.

"Can we do that again?" Emma asked.

"On Thursday," Christy told her.

"I want to talk before then."

Arranging a time to coordinate with school events, homework, dance lessons, and soccer practice had been tough, so everyone had agreed to plan their calls near the children's bedtime. Unfortunately, with the seven-hour time difference, it meant Gail and Ty they had to call at three a.m. local time, which explained why they'd looked a little bleary-eyed.

"I know you do, but your mom and dad have to wake up in the middle of the night to talk to us. They can't do that every day."

"But I didn't tell Mama about the caterpillar I saw and Daddy doesn't know about my loose tooth."

"I'll help you email them," Linc offered. "How does that sound?"

Emma frowned, her bottom lip quivering as if she wouldn't need much encouragement to break into a wail.

He tugged on the little girl's earlobe. "Did you lose your smile? You'd better find it quick because you'll need it for school tomorrow. You don't want your teacher calling me and saying that Emma Maguire is being grumpy today, do you?"

"No."

"Good. Now, run and get ready for bed." He glanced at Christy. "Whose turn is it tonight? The princess or the knight?"

"The princess," Emma stated firmly. With Linc's one, innocently phrased question, eagerness replaced her downcast expression.

Christy was impressed by the way he'd turned his niece's ill-humor completely around. Was his success born out of experience or did he have an innate gift for handling children? Given his past, she suspected a combination of both were responsible.

"Okay, then. Off you go. The longer it takes you to get ready for bed, the shorter the story will be."

The two dashed off and Christy felt Linc's gaze. "What's wrong?" she asked.

"Nothing. I just wondered if you felt better now."

"I've felt fine all evening," she said, puzzled. "Why?"

"You were as fidgety as the kids. I assumed you were nervous."

She sank onto the sofa, surprised he'd noticed. "I was. I wanted everything perfect so Gail wouldn't worry about them or wonder if they'd made the right decision when they asked me, *us*, to watch them."

"Trust me, she saw two happy, healthy kids who were coping with their parents' absence quite well."

"I'm glad you think so."

"I do."

"Unca Linc!" Derek called from his bedroom. "We're ready!"

Laughing, he rose. "Now, if you'll excuse me, my fans await."

For a few minutes Christy listened to Linc's deep voice as he began his story. She couldn't hear the words, but she heard the tone and it touched her in ways she hadn't expected.

Idly, she wondered how Linc would deal with a diagnosis such as hers if delivered to *his* wife or girlfriend. Would he decide, as Jon had, that he hadn't bought a ticket for that particular movie and wasn't interested in doing so? Or would he see her through the entire process—the surgery, the chemo, more surgery, the endless waiting for test results?

She suspected he wouldn't leave his significant other hanging in similar circumstances. A man who'd taken on the care of his younger siblings as well as his grandmother while barely in his twenties wouldn't walk away from a woman he loved.

On the other hand, after taking on so many responsibilities at such a young age, he obviously wasn't interested in tying himself down because he was in his late thirties and didn't seem interested in changing his marital status. His career *was* both wife and mistress, so imagining him in Jon's place was pointless.

Life was what it was and fate had given her a fellow whose love hadn't been strong enough to face the challenges that had presented themselves. In hindsight, she was grateful to have discovered his character flaws before their relationship had become legal.

As for the future, self-preservation ruled the day. She wouldn't allow any man to get close until she received her five-year all-clear report. Without that medical reassurance, it wouldn't be fair to dump such a heavy burden on a guy. Waiting until then would also save her the trouble of dealing with heartache in addition to cancer, round two.

Aware of the hour, Christy tidied the living room, sent Ria outside for her last trip outdoors, then delivered her own share of goodnight hugs and kisses to Derek and Emma. For some reason, though, when they both turned away to leave Emma's bedside, the little girl clung to Linc and whispered in his ear.

"You should tell her," she heard him say.

"Please?" the little girl begged.

"Okay. I'll do it, but next time you have to 'fess up yourself."

"Thanks, Unca Linc."

Curious about what Emma considered so terrible that her uncle had to divulge it on her behalf, Christy held her questions until she'd called in Ria and they were both relaxing on the living-room sofa with the television volume turned low.

"What couldn't Emma tell me about?" she asked as she sipped on her cup of herbal tea.

"She went into your room today."

Considering all of her medications, vitamins, and supplements, which might pique a child's curiosity, Christy panicked. "She didn't swallow anything, did she? Ria didn't eat—"

"No, nothing like that."

She relaxed. "Good."

"Apparently Emma has this horrible fear you'd be furious if you knew she went into your room. She believes she's facing a fate worse than death and asked me to beg for mercy on her behalf."

Christy smiled at Linc's wry tone. "I told them I had things in my room that could make them or Ria sick, so it would be best if they didn't go inside unless I gave them permission." She didn't intend to explain what those things were; she simply hoped Linc would accept her simplified explanation as the kids had.

"Emma understands that, which was why she was worried."

"Out of curiosity, how did she end up there, anyway?"

"She and Ria were playing and somehow the two of them ended up in your room. In their exuberance, some of the bottles on your dresser rolled off. Nothing broke, so you shouldn't worry about that."

"Then no harm done, I'm sure," she said lightly.

"The problem was," he continued, "a few vials rolled behind and she couldn't reach them."

"Thanks for telling me. I would have wondered why some had disappeared. Before I go to bed I'll—"

"The lost have been found. I put the vials on top of your dresser with the others."

She swallowed hard. "You...did?" Then she plastered a wide smile on her face and pretended nonchalance. "How nice of you. Thanks."

"You're welcome."

At first, she believed she'd skated through that awkward moment with ease, but the compassion she saw on his face said otherwise. He might not ask questions—it would be rather forward of him to do so—but whether he did or didn't, his eyes held a *knowing* look that hadn't been present before.

Of the pills he'd retrieved, only one would have generated the curiosity and sympathy in his gaze—the one easily recognizable as a cancer treatment.

If she didn't say a word, she sensed he'd drop the subject, but it seemed cowardly not to address the obvious. It would become the elephant in the room they both tried to ignore and she would analyze his every remark and every glance for a hidden meaning.

She could handle anything from him except pity.

No, she didn't want that. Better to face the situation head-on.

"You know, don't you?" she asked.

CHAPTER FIVE

You know, don't you? Christy's question echoed in Linc's head and he paused to debate the merits of pretending ignorance. However easy it might seem in the moment, honesty had been and always would be the best policy.

Her eyes held resignation, as if she hated that her secret had been revealed, and he softened his own gaze. "I wasn't being curious. I didn't intend to read the label, it just happened."

From the way Christy visibly hunched her shoulders in an effort to draw inside herself, Linc knew he'd thrown her off balance. He had plenty of questions, but there were times to speak and times to listen. At the moment, listening seemed to be the most appropriate course of action.

Had anyone else told him news of this sort, he would have reacted in a most clinical, detached manner. With Christy, however, his detachment had flown out the window.

Sensing her mental turmoil, he scooted closer to lend his comfort and encouragement. She stiffened in his one-armed hug as if she didn't want to accept his support, but gradually the tension in her body eased.

Silence hung in the air as she continued to cradle her teacup, but Linc waited.

"You're probably wondering why I never told you," she began.

"Not really." At her startled glance, he explained. "I'm not your physician or..." He wanted to say *your lover* but caught himself. "Or more than a casual acquaintance, so I understand why you haven't shared your personal issues with me. I assume Gail knows?"

"We hadn't shared too many yoga classes before I told her. One doesn't keep many secrets from the ladies at the gym," she said wryly. "For the record, though, my having breast cancer doesn't diminish my ability to look after Derek and Emma."

"Of course not," he answered quickly, to soothe her obvious fears that somehow he'd find her lacking. It also made sense as to why she'd been so worried about the children's appearance for tonight's internet call and had driven herself frantic to make everything perfect. She wanted to prove she could handle the job.

"Good, because for the time being I'm perfectly healthy."

His mental cogs clicked together. "Then Emma wasn't far off the mark, was she? The pet she'd heard you mention was a PET *scan*, not a four-legged animal."

She nodded, a small smile curving her vulnerable mouth. "Yes. My five-year check-up is due a few days after Gail and Ty return, so you don't have to worry about—"

He snagged onto the time frame she'd divulged. "Five years?"

"I was twenty-four when I was diagnosed, which gives me the dubious honor of being one of those rare young people who develop breast cancer. Mine was a particularly aggressive type, so I opted for a double mastectomy."

Knowing what he did about the drug she was taking, her tumor had also been estrogen-receptor positive, which meant estrogen fueled the cancer. Tamoxifen would stop production of the hormone so the abnormal cells couldn't multiply.

"Speaking from a medical standpoint, you made a wise decision."

She shrugged. "It was the only one I *could* make. Because you're curious, as are most men, all this..." she motioned to her chest "...is courtesy of a skilled plastic surgeon and reconstruction."

Admittedly, he enjoyed seeing those curves and fantasizing about them, but he considered himself more of a leg man. Picturing her long legs and those miles of smooth skin wrapped around his waist was one strong image that would keep him awake at night. "I'm not most men."

She grew thoughtful. "You're not, are you?"

He wasn't sure if she was paying him a compliment or not. "As for worrying about your ability to look after Derek and Emma, I'm not. I merely wanted to say that whatever you need to do, whenever you need to do it, we'll handle the logistics."

"Thanks, but for now I only need to swallow my pills, eat right, and take care of myself, which is what every other person on the planet should do."

"True." Thinking of his upcoming week, he leaned forward. "About the taking-care-of-yourself part, one of my colleagues is still on vacation. I won't be able to pull my share of the load until next weekend so unfortunately you'll have to carry the extra burden. After that, things should settle down considerably."

In light of Christy's revelation, he'd make sure he was available after that. Although he sensed she wouldn't appreciate being treated as gently as if she were blown glass, he'd make a point to stay alert and step in whenever she needed extra help. Gail and Ty really had been smart to ask them to share parenting duties. They'd obviously foreseen areas of potential problems and had prepared for them. Now it was his turn to do the same.

"Thanks for the warning," she said.

"Meanwhile, I don't want you to physically do more than you should. You don't have to be Super-Aunt. No one is holding you to an impossible standard, least of all me."

He'd expected her to appreciate his support, but instead she bristled. "I'm quite capable of taking care of the kids, maintaining the house, and doing my job at the hospital. This is precisely why I don't blurt out my history to everyone I meet. People tend to wrap me in cotton wool and treat me like an invalid, but I'm *not*."

"Of course you aren't," he said, realizing she'd misinterpreted his intent. "I was trying to be considerate. That's all. I don't want you to be afraid I'll complain if I come home and find dishes in the sink."

Her hackles seemed to drop. "Sorry. I get a little defensive sometimes. It really bugs me when I'm told I can't or shouldn't do something because I had cancer."

So many things now made sense, from her can-do, full-steam-ahead attitude to the myriad daring activities that most people would shun. "Offends your overdeveloped sense of independence, does it?"

Color rose in her face. "It does," she admitted. "That's why…"

When she stopped in midsentence, he filled in the blanks. "That's why you go skydiving, white-water rafting, and all the other physically challenging hobbies you're known for."

Her eyes widened. "How did you know?"

"It was a logical assumption. Anyone trying to prove themselves usually chooses a task that most people wouldn't dream of doing."

"I haven't done anything *that* bizarre or unusual," she pointed out. "Lots of people go white-water rafting."

"Sure, but skydiving?"

"Okay, so that's not quite as popular, but my little excursions are my way to celebrate a good medical report. Some people reward themselves with chocolate. I work on my bucket list."

He was relieved to know she wasn't a thrill-seeker, as he'd thought; she was only working her way through a list of experiences. He instantly felt small for misjudging her motives.

"So what's on tap for this year?" he asked. "Bungee-jumping? Swimming with sharks? Diving for sunken treasure?"

"My list consists of things I want to do before I kick the proverbial bucket, not the things that would kill me in the process," she said wryly. "The first two you mentioned are definitely out, although..." she tapped her mouth with her forefinger "...the sunken treasure idea has possibilities, provided I find time to learn how to scuba dive."

He chuckled. "I stand corrected. So what's left?"

"A trip to Paris. Walking on a glacier. Yodeling in the Swiss Alps. Watching my nieces and nephews graduate from college. They're younger than Derek and Emma—my sister has two boys and my brother has two girls and a boy. It'll be a while until I can cross off that entry and I intend to be around until I do."

He smiled at her determination and applauded her for it. "Do they live around here?"

"They live in the Seattle area near my mom. My family wasn't happy when I moved to the Midwest, but they understood."

He suspected she'd relocated as a way to assert her independence. However, it didn't take much imagination to picture the resistance Christy had encountered when she'd announced her plans to leave the bosom of her family. He'd spent weeks trying to convince his own sister to accept the promotion her company had offered here in Levitt Springs, but she'd wanted to strike out on her own, too. He would have preferred having her only fifteen minutes away instead of ninety, but she had to live life on her terms, not his. In the grand scheme of things, however, she was relatively close and he could bridge the distance with a mere hop and a skip.

"Then your family was your support group?" he asked.

"I don't think I would have kept going if not for them and my friends. They drove me to doctors' appointments and chemo sessions when I couldn't, loaded my refrigerator with chicken soup, and took me shopping at Victoria's Secret when my reconstruction was completed. They were the greatest. Everyone should have support like I did."

That explained the scrappy underwear he'd found. Unfortunately, being reminded of her lingerie made him wonder what color she was wearing today.

Yanking his mind off that dead-end track, he noticed one significant absence in her list of supportive people. "Assuming you had a boyfriend, where was he in all this?"

She let out a deep sigh of apparent resignation. As if recognizing her mistress's inner turmoil, Ria padded to the sofa and rested her jaw on Christy's knee. She scratched the dog's ears and met his gaze. "He took off."

He wasn't surprised; he'd seen enough in his own practice to know that some people simply couldn't handle illness, whether it was their own or their spouse's, but the idea of leaving someone under those circumstances was beyond his ability to comprehend.

"What happened?"

"Jon seemed to accept my diagnosis through the talk of lumpectomies, chemotherapy, losing my hair, et cetera, until the word 'mastectomy' was mentioned. When 'double' was added to the table as the best course of action, even though he knew I planned to undergo reconstruction so I'd have my figure back by Christmas, he freaked out."

"So he left."

"Not immediately. The final straw came when he learned I'd need hormone suppression therapy for at least five years and my ovaries might or might not wake up and be ready to work. He wanted kids of his own, through the usual method and not through special medical means, so he wished me luck, kissed me goodbye, and I never saw or heard from him again."

In his disgust Linc muttered an expletive that would have shocked the most hardened longshoreman.

She burst out laughing, clapping her hands over her mouth as her eyes twinkled the entire time. "My, my, Dr Maguire. I'd scold you for your language but those are my sentiments exactly."

He grinned. "It's nice to know we're on the same page." After a brief hesitation he spoke again. "He's the reason you won't date until your next scan, isn't he?"

"I date," she protested mildly. "Just not often and it's never serious. I make that plain from the beginning."

"Do you explain why?"

She looked at him with a measure of horror. "Of course not. Actually, that's not quite true. I'd gone out with someone before I moved to Levitt Springs two years ago."

Instinctively, he knew this story wouldn't have a happy ending either, but knowledge was power and he wanted the facts so he knew exactly what demons she was fighting. "What happened?"

"Nothing. I shared everything I've told you—maybe not quite *everything*..." her smile was rueful "...but Anthony knew about my cancer and the surgeries. We had a wonderful evening."

She paused and he sensed a "but" was coming.

"After he took me home, I never heard from him again," she finished.

He cursed under his breath and she smiled. "It wasn't that

bad," she told him. "We only went out once. When I realized he wouldn't call, I was disappointed but not crushed. After that, I moved here and decided to keep my tale to myself. Some women tell everyone they meet about their cancer experience and I understand why they do. The more women realize it could happen to them—at any age—the better, but for me, I want people to see me for who I am, not for what I've gone through in the past or might in the future."

"Aren't you selling us short? You shouldn't assume all men are as weak-willed and lacking in character as those two."

"I know," she admitted, "but I can't take the risk. If a particular relationship is meant to be, it'll happen at the right time, under my terms."

He hated that she'd lumped all men in the same category, himself included. "When did Ria appear on the scene?"

"After Jon disappeared to find the new love of his life, my brother brought me a puppy. She was beautiful, happy, and loved the water, so I named her Ria. She also had the biggest paws, which made me afraid she was part horse, but in the end she was my best friend and was there whenever I needed a warm body to hold on to."

Once again, he had an uncommon urge to hunt down this Jon character and do him bodily harm. As special as Ria was, Christy should have had a real person holding her during those dark days and nights. In fact, he wished he'd known her at the time because he couldn't imagine leaving her. A person didn't desert the one he loved.

Yet he was glad this guy had decamped, otherwise *he* might never have met her. The possibility of living the rest of his life without her waltzing into it drove the air out of his lungs like a fist to his solar plexus.

"Now you know my whole sordid tale," she said lightly, "and why fundraising for the cancer center and the Relay for Life organization is important to me."

"You could be the hospital's poster child for the event," he pointed out.

"I could, but I won't. I'll leave that to someone else." She grinned. "I'm going to be too busy getting my dance partner up to speed for the competition."

"Speaking of which, did you have to drag *me* into your plan?" he said in mock complaint.

"I did," she stated innocently, although her eyes sparkled with humor. "You always walk into the unit so completely focused on nursing notes and lab reports that I decided you should get involved on a more personal level."

"I'm involved," he protested mildly. Being conscious of her fragrance and the softness of her skin, he could think of at least one other activity in which he'd like to involve himself. "I write a check and it comes out of my *personal* bank account."

One of her eyebrows arched high. "Writing a check is nice, but it isn't *participation*."

"Well, thanks to you, I'm participating now," he complained good-naturedly.

She giggled. "You are, aren't you?"

While his apprehension about sailing around the floor in front of a group of people hadn't faded, it seemed small and insignificant when compared to Christy's challenges. Spending an evening in the company of a woman who embraced life to the degree that she did wouldn't be the royal pain in the backside that he'd first thought. Perish the thought, but, to borrow her phrase, it would probably be...fun.

"I'm warning you, though. After this week, when I don't have to cover so many extra shifts, we're going to start practicing," he said firmly. "And I do mean *practice*."

A small wrinkle formed between her eyebrows. "I was only teasing about getting my dance partner up to speed."

"You have may have been teasing, but I'm not."

"Need I remind you this is only a friendly event? No one is expecting you to be Patrick Swayze."

"If they are, they'll be sorely disappointed, but if something is worth doing—and you keep telling me it is," he added wryly, "then we're going to do it well."

As he saw her smile, he asked, "What's so funny?"

The grin disappeared, but the humor remained in her eyes. "Nothing," she said innocently. "If you want to practice, we'll practice."

The cuckoo suddenly chirped eleven times, which caught Linc by surprise. He wondered where the hours had gone, but he'd been so engrossed in Christy's story that he hadn't noticed how quickly the evening had passed.

"I'd better start the dishwasher before I forget." She rose out of his loose embrace. "Then I'm turning in."

As he followed suit, his arm felt empty and almost unnatural, as if his body sensed what his mind could not—that she belonged there. Not just for a few minutes or over the course of a conversation, but for years and years.

Perhaps it was time he reconsidered a few points he'd etched in stone. The ideal woman he'd hoped to find—the one with steady, dependable traits—suddenly didn't seem quite as attractive she had a few weeks ago. Being with Christy had made his nameless, faceless future wife seem so…colorless, so black and white.

He now wanted color in his life.

Out of habit, he checked the front door to be sure the deadbolt was thrown, and armed the alarm system.

It was such a husbandly sort of thing to do, he decided as he waited for her to return so he could turn off the lights. Yes, he knew she could flick the switch as easily as he could, but he'd reverted back to his early days when his family had been together. He had always been the last to go to bed because, as the man of the house, he'd accepted the responsibility of securing their home for the night. Old habits, as he'd told Christy, definitely died hard because he'd fallen back into them as if it were only yesterday.

He heard the water running into the dishwasher, then the rhythmic swish as it circulated, but she still hadn't reappeared. Wondering what had delayed her, he meandered into the kitchen and found her with her hands planted on the counter, head down.

"Is something wrong?" he asked.

She straightened immediately and turned toward him, but he saw the too-forced smile. "Why do you ask?"

"You looked as if you were a few hundred miles away."

Her smile was small. "I suppose I was," she said slowly. "For years I haven't thought about some of the things I shared tonight. I'd pushed Jon and the incident with Anthony completely out of my mind, but remembering the way it was... now my emotions are a little tangled."

He didn't believe she had pushed those two experiences out of her head as much as she thought she had. The fact that she intended to hold any fellow at arm's length until she passed her magical five-year date proved that both men's rejections continued to color her relationships.

"Understandable," he said, "but I'm honored you opened up to me. For the record, though, if you hadn't have volunteered the information, I wouldn't have pressed."

"The story was bound to come out sooner or later. You can't share a house with someone and keep any secrets," she said ruefully. "I trust, though, you'll hold everything in confidence? It's not that I don't want anyone in Levitt Springs to know, but I'd rather tell people in my own time and in my own way."

"I won't say a word."

"Thanks."

He sensed the absence of her normally confident air and

he felt somewhat responsible. If he'd pretended ignorance about the pills, denied any knowledge of what he'd seen, she wouldn't be reliving the sting of her ex-boyfriend's rejection.

Impulsively, feeling as if he needed to comfort her as he would a distraught Emma, he covered the distance and drew her against him. "Jon was, and still is, an ass," he murmured against her hair. "For that matter, so is Anthony."

She shook in his arms and he didn't know if she was laughing or crying until she spoke. Then he heard the hoarse, telltale quiver in her voice. "They are."

"You're better off without them."

"I am," she agreed.

"Jon definitely didn't deserve you."

"He didn't."

She sounded as if she was repeating the arguments she'd used before. He pulled away just enough so he could tip up her chin and stare into her chocolate-brown eyes. "A fellow with any brains would be happy to call you his, cancer diagnosis or not."

She licked her bottom lip before squeezing out a weak smile. "Thanks for the thought."

His gaze landed on her mouth and he instantly realized she was definitely *not* Emma by any stretch of his imagination. He had an uncontrollable urge to determine if her lips would fit his as well as her body did, and if they tasted as delicious as he suspected. Before he could restrain himself, he bent his head and kissed her.

It was a chaste kiss, one meant to console, but not only did that contact pack a powerful punch, it also ignited a hunger inside him.

Gradually, he increased the pressure, waiting for her to respond to his lead, and to his utter delight she did. He caressed her back, carefully encouraging her to lean closer until he finally felt her weight settle against him. Little by little, he inched one hand toward her bare shoulder. Entranced by the smooth skin, he trailed his fingers along the bones before stopping at the hollow of her throat.

He'd run his fingers along the skin of countless patients, but his touch had been clinical as he'd felt for lumps, bumps, and other signs of illness. This time it was different. This time his sensitive fingertips noticed softness while his nose picked up the fresh, floral scent that was pure Christy.

Stopping was impossible; it seemed crucial to catalogue every inch of her, although he was cautious of what he suspected were her well-defined boundaries. But her skin was warm and his five senses conspired against his good sense until his fingers traveled an inch lower and she suddenly pulled away.

Puzzled, he stared at her, wondering if he'd touched a tender spot, but as he glanced at the point where his hand had roamed on her sternum, he mentally kicked himself for his insensitivity. Clearly, she thought he intended to stray deeper into what she considered forbidden territory.

"I should go to bed," she said, her voice breathy as if she'd been jogging for a mile. "Goodnight."

"Goodnight," he answered to her back as she fled. His night, however, couldn't end with him in his current state. He'd work off his tension in Ty's basement weight room and if that didn't resolve his problem, a cold shower would come next.

All because of the sixty seconds she'd spent in his arms.

Christy spent the next twenty-four hours scolding herself for overreacting to Linc's touch. His gentle caresses hadn't been inappropriate and yet she'd jumped like a frightened virgin.

The truth was she'd enjoyed being in his arms far more than she'd dreamed possible. He was solid and warm and comforting, which gave her such a deep sense of safety—

almost as if she was being protected from the latest of life's impending storms. More than that, though, he reminded her of a steady rock she could lean on whenever the need arose.

In spite of all that, she'd jumped away from him like a startled rabbit, she thought with disgust.

She might have apologized, but she didn't see him at all on Monday, although she knew he had come home because he'd left a glass in the sink and a scribbled note on the counter, asking her to pick up his clothes at the dry cleaner's. *Please*, he'd underlined in thick, bold strokes.

On Tuesday, she saw him at the hospital, but other than a quick "How are the kids?" their conversation had been limited to the status of his patients.

She didn't see him at all on Wednesday, but once again she'd found a note. This time he'd stated how much he'd liked the oatmeal cookies she'd left for him. She'd seen his distinctive scrawl before and thought nothing of it, but his personal message—his compliment—brightened her day. Because she was off duty and intended to spend her hours on household chores and laundry, she needed that bright spot.

Since the kids were in school, she vowed to tackle household projects. She cleaned furiously, debating for the longest time if she should go into Linc's room in case he'd think she was invading his privacy. Finally, after she'd cleaned bedrooms and the community bathroom, she caved in to her own arguments. The man hardly had time to breathe, so he certainly wasn't going to spend his free hours dusting and scrubbing the tub. As neat as he was, he wouldn't notice she'd been in his domain, anyway.

She, however, certainly did. The masculine scent of his bath soap hovered in the bathroom and clung to his towels. Even his bed sheets retained his personal fragrance.

He left more than his scent behind, though. She found other clues that fit the man she knew him to be. The unmade bed suggested he'd been called out early, but even the rumpled bedding testified to Linc's control. A faint indentation of his head on the pillow and one corner of the sheet pulled out from under the mattress hinted that he wasn't a restless sleeper—probably because when he finally closed his eyes, he was too exhausted to move.

Idly, she wondered what he'd be like to sleep with. Would he snuggle up close, like Ria did when it was cold outside, or stick to his side of the bed? Would he pull her toward him or move to the center to meet her?

As she caught herself in her own daydream, she chuckled with embarrassment and was grateful that he wouldn't walk in and discover her locked within her own wicked imagination.

She stripped the bed, forcing a clinical detachment to complete the job.

His full laundry hamper presented another problem. It seemed a horrible waste of water to ask him to launder his things separately—again, when would he even have time?—so she gathered his washables and added them to her other loads, all the while trying not to notice how wifely it felt for his T-shirts and unmentionables to mingle with her own.

Determined to keep her thoughts occupied, she dusted and scrubbed and vacuumed until Ria fled the house for the quiet safety of the back yard. She left nothing unturned, and had even gone into Ty's basement weight room where she'd found a few dirty towels. By the time Emma and Derek were out of school, the place was spotless and she was literally exhausted.

They strolled to the park to exercise Ria and came home at dinnertime, but once again Linc didn't put in an appearance. She didn't see him until the next day at the hospital and then she was certain it was only because Thursday was his normal scheduled surgery day. One of his patients had just been wheeled to a room after waking up in Recovery and Linc had walked in to talk to the man's wife, wearing his green scrubs.

After they'd dealt with the usual order of patient business, he pulled her aside. "When can you get away for lunch?"

"It's hard to say," she admitted. "We're swamped today."

"Make time."

She was tired enough to bristle at his demand—between keeping up with two busy children, a house, and working a short-staffed twelve-hour shift, she now understood why her working-mother colleagues had fragile tempers by the end of the week—but she had to eat and if she didn't take a break soon, her feet would revolt.

"Maybe by one or so," she began.

"Okay. I'll see you then."

He strode away before she could recover from her surprise. As far as the gossip mill had reported, the man rarely took time for himself between his surgical cases and when he did, he usually ate on the run. Could it be he was finally loosening up and becoming more approachable? She smiled at the thought.

Yet as she watched him pause to talk to a pharmacist, then laugh at whatever she'd said, her self-satisfaction dimmed as an unreasonable combination of curiosity and jealousy flooded over her.

Was this the woman he'd mentioned he'd wanted to get to know? If so, then her plan to convince him to enjoy life's simpler pleasures might drive him into another woman's arms.

It was silly of her to consider the possibility. After all, she didn't have any illusions that she was his type.

But, oh, it was nice to dream...

Linc's work schedule for the week hadn't been that unusual for him, but throughout the day—especially during the evenings—he'd caught himself wondering what Christy and the kids might be doing. Knowing that he was missing out had made him impatient at times and he'd earned a number of startled glances from his staff who obviously wondered what had twisted his surgical gloves into a knot.

Each night as he came home he half hoped Christy would be waiting for him, as she had on that first night. Logically, he knew he was expecting too much. Ten-thirty or eleven was late for someone who went to work at five a.m. Not being accustomed to keeping up with two active children, she probably ended her day as soon as Emma and Derek did.

Illogically, he still hoped.

Whenever he walked into a quiet house, those hopes deflated, although he was pleased by her gesture of leaving the kitchen light blazing so he wouldn't stumble in the dark in the somewhat unfamiliar surroundings.

While she might not physically make an appearance, he felt her presence in other ways—a plate of food in the refrigerator, a pan of frosted brownies on the stove, clean towels in Ty's weight room. Only one thing could have topped them all—if he'd been able to slip into her bed instead of his.

With great relief, he saw his hectic week finally drawing to a close. He could hardly wait another day to talk to her in person instead of through hastily scribbled notes left on the kitchen counter. Yes, he'd seen her a few times at the hospital, but they'd both been coming and going, so conversation had been limited to medical issues.

Today, though, he'd decided to make a change. Before his last case, he'd shocked his surgery staff when he'd announced a thirty-minute break between patients, but he didn't care that he'd wrecked his own routine. He only knew he couldn't wait until Friday night or Saturday morning to see Christy again, and maybe…steal another kiss.

In fact, he couldn't remember the last time he'd been this eager to meet someone. His job had meant so much to him that it had consumed his existence until most of the personal side of his life had faded away. He'd become somewhat aware of the situation—his time with his brother's family had pointed out what he was missing—but he hadn't discovered a compelling reason to change the habits he'd formed.

Christy had provided it.

A week ago, he'd believed she wasn't right for him with her daring, impulsive approach to life. Oh, he'd been drawn to her like a hapless bug flew toward light, but, given enough opportunity, he was certain he'd eventually purge her from his system. Now, a mere seven days later, it was the last thing he wanted.

His attitude was odd, really. They'd spent more time apart than together, and yet everything he'd seen, everything he'd heard, and everything he'd done only whetted his appetite for more.

The good news was, "more" hung right around the corner.

He returned to the surgery floor at the appointed hour with five minutes to spare, then waited for her to swap an IV fluid bag that had run low. He chafed at the delay, but he was only minutes away from having her to himself, relatively speaking, so he hid his impatience by accessing several lab reports while he listened for her footsteps.

When she returned breathlessly, as if she'd hurried on his account, her smile was worth the wait.

In the cafeteria, he steered her toward a table for two in the corner near the aquarium. Aware of the curious glances directed toward them, he simply ignored everyone and focused on Christy.

"You look tired," he said without preamble as she poured her low-fat dressing over her chef's salad.

"Is it that obvious?" she asked ruefully.

He shrugged as he dug into his roast beef special. "Only to me. You aren't doing too much, are you?"

"Probably, but that's how it works," she quipped. "To be honest, you're looking a little frayed around the edges, too. You aren't the only one with keen powers of observation."

"Apparently not," he answered dryly, surprised she'd picked up the signals others had overlooked. He immediately wondered what else she'd deduced about him. If she had any idea of how easily she triggered a surge in his testosterone level, she'd probably lock herself in her bedroom and never come out.

"I don't know where I'm busier—here at work or at home with the kids. We haven't had a dull moment."

"I've seen the calendar Gail left for us. Next week will be better."

"I don't see how. Between soccer practice two nights and a Cub Scout meeting—"

"I'll be available to help," he interrupted. "The load won't fall completely on you. I'm sorry it did this week, but it won't happen again."

"Don't apologize. A doctor's life doesn't run on a schedule. If it's any consolation, the kids have missed you."

"I've missed you all, too. How did the internet call go last night? No tears when it was all over?"

"A few, but not many. Emma's having a ball, sending emails. You created a monster when you created her own account and showed her how to send letters. I think she's singlehandedly trying to fill her mom's in-box."

"Maybe we should limit her to one or two a day."

"Keeping her too busy to think about sending a message would be better. Forbidding her to contact Gail will only make her more homesick and she'll dwell more on her parents' absence than she should."

He considered her comment. "You're probably right."

"Don't worry. She'll get past this. We simply need to be patient."

"How did you get to be so wise with kids?"

She tipped her bottle of lemonade and drank deeply. "I learned a lot from watching my brother and sisters interact with their children. How about you?"

"My parents constantly reminded me that as the oldest I had to look out for the younger siblings no matter where we were or what we were doing. I'm afraid I wasn't always tactful," he said wryly.

"Ah, you were the bossy older brother."

"Afraid so. I suppose I had more of a dictatorial style, but I think that came from being left in charge so often. My mom had a fantastic voice and a dream to make it big in the country-music scene, so my dad hauled us all over so she could perform and it was my job to keep the little ones busy. As soon as I turned thirteen, they left the three of us at home."

"What did you do to occupy the time?"

"Board games, cards, whatever. You name it, we played it. If I had a dime for every round of *Chutes and Ladders* or *Sorry*, I'd be a wealthy man," he said wryly. "In any case, our main goal was to be awake when our parents came home."

"Were you successful?"

He shook his head. "No. Joanie would usually conk out around eleven, Ty would fall asleep at midnight, and one was my limit."

"Did they do that often? Leave you home alone?"

"Every Saturday night."

"That must have been tough."

He considered for a moment. "It wasn't as tough as it was frustrating. The little kids needed their attention, not mine. I knew my parents loved us, but at times I resented how easily they left us to chase their own dreams."

And that, he knew, was the main reason why he hadn't been in any rush to look for Mrs Right. Although his job guaranteed there would be times when he'd be gone at night, just as his parents had been, he wanted the mother of his children to be a mother twenty-four seven, not just when it was convenient.

"Regardless of their actions, they must have done something right," she said softly. "You and Ty both turned into responsible adults."

They had, hadn't they? he thought.

"Your story does explain why you take life so seriously," she remarked. "Didn't you ever do anything just for fun?"

"Sure. I hung out with my buddies on Friday nights after football and basketball games. Band kids had to stick together."

"Marching band?"

"I was quite the trumpet player in my day," he said proudly.

"Can you still play?"

"I doubt it." He grinned. "Fortunately for you, I sold my trumpet so we'll never know. By the way, the house looks great. You've been busy."

"I'm surprised you could see a difference. You haven't been home much."

He couldn't tell if she was peeved by his absence or surprised that he was aware of his surroundings even if he came home during the wee hours. He grinned. "You'd be surprised at what I notice. Speaking of which, I don't expect you to clean my room or do my laundry."

"I'm sure you didn't, but I couldn't very well let your room turn into a pigsty, could I? Gail would kill me."

"Actually, she'd kill *me*," he said wryly. "Regardless, I don't want you taking on more than you need to. I'll ask my housekeeper to add us to her list and—"

"You'll do no such thing." Her voice was firm. "I'm perfectly capable of performing a few chores."

"It isn't a matter of capabilities." He had to tread lightly because he hated to offend her independent spirit. "It's a matter of having enough hours in the day."

"We'll make time. If everyone pitches in, cleaning won't take long at all. 'Many hands make light work,' my mother always says."

"Yes, but, as far as I'm concerned, paying a housekeeper is money well spent."

"I'm sure it is, but I wouldn't feel right if you footed the bill. We're in this together, remember, and, as far as I'm concerned, it's an unnecessary expense."

Her light tone didn't disguise the steel in her voice. He wanted to continue to argue his point, but his gaze landed on the fraying edge of her scrub top's neckline. Nurses might be paid well these days, but thanks to the associated expenses of her illness he suspected money was still tight.

Although he wanted this to be his contribution to the household, he didn't press the issue. "Okay, we'll do it your way. For now," he tacked on his proviso.

"Fair enough."

"So you know, if I had my choice as to what I'd like you to do—cook or clean—I'd choose cooking. What are the odds of getting another batch of those cookies?"

She laughed, clearly amused by his hopeful tone. "That depends on when Derek is scheduled to provide treats for another soccer game."

"Ah, that explains why I couldn't find any more. You gave them away."

She finished her salad. "I did, but you liked them, did you?"

"The best oatmeal cookies I ever tasted."

"Somehow I never saw you as having a sweet tooth."

"I do, which is why I work out three or four times a week. I'm surprised you haven't heard me in the basement."

"You actually exercise when you get home?" She sounded incredulous.

"Sometimes," he admitted. "Lifting weights helps me work out the kinks if I've been in surgery all day. Sometimes I'm too keyed up to go to sleep, so pumping iron helps."

"Wow. I usually stare mindlessly at the television when I'm exhausted. I'm impressed you're that...disciplined."

"Impressed enough to make another batch of cookies?"

She giggled. "Okay. I'll let you get lucky this weekend."

If she didn't catch the double entendre of her own words, he certainly did. As he glanced at the aquarium and saw those same fish kissing again, he realized his craving went beyond mere cookies. He wanted another taste of Christy and he wanted it as soon as possible.

Getting that taste wouldn't be easy. Underneath her bubbly personality and a layer of friendliness lurked a skittish woman who'd been hurt by someone she'd trusted.

It would be up to him to prove that he was someone she could trust.

CHAPTER SIX

By Friday, Christy knew she was in trouble. Dredging up the old memories of Jon had fueled her determination to prove that just because she'd had cancer, she was still capable of doing everything any other woman could do. As a result, she'd pushed herself too hard and was paying the price with her nauseous stomach and the headache behind her eyes. She should have been at home because it was her day off, but someone had called in with a family emergency, so as soon as Christy had sent the kids to school, she'd reported to work.

She would have rather spent the day in bed.

There was one silver lining to this dark cloud—she'd arrived on duty after Linc had already made his rounds, otherwise he would have taken one look at her and with the telltale twitch in his cheek to indicate his unhappiness he would have insisted she return home. Naturally, she would have had to disobey his command on principle. She was still her own woman and made her own decisions even if, in this case, he was right.

Fortunately, her supervisor had also arranged for a second-shift nurse to come early, so Christy was able to leave as soon as Derek and Emma's school day ended.

She swallowed several anti-inflammatories and painkillers, and soldiered on through the rest of the afternoon—even making Linc's requested cookies—but by dinner's end her own food refused to stay in her stomach and she finally had to face facts. Her body had reached its limit.

"Are you guys ready for bed?" she asked, hoping she sounded brighter than she felt.

Derek was horrified. "We never go to bed at seven, even on school nights. Fridays is our night to stay up late 'cause Mom wants us to sleep in on Saturdays."

"Yeah," Emma chimed in. "It is."

"Then you do sleep late on Saturdays?" Christy asked, because so far they hadn't.

Derek's grin was sheepish. "Sometimes, but if we don't and Mom or Dad aren't awake, we know not to bother them."

Thank you, Gail, for training them properly, she thought with some relief. "I'd suggest you snooze as long as you can. We have a full day tomorrow."

Derek was suspicious. "Doing what?"

She had no idea, but surely Linc had a plan. "I have to discuss it with your uncle first," she prevaricated.

"We can watch a movie now, can't we?" Derek asked.

"Yeah." Emma's head bobbed enthusiastically. "Mom lets us on a Friday."

She hated to park them in front of the television, but common sense told her that Gail and Ty allowed them to watch their movies if the size of the children's collection was any indication. As for leaving them alone, she also knew their parents didn't hover over them every second. They were school-aged children, not toddlers who required constant supervision.

"Okay, but after that, it's bedtime."

"Sure." Emma peered at her. "You don't look so good, Christy. Are you sick?"

She managed a smile. "A little. I'm going to lie down, but I want you to get me if you need anything. Anything at all. Is that understood?"

"Sure."

"And don't eat all the cookies. Save some for your uncle."

"We will," the two said in unison.

"Don't forget to wake me in half an hour or when your uncle arrives, whichever comes first."

"We will."

As the opening credits appeared on the screen, Christy dropped onto her bed. Ria padded in and curled against her in her usual, I'm-here-for-you-because-I-know-you-don't-feel-well position.

Christy patted the dog's head in gratitude for her faithfulness before she promptly closed her eyes and tried to relax.

"All I need are thirty minutes," she murmured aloud. "Just thirty minutes and I'll be ready to go. Linc will never know I couldn't keep up. How much trouble can two kids cause while watching a movie, anyway?"

Linc was more than ready to be home. His hospital patients were stable, including the emergency splenectomy case, and, barring a car accident, he should have a quiet evening ahead of him.

He strode into the house at seven forty-five, expecting to see three smiling faces eager to enjoy the remaining daylight. Instead, he walked into a kitchen that resembled a disaster area, with stacks of dirty pots and pans, spilled juice, and a popcorn trail that led into the living room.

Before he could wrap his head around the unusual scene, Emma came running and launched herself into his arms.

"Unca Linc's home!"

"Hi, sprout. How are you?" he asked as he settled her on his hip.

"I'm fine. Christy's sick."

Emma's revelation explained the mess. Immediately, he tried to recall what bug was making the rounds now, and came up blank. "She is? Was she sick all day?"

Emma shrugged. "Just since dinner. She's in bed so you hafta be quiet. Derek and I are watching a movie. We missed you, Unca Linc." She flung her arms around his neck and hugged him.

Not for the first time in his life, Linc was envious of his brother. This was what Ty came home to every night, not an empty house with a radio or television for company.

This, he decided—coming home to a wife and kids and even an occasional mess—was what he wanted, too. Preferably sooner rather than later.

"We missed you."

"I missed you, too." He prodded for information. "What's wrong with Christy?"

"I think it's her stomach because I heard her throwing up. She told us to wake her when you came home. Do you want me to get her?"

"That's okay. I'll check on her myself," he told her as he lowered her until her feet touched the floor.

"Christy left a plate for you in the 'frigerator," Emma offered helpfully, before she headed for the living room. "I'm gonna watch the rest of our movie."

Whatever Christy had served definitely smelled delicious and from the looks of the pots and pans on the stove, she'd served spaghetti. Although he wanted to dig into his own serving, he chose to wait until he discovered what was wrong with Christy.

He strolled through the living room, past the two children, who were engrossed in their movie, and stopped at Christy's door. When she didn't answer his knock, he peeked inside and saw her lying in bed with a watchful Ria at her side.

"Christy?" he asked softly.

She stirred. "Linc?"

"It's me," he assured her. "I hear you're not feeling well."

"I'm okay. Dinner's in—"

"The refrigerator. Emma told me." He strode in and stood next to her bed, worried that whatever had hit her had laid her so low and so quickly.

"I still need to clean the kitchen." She grimaced as she tried to rise.

"The kitchen can wait. Do I need to phone your doctor? Call in a prescription?" He imagined all sorts of possible causes and treatments—some dire, some run-of-the-mill—as he gently placed his hand on her forehead. Her skin felt cool, which eased his worries to some degree.

"No. Please, no. It's nothing."

He disagreed. "What's wrong? Stomach flu?" He'd already ruled out a chest cold because she breathed easily and her nose wasn't running.

"No, just overtired."

"Overtired?" His momentary panic eased. "I thought you agreed to pace yourself."

"I know, and I tried, but I felt so wonderful and thought I could do it all, so I did. Unfortunately, pushing my limits caught up to me today." She met his gaze for an instant before she closed her eyes. "I know you want to, so go ahead and scold."

She sounded defeated as well as sick, so he opted for mercy. "I'll wait until you're feeling better," he teased. "It's tough to kick a man—or woman—when she's already down."

"Thanks. Just give me another hour or so. I'll feel better by then. Honest."

Linc doubted it. Her face was too pale and the circles under her eyes too dark for him to believe a mere hour's nap would solve her problems, but he didn't intend to argue with her.

"Okay," he said evenly. "Can I get you something in the meantime? Hot tea? Aspirin?"

"I'm fine, thanks, although I'd appreciate it if you could let Ria outdoors. She hasn't had a bathroom break for a while."

"Will do." He snapped his fingers. "Come, Ria. Outside?"

Ria perked her ears as if she wanted to obey, but from the way she glanced at Christy, then back at him, she was torn between obeying nature's call and comforting her mistress.

"Come on, girl," he coaxed. "Take care of business and you can join Christy again."

Reluctantly, Ria rose, stretched, then gracefully leaped off the bed. Linc opened the patio door and as soon as Ria returned from a trip to her favorite bush, she ignored the tasty popcorn trail and disappeared into Christy's bedroom.

Certain the animal was now cuddled against her owner, Linc had one thought as he microwaved his dinner.

He was jealous of a dog.

After he'd eaten, washed the dishes, changed into a pair of comfortable gym shorts and an old T-shirt, he carried in a cup of tea prepared the way she liked it—with one teaspoon of honey—and stayed with her until she drank it.

He spent the rest of the evening watching movies, playing a few hands of *Go Fish* and *Old Maid* with Derek and Emma, and checking on Christy.

"I'm going to float away," she grumbled as he helped her sit so she could drink another cup of tea.

"Better that than getting dehydrated," he said cheerfully. As soon as she'd emptied most of the cup and lay down again, he returned to the living room and found both children fighting to stay awake.

For the next hour he oversaw their bedtime ritual and read the obligatory two stories, with an extra book for good measure.

"Christy said we had big plans for tomorrow," Derek mentioned as he crawled between the sheets. "What are we doing?"

Linc thought fast. "We'll see how she feels," he hedged,

"but I thought we could spend the day at my house. My weeds are probably knee-high by now."

"Can I ride the mower with you?" Derek asked, his tired eyes brimming with excitement.

"Maybe," he said. "Now go to sleep and we'll talk about it in the morning."

Outside Christy's room, he paused in indecision, but a noise in the kitchen drew him there instead. He found Christy leaning against the counter, a cupboard door open, as if she'd been trying to retrieve a glass but hadn't quite managed it.

"How are you feeling?" he asked.

She straightened with obvious effort. "Better. I came to wash the dishes, but everything's done."

Because she sounded almost irritated, he fought back a smile. "It gave me something to do while the kids finished their movie."

"Where are they?"

"In bed, ready to wake up at the crack of dawn for a fun-filled, action-packed day at the Maguire house." He motioned to the cupboard. "Can I get you something?"

"Water, please."

He filled a glass and placed it beside her.

"You should have left the dishes for me," she said in between sips. "I said I'd—"

"Yes, I know, but I didn't mind," he said calmly. "There weren't that many, so it didn't take long. I didn't even get dishpan hands. See?" He held up his hands to show her.

To his surprise, then dismay, a few tears trickled down her face and she swiped them away with her fingertips. Oh, man. She was *crying*.

"Hey," he protested. "Washing a few pots and pans isn't anything to get upset over."

"I'm not." She sniffed.

From where he was standing, she certainly seemed as if

she was. "If you're not upset," he said carefully, "then what's wrong?"

"I'd wanted everything to be perfect when you finally came home."

"It was," he assured her. At her skeptical glance, he corrected himself. "Maybe not *perfect*, but it was close."

"No, it wasn't."

"Hey, the kids were fed and my dinner was waiting for me. Having only a few dirty dishes waiting was pretty darned good, in my opinion."

"That's not the point. I—"

"If you were afraid I'd find fault, I apologize. You don't have to impress me, Christy, because I've been impressed since our first weekend."

She met his gaze, her smile wan. "How could you be?"

"Trust me. I am."

Her expression revealed her skepticism. "I truly wanted to amaze you with what I could do and how well I could keep up, but I'd really wanted to convince myself." She raked her hair with one hand. "And I failed."

She'd caught him off guard. "You wanted to impress yourself? Why?"

"After thinking about Jon the other night, I realized that all this time I've been trying to prove him wrong—that my cancer treatments wouldn't make me less of a woman than any other. That I could still juggle the same things every other woman juggles in her life, even if I lacked a few body parts and didn't have the same hormones swimming around my system. He'd never know if I'd succeeded or not, but *I* would know the truth." She paused and her shoulders drooped. "I'm beginning to think he was right."

Furious with Jon's insensitivity and angry at himself for dredging up enough of the past to rob her of her confidence, he held her by her shoulders. "Absolutely do *not* mention or think about that man's narrow-mindedness again. You've done a remarkable job when it comes to balancing work and children and a house. Do not *ever* suggest or even *think* otherwise. Got that?" he ground out.

She blinked several times before she nibbled on her bottom lip.

He squeezed her shoulders and gave her a slight shake. "Did you hear what I said?"

"I heard. But—"

He gentled his hold as well as his voice. "You have nothing to prove to me or to anyone else, and I don't want you to try." He nudged her chin upward with his index finger so her gaze could meet his. "You're tired and aren't feeling well, so it's easy to let your imagination and your fears run wild, but, honestly, no one in this house has any reason to complain about what you have or haven't done, least of all me. I'm the one who's been absent without leave for the past five days."

She hesitated, her face pensive as if she was giving his words some thought. "So you're saying I should complain about you?"

"If it'll make you feel better, yes."

Her chuckle was weak but, nonetheless, it was still a chuckle. "I'll pass."

"Good, because I'm not sure my fragile ego could take it. For the record, there's no shame in recognizing one's limitations and delegating accordingly. If we could manage everything ourselves, we wouldn't need each other, would we?"

Her downcast expression suddenly turned thoughtful. "I suppose not."

"Good. Now, finish your water and hop into bed where you belong. Tomorrow will roll around soon enough and I have a few plans on how we'll spend the day."

She nodded, but didn't move. Instead, her gaze continued to rest on him until he felt almost uncomfortable.

"Do I have spaghetti sauce on my chin?" he joked.

"No, but this is the first time I think I've ever seen you so passionate about something. Normally, you're so...so *controlled*."

"People respond better if their surgeon is controlled and doesn't rant and rave like a lunatic when he's aggravated," he said lightly.

"You can be passionate without being out of control. Watching you express your emotion is...comforting, I guess. You seem so much more...*natural*. I like seeing you less formal."

He could think of many other ways to show her just how passionate he could be, but now wasn't the time and the kitchen wasn't the place. It was, however, reassuring to realize he didn't have to hide his innermost feelings around her. He could relax and be himself, such as he was.

"You'll see my emotional side more often in the coming weeks after we all start to get on each other's nerves," he said in a dry tone. "In the meantime, you need your rest."

"I'm tired but I'm not sleepy. Does that make sense?"

"It makes perfect sense," he said as he led her toward her room, "but I'll tell you what I tell the kids. Get ready for bed and by the time you're finished, you'll change your mind."

He turned down her sheets while she slipped into the bathroom, then returned to the living room where he sprawled on the sofa and debated if he needed another trip to Ty's weight room before he called it a day, too.

However, when she appeared wearing her sleepshirt that hit her midthigh, every part of his body seemed to notice just how long her legs were. "Do you need anything?" he asked her, hoping his voice didn't sound as hoarse as it did to his own ears.

"Stay with me," she said.

He froze, certain his hearing had suddenly and inexplicably failed. "Stay?" he echoed as surprise paralyzed his lungs for a few seconds.

"Talk to me until I fall asleep," she said. "Please?"

He simply rose and followed her like a lemming. He couldn't explain why he obeyed—perhaps it was the plea in her voice and on her face. Perhaps he was just a glutton for punishment. Whatever the reason, he knew he couldn't refuse.

As he watched the slight sway of her trim hips, he decided that he deserved a sainthood for what he was about to do. His discomfort increased as she crawled into bed with her night-shirt riding dangerously high over her delightful backside, and he hardly noticed Ria standing at the foot of the bed, watching what her humans would do next.

The instant Christy scooted across the full-sized bed that was hardly large enough for her and patted the spot beside her, he immediately lost his ability to breathe or swallow. He'd expected to sit beside the bed, not share it.

"Please?" she asked.

Considering how she'd nearly jumped out of her skin when he'd touched her the other day, her request seemed out of character. Only able to arrive at one reason for her change of heart, he narrowed his eyes to study her with a physician's objectivity. Her pupils appeared normal, but he still had to wonder if she was acting under the effects of a drug or suf-fering from some sort of chemical reaction.

"What have you taken?" he asked, suspicious.

"Over-the-counter stuff," she said. "Why?"

Telling her that he thought she was high on drugs wouldn't win him any brownie points.

"No reason," he said, resigned to a very long workout after she'd dozed off.

"I know I'm asking a lot of you but, as comforting as Ria is, our conversations are one-sided. If you don't want to, though..."

He wanted to, and if she knew how badly he wanted it, she'd have locked her door before he'd come inside. However, he must have paused too long to answer because she suddenly sat up and wrapped her arms around her knees in a protective gesture.

"Forget it," she said. "I shouldn't have asked. I knew better, but I'd hoped you were comfortable enough…"

Once again, he mentally kicked himself. She'd seen his hesitation as a sign of distaste when in reality he was simply trying to keep his body under control.

"Trust me, I want to be here, beside you," he said as he lowered his weight onto the bed. "If you knew how much, though, you'd rethink your request."

Idly, he noticed Ria had disappeared but the tell-tale sound of her scratching her pallet as if making her nest told him the animal had accepted his place in Christy's bed.

Christy hadn't responded. Thinking she might be reconsidering her request, he glanced at her and saw her eyes wide with disbelief. "Really?" She hesitated, her teeth worrying her lower lip, "You're not just saying that because you feel sorry—"

"Sweetheart, right now I'm feeling a lot of things and 'sorry' isn't on that list." He held out his left arm as an open invitation and she slowly curled against him.

It was heaven. It was hell. He persevered as she wriggled to find a comfortable position with her head resting on his shoulder and her body plastered against his. He inhaled sharply, but that, too, was a mistake because her sweet scent filled his nostrils.

Hoping conversation would focus his attention on subjects other than her physical presence and how great she felt in his arms, he asked, "What should we talk about?"

"I don't care. Whatever you like."

He wanted to point out that she was the one who'd requested conversation, but didn't. He simply had to think of this as being similar to sitting beside Derek or Emma as he read or told bedtime stories.

Unfortunately, the circumstances weren't the same; they didn't compare in any way, shape, or form.

"Okay," he said, casting about for a place to start. "Do you always get physically ill when you're overtired?"

"No. I wasn't like this B.C., before chemo. I keep hoping it'll fade, but it hasn't. Normally, I do a better job of pacing myself, but taking care of Derek and Emma is like a dream come true. I was like the Energizer Bunny. I kept going and going and going."

"Why? You have two months to fill Gail's shoes."

"Two months in which to pack a lifetime of mothering," she corrected. "If I never have kids of my own, I have to store up the memories when I borrow someone else's."

"You don't know that you won't ever be a mother."

"I also don't know if I will."

"No one has guarantees," he pointed out. "I hate to break it to you, but you're like the rest of us. Fertility for anyone isn't a given. If it were, there wouldn't be specialty clinics all over the country."

"Hmm. I never thought of it like that. But you have to admit the odds of my hormones staying on a permanent sabbatical are much greater."

"People beat the odds every day. However, if you don't…" he shrugged "…there are a host of other ways to have a family. Your real problem is that you worry too much."

She snickered. "I do, don't I? So tell me, why don't you let anyone see your emotions and the passion inside you?"

It took him a minute to follow her conversation shift because she'd started rubbing her fingers against his heart and the contact was doing crazy things to his nerve endings. He placed his hand over hers to stop the gentle torment as he spoke.

"People trust me with their lives. They want to feel confident about the person who's cutting them open and messing around with their insides. Patients prefer a surgeon who is cool, calm, and collected under fire, not one whose emotions are constantly on display."

"I suppose you're right." She burrowed deeper against him and sighed like a contented kitten, which effectively sent a fresh surge of blood into his groin.

"I know I am."

Her words came slower, which made him think she was finally starting to doze. A few seconds later, she spoke again.

"Why aren't you married by now?"

"I haven't found the right woman," he answered.

"Have you been looking?"

"Not seriously," he admitted.

"Why not?"

There was something about the darkness that made it easier to share things he only admitted to himself. "I had this idea to wait until I was forty."

"Forty? Gracious. Your life will be half-over."

He grinned at her affronted tone. For a woman who wrung every minute of joy from her day, he was surprised she had such a glass-half-empty attitude. Then again, if he'd endured what she had, aware that any day could be his last, hindsight would paint those years as wasted, too. As he'd already pointed out, life didn't come with guarantees.

Unsettled by his epiphany, he went on to explain. "I suppose I wanted my future spouse to be settled in her career like I was, wanting the same things I did when it came to raising a family. I'd met a few women who'd interested me, but there always seemed to be something missing."

"No passion?"

Was that it? Possibly. Probably. Whatever the reason, he'd never felt compelled to pursue them. Christy, however, was the exception.

"What about the lady you told me about?"

"Which lady?"

"You know. The one you said you wanted to get to know."

He had to think a minute to remember…and when he did, he was grateful the room was too dark for her to see his grin. "Oh, *that* woman."

"So, Romeo, are you going to ask her out?" Her body tensed, as if bracing herself for his answer.

"Definitely."

Because it was dark, he sensed rather than saw her disappointment. "That's nice," she answered, although her words lacked sincerity.

He wanted to believe she was jealous; he certainly hoped so because it meant she had feelings for him. His for her were certainly multiplying at an exponential rate.

"What's she like? Is she pretty?"

"I think she's beautiful, but I get the impression she wouldn't agree."

"What attracted you to her? I'll bet she has a great body. Doesn't have a single scar either."

Once again, he heard her mournful tone. "She has scars, but I'm a surgeon so they don't bother me. I think of them as badges of courage."

"Oh, what a great description. What else can you tell me about her?"

"She's sweet." As she snorted at that remark, he continued, "And kind. She'd do anything for her friends. She loves kids and is definitely a dog person."

She sighed. "She sounds perfect."

"Oh, she has her flaws, but to me no one else compares."

"Where will you take her on your first date?"

"I haven't decided yet. Where would you suggest?"

"My choice would be Grant's Point," she said, her voice growing softer. "It's a very peaceful, romantic spot. You can reach out and touch the stars while you hear the wind whisper through the trees and smell the pines. There's no place better."

If memory served him, the landmark was a famous place for couples to visit. Local folklore suggested the majority of Levitt Springs' population had been conceived on that overlook. Regardless, if the hill was Christy's choice, he'd take her there.

However, she seemed to be speaking from experience and he hated the idea of another guy taking her there, even if only for a platonic let's-see-the-local-hot-spots trip.

"You've been there before?"

"Ria and I drove there one night and watched the stars come out. It was great. You and your lady friend will enjoy it."

He was uncommonly pleased to hear Ria had been her date. "I'm positive we will."

"If you want, she can take my place as your dance partner." Her reluctance was evident, as if she didn't want to extend the offer but good manners demanded it.

"I'm happy with the partner I have."

"If you change your mind..."

"I won't," he assured her.

"Thank you."

He wondered what she was thanking him for—for not changing his mind or for being happy to have her as his partner. Maybe it was simply because he wasn't rejecting her in favor of another woman.

For a long minute he only heard her gentle breathing and he thought she'd finally fallen asleep, but before he could move a muscle, she spoke again.

"I'm sorry for jumping out of my skin the other night when you touched me." She slurred her words and he wondered if she realized she was speaking.

"It's okay. I understand."

"It's not okay. I wanted you to do what you did, but—"

"But what?"

"I don't feel anything," she said flatly. "Men expect a woman to respond, but I can't because they aren't feeling *me*. If you don't mind, I need your help."

Clinically he understood her dilemma, but personally he sensed a minefield had appeared in front of him. He could only hope she wouldn't remember this conversation in the morning. "Help with what?"

"Help me so I don't jump next time," she said. "We could practice."

He swallowed hard. "Practice?"

Her nod felt as if she was nuzzling his shoulder with her nose. "That way, if I ever meet a fellow and he—"

The idea that she wanted him to condition her to handle another man's touch nearly made him growl with frustration. As uninhibited as her exhaustion had made her, if she'd asked to begin now, *he* would be the one jumping out of his skin, not to mention her bed. Although he was male enough to be grateful she had asked *him* for help.

"Sorry, but that isn't something we should do. You'll have to wing it when the time comes."

Once again, she sighed. "You're right. Your girlfriend wouldn't understand, would she?"

For lack of anything else to say, he resorted to, "No, she wouldn't."

"You know something?" She slurred her words. "I was prepared to dislike you, but you're a very nice man."

He grinned like a loon. "I'm glad you think so."

"It's too bad, though."

"Oh?" he asked.

"Because it wouldn't take much for me to fall in love."

His breath froze in his lungs. "Would that be so terrible?" he asked softly.

"Not terrible," she murmured. "It would be wonderful. Not a good idea, though."

"Why not?" he asked.

One minute of silence stretched into two, then into five, but she didn't answer. He wanted to nudge her awake so she could reply to his question, but he was reasonably certain she wouldn't remember what she'd said.

He, however, wouldn't forget.

Another five minutes went by. With great regret, Linc eased out from under her, covered her bare legs with a sheet, then tiptoed from the room.

He'd never imagined the evening would end with the two of them engaging in pillow talk. If another woman had said she could fall in love with him, he would have run for the nearest exit, but hearing Christy admit those feelings only reinforced his determination to hold on to her in any way he could.

Aware of his lingering arousal, he headed once again to the basement. At the rate he was going, he'd develop a body-builder's physique before Ty and Gail returned.

CHAPTER SEVEN

"I THINK Jose is well enough to go home, don't you?" Linc said to Christy after he'd reviewed Jose's chart five days later.

"He's doing remarkably well," she agreed. "He's complaining about the food again, so he's definitely feeling better." Between the filter that had been surgically inserted and medication adjustments, his most recent tests showed the clot in his leg was nearly dissolved.

Linc clicked a few final computer keys before he logged off the terminal. "I'll break the news to him while you get things rolling."

"Will do."

He scooted his chair away from the counter. "You have a sitter for tonight, right?"

"Heather's coming over at seven," she told him. Heather was the sixteen-year-old high-school girl who came early on the mornings Christy had to work and oversaw Derek and Emma getting ready for school. Sometimes Linc was still there, but more often than not he'd left early, too, so Heather's presence was a godsend.

"Although I still don't understand why we need a sitter while we practice a dance routine," she grumbled good-naturedly. "Derek and Emma won't bother us."

He raised an eyebrow. "If they don't, it would be a first," he said wryly.

"I agree they're rather clingy, but they're still adjusting."

"I understand that, but even if by some miracle they would give us an hour to ourselves, I'd rather not risk it. Constant interruptions aren't conducive to learning what we need to learn. The competition is only six weeks away."

As if she needed reminding. She'd fielded more questions about being Linc's partner, and from some of the comments she'd overheard, most were surprised to hear of his participation. Speculation and curiosity had increased ticket sales, as she'd suspected would happen. She only hoped Linc hadn't heard those same rumors because, knowing his determination to excel, he'd insist on incorporating a more advanced routine than necessary.

"Regardless, everything is set for tonight," she said.

"Great." With that, he rose and headed to Jose's room.

Less than a minute later, one of the other nurses, Rose Warren, strode into the nurses' station, looking over her shoulder with eyes wide and her jaw slack.

"I can't believe it," she remarked to Christy. "Did you see him?"

"See who?" Christy answered as she pulled the appropriate discharge forms and patient home-care instructions from various folders.

"Dr Maguire." Rose stared in the direction she'd come. "The man *smiled* at me."

Christy grinned. "How absolutely terrible."

"I wonder what's happened? I mean, he's always been courteous but he's never gone out of his way to be friendly."

"Yes, he has," she protested mildly.

"To you, maybe. To the rest of us, he's just...*polite*."

Was Rose right? Christy thought for a moment and suspected there was some truth to her observation, but if Linc spoke to her more often than anyone else, it was only because most of the staff didn't bother including him in their conversations. Granted, they'd probably tried at one point and his usual monosyllabic answers had eventually convinced them to stop trying, but she'd been undaunted. She'd always forced him into a discussion that didn't involve treatment plans or patient symptoms and over the two years she'd known him they'd progressed to single sentences. Now, though, he didn't wait to speak until spoken to, which was quite an achievement, in her opinion.

"He's a very quiet, reserved person," she countered, "but once you get to know him, he's a great guy."

"Well, whatever you're doing to put the smile on his face, keep it up."

She wasn't doing anything in particular, although she had to admit that ever since Linc had sat with her while she'd fallen asleep, she'd caught him staring at her with the most amazing twinkle in his eyes. She must have said something amusing, but she couldn't remember what it must have been. She recalled asking him why he hadn't married, as well as a host of other questions regarding the woman he wanted to get to know. In a fuzzy corner in her memory she thought she'd apologized for jumping out of her skin when he'd touched her, and had told him why, but the rest was a blur between reality and a dream.

However, when she pressed him for details, he simply smiled, which made her wonder if she'd talked in her sleep.

It was probably best if she didn't know what she'd said while her defenses had been down because she'd never be able to face him again.

"I wonder if he's seeing someone," Rose said thoughtfully.

The idea gave her a moment's pause, but unless he carved out time in his already busy days, she couldn't conceive how it might be possible. Although she wasn't trying to keep him from his lady friend, she was, however, pleased that he'd devoted his evenings to her and the children.

"Could be," she said in a noncommittal tone.

Rose's dark eyes grew speculative. "Aren't the two of you looking after his brother's family while they're out of the country?"

"Yes."

"How's that working out?"

Christy was nothing if not circumspect. "Fine. You know how it is with kids, there's hardly time to breathe."

Once again, Rose glanced in the direction he'd disappeared. "If a love interest hasn't lightened his mood, then being around you must have done the trick."

Linc *had* spent far more time at home than she'd initially expected. While he still had definite ideas about how and when things should be done, he'd also been more willing to compromise than she'd dreamed possible.

"Unless..." Rose stared at Christy thoughtfully "...you two are having a romance."

Christy fought the warmth spreading up her neck and into her face. "Don't be ridiculous. He's just getting into the spirit of the hospital fundraiser," she prevaricated. "Have you bought your tickets yet?"

"I have. Dean and I are looking forward to a night out." She grinned. "Even if we have to spend it with the same people we work with."

"Oh, the sacrifices one must make."

"Where are you going on your vacation this year?" Rose asked. "Let me guess. You're running the bulls."

Christy laughed. "Sorry, that's in July and I've missed it for this year."

"Maybe you can do one of those Ironman events."

"I'm not in shape for it."

"You're not in shape for what?" Linc's voice interrupted.

"An Ironman event," Christy explained. "You know—

those endurance events that involve swimming, biking, and a marathon run."

"We were discussing ideas for her annual adventure," Rose added helpfully. "She's already missed running with the bulls, but I suppose she could always do something wild like climbing Mount Everest."

"Sorry," Christy answered cheerfully, noting how Linc had suddenly tensed. "Too cold."

Rose turned to Linc. "Do you have any suggestions for her, Doctor?"

A predatory gleam appeared in his eyes as he met Christy's gaze and the heat she saw caused all her nerve endings to tingle.

"Not off the top of my head," he said. "But I'll give the subject some thought."

Hearing that Christy was looking for a new adventure activated a fiercely protective streak he hadn't noticed before. He didn't want her choosing a dangerous pastime and he certainly didn't want her getting her thrills in the company of some other guy, no matter how innocent the circumstances might be.

As for suggesting an exciting activity, he had an idea and it had driven him to the weight bench on several occasions. It involved the two of them, alone on a deserted island and surrounded only by the sun, sand, and the sea. Unfortunately, the rest of his mental picture wasn't suitable to mention to a relative stranger and he was certain Christy wasn't ready to hear it either.

Some things a man had to keep to himself until the proper moment.

However, he'd planned an adventure of another sort for this very evening—Christy didn't know about it, yet—and he spent most of his afternoon keeping close tabs on the clock.

If his office staff thought he was unusually eager to leave, they were too polite to comment.

At six forty-five, after promising Derek and Emma that he'd make up for missing their bedtime story, Linc promptly ushered Christy into his car. Tonight was their first private dance lesson and he couldn't decide if he was dreading the experience or looking forward to it. He hoped the instructor would be as good as his billing because he didn't want to disappoint Christy with his two left feet.

He passed the street leading to her apartment, then turned in the opposite direction from his house when she spoke.

"Linc," she said carefully, "I thought we were going to practice a dance routine."

"We are."

"Then where are we going?"

He made a right turn. "I've scheduled private lessons for us at the You Can Dance studio."

Her jaw visibly dropped. "However did you manage that? They're booked for weeks in advance and that's just for a *group* lesson. I can't imagine what one would have to do for a private session."

"Yeah, well." He shrugged. "It's who you know. In my case, one of my patients is a relative and he put in a good word for me."

"I should be angry with you," she said without heat. "First you announce at dinner that your housekeeper will come by every week and now you've arranged for private dance lessons? What's next? A caterer?"

He chuckled at her obvious frustration. "Catering is definitely out, but we have a dance routine to perfect," he reminded her, "and that won't happen overnight. So, to be sure we have time to devote, it only makes sense for Paullina to take on a few of our housekeeping chores. It isn't a reflection on you, I swear."

only yours. When you move securely in that knowledge, your feet will go where they need to and she will follow."

Yours and only yours.

He liked the sound of that. Furthermore, he suddenly realized that he wanted far more than only a moment. He didn't know how or when it had happened, but he wanted weeks, months, and *years* with her. He also wanted the clock to begin now, not later after her check-up.

"Shall we try again?" Mario asked.

He drew a bracing breath. "Okay. Let's do this."

The instructor clapped his hands. "Good. Then we begin."

By the end of the session Linc was exhausted and he was certain Christy's head was spinning from all the turns they'd practiced, but as soon as he'd put Mario's advice into play, he'd felt himself become more sure-footed.

Mario pulled him aside as they were leaving. "Well done. I can see your confidence growing, no? Perhaps when you return you will be the teacher and I will be the student?"

Linc laughed. "I appreciate the thought, but that would take a miracle."

Mario smiled, his teeth white in his tanned face. "Stranger things have happened, no? Now, go home and practice. We will see your progress at the next session."

"Linc," Christy cried three nights later as she collapsed on the sofa after another set of spins. "No more. Please."

Linc grinned. "You aren't wimping out on me now, are you? What happened to the woman who's looking for an adventure?"

"She's tired and if she turns one more time, she's going to do something horrible, like deposit her dinner on your feet." She rubbed her midsection in an effort to calm her stomach.

He sank onto the cushions beside her. "Poor baby. I have been working you hard, haven't I?"

"To put it mildly. You haven't forgotten this is just a friendly competition, have you?"

"No, but anything worth doing…"

"Is worth doing well." She finished his saying because if she'd heard it once, she'd heard it a hundred times. "Now I understand how you became such a brilliant surgeon. You give new meaning to the word 'single-minded.'"

"Thanks. I think."

"You're welcome. The good news is that Mario and Carmen should be pleased when we see them tomorrow night."

"They certainly should be," he said, sounding pleased with himself. "We're positively awesome."

She had to admit, they were. Of course, Mario and Carmen had only assigned them a few steps to perfect, but they had learned those well. While she'd always had a good sense of rhythm, Linc had completely surprised her. He moved so naturally to the music, she couldn't believe she'd ever thought him stilted and straitlaced.

"You never did say why Mario pulled you aside," she said, curious.

"He gave me a pep talk. He said I was trying too hard."

"You were." She'd seen him struggling and she'd found his determination endearing. She'd also been tempted to suggest they try something less complicated, but Carmen had stopped her.

"Men are simple creatures," she'd said. *"They give gifts to the ones they care about. He wants to do this for you, so you must not deny him the chance."*

Now, three days later, the notion that he might care about her made her smile with delight. On the other hand, when she wasn't reveling in those female feelings, she was having a panic attack. She didn't want to fall in love with him, even though she feared she'd already marched halfway down that path.

Besides, Carmen must have misread Linc's signals because someone else had already captured his eye. If Linc seemed determined to master this particular dance, proving that he could was his only motivation.

She pinched her thumb and forefinger together. "By then, I was this close to suggesting we stick to a simple waltz."

"Won't happen," he said firmly. "I'd already made up my mind."

Once he'd reached a decision, she knew nothing short of an act of God would convince him to change his mind. "What exactly did Mario say to get you to relax?"

"That I'd be the envy of every man watching, so I might as well enjoy myself. Those weren't his exact words, but they're close."

Certainly the women in the audience would feel the same about her, she thought. It was inevitable as she would have the most handsome man in the hospital at her side.

"By the end of the evening, you'll be on every single woman's radar," she said lightly.

"Won't matter," he said firmly. "There's only one on mine."

She ignored the instant pain she felt. "When *are* you going to ask out this paragon of virtue?"

"Soon."

"How soon?"

"You seem awfully concerned about my dating habits."

"Only because I don't want to stand in the way of true love," she quipped. "Derek and Emma have been invited to a sleepover on Friday night. Why don't you taking her out then? With the kids gone, I wouldn't slap a curfew on you."

He laughed. "Good idea. I could arrange a date." He paused. "What will you do?"

She didn't want to think about the long hours she'd face in her apartment, but whether he brought his date here or to his own house, she definitely wouldn't stick around to meet her.

"Girl things," she answered promptly, thinking she was overdue for a facial and a long bubble bath complete with candles, soft music, and a romance novel.

"I see. Then I'll plan my evening."

"Yes, do." She pasted a smile on her face, painfully aware of unreasonable jealousy gripping her soul.

Christy touched the homemade beer-and-cucumber mask she'd applied to her face and decided it was time to wash off the residue. As Friday night activities went, indulging in a facial wasn't high on the excitement meter, but her pores said it was long overdue. Although her great-grandmother's recipe probably didn't have any real scientific basis for giving a peaches-and-cream complexion, knowing she was one of a long line of women in her family to engage in the ritual was comforting.

Tonight, more than ever, she needed to feel as if she weren't alone.

Puréeing the cucumbers and blending in the other ingredients had also given her something to concentrate on other than Linc's date.

Ever since she'd dropped off the children at their friends' house—fortunately Derek and Emma's buddies were a brother and sister—her thoughts had drifted in a most fruitless direction. It was too easy to create a mental minute-by-minute scenario of Linc's evening.

He *should* spend time with the woman who'd caught his eye, she told herself fiercely. She *should* be happy because he'd finally realized his work was a cold-hearted mistress and was seeking one of flesh and blood. If she'd convinced him to stop postponing his plans for his personal life, then she should pride herself for nudging him along.

Vowing to find a constructive activity, she'd tried to read two different books, but neither held her interest.

She'd lounged on her postage-stamp-sized balcony to enjoy the fall weather and the last few rays of direct sunlight in the quietness, but even nature conspired against her. Birds called to their mates, crickets answered each other's chirps, and the distant sound of children laughing only emphasized her loneliness.

She'd also considered whipping up a batch of cookies, but couldn't because her cupboards were literally bare. Although running into Linc and his date at the grocery store was highly unlikely, she didn't want to risk it.

For a woman who didn't want romance, who was positive she hadn't found a man strong enough to cope with her uncertain future, she was acting completely ridiculously.

She shook off her gloom with great force of will and planned the rest of the evening. As soon as she finished her beauty treatment and slipped on her running shoes, she would take Ria for a romp around the park. By the time they came home, she'd be too tired to imagine what Linc might or might not be doing.

Not knowing was part of her problem, she decided with some irritation. She'd pressed him for details about his prospective girlfriend and his itinerary, aware that asking was similar to probing a sore tooth, but he'd been remarkably uncommunicative.

"I'll leave it up to her," had been his reply, so she'd finally held her questions. Yet she hadn't stopped wondering...

She hoped his mystery woman deserved him.

The doorbell—and Ria's answering barks—interrupted her thoughts. She was inclined to ignore her unexpected visitor, but Ria bounded into the bathroom and began barking in her familiar follow-me style.

"Okay, okay," she grumbled as she patted her face dry, hoping she'd removed all traces of crustiness and didn't smell as if she'd fallen into a distillery vat.

Ria nudged her toward the stairs and stood beside Christy as she unlocked the door.

The man on the stoop caught her by surprise. "Linc!" she exclaimed. "What are you doing here?"

"May I come in?"

"Certainly." She stepped aside, both happy and puzzled that he'd dropped by. "Where's your date? Or should I ask *when* is your date?"

His grin was broad as his gaze traveled down her entire body. A second later, he flicked at a dried flake on her T-shirt. "I came to pick her up, but I'd say she isn't ready."

Her heart pounded and she couldn't breathe. "You came for *me*? But…"

"You're my date." His mouth curled with amusement. "Now, run along and get dressed. I'll occupy Ria's attention so she won't hide your shoes."

Shock, as well as suspicion that she'd somehow misunderstood, had rooted her feet to the floor. "You mean…*I'm* your mystery woman?"

He nodded.

"*I'm* the woman you want to get to know?"

"Yes."

Although her spirits wanted to soar into the stratosphere, she held a tight rein on them. "I don't understand. I thought you cared about…"

"Someone else?" he supplied helpfully.

She hesitated. "Well, yes."

"You were wrong. There isn't anyone else. *You're* the one I care about—the one I want to spend my evening with."

She wanted to cry tears of joy as well as frustration. "You shouldn't want that—"

"Of course I should," he interrupted. "You're a kind, generous, thoughtful woman and every bachelor I know would trade places with me in an instant."

"It's a nice thought, but—"

"Whatever has happened in the past or will happen in the future doesn't matter. The current moment is what we have, so we're going to focus on it. The real question is, have you eaten yet or…" he leaned closer to sniff "…have you been drinking your dinner?"

Her face warmed. "I suspect the ingredients in my great-grandmother's facial recipe were chosen for their, shall we say, *medicinal* qualities." She grinned. "According to Grandma Nell, her mother faithfully applied her facial every Saturday night. Her private time probably included sampling the ingredients while she pampered her skin."

He chuckled. "I don't blame her. Life was hard a hundred years ago and she probably deserved a beer or two at the end of her week."

She smiled. "It makes for an interesting story, doesn't it?" Then, because she didn't want to think about not having descendants who could pass on the tale, she changed the subject. "As for dinner, I haven't eaten."

"Good, because I'm starved. Now, put on your glad rags and let's go."

She should protest, and she was inclined to do so, but she didn't. Perhaps she held back because he acted more like a friend than a guy who was seriously intent on a commitment. Maybe it was only because she was relieved she didn't have to share him with anyone else. She was certainly flattered he'd asked *her* when he could have chosen from a host of eligible women.

It was also far too easy to remind herself she was mere weeks away from her five-year check-up and the end of her self-imposed moratorium on romantic relationships. She could go out, keep the mood light, and just enjoy being in the company of a handsome fellow.

The more she considered, the more enticing an evening of Linc's undivided attention sounded.

"Casual, I assume?" she asked, eyeing his jeans and noticing how fantastic he looked in denim and a cotton shirt.

"Whatever's comfortable," he agreed. "Keep in mind it'll be cool after dark."

She changed in record speed, although she was so excited it took her three tries to successfully brush on her mascara and apply lip gloss.

"I'm ready," she said breathlessly when she emerged fifteen minutes later, wearing her favorite low-cut jeans, a sleeveless white cotton shell and her favorite pearl earrings.

He held out his arm. "Then shall we?"

Before she could pat Ria one final time, he snapped his fingers. "Let's go, Ria."

The dog raced to the door while Christy stared at him. "We're taking her with us?"

"Not to dinner. We'll drop her off at my place on the way. She can chase rabbits and hunt squirrels while we're gone."

"She could stay here. She's used to being alone."

"She could," he agreed, "but wouldn't you rather let her run in a huge yard instead of relegating her to a tiny apartment? Do you really want to deprive her of one of our rare days of nice weather?"

She couldn't refute his argument, although he obviously intended to end up at his place at some point. Was he giving her the opportunity to spend the night by ensuring she couldn't use Ria as an excuse to refuse?

He must have read her mind because he pulled her close. "Before you get all righteous and accuse me of having an ulterior motive, I want you to remember this. However long our night lasts, whether it ends at ten o'clock or in the wee hours, nothing will happen that both of us aren't ready for."

She knew he wouldn't push her beyond her comfort zone—

he wasn't the sort who notched his bedposts—but nevertheless she had to ask. "You won't be disappointed if we have an early night?"

His smile was tender as he cupped her face. "I'm a guy. Of course I'd be disappointed, but tonight isn't about me. Tonight is for you."

He was being so sweet, she wanted to cry. More than that, though, she wanted him to kiss her. He obviously wanted it too because he bent his head and she felt his breath brush against the bridge of her nose. Unfortunately, in that split second before his lips met hers, Ria barked impatiently.

He grinned and instead of the lingering kiss he'd been so obviously prepared to give, he delivered a swift peck on her cheek. "We're being paged, so hold that thought."

She did.

CHAPTER EIGHT

"THANKS for letting me share your dinner," Christy said as ninety minutes later they left Rosa's Italian Eatery, the mom-and-pop restaurant he favored for its authentic cuisine and intimate dining atmosphere.

"You're welcome." He'd never divided his dinner with a date before, but Christy had eyed his chicken and eggplant parmesan with such curiosity that he'd given her a sample. In the interest of fairness, she'd shared a taste of her vegetable lasagna and before he knew it, they'd split both meals between them.

"How long have you known Rosa and her husband?" she asked.

He thought for a minute. "Several years. I first met them when their sixteen-year-old son, Frank Junior, had been in a car accident. After I put him back together, Rosa insisted on showing her gratitude by catering a meal for my office staff. The food was fabulous and now, if I want Italian food, her place is at the top of my list."

She stopped in her tracks and he felt her gaze. "You really amaze me," she said.

He grinned, pleased she was seeing him as a good guy and not of the same ilk as the infamous Jon. "Why? Because I prefer eating at great places?"

"No, because your patients aren't just patients. The ones

I've met have always spoken highly of you, and I'd assumed it was because of your surgical skills and the stories of how, no matter how busy you are, you find time to see someone who needs you."

"I try," he admitted, "but I have a few favorites, as I'm sure you do, too."

"Yes, but, unlike you, I don't usually see them again."

They'd reached the car and because Linc had been keeping tabs on the weather, he noticed a bank of clouds building in the west.

"Looks like the weatherman might be right about the rain," she commented.

"That's what I was afraid of."

"Oh? You don't want the moisture? For shame, Dr Maguire. Don't let the farmers hear you utter such blasphemy," she teased.

"I don't want it *tonight*," he corrected. "I need nice weather for what I had planned."

"Then you *did* organize your evening," she accused good-naturedly. "You told me you were allowing your date to plan your activities."

He grinned. "I did, more or less. She told me what she'd like to do and I took her suggestions to heart."

"I didn't give you any suggestions."

"If I recall, you mentioned Grant's Point."

Her face lit up like the mall's Christmas tree. "Is that where we're going? I can't believe you remembered."

"You'd be amazed at what I remember," he said lightly. In fact, he remembered a lot more than she thought he did. "The only problem is…" he pointed to the sky "…we won't have much time out there before we get wet."

"Bummer."

"Yeah, but if you're okay with waiting, we'll save that

excursion for next time." It was a subtle mention of his intention to take her out again, and he waited for her reply.

"I'd like that."

Hiding his satisfaction over her response, he helped her into the car, then walked around to the driver's side.

So far, everything was turning out better than he'd hoped. He'd worried how Christy would react when he arrived on her doorstep unannounced and had half expected her to refuse to go at all. She'd seemed determined to shun a personal relationship until she'd reached the magical date she'd set, which was why he'd used the just-friends approach.

However, his ultimate goal was to show her that friendship would never be enough. For himself, he already wanted more because he didn't want to return to his previous life when everything he did revolved around his work. He wanted his days—his future—revolving around her because he couldn't imagine facing a day without her.

A short time later, Linc escorted Christy into his house and once again she was filled with a sense of belonging, as if she "fit" in this house. If she'd had the finances, not to mention the time and strength, to maintain a place like his, she'd buy it. Her feelings had nothing to do with the owner.

Oh, who was she kidding? She enjoyed being around Linc whether they were at the hospital, Gail and Ty's house, or his place. If the truth were told, she enjoyed being with him far more than she should at this point in her life.

She paused in front of the patio door. "I'll get Ria so we can go."

"How about a glass of wine first?"

She hesitated. Returning to her empty house wasn't nearly as attractive as staying here with Linc, but, given how easily she was falling for him, it wasn't wise to stay.

"I bought this bottle specifically for our star-gazing," he

coaxed. "We may not be able to see too many stars from my patio, but we can't let it go to waste."

Rather than argue that a sealed bottle of wine would keep indefinitely, she gave in because deep down she wanted to stay and pretend she possessed a future as secure as any other twenty-eight-year-old woman's. "One glass, on the patio, please."

If she'd refused, she was certain he would have been chivalrous and obliged, but his broad smile suggested her answer had pleased him. He grabbed two wine glasses and the bottle he'd brought in from the car then accompanied her outdoors.

As soon as she stepped outside and called for Ria, the Lab raced toward them, only to stop abruptly in front of Linc and nudge his leg in an apparent attempt to receive his personal attention, too.

He laughed as he tucked the wine bottle under one arm, then obliged. He'd obviously found the right spot because the dog extended her neck as if to encourage him to shower his attention over a much larger area.

"Don't I get a hello?" she asked her pet lightly, disappointed Ria had transferred her allegiance to Linc so quickly.

Ria wagged her tail and continued to lean into Linc's touch.

"Apparently not," he said. "You know I can find the right spots, don't you, girl?"

"Yes, well, you're going to spoil her with those magic fingers of yours." Remembering his touch on several occasions, she wished she was on the receiving end instead of her dog. "Ria," she asked, "are you almost ready to go home?"

A rabbit darted across the yard and slipped through a small opening in the wooden fence. Ria gave a sharp woof before bounding to the same corner to nose the ground where her prey had escaped.

"I think her answer was 'No'," Linc said as he handed her an empty glass, then popped the cork on the bottle.

"You do realize she'll be willing to spend hours in your yard?"

He grinned. "She's a dog. Of course she will."

"Yes, but we shouldn't wear out our welcome."

"You won't," he assured her. "If the weather hadn't interfered with my original plan, she'd be spending hours doing what she's doing now."

"Yes, but—"

"Do you have something special to do when you get home?"

"No," she said slowly. "But—"

"But nothing," he said as he poured both glasses half-full. "We may have postponed our Grant's Point trip, but the evening is still ours. *And...*" he emphasized the word "...I have a Plan B."

"Which is?" She sipped her wine.

"We haven't practiced our dance steps today," he reminded her.

"No, we haven't, but one day won't matter."

He lifted an eyebrow. "Speak for yourself, my dear."

She smiled at his grumble. "Mario was quite impressed with you at our last lesson."

"And I want him to stay that way. Or are you trying to get me in trouble with the teacher?"

She laughed. "I can't believe you ever got in trouble at school."

"Contrary to what you might think, I had my moments of infamy. Unfortunately, my stories can't leave this property. They would ruin the 'perfect son' standard I projected to Ty and my sister." He grinned.

She laughed. "I promise. What did you do?"

"Nothing malicious. Mostly stuff like hiding red pens on test days, rearranging the books on the teacher's desk, hiding the dry-erase markers in another classroom so she couldn't post assignments on the board."

"Did your ploys work?"

"Once," he admitted, "but my teachers were a wily bunch. They kept extra red pens and markers in their file cabinets. If one disappeared, they simply pulled another one from their stash or borrowed from another instructor." He smiled. "But my tactics gave us a few minutes' reprieve and to an eight-year-old a few minutes' delay was a coup."

"Did you go to school in Levitt Springs?"

He shook his head. "We grew up about three hours from here. Fortunately, my hometown had a college, so I earned my undergrad degree while Ty and my sister finished high school. After that, we went our separate ways. I began med school, Ty and Joanie entered different colleges and Gran had died by then, so splitting up was inevitable. We kept in touch with weekly phone calls, though."

"How did you and Ty both land in Levitt Springs?"

"Ty had gotten a job with an architecture firm here after he finished his education. Eventually, after I'd completed my surgery residency, I looked for a place to go. I'd narrowed my job offers down to two—one in St. Louis and one here."

"And you chose Levitt Springs."

"My niece and nephew swayed my decision," he admitted. "They don't have grandparents, so it seemed important to give them a doting uncle. I would have moved to be near my sister, too, but she's a buyer for a department-store chain and spends most of her life on the road."

"A win-win situation for everyone," she remarked.

"It is," he agreed. "Being surrounded by family after all those years of only getting together for Memorial Day or Christmas is wonderful. Of course, I'm busy enough that I don't see Ty and his kids as often as I'd like, but we manage to get together at least once a week, even if only for an hour or so."

"Family means a great deal to you," she guessed.

"It does. Although I've watched the kids before on weekends, filling in for Ty makes me eager to have a Derek and Emma of my own."

In another lifetime she would have been thrilled to hear him confirm that his philosophy mirrored hers. However, her future was too uncertain to rejoice in those similarities.

She drained her glass because she couldn't think of a suitable reply.

"More wine?" he asked.

"No, thanks. Our steps are difficult enough without having impaired coordination."

He rose to click a button on his iPod player. The music began and he smiled at her. "Shall we start?"

Regardless of what her future held, her heart skipped with excitement as she set her glass on the end table and walked into his outstretched arms. "Of course."

For the next thirty minutes she turned and twirled, conscious of his strength as he caught her. Occasionally he stepped on her toes or she stepped on his but as time went on, those incidents occurred less and less.

Finally, they'd managed to make it through the first half of their routine without a single misstep.

"Are we getting good or was that a fluke?" she teased him.

"I vote we try once more," he told her.

So he started the music once again.

To Christy's delight, they repeated their steps perfectly, ending with a final spin that required him to catch her.

For a long minute he simply held her against him, making her aware of how his labored breathing matched hers.

The patter-patter of rain on the roof punctuated the silence and the fresh, clean scent it brought mingled with Linc's masculine fragrance. He exuded warmth, and while that was pleasant, as the air suddenly carried a coolness she hadn't noticed before, she was more impressed by his strength and rock-solidness.

In that instant Linc no longer seemed like a friendly dance partner. He was an attractive, virile man in the prime of his life.

She should push herself away, but she couldn't. The intensity in his gaze was too mesmerizing and savoring this moment too important for her to move.

"That was awesome," he murmured.

"Oh, yes." She didn't know if her breathlessness was due to physical exertion or from being in his arms. She was playing with fire, but it had seemed like for ever since she'd felt as carefree and as attractive as she did at this moment.

It was also a bittersweet moment. She hated to be realistic with romance simmering in the air but she had to control her attraction because these feelings could never grow. Not yet, anyway, and, depending on her doctor's findings, maybe never.

"I suppose we should stop practicing while we're ahead," she said lightly. "End the session on a high note, so to speak."

"Probably."

Yet for the next sixty seconds he didn't release her and she didn't push the issue. The moment would end soon enough and she wanted to enjoy it for as long as it lasted.

"It's raining," she commented inanely, wishing she could go back to her carefree youth when the *C* word only applied to other people. "We should call Ria and go inside."

"I'd rather kiss you," he said.

Her gaze landed on his mouth and although her small voice cautioned her about the wisdom of it, she raised her chin to meet his lips in a kiss so fierce her toes curled and her inner core ached.

"We shouldn't do this," she murmured when he gentled his mouth and inched his way to the sensitive area behind her ear.

"Of course we should."

Her mind barely registered his words, she was too consumed with the sensation of being pressed against his entire length to make sense of them.

Suddenly he pulled away just enough to meet her gaze. The hunger in his expression warmed her down her to her toes. "Have you thought about what we'll do after Gail and Ty return?"

"The Fall Festival is the same day," she pointed out. "The next afternoon I leave for Seattle so I can be bright-eyed and bushy-tailed for my doctor's appointment on that Monday. With a hectic schedule like that, I haven't thought past that weekend."

"We should," he said.

Instinctively, she sensed he was referring to a topic she'd been purposely avoiding. "I imagine we'll go back to the way things were before," she said lightly. "We'll see each other a few times a week at the hospital."

"I don't think so. Too much has changed."

He had a point. Between their shared parenting responsibilities and the dance competition, whenever she saw him on her unit, she treated him differently. Oh, she still gave him the respect he deserved, but now she joked and teased and asked personal questions that she'd never had the courage to ask before. He'd also loosened up enough to join in staff conversations without prompting. Rose hadn't been the only person who'd noticed the change.

"You're right. Things are different. In fact, *you're* so different that several single women have mentioned they'd love to go out with you. If you like, I can give you their names."

She struggled to make the offer because she felt rather

possessive about him, but she had no right to that particular feeling. Yes, she'd dragged him out of his shell and convinced him to stop putting his professional career ahead of his personal life, but those lessons would simply prepare him for the woman of his dreams. When he found her and eventually had his own Derek and Emma, and maybe even a Nick or a Beth, she could take pride in the role she'd played.

"You're pulling my leg, right?"

"Not at all. Theresa in Respiratory Therapy, Monica in the Recovery Room, and—"

His hold around her waist tightened. "Their names don't matter because every one of them will be disappointed. Maybe you didn't hear me when I came by your house. I want to spend my time with you—no one else."

It was a wonderful thought and her heart did a happy dance, but the implications scared her. He was asking too much, too soon. "That's sweet of you to say, but—"

"I know you're worried about your upcoming appointment but, whatever happens, I'm not going anywhere. I'll be with you every step of the way."

Christy stiffened, and Linc sensed her mental withdrawal. Any second she'd bolt, and he imperceptibly tightened his hold. She felt too good right where she was and he wanted to show her both literally and figuratively that he wouldn't let her go without a fight.

There would be no turning back.

He could have said nothing and let the days roll by, but she needed to know that *this* time she wouldn't face her future with only Ria as her companion. His intentions were to prove he had more staying power and more strength of character than the other jerks who had walked into—and out of—her life.

Moisture glistened in her eyes and she blinked rapidly. "I know you mean well, but please don't make any promises."

"I already have."

"I won't hold you to them," she warned.

"Are you giving me an escape clause?"

"Someone has to."

"Do you really think I'm the sort of guy who runs at the first sign of trouble?"

Her shoulders slumped before she shook her head. "No, but it's too risky to say what you might do when or if the situation changes."

He disagreed, but she wouldn't change her opinion in the space of this conversation. "Okay." He spoke evenly. "We'll continue our discussion after your appointment, but I happen to believe we have a future. Don't let fear hold you hostage."

For a long minute she didn't move, until finally she nodded ever so slightly. "I'll try."

Pleased by his small victory, he stepped forward and lightly brushed her cheekbone with his lips. "That's all I ask."

At times over the next three weeks Christy wondered if she'd imagined that particular conversation because Linc never referred to it again. However, every now and then she'd catch him studying her, sometimes with curiosity and sometimes with a speculative gleam, but no matter what she saw in his eyes, he always smiled his lazy grin that turned her insides to mush. She tried to do as he'd asked—to think about a life after she received her five-year medical report—and it was easy when he was nearby. In the wee hours of the night, however, when darkness had closed in and she had only Ria to hold her fears at bay, it wasn't. Fortunately, those instances didn't happen often. She was simply too busy trying to stay on top of their schedule and keep the household running smoothly to reflect past the upcoming weeks.

Time, however, was marching on and the kitchen calendar reflected it. Emma had circled the date of her parents' return with a red magic marker and, thanks to the huge black Xs she marked in the squares at the end of each day, Christy could count the remaining white spaces at a glance.

There were fourteen of them.

Her time of sharing the house with Linc and playing a mother's role was drawing to a close, so she savored every moment, including those less than idyllic times...

"Christy." Derek raced into the kitchen while she was finishing the dinner dishes. "Emma keeps bugging me. She won't stay out of my room."

"He took my doll's car," Emma wailed, "and I know he's hiding it under his bed. I want it back."

"I didn't take it. It's probably buried under all your doll junk." His disgust was obvious.

"My stuff is *not* junk." Emma's lower lip quivered.

"Is, too."

"Is not."

"Guys," Christy warned. "Both of you, calm down."

"He called my stuff *junk*." Emma was clearly affronted. "I don't make fun of his toys." She poked a finger in her brother's chest. "Take that back."

"Will not. And quit touching me."

He shoved his sister and Emma began weeping. "You're being mean. I want my mommy! She'd make you be nice to me!"

Christy abandoned her task to hold the little girl as she sobbed on her shoulder. "Oh, sweetie, your mom will be home in two weeks. That's only fourteen days. Don't forget about tonight being our phone call night. You don't want your mom and dad to see you with red eyes and a runny nose, do you?"

Emma sniffled.

"You're just being a baby," Derek complained in a typical big-brother voice.

"Am not!"

"Stop, you two," Christy scolded. "We'll straighten this out in a few minutes."

Linc had been outside watering the shrubs and walked in as Christy delivered her warning.

"What's going on?" he asked.

Emma pointed a finger at her brother. "He started it."

"Did not."

"Quiet. Both of you," Linc ordered. "Will someone tell me what's going on?"

"Emma can't find her doll's car and she thinks Derek took it," Christy explained.

"I didn't," Derek insisted.

"Did, too!"

Linc held up his hands. "There's only one way to solve this. We'll look for the car right now."

"It's in Derek's room," Emma informed them.

"Is not."

Christy exchanged a glance at Linc over their heads and shrugged. "They've been like this all afternoon."

"Off you go to your rooms," he commanded as he pointed. "I'll be there in a minute."

As each child stormed to their private corners, Linc paused. "All this drama is over a lost car?"

"That convertible is very important to Em," Christy said with a smile. "The main problem is they both miss their parents. She reacts with tears and Derek hides his feelings behind aggression."

"I didn't realize. Everything was going so smoothly I'd hoped we'd passed that stage."

"We did, but two months can seem like for ever to a child. A time out for both is in order, I think." A distant door slammed and Christy smiled. "Do you want to deal with that or should I?"

"I will," he said.

He returned less than ten minutes later. "The mystery of the missing car is solved."

"Where was it?"

"Under Emma's bed. She'd decided the space was the perfect place for a 'garage' and forgot. She apologized to Derek, so life is good."

"Will you be able to handle them by yourself tomorrow?"

"Considering they'll be in school most of the day, I'd say so," he said wryly, "but I've been thinking. I could go with you."

His offer surprised her because when she'd mentioned her upcoming trip a week ago, he'd simply nodded. "I'm flying to Seattle for the usual battery of tests, not open-heart surgery. Don't you have patients to see?"

"None that couldn't wait until next week," he said. "I've been rearranging my schedule, just in case."

"You have?" She could hardly believe he'd go to the trouble. "Whatever for? You'd go crazy sitting in waiting rooms all day."

He grinned. "Probably, but I'd do it. For moral support."

She wanted to cry at his thoughtfulness. "Thanks, but my mom has planned to spend the day with me. She's used to the routine."

"Good, because I don't want you to be alone," he stated firmly.

It seemed strange to have someone other than her own family fuss over her. His concern gave her a warm, fuzzy feeling that was far better than hot cocoa and a warm blanket on a cold winter night.

"I won't be," she assured him. "This way is best for the kids, too. After tonight's outburst, they need you, not a sitter."

"Maybe, but I still don't understand why you want to travel so far for your tests, only to turn around in another two weeks to visit your doctor. We run the same procedures here, you know."

His voice and expression revealed his frustration quite clearly and she tried to explain her reasons. "This seems silly, but all my records are there and I'd like to have the same people looking at my scans. As crazy as it sounds, they've given me good reports and I don't want to jinx myself."

He fell silent for a few seconds before he finally nodded. "If that's what you need for peace of mind, then that's what you should do."

She was half-surprised he didn't try to convince her otherwise. "You aren't going to tell me I'm being illogical and superstitious?"

"I could," he admitted, "but having faith in one's medical team is crucial to a patient's recovery. If you aren't ready for someone else to run your tests, you shouldn't. Otherwise, whatever the outcome, you'll always question the results."

"Thanks for understanding."

"What I don't like is how you're going to be exhausted when you return."

"It's sweet of you to worry, but I'll be fine."

He frowned. "I don't see how you will be. You're taking the red-eye flight in the morning, spending the entire day being poked, prodded and scanned, then jetting back late at night. At least stay a little longer and fly home Saturday."

"I scheduled my flights months ago. I can't change them now without huge penalties."

"Screw the penalties. I'll pay the difference."

"I can't have you do that. Honestly, I'll be fine." She grinned. "Keep the light on for me, okay?"

"I'll do better than that. I'll be waiting up."

CHAPTER NINE

CHRISTY kissed her mother on the cheek as soon as she met her at the baggage claim the next morning. "Hi, Mom. It's great to see you."

"You, too, hon," her mother said. At a very young-looking fifty-four, Serena Michaels was dressed fashionably smart in spite of the early hour and their final destination. Although Christy had told her repeatedly that no one expected her to look as if she was heading for a photo shoot instead of a day at the hospital, her mother had disagreed.

"If you look great, you'll feel great, too," had been her mantra, so Christy had taken a few special pains herself. Instead of wearing blue jeans and a T-shirt, she'd worn a comfortable pair of dress slacks, one of her favorite designer shirts, and a matching sweater.

"Did you have a good flight?"

"No problems," she answered cheerfully, preparing for the inevitable question that would come next.

"How are you feeling?"

She'd trained herself over the years to not worry about cancer invading again if she didn't feel well, but her mother hadn't learned the same lesson. She still needed the reassurance that as long as her daughter felt healthy, then it must be so.

"Never better," Christy answered. "I really appreciate you taking the time away from the restaurant today."

"Of course I'd take the day off," Serena assured her as she ushered her to the parking garage. "We may as well use the time in between your tests to catch up. I want to hear all about your side job as a live-in nanny and this dance competition you've told me about."

While Christy filled in the details, she soaked up the ambience of the city. She'd grown up here, and while it was home, it also wasn't. Oddly enough, she felt more rooted in Levitt Springs and she wondered if Linc had made the difference.

Throughout the day Christy shared story after story between her sessions of blood draws, PET and bone-density scans, and every other test her physician had ordered. She didn't realize Linc had figured prominently in every tale until her mother commented.

"You've talked about this Linc a lot lately. Is he someone new?"

"I've been acquainted with him since I moved to town, but I didn't really *know* him until we began taking care of his brother's children."

"He sounds like a special fellow," Serena remarked.

"He is. He even offered to rearrange his patient schedule to come with me today."

A knowing smile appeared on her mother's face. "He's that taken with you, is he?"

"He seems to be, but…" she hesitated "…I'm not sure it's wise."

"Why not? You're healthy, attractive, and—" Serena stopped short. "You've told him about your history, haven't you?"

"Yes, Mother."

"The news didn't scare him away?"

"It should have," she said honestly, still amazed by his tenacity, "but it hasn't so far."

Serena's eyes glowed with happiness and she leaned over to hug her. "You're going to keep him, aren't you?"

"A relationship isn't that simple for me, Mom. There are long-term consequences to consider."

"He's a physician, Christy. Of course he knows the consequences."

"I'm just trying to protect him from making a mistake he'll regret, especially if my ovaries never wake up and he can't have the son or daughter he wants."

"I may not be in the medical profession, but even I know there are plenty of ways around that particular problem. Do you love him?"

Christy pondered for a moment. Her feelings for Linc were much stronger and deeper than those she'd felt toward Jon, but she wasn't ready to admit she was in love.

"I care about him," she said simply. "More than I'd expected I would. Probably even more than I should, which is why I can't be certain he really knows what he's getting into. Yes, he has all the medical knowledge, but I'm not sure his heart knows what he's getting into."

"You want to protect him."

Linc had called her tactic "giving him an escape clause". However anyone described it, her mother had pegged her correctly.

"Yes."

"You can be right about so many things, but in this you're wrong. Call your excuse for what it is, daughter. You're not trying to protect him as much as you're trying to protect yourself."

Christy mentally argued against that notion throughout the day, but by the time she was back on the plane and flying home, she finally conceded her mother's assessment might have merit.

She'd always thought she was being altruistic by spelling everything out early in her relationships. Full disclosure early on was in everyone's best interests because if a fellow couldn't deal with her situation, she'd rather learn it early in a relationship. Maybe she *was* only protecting herself, but her method worked.

With Linc, however, it hadn't. He wasn't reacting true to form.

I'll be with you every step of the way, he'd told her. She wanted to believe him, but she couldn't take that leap of faith. He was the one man who, if he ever changed his mind and walked away, would devastate her to the point where she'd never recover.

As the evening dragged on and bad weather delayed her flight, one thought kept her going—she was heading home.

As the hours ticked by, Linc found it more and more difficult to wait patiently for Christy's return. Every light in the main part of the house blazed because he wanted her to see the beacon as soon as she turned onto their street.

He'd expected her at nine and wished he could have met her at the airport, but he couldn't leave Derek and Emma unattended. He'd tried phoning her, but his call had gone straight to her voice mail. A check on her flight status via the internet told him she'd been delayed due to bad weather. He might have wished the airline had cancelled the flight so she wouldn't endure such a long travel day, but he wanted her safe at home and he wouldn't rest until she was.

Finally, he heard the distinctive sound of the garage door mechanism and his shoulders slumped with relief.

"You made it," he said inanely as he greeted her with a heartfelt hug and a brief kiss.

"Finally," she muttered. Her body drooped with apparent exhaustion, her smile seemed forced, and she leaned on him as if the sheer act of standing required more energy than she could summon. She made no effort to leave his embrace, which suited him just fine.

"It's past midnight. I can't believe you waited up for me. You didn't have to, but I'm glad you did."

He grinned. Those few words made the hours of impatience worth it. "I said I would. I couldn't go back on my word, could I?" he said lightly, hoping she'd see this incident as another example of his trustworthiness. "I couldn't sleep anyway until you got home."

She chuckled. "I'll bet you stayed awake when Ty or your sister went out, too."

"Sometimes," he admitted, although waiting for his siblings didn't compare to waiting for Christy. Not knowing where she was or what might be happening had made it impossible to close his eyes. The saying "Ignorance is bliss" didn't apply where Christy was concerned.

He changed the subject. "How did your tests go?"

"Like they usually do. I didn't do a thing except lie on the X-ray tables or sit in chairs. Machines and the staff did all the work."

"Are you tired?" he asked, already knowing the answer.

"Very. You'd think, though, after sitting or lying down all day, I wouldn't be."

"It's a good thing tomorrow is Saturday," he told her. "The kids and I will watch cartoons so you can sleep late."

"That isn't necessary," she began.

"Yes, it is," he insisted. "I'm repaying the favor."

As a sign of her exhaustion, she capitulated. "Okay, but no later than nine," she warned. "Derek has a soccer game at eleven and I have a few things to do before then."

"Nine a.m.," he repeated. "Can I get you anything now? A cup of herbal tea? A glass of water?"

"No, thanks."

"Okay, then. Pleasant dreams."

"You, too," she murmured, before disappearing into her room.

As he performed his final walk-through of the house for the night, his own exhaustion tugged at him and he realized he was ready for the day to end. Now, though, it could, because Christy had come home.

Christy didn't report to work until Tuesday, but the thought of what Linc and the children had done for her this past weekend still brought a smile to her face. Promptly at nine a.m. on Saturday, Emma had knocked on her door and Linc had barged in, carrying a breakfast tray. The plate had contained several misshapen pancakes, a small bowl of fresh strawberries and blueberries, and a cup of her favorite herbal tea prepared specially for her by Emma.

The day had been declared a "Coddle Christy" day and the trio had done so with great enthusiasm. She'd been encouraged to do nothing but eat and sleep and although she'd been certain she didn't need a nap, she'd found herself snoozing in Linc's lounge chair when they'd gone to his house to water his flowers.

His thoughtfulness had given her a few bittersweet moments because their time of sharing a house would be ending soon. While it wouldn't be long before she'd only have her memories to sustain her, what fun it was to create them.

Her good mood faded, however, as Linc pulled her and her supervisor, Denise, into a treatment room during his morning rounds and closed the door.

"I want Christy to look after Mrs Connally this week,"

he informed Denise in his typical, authoritative physician's voice.

Shocked by his request, Christy listened with a combination of horrified surprise, embarrassment, and anger at his high-handedness. "I appreciate your request, Doctor," the charge nurse said diplomatically, "but I can't honor it. If I allowed the doctors to pick and choose which nurses would look after their patients, I'd have a staffing nightmare."

"It's in Mrs Connally's best interests for Christy to be her nurse," he argued. "Have I ever asked for a favor before?"

"Well, no, but I can't establish a precedent. If the other doctors—or the nurses—learned I gave you a special favor, I've have a mutiny on my hands."

"Who has to know?" he said. "This is strictly between the three of us."

"I realize the medical staff each has his or her favorite nurses, but I work hard to spread the difficult cases around. Christy already has several. I can't load her with one more."

"Then pass one of hers to someone else."

"I could, but why do you want her for this particular case?" Denise asked, ever blunt. "I have more experienced nurses—"

"This woman and her family need Christy right now."

"I don't understand."

"You don't have to. However, I know what I'm talking about."

Denise frowned. "I'm sorry, but if you want me to bend the rules, I need a good reason to do so. Why is Christy the only nurse who can take care of your post-mastectomy patient?"

Christy's anger and embarrassment faded as the reasons were painfully obvious. To Linc's credit, he didn't divulge her story but simply reiterated his stance.

"Because I believe she is," he said. "Let's leave it at that, shall we?"

Seeing Denise's mulish expression, Christy knew her

supervisor wouldn't give in. Linc wasn't trying to draw attention to her but he must be concerned about his patient to ask for such an unusual favor.

"I can explain," she addressed her supervisor quietly. "I had a double mastectomy myself."

Denise's argumentative expression vanished and she looked as shocked as if the floor had disappeared underneath her feet. "You?"

"Yeah. About five years ago."

"My patient needs to see she can still have a full and happy life," Linc added. "Because of her personal experience, Christy can show her that in a way few others can."

Denise let out a deep breath. "Okay. You've been reassigned. Tanya can take Mr Wiseman." She paused, peering over her reading glasses. "You should have told me about this before now."

She shrugged. "I've told a few of my patients if they've had similar surgeries, but I didn't necessarily want it to be common knowledge."

"You do realize I'll take advantage of your experience in the future, don't you?"

Christy nodded. "Yes, ma'am."

"Then it's settled." Denise addressed Linc. "Are you satisfied, Doctor?"

He worked his mouth in an obvious attempt to hide a grin. "Absolutely."

"Good." Denise strode from the room, leaving Christy alone with Linc.

"I'm sorry for putting you on the spot," he began, "but Renee Connally is having a difficult time coping with her diagnosis. She's forty years old, has three children, and is convinced her life is over."

"Is it?" she asked.

"The cancer is invasive, but we caught it early and her

sentinel lymph nodes are clear. You were the first person I thought of who might convince her that she can get past this. I'm sorry I outed you."

"The news was bound to break sooner or later," she said, "but don't worry about it. Meanwhile, I'll talk to her."

"Thanks," he said. "The sooner you get her to look positively at her future, the better."

Christy found Renee dozing, her husband in the chair beside her bed. As soon as she walked in, the woman opened her eyes.

"I'm Christy and I'll be taking care of you," she said calmly. "Are you staying ahead of your pain?"

"For the most part."

Christy chatted about non-consequential topics while she checked Renee's drain and offered to teach her how to maintain it as soon as Renee was able. After discussing a few other physical issues with her, Christy said cheerfully, "Doctor says we have to get you moving, so I'm going to bump your hubby from his chair. You can sit there for a while."

As her husband jumped up, Renee shook her head. "I'd rather not. There isn't any point, is there?"

"Of course there is. Lying in bed won't help you return to your normal life."

"That's the point. My life isn't normal any more, is it?"

"Not by your old standards, but whatever treatment you face won't last for ever. You're facing a tough period, to be sure, but you can get past this. You have to, for your children's sakes."

"I know you mean well, but save your Pollyanna attitude for someone else. You have no idea what I'm going through."

"Actually, I do," she said bluntly. "I had a double mastectomy five years ago and I'm proof that life goes on." She pulled up a nearby folding chair and began to tell her story.

* * *

By the end of the week, Christy was pleased with Renee Connally's progress. She had begun to take an active interest in her own nursing care and her entire outlook seemed much improved.

She'd also learned something from Renee and her husband as well. As she watched her walk the hallway with his help and sometimes caught the two of them in the room with their heads together, she came to a startling conclusion.

Jon hadn't loved her.

Oh, he'd been good company and they'd got along well, but true love had staying power. When the going got tough, love allowed two people to endure. It didn't encourage one person to abandon the other.

I'm not going anywhere.

Linc's words resurfaced in her memory. For the first time she began to believe it was possible—that there *were* men who stood by their wives and girlfriends during difficult times. That fellows like Jon were the exception, not the rule.

Unfortunately, her revelation came at a time when she had to shelve her personal concerns and focus on the job at hand. Gail and Ty were due home on Saturday and Christy had a million things to do before they arrived. Not only was the dance competition on her mind but she wanted everything in the house to be in perfect order, from the housework to the laundry. To that end, she created lists of chores for everyone until Linc complained as loudly as the children.

Naturally, Derek and Emma were wild with anticipation.

"We should visit the park so Ria can run off their energy, shouldn't we?" Linc said on Wednesday evening.

"I think so," she said ruefully. "The sad thing is, they're like Energizer Bunnies. Poor Ria is so tired her tail drags most of the time."

"After Saturday, Ria can resume her quiet life." He paused.

"If their flight is delayed again for any reason, we'll cut it close to get to our event on time."

"We'll manage. If nothing else, we'll leave their car and they can drive themselves home."

"Let's hope we don't have to. Derek and Emma would be crushed if they weren't able to greet their parents as soon as they land."

Christy didn't understand what had caused the airline to bump Gail and Ty to a later flight, but she was relieved to have the extra hours' reprieve. Truth was, she wasn't looking forward to returning to her quiet little apartment after being a part of a boisterous family atmosphere.

"I've been spoiled the past two months," Linc commented.

"Spoiled? How?"

"As crazy as it sounds, I liked having all the commotion when I came home at night. It'll take time to get used to peace and quiet again."

"I agree." She grinned. "Maybe we can borrow Derek and Emma for the occasional weekend."

"It's a deal," he said.

Suddenly both children raced through the house, doors slamming, with Ria barking at their heels as they rushed into the back yard.

Linc visibly winced. "I was going to ask if you wanted to run through our dance routine again, but we'd better save that for later. Unless you think we don't need the practice."

She hated the idea of never dancing with him again, so she intended to make the most of her opportunities.

"'Practice makes perfect,'" she quoted. "I'll pencil you into my schedule after the kids are in bed for the night."

"I can't wait."

Neither, it seemed, could she.

* * *

On Saturday at two, Linc herded his group through the airport to the baggage claim where they waited for Gail and Ty to arrive. According to the monitors, their flight would land in a few minutes, so they still had plenty of time to wait. Linc would have preferred spending the extra hour at the house, but every five minutes Derek or Emma had asked, "Can we leave yet?"

Although he'd miss the time with the children, Linc was glad his brother would be home again. He looked forward to giving Christy his full attention.

"Are you okay?" he asked her as they milled around the open area along with others who were also waiting for their friends and family to appear.

"Sure. Why wouldn't I be?"

He suspected the reason went far beyond her desire to create a perfect homecoming. She'd been in her element taking care of Derek and Emma and she was probably sad because her opportunity would end within the next few minutes. Little did she know, though, that he intended to keep her busier than ever.

"You look a little stressed," he hedged.

"Too much on my mind, I guess. Oh, look." She pointed to the group of passengers descending on them. "They're here."

As both children broke away to run toward their parents, Linc remained at Christy's side, his arm slung around her waist. From the way she swiped at the corner of her eyes, he knew his brother's family reunion bothered her more than she let on.

He remained rooted to the spot, determined to show her that no matter the situation, she could lean on him.

"My word, Christy!" Gail exclaimed as she walked into her house a short time later. "This place looks better than when I left."

Christy laughed at her friend's awe. "I wouldn't go that far, but everyone worked hard to get ready for you. We also went grocery shopping and stocked the refrigerator so you won't have to fight the stores for a few days until you recover from jet lag."

"You've thought of everything," Gail marveled. "So tell me quick while the men are unloading the suitcases—how did things go with you and Linc?"

"Great."

Her gaze narrowed. "You're not just saying that, are you?"

"No, I'm not. In fact, things went much better than I'd ever dreamed they would. You were right. He really is a great guy. In fact, I'll probably miss having him around on a daily basis, dirty socks and all," she finished lightly.

Gail eyed her carefully. "Oh, my gosh. You've fallen in love with him, haven't you?"

Christy wanted to deny it, but she couldn't—not to her dearest friend. She didn't know when it had happened, but it had. "I think so," she said.

"How does he feel?"

She smiled. "He says he isn't going anywhere."

Gail clapped her hands and crowed. "I *knew* you two were meant for each other. This is absolutely *wonderful*."

"No, it isn't," she said flatly. "We have so many potential problems ahead of us. It wouldn't be fair to ask him to face those when he doesn't have to."

"Don't you think he's already weighed the pros and cons? He's an adult and can make his own decisions," Gail informed her. "He doesn't need you to think for him."

"I know, but how can I be sure he won't change his mind when the going gets rough?"

"Some things you have to take on faith."

Unfortunately, when it came to something this important, her faith was practically non-existent.

"Are you worried about your doctor's appointment? Is that why you can't think reasonably?"

"I'm concerned, not worried, and I *am* thinking reasonably."

The sympathy in Gail's eyes suggested that she didn't agree. "You've been feeling okay, haven't you? You don't have any symptoms that you're not telling me about?"

"No symptoms and, yes, Mother, I've been feeling fine. Thanks for asking."

"I'm sounding mother-hen-ish, aren't I?"

"A little, but I know you mean well." She hugged her friend. "I'm glad you're back," she said sincerely, because she *had* missed her. "Thanks again for the opportunity to look after your kids. We had a wonderful time and I'll never forget it."

"I'm glad. We couldn't have enjoyed ourselves as much as we did if we weren't confident Derek and Emma were taken care of."

Linc walked in with a suitcase in each hand, his brother behind him equally laden. "I hate to rush away without hearing about your time in France, but Christy and I have a fall festival to attend."

Gail snapped her fingers. "That's right. The dance competition is tonight. I'd forgotten."

"We haven't, because, oh, by the way, we're going to win." Linc grinned.

Christy laughed. "Spoken like an overconfident surgeon. Seriously, though, we're quite good."

"I left four tickets on the counter if you decide you'd like to watch our performance," Linc informed his brother and sister-in-law. "We're the very last couple on the schedule, so it'll be close to nine o'clock. After that, the disc jockey will provide music and open the dance floor to everyone."

After a quick round of goodbyes, Christy allowed Linc to

escort her and Ria to her car. Her suitcases were already in the trunk and as soon as he opened the passenger door, Ria bounded inside.

"I guess this is it," she said.

"Only for now," he said firmly. "I'll pick you up at your house in two hours. That will give you time to rest before our big evening."

"You mean time to get nervous?"

"You aren't nervous, are you? This can't be coming from the woman who assured me this fundraiser was all in the spirit of fun."

"I lied," she said promptly.

"Surely my fearless partner—the same lady who jumps out of airplanes and rides the rapids—isn't suffering from cold feet, is she?"

"As crazy as it sounds, yes."

"Silly woman," he said with obvious affection. "Win or lose, we're going to be great."

She eyed him carefully. "Somehow I'd always imagined that I'd give *you* the pep talk tonight. Are you the same Lincoln Maguire who had to be coerced into participating?"

"One and the same, but we've practiced until we could both dance our steps in our sleep and sometimes I have. If we trip or miss a step, we've already practiced that, too." He grinned. "We'll recover."

His humor was infectious. "We will, but why don't I save time and meet you at the convention center?"

"I seem to remember having this same discussion once before," he said sternly, although the twinkle in his eye minimized the sting, "but now, like then, my answer is no. We're partners. We'll arrive and leave together."

His description made her realize how badly she needed him to understand what a partnership with her would mean. Somehow she had to make certain he looked at a future through regular lenses and not rose-colored glasses. However, she'd save that discussion for later.

She gave in. "If that's what you want to do."

"It is. Now, drive home safely, and I'll see you soon."

She couldn't stop her pulse from leaping with anticipation, although she knew tonight's dance competition might only be the beginning of the end.

CHAPTER TEN

LINC strode into his house and hardly noticed the quiet. He was too busy replaying the last few hours they'd spent together. From the moment they'd got into the car and headed to the airport, he'd sensed Christy's mental withdrawal. At first, he'd thought it was because she simply didn't want to say goodbye to the kids, but his gut warned that it went much deeper. She intended to distance herself from *him*, probably out of an altruistic notion that she would save him from himself.

He wasn't going to let her because he intended to stick to her like glue. The only way she'd get away from him would be if she moved to another city, and he wasn't averse to following her. In the space of a few weeks he'd come to the point where he wanted her to be a part of his every day. He didn't want some steady, dependable sort, although Christy was all that and more. He wanted the Christy who fearlessly faced life with joy and grace because…

Because he loved her.

The realization hit him hard, but it was true. He loved her, and he'd do anything within his power for her, just as his father had done for the love of *his* life. As he looked at his childhood with new eyes the weight of his old resentments dropped off. He couldn't let the day end without telling Christy how he felt.

She'd probably tell him he was mistaken or try to convince him of her shortcomings, but she didn't understand the most important thing. He needed her just as she was.

They were by no means late and, in fact, had arrived at the convention hall a little early, but Christy was amazed by the crowd of people who'd already gathered.

"You're at table five, near the front," the woman at the check-in desk informed them. "Enjoy yourselves and good luck with the competition. We have a packed house tonight."

The news didn't come as any surprise. Christy had suspected people would come in droves and it was nice to know she'd been right.

"Let's find our table before we mingle," Linc said in her ear because the noise level already made hearing difficult.

"Good idea," she said, conscious of his hand on the small of her back as they wound their way through the tables and groups of people. The skirt of her red silky dress, purchased specifically for tonight's occasion because it flared and flowed in the right places, swung provocatively over her sashaying hips. The spaghetti-strapped bodice was covered in glittery sequins and would sparkle like diamonds under the spotlight. The garment fit perfectly and although Linc's hand didn't stray from the base of her spine, her skin sizzled under the heat of his fingers.

She'd proved her mother's belief about clothing, she decided. She felt as sensational as the dress, and Linc's admiring gaze when he'd arrived at her house had told her it had been money well spent.

Linc had earned her admiring gaze, too. She'd seen him wearing scrubs, casual work attire as well as workout clothes, but, as wonderfully as he filled out those garments, he was positively awesome in his black tuxedo pants and the long-sleeved dress shirt he wore open at his neck.

Christy meandered past various groups and mingled with others, conscious of Linc remaining at her side. She was surprised he didn't veer off to visit with his own friends and colleagues and leave her to her own devices. Instead, if he wanted to speak to someone, he'd grab her hand and drag her along. If she saw someone and headed toward them, he followed.

The truth was she was thrilled he didn't leave her. At this moment they were a couple. A pair.

Partners.

I'm not going anywhere, he'd told her on several occasions, and since then he hadn't. For the first time she began to believe that it might be true—that he wouldn't leave her when or if the going got rough.

By the end of the hour the hall was packed and they took their seats at the same table as several of Linc's partners and their wives.

Janice Martin, a distinguished lady in her mid-sixties, who was seated on Christy's left, leaned close. "I'm pleased you convinced Linc to participate in this event. The man is too young to work twenty-four seven. He needed an interest outside the hospital and I'm delighted you gave him one."

"Thank you, but it was more a case of bullying him into it rather than persuading him to volunteer."

Janice patted her arm. "However you managed this miracle, I'm glad you did. Why, he looks like a new man."

Christy glanced at Linc, who was chatting with Dale Zorn, a cardiologist, on his right. The version of the Lincoln Maguire beside her bore little resemblance to the man she'd known a few weeks ago. That fellow had been tense, extremely focused, and didn't smile. Now his face was animated and his body relaxed, as if he didn't have a care in the world.

"Being a temporary father to his nephew and niece had a lot to do with his transformation," she told Janice.

"Ah, yes. My husband told me you two were looking after his brother's kids. How did you enjoy being parents?"

How could she possibly describe the best experience in recent memory? "I had the time of my life," she said simply.

As soon as she'd voiced those words, she realized how appropriate it had been for Linc to choose that particular song for their dance routine. It was a fitting end to their two months together.

Selfishness suddenly reared its head. Because of all the potential obstacles facing them, ending their relationship might be for the best, but every fiber of her being warned that it would be a mistake—one she would regret for the rest of her days. Truth was, she wanted what the Connallys had—a partnership that saw them through the good times as well as the bad.

Their partnership was more than a simple agreement between two people. Love had knit them together; love had made the difference—the same type of love she felt for Linc.

Then you know what you have to do, her little voice chided her. *Take the risk.*

She wanted to ponder her choices and replay all of her what-if scenarios, but the master-of-ceremonies interrupted her thoughts as he began the event. Linc turned to her. "Nervous?"

"A little. You?"

"Never better."

For the next thirty minutes Christy and the rest of the guests were entertained by the various teams who performed. Some were good, others fair, still others were perfectly awful or downright hilarious, but through it all she was conscious of Linc's arm resting on the back of her chair, his hand curled around her shoulder.

She simply couldn't imagine going back to the way things had been before. In the hours prior to tonight's event, her apartment had seemed so sterile and lifeless and the thought of facing that existence day after day was too horrible to imagine.

She wanted to be with Linc, morning, noon, and night. She wanted him to tease her about how she squeezed her toothpaste, rave over her meals, and pamper Ria as much as she did. She needed him in more ways than she could ever list, and she needed him like she needed air to breathe, because she loved him.

So focused was she on her epiphany, she hardly noticed he'd moved until he whispered into her ear, his breath warm against her neck. "We're next."

She nodded. The butterflies in her stomach suddenly settled as she resolved to express her feelings during their song. She realized how diligently he'd been working to convince her to trust him and now seemed the perfect opportunity to show him what lay in her heart. The words would come later, when they were alone.

The performance ended, although Christy had been so focused on her private thoughts she hadn't paid attention to her competition. After the applause died down, the MC announced their names.

Linc grabbed her hand and led her to the dance floor. Before he left her to stand alone center stage, he squeezed her fingers and winked.

She laughed at his irreverence while he moved to stage right. The crowd fell silent as the familiar melody began.

Christy allowed the music to wash over her, paying careful attention to the lyrics as she poured out the emotions that matched those expressed in the song.

Through the basic grind that brought a few catcalls, then the flamenco, various dips and spins, the spectators faded into nothingness as she focused on Linc.

He clearly did the same because his gaze had locked on

hers. Easily, effortlessly, she glided through the steps. As the music drew to a close, the final spin brought her into Linc's embrace.

Barely conscious of the thundering applause, she only had eyes for Linc. He traced her jaw, then bent his head and kissed her in such a lingering manner that her toes tingled and the crowd went wild.

As the announcer came to the microphone, Linc broke contact and they made their way back to their table. Christy's heart pounded as much from his kiss as from the exertion and she felt so marvelous she was certain her feet didn't touch the floor. People nodded to her as they clapped while others pounded Linc on his back for a job well done.

"Okay, folks. Based on the amount of applause, I think it's easy to tell which team is our winner. Dr Lincoln Maguire and his lovely partner, Christy Michaels!"

The hired DJ began a music set and encouraged everyone to participate. The mood in the building was high and from the numbers of couples who took to the dance floor, they'd been energized by Christy and Linc's performance.

"Do you want to stay?" Linc asked her.

She hesitated, trying to read him and failing. "Would you mind if we didn't?"

His slow grin was the answer she wanted. "Not at all."

Although Linc graciously accepted everyone's congratulations on their way out, he chafed at the delay. He wanted to simply toss Christy over his shoulder and walk through the throng, but he'd already pushed his limits when he'd kissed Christy in front of five hundred spectators. People he knew and those he didn't remarked on his memorable performance, although he didn't know if they'd been impressed by his dancing ability or because he'd kissed his partner with such fervor.

Either way, the first *Dancing with the Docs* event would go down in hospital history.

"Would you like to come inside?" she asked as he pulled into a parking space outside her apartment.

"I'd like that." His gut warned him that something monumental would take place and, if his suspicions were correct, it wouldn't be good.

"My selection is limited tonight," she said as she headed for her kitchen. "Would you like water or wine?"

The wine could wait until they had something to celebrate. "Water, please." As she handed him a glass and they headed into the living room, he asked, "What's on your mind? And don't say 'Nothing' because I can read you too well."

"Okay." She placed her glass on the coffee table before she sank onto her sofa. "Here's the deal.

"This afternoon, I'd contemplated how we should go our separate ways."

He nodded. "I suspected as much."

"It seemed the right thing to do. You want things out of life that I might not be able to give you—two point five kids, a minivan, becoming soccer parents, and the potential to celebrate a fiftieth anniversary, to name a few.

"My mother told me I was trying to protect myself from being hurt, and deep down I was. I'd done a good job, too, until you came along," she said wryly, "but you wiggled through my defenses and I did the unthinkable. I fell in love with you."

After bracing himself for the worst, relief swept through him to the point he couldn't speak.

Her mouth trembled as she met his gaze. "Whatever happens next is up to you."

Rather than act on her cue to leave if he so desired, he drew her against him. "I'm not going anywhere."

"You're sure? Think long and hard about your decision," she warned.

"I already have. I love you too much to be intimidated by the obstacles we might face."

Tears glistened in her eyes. "Oh, Linc."

"You should know that I'd anticipated this conversation ever since you left Gail and Ty's. In fact, I'd intended to seduce you if that's what it took to persuade you of my sincerity."

She chuckled. "Wow."

"In fact, I may do it anyway." With that, he kissed her.

When Christy finally came up for air, she scooted away. "Before we take this to its logical conclusion, I want everything perfectly clear between us. My cancer could return. Derek and Emma might never have a cousin or two. We could—"

"Whatever happens, I'm going into our relationship with both eyes open," he assured her. "Do I need to sign your list in blood or is my word good enough?"

She smiled. "Your word is enough," she said simply.

"Good. While we're tossing out worst-case scenarios, I could develop a life-threatening disease in five, ten or twenty years. I had mumps as a child and could be sterile. What if I walk into the hospital parking lot and a runaway car runs me down? Could you deal with *my* issues if they ever happen?"

His points made her realize she might be making more out of her worries than necessary. "Yes. However, there's one more thing for you to consider."

"Christy," he said kindly, "whatever your concern, it isn't as important as you think it might be. I love you for the woman you are."

"That's sweet of you to say, but I want to give you one last chance to change your mind. You may not need to see this, but I need to show you."

She led him into her bedroom and turned her back toward him. "Unzip me, please. I can't reach."

"This is completely unnecessary."

"I don't agree. Just do it."

As soon as he tugged down the zipper, she turned around to face him. Slowly, carefully, she let the gown drop to the floor.

"I want you to see exactly what you're getting," she said softly. "If you're repulsed—"

She held her breath and watched his expression as he gazed at her manmade curves. She saw interest and awe, but not disgust, and she finally allowed herself to breathe.

He traced her collarbone with a feather-light touch before trailing his fingers down her breastbone. Meeting her gaze without flinching or hesitation, he suddenly pulled her against his chest and covered her back with his hands.

"I see the most beautiful woman in the world."

Although logic said otherwise, she was thrilled he thought so. "Will you stay with me tonight?"

He nodded. "On two conditions."

She raised an eyebrow. "And they are?"

"One, I won't leave until morning. In fact, I won't leave until it's time for our flight."

Surprised by his comment, she asked, "Do you want to come along?"

"Nothing could keep me away. In fact, I bought my ticket two weeks ago. I had planned to go with you, one way or another."

If she'd needed final proof that he would stick by her, no matter what, he'd just provided it.

"What's the second condition?"

"That you agree to marry me. I want you to know beyond all doubt that I won't be influenced by the outcome of your appointment."

Although she'd suspected as much, until now she'd been afraid to believe. "I know you will," she said simply. "And, yes, I'll be your wife."

His grin instantly stretched across his face before he stepped back and began unbuttoning his shirt. "Good. Now that we've addressed those minor details, I want to make love with you."

She wanted to cry with happiness and all she could do was nod her agreement.

"I hope you got a nap this afternoon," he added, "because we won't be sleeping most of the night."

Christy helped with his buttons, enjoying the feel of his hard chest beneath her fingers. "Is that so?"

"Oh, yes," he assured her, before he stepped out of his trousers and drew her against him once again. "It's a promise."

Christy sat in her oncologist's private office with Linc beside her as they waited for Dr Kingston to walk in. He'd conducted his exam in his usual noncommittal manner and after he'd finished, he'd suggested she join him in his office as soon as she'd dressed.

She pulled on her clothes in record time.

As she sat in front of the doctor's desk, outwardly she was calm, but inwardly she was a bundle of nerves.

"Whatever he tells us, we'll deal with it," Linc assured her as he held her hand in his strong one.

She managed a smile. "I know, but—"

"Think optimistically," Linc told her.

The door swung wide and Dr Kingston entered. He was tall, thin, and reminded her of an oversized scarecrow, but his eyes were full of compassion. He also seemed older than she remembered, but she supposed his job was more difficult and more stressful than most.

"Sorry for the delay," he said in a kindly voice that matched his expression. "I had to take a phone call."

Christy introduced Linc, then waited for the oncologist to open her chart on his desk.

"You're doing well?" he asked. "Still enjoying your job?"

"Oh, yes."

"My wife insists I need to take a vacation. Maybe we should travel to the Midwest. I haven't been in the area in years."

"It's a wonderful part of the country," she agreed, fighting her impatience.

"I imagine it is. But, then, you aren't here to listen to my vacation plans, are you?" Without waiting for her response—which was a good thing because she suddenly couldn't breathe—he opened her folder. "Ah, yes. I remember now. Your results came in a week ago."

"And?" she asked, her palms suddenly moist.

He leaned back in his chair and steepled his fingers. "Your scans are clear. No sign of any abnormalities."

Christy's shoulders slumped and tears came to her eyes as Linc hugged her.

"Your tumor marker levels haven't changed either, so I'd say you passed your five-year check-up with flying colors."

"Thank you," she choked out.

He smiled. "I'll be happy to take the credit because I don't often have the opportunity to deliver good news. Out of curiosity, though, I know you celebrate your anniversary with an adventure. What did you plan for this year?"

Christy looked at Linc and smiled at him with all the love in her heart. "A wedding."

* * * * *

SEDUCED BY THE HEART SURGEON

CAROL MARINELLI

CHAPTER ONE

'YOU ALREADY KNOW, don't you, Freya?'

'Know what?' Freya frowned as she attempted to pull up the zipper on her friend Beth's wedding dress. It had slipped up easily at the final fitting just last week so Freya gave it another tug but it refused to budge. 'Have you…?'

Freya stopped herself from continuing with the question. She, more than most, knew just how much damage that a throwaway comment about weight could cause and she certainly didn't want to inflict that pain on Beth. Especially not on her wedding day, but, hell, the dress was tight.

Then it dawned on Freya why she was having so much trouble getting Beth into her wedding dress. Beth had declined Freya's offer of champagne as they prepared for her late afternoon wedding and the girls' night in at Freya's apartment last week had been a very tame affair.

Freya worked it out just a split second before her friend said it.

'I'm pregnant!'

Oh, Freya was very grateful for that split second because her eyes had screwed closed as yet another friend revealed their happy news, but by the time Beth had turned around, Freya had composed herself and was smiling.

'That's fantastic news, Beth.'

'Don't pretend that you didn't know.'

'I honestly had no idea,' Freya admitted.

'I didn't have even one of the cocktails you'd made!'

'I thought it was a bit odd,' Freya admitted, because Beth loved a drink. 'I just believed you when you said that you were detoxing for the wedding.'

Oh, it had been a tame night. Two of the women were pregnant, one was breastfeeding and now Freya understood why Beth had also declined the cocktails that Freya had prepared. For Freya, it had been a long night of being told, *It will be your turn soon,* and asked, *Are you still not seeing anyone?* Her friends didn't know about her fertility issues, so they hadn't been deliberately insensitive. She could have told them that day that she'd had blood work done and when Hilary was back from her trip she would be having some further tests to see if she might be a candidate for IVF through an egg donor.

Freya didn't really open up to anyone, though, not fully.

'So when did you find out?' Freya asked Beth.

'Two weeks ago. I was devastated at first, I have to admit.'

'Devastated?' Freya checked. She knew very well that Beth and Neil both wanted a family and so she wondered if they had found out that there was something wrong with the baby.

'Well, I was very upset,' Beth clarified. 'We've been saving up for the honeymoon for ages and had paid for all drinks to be included...' Beth rolled her eyes at the perceived inconvenience. 'I'm fine about it now.'

Fine!

Freya did her best not to dwell on that word.

Finally the zip was up and she arranged the huge bow on Beth's dress.

Freya knew that she overthought everything but, really, to use the word *fine* to describe the news that you were pregnant irked her!

'Have you told your parents?' Freya asked once she had unclenched her jaw.

'Not yet. Neil's going to reveal the news during the speeches, so we can capture everyone's expressions. Can you warn the cameraman?'

'Sure.'

'You won't forget?'

'I never forget,' Freya said. 'That's why you've got me planning your wedding, remember!'

Oh, Freya was on edge and trying not to be but Beth really was a bridezilla.

'Okay, done. Wow. You look amazing!' Freya said. 'Simply stunning.'

No one could ever tell when Freya was lying. It was why she was so successful in PR.

The dress that Beth had chosen was a long sheath of ivory tulle, tied in the middle with a huge satin bow.

Like an oddly wrapped parcel, Freya thought.

Worse, Beth had chosen similar for Freya to wear. Hers was knee-length, though, and the shade of Freya's dress was Antique White. Freya felt as if she was wearing an old teabag. Her brunette hair had been teased into curls and Beth had insisted on red lips for them both. The only saving grace was that the bow on Freya's dress was smaller.

They looked like two poodles who'd been badly clipped, Freya thought as she stared at their reflections.

'Are you wearing a bra?' Beth checked.

'It didn't work with the dress,' Freya said.

'Well, put some plasters on them,' Beth said. 'I don't want *your* nipples in *my* photos.'

There was a knock at the door and, of course, brides didn't answer doors, so Freya opened it and smiled when she saw Beth's father, realising it was time for her to head down and check the last-minute details.

'Right, I'm going to go down and make sure everything is in place,' Freya said. 'Enjoy every moment and leave all the worrying to me.'

'I shall.' Beth nodded. 'It's all set for midnight?'

'It is.'

'I want everyone watching us kiss as we ring in the New Year.'

'They shall be.'

'Thanks for organising everything.'

'Well, it's been a lot more fun sorting out flowers and table plans than getting everyone at The Hills to glam up for the new brochure…'

'They're already a glam lot.'

'I know they are.' That hadn't been what Freya had meant but there wasn't time for all that now. 'I'll see you down in the hotel chapel.'

'Don't forget the plasters,' Beth reminded her. Freya smiled and picked up her posy of red flowers to match her red lips then stepped out of the room and let out a very long breath.

Again she had lied. This wedding had been *hell* to organise.

Two of the hotels that Beth and Neil had chosen as potential venues had explained that their stairways and escalators were for all of their guests, especially on New Year's Eve. It had been difficult to find somewhere to accommodate all their demands but Freya had achieved it.

The wedding was at five, then dinner and speeches,

but instead of being able to relax afterwards she had to keep the cameraman and photographer sober, as well as get two hundred guests out of the ballroom and onto the main staircase. Oh, and her ex, Edward, was going to be there.

As he had been at three other weddings she'd attended this year.

Freya was so over weddings!

She knew that her PR skills were a very large reason that Beth had chosen her to be bridesmaid.

It didn't offend Freya.

To survive as top PR consultant in LA, you needed to keep in with your contacts. Beth was a journalist, and the many hours that Freya had spent organising the wedding would be returned in kind.

It was called networking and Freya was very good at that.

Freya got to her hotel room to freshen up. She checked her make-up and wished she hadn't—it was far too much.

She really didn't like this dress and how *much* it revealed of her shoulders. Her upper back was bare too and she felt exposed. Freya turned and craned her neck and told herself that everyone in the chapel would be looking at the bride rather than the bridesmaid's spinal column.

As always, she checked her phone and saw that there were several messages and missed calls from her brother, James.

Work.

Freya knew that it would be.

James Rothsberg was *the* cosmetic surgeon in LA and for the past six years he had poured everything into The Hollywood Hills Medical Center. It was an amazing facility frequented by the rich and famous. Affectionately known as The Hills, it had everything from obstetrics to intensive care and was the top tier of health care. Two years ago James had asked Freya to come on board and she had put her PR skills to excellent commercial use.

Till now.

It was time to give back, she had told James.

And he'd listened.

Which was why, instead of rolling her eyes at being called late afternoon on New Year's Eve, Freya called her brother.

'Hi, James,' Freya said. 'You've been trying to get hold of me.'

'I have,' James said. 'Freya, I need you at The Hills tomorrow at nine.'

'On New Year's Day?' Freya checked.

'I've just taken a call from Geoff, and Paulo's condition has deteriorated. I've just spoken with Zackary and he's agreed to come in and be interviewed tomorrow instead of waiting till Monday.'

Freya's eyes screwed closed as James carried on talking.

'I need you to be at the interview.'

'Me?' Freya tried to keep the quake from her voice. 'Since when did I sit in on the hiring of medical personnel?'

'Since you talked me into taking on charitable cases,' James answered tartly. 'And, given we're going to be asking him to donate his skills for nothing…'

'He already knows that he'll be doing some pro bono work.'

'Freya?'

She could hear the question in her brother's voice at her reluctance to sit in on the interview. After all, Freya had been the one pushing for The Hills to embrace this. Freya had been the one looking into a suitable charity to properly support and now things were finally moving along. But what James didn't understand was that the very seemingly together, always-very-much-in-control Freya had got herself into a little pickle that her older brother didn't know about.

There was a big pickle her brother didn't know about either, namely that the charity she'd found was headed by his ex, Mila Brightman, but it was the other pickle in the jar that Freya was wrestling with now.

She had already been dreading meeting the hotshot cardiac surgeon Zackary Carlton.

Or Zack, as she'd found out he'd prefer to be known.

They had flirted via emails.

Not much.

It felt massive to Freya, though.

'I need you there tomorrow at nine,' James said. 'I'm sure he's going to have questions about the promotional side of things and I want a press release out saying that we have Zackary on board.'

'Zack!' Freya said. 'He prefers to be called Zack.'

'Noted,' James responded. 'I'll see you tomorrow at nine. I'll flick over some details tonight.'

'Thanks.'

Oh, God.

After the tame girls' night with her smug married friends, Freya had poured another cocktail and opened up her laptop and located a certain series of emails.

She never got involved with people she worked with. Actually, Freya really didn't get too involved full stop. But this teeny tiny flirt had been fun and Zack had outright asked if she was single.

Several daiquiris later, when Freya, who took her health seriously and didn't often drink, had decided to embrace the merits of *not* being married, she had typed her response back.

Very single. (Don't tell James.)

And now, tomorrow, she had to face him.

His response had made her blush and it was making her blush now.

I never kiss and tell.

Hopefully he wouldn't get the role, Freya thought, but who was she kidding? James wanted Zack Carlton on board, so much so that he had him currently housed in a luxury apartment that The Hills owned and was interviewing him on New Year's Day.

It had been a stupid flirt, a tiny one, but it had been completely out of character for her, and not just professionally. Freya wasn't a flirty person at all, she was far too controlled for that.

Blame it on the daiquiris.

Actually, she couldn't because the flirt had started a couple of emails prior to that.

She sighed. He was probably fifty and married with sixteen children. She'd blush about it tomorrow, but right now she had to deal with the wedding.

First, though, she texted her neighbour Red. Freya had a late checkout but hadn't been intending to use it as she wanted to get home to her little dog, Cleo. Instead, she asked Red if he would let her out and feed her in the morning.

With that sorted she went to go but then Freya caught sight of her bare shoulders; she turned and looked again at her spine.

It had been that sight that had terrified James. Freya could still remember his shocked reaction as he had sat her up so that the doctor could listen to her chest.

'Freya!'

She had always kept this part of her body covered, hiding her secret, denying to everyone she had a problem, partying her way through her parents' appalling divorce and pretending she didn't care.

It was hard enough having high-profile actors as parents and wearing the Rothsberg name, but when that marriage had ended, to have it played out over the media had been agony.

And when a journalist had pointed out that Freya was just a little bit younger than her father's latest girlfriend, a magazine had taken it one nasty step further and pointed out that Freya was also considerably larger.

Her comfort during the very public break-up had, till then, been food and she'd had to endure the spotlight that had shone on her parents suddenly widening to accommodate both herself and James.

She had rigorously denied herself the comfort of food.

Very rigorously!

And she had also partied hard.

James had hauled her out of a nightclub and, too weak to row with her brother, Freya had collapsed and been rushed to hospital.

There she had been stripped and put into a gown and then James had been allowed back in, and that was when he had seen her spine and the true extent of her problem had been exposed.

Now, fourteen years later, she would stand today with the most loathed part of her body on show and, joy of joys, eat at the top table.

Freya was better now—so, so much better.

Recovered, healed, whatever the best word was, but there were still hurts and repercussions that she had to deal with, and one of the big ones was that she rarely had a period.

Seriously rarely.

Once, maybe twice a year.

'It's your own fault,' Freya told her reflection, and then came away from the mirror and headed out to the elevator.

She got in and closed her eyes, resting against the wall as she angled her neck to release tension. When she opened them, instead of being on the mezzanine level, she was on the ground floor, and looking into the eyes of Him!

'Well, you prove my theory,' he said in a deep, sexy voice.

It was Him!

The man she had seen a few days ago.

Freya had been speaking with the hotel's events co-ordinator and working out how long they would need to freeze the escalators for, when they'd both stopped talking as the sound of Cuban heels had rung out on the marble floor. And they had stopped talking with good reason. Tall, tanned, with shaggy, curly black hair, he had walked past them in dark jeans and tight T-shirt, carrying a large backpack. He had been just so sexy that he'd simply stopped conversations. Both women had watched him go up to the desk to check in and then shared a guilty smile once they'd finished checking him out.

And now Freya was in the lift with Him.

'And your theory is?' Freya asked.

'That all the good girls are taken.' He asked her which floor she wanted. 'I've already pressed...' Actually, no, her selection had been erased. 'The mezzanine level.' She watched as long suntanned fingers pressed said level and then he pressed for floor twenty-eight and she wished, how she wished, she had given the thirtieth floor as her choice of destination, just for a minute or two more alone with him.

'Shouldn't brides be smiling on their wedding day?' he asked, and Freya tried to place his accent.

'Believe me, the bride is smiling,' Freya said in a dry voice. 'I'm the bridesmaid.'

'Did I hear the word *maid*?'

Freya laughed at the cheeky inference and the slow smile he gave in return had her stomach tighten. Sexy green eyes were looking right at her, and he didn't make her feel like an old maid in the least...

Freya blinked at her own thought process.

The hotel events coordinator had, when they'd been watching him, sighed that he was probably gay and Freya had said if that were the case, *again*, then she really had to get out of LA.

Oh, he was so not gay. His eyes might as well be blow-torches because he had her face just turn to fire.

Sadly the doors pinged open.

'Enjoy the wedding...' he said.

'Oh, I shan't, it's going to be a very long evening,' Freya replied, peeling herself from the wall, when she really didn't want to get out.

'Yeah, I get it.' he said. 'I do my best to avoid weddings.' He met her eyes. 'Especially my own.'

Was he telling her that he was single?

She thought back to the flirty emails that she would live to regret tomorrow, but flirting was kind of fun, Freya was finding out, and she was *very* single.

'And me,' Freya said.

The elevator doors were open but the conversation

wasn't closed and he put one big boot out to keep them open as he asked Freya a question. 'Why did she want a big white wedding on a Thursday?'

'Because it's New Year's Eve.'

'So it is! Well, thanks for reminding me, I'd be in trouble if I didn't call home.'

'You're Australian?' Freya asked, now that she'd placed his accent.

He nodded.

'LA's a long way from home.'

'It is,' he answered. 'And I'm suddenly lonely.'

He didn't look lonely in the least, not with that smile.

'Poor you,' Freya replied, and met his smouldering gaze. His deep green eyes were thickly lashed and she looked down to a dark red mouth and stubbled jaw.

He was so hot, so direct, so bad, so sexy and her reaction to him so acute that Freya could possibly have forgiven herself if she'd hit the button to close the doors and leapt up onto those lean hips.

'I'd better go,' she said, because, yes, she'd better. 'It was nice to meet you...' Freya fished for his name.

'We don't need names, do we?'

She ought to have been offended, Freya thought. She ought to be very, very offended and yet she wasn't.

'Enjoy the wedding,' he offered, 'and thanks for messing up my theory.'

'But I haven't,' Freya said, simply unable to resist prolonging this delicious, rare flirt and, just as when she had hit 'send' on that blasted email, she offered a verbal response that would be just as hard to retract. 'I'm not a good girl.'

'It would seem that you are,' he answered smoothly, 'given that you're about to get out.'

The bow around her middle was killing Freya. She

wanted to tear it off, and the dress too, and stamp on them. Instead she stood as his eyes performed a long and slow perusal of her aroused body and Beth would be furious because her nipples were throbbing. They needed his mouth. Oh, yes, they did.

Oh, she was in no position to take offence as his gaze lingered and lingered, because Freya was doing the exact same thing to him. Down that wide chest her eyes went. He was wearing a silver-grey T-shirt and he too had two nipples, she knew that because she counted them slowly and carefully. Then she looked down to his flat stomach. His T-shirt was half-tucked in and she fought not to lift it free. He had on a heavy leather belt that made her thighs want to press together. She looked at the thick bulge in his jeans and was frustrated by the button-up flies, because she'd break her nails tearing at them just to get to him. What the hell was happening? Freya wondered. Because she completely wanted to sink to her knees and to do just that.

It was, for Freya, the oddest feeling. She wasn't very free in bed and she wasn't the most generous lover. She just hoped to have her needs met. 'One for you, one for me' type of thing, and if her needs weren't met then she'd lie twitching with resentment. Actually, even if they were met, it was so underwhelming that she lay twitching anyway, wondering why she couldn't enjoy it. Freya controlled everything that went in her mouth and what she was looking at now wasn't one of them.

Freya licked her lips, not deliberately but very provocatively, it would seem, because he just grew before her eyes. She watched as that lovely hand that had earlier pressed the button had no choice but to make a little room and he rearranged himself to her eyes.

Freya tore them from his bulging crotch and he gave

her a slow, appreciative smile in reward for her lovely effort to get him so hard and so soon.

'I'm impressed,' he said.

'With what?' Freya breathed. She could hardly speak.

'It takes great skill to be such a turn-on in that dress.'

And Freya had more than seen just how turned on he was. 'I have to go.'

'Then go.'

He didn't remove his boot from the door, and Freya could either step over his leg or walk around him. The scent of him mingled with her arousal and Freya had this terrifying moment of absolute conviction that she wasn't going to make it to the chapel in time.

He was sex.

And suddenly, for the first time in her life, so was she.

Freya didn't walk around him, she put one high-heeled foot over his calf and proceeded to step over the hurdle.

She'd never gotten over them at school and was having the same trouble now.

He was terribly polite, for such a filthy animal he really was extremely polite, because his hand settled on her arm to help her over.

Oh, she needed help because the feel of his warm fingers on her bare skin had Freya wanting to straddle his calf and she knew that the bastard knew it.

'Do you want to come up for a drink?' he offered in that low, sexy, deep voice but, really, why bother attempting to be polite? Freya thought. A drink was the very last thing on either of their minds.

'I have a wedding to get to,' Freya croaked. 'I really do.'

'Then you'd better go, or you're going to be extremely unpresentable very soon.'

Oh, those eyes, Freya thought, unwilling to leave the

heat of his gaze, but then she looked at his mouth as he stated what he'd already achieved.

'I want to mess you up,' he said. 'I want you dishevelled.'

She deserved a gold medal and the national anthem sung in her honour because she had made it over his leg. Freya tried to walk off, she really did, but her muscles were protesting and her damp knickers were demanding that she take them off.

'Hey,' he called to her blushing shoulders. She could feel his eyes on her spine and it didn't make her feel ill, instead it made Freya, foolishly, dangerously, turn around. 'If the wedding gets to be a bit...' He shrugged. And then, with utter and no doubt practised ease, he gave her a free pass to heaven. 'Room 2812.'

CHAPTER TWO

'FREYA?' THE HOTEL'S events coordinator prompted when Freya didn't answer her question.

'I was just taking it all in,' Freya said, rather than admit her mind was still back in the elevator. She looked around the ballroom. 'Yes, Beth's going to be very pleased.'

The tables were dressed in red but instead of having flowers as centrepieces Beth had decided on huge bows. There were bows on the chairs too. Freya's carefully worded response told the hotel events coordinator that she had done an amazing job with terrible directions.

They shared another small smile and Freya nearly burst out laughing, a part of her wanting to tell the other woman about her little…er…encounter with the man they'd been admiring a few days ago. Instead, she headed off to the chapel where guests were starting to arrive, hugging the memory to herself and smiling. It had been fun and Freya had never had fun like that.

Freya knew that she was a private, prickly person.

She was, thanks to her psychology degree that lay languishing unused on her résumé, very self-aware. And her very self-aware self knew why she didn't let her guard down.

Freya didn't trust anyone with her feelings.

And walking towards her was yet another reason why. Edward!

'Freya, we have to stop meeting like this.' He smiled.

'Well, now that all our friends are married, we shall,' Freya answered coolly.

'Won't I be getting an invite to yours?' Edward asked.

'That would be a no,' Freya said.

'Are you here with anyone?'

Freya was not going to prolong this conversation so she gave him a very tight smile and walked off.

Oh, how she loathed him.

He was married now and had twins but that hadn't stopped him from trying to chat her up at the last wedding they'd been at. Freya knew, because she'd been dealing with the RSVPs, that Cathy, his wife, wasn't attending tonight as one of their children was unwell.

Oh, a come-on from Edward she so did not need.

Not when she had Mr Room 2812, Freya thought with a sudden smile.

Of course she wouldn't be taking him up on his offer but it had been such, *such* a nice offer to have that it got her through the wedding and then the meal.

The endless five-course meal at the top table.

It was hard to explain, even to herself, but set menus were for Freya the hardest.

Chicken or beef was served alternatively and Freya let out a small breath of relief that she was given chicken, which would have been her choice.

'Would you mind…?' Beth's mother said. 'I don't like red meat.'

'Of course.' Freya smiled, to show that it didn't matter in the least to her, and they swapped plates.

She had been worried about the meal at the wedding and had thought about talking to her friend, Mila, about it. She sometimes discussed her eating disorder with Mila, because Mila didn't treat Freya as if she had two heads and tiptoe around her. But weddings were a bit of a touchy subject between Freya and Mila, given James had jilted her friend at the altar. Also, she was avoiding Mila a bit at the moment, because Freya still hadn't told James that the Bright Hope Clinic charity was run by his ex-fiancée.

James didn't even know they'd remained friends.

Oh, it was a long dinner and then came the speeches.

Freya glared at the cameraman, who was getting stuck into the champagne. She would have preferred Beth to have chosen someone else, but the wedding budget was getting tight, Beth had said. Freya had gently suggested losing a few bows but that hadn't gone down well.

'My wife and I have an extra surprise for you all,' Neil said. 'You'll be thrilled to know that the stork arrived early....'

The whole room melted and clapped and the cameraman must have seen Freya's stern glare because he panned to the guests and then back to the happy couple. Neil made a joke about more free cocktails for him on their cruise. This had Freya's jaw tense.

Then the dancing started but Freya still couldn't relax as Beth had yet more requests.

'I want him to film messages for us from all the guests.'

'I know that you do.'

'But I don't want the messages to just be about the baby,' Beth said. 'I want them mainly to be about me.'

Me, me, me, me, me, Freya thought as she nodded and smiled.

Freya took a glass of champagne from a passing waiter

and then Edward came over. 'You're looking gorgeous, Freya,' he said.

She looked terrible, as Mr Room 2812 had so sexily pointed out!

'Can I get you another drink?' Edward offered.

'No, thank you.'

'You were blonde last time I saw you,' he said. 'You've gone back to brunette.'

'Really?' Freya's response was sarcastic. 'Thanks for letting me know.'

'I'm actually staying here tonight,' Edward said. 'How about a dance for old times' sake?'

'How about I throw this champagne in your face?'

Freya walked off with her drink and headed outside to drag the cool night air into her lungs. She loved LA in winter and she promised to take herself riding some time soon. It was her best method for relaxing and she had been introduced to it when she had been in rehab.

Freya never cried.

Not even in rehab had she let them break her but tonight she suddenly felt close.

It wasn't Edward, she harboured no hidden feelings for him—well, no nice ones.

It was how they'd ended things that still stung, all these years on.

Her long stint in rehab had been spread far and wide across the media and everyone had thought she'd been on drugs. At the age of twenty-three, when they'd started dating, he'd asked about it and Freya had told him about her eating disorder.

It had been hard to reveal but she'd pushed on and had told him she was recovered, or healed, or whatever the best word was. But when she'd told him that she probably couldn't have children he had, on the spot, dumped her and accused her of stringing him along. It had felt as if Edward had only been dating her on the assumption that one day she'd be pregnant.

'I thought we were enjoying each other's company,' Freya had said. 'Not looking for future mating partners.'

'Well, it's preferable to have that option,' had been his callous response.

It had hurt, it had been such a horrible blow to her recovering self, but she had refused to let it plunge her back into hell.

Freya knew she should go back inside but she could not face Edward.

Did he think she'd have an affair, that married men were all that was left? Oh, no, she would rather, far rather, get in that elevator and...

Why not? Freya thought.

They'd both, in that brief exchange, stated that they were single.

And she'd promised this coming year to do more of the things she liked and to try new things.

No.

Freya simply couldn't see it.

Going up and knocking on Sexy Bastard's door just for sex.

Or maybe he'd left it open and she would just slip in.

Actually, Freya could see it.

And she *had* promised to keep her New Year's resolutions...

New Year.

Yikes! Freya remembered a little too late that she had to get everyone out for the photo shoot and the next twenty minutes were frantic indeed.

It had been a long and difficult night, Freya thought,

and a part of her longed to just head upstairs and to find out what simply letting go and having fun actually meant.

An aching part of Zack had really wished she would head up!

He'd arrived back in his room so turned on and waiting.

Come on, he'd thought.

God knew, he'd needed the distraction.

He'd unlatched the door and lain on the bed, hands behind his head.

She was stunning.

Dark eyes, dark hair and that mouth… She'd looked a little familiar but all he had ever seen of LA till now had been the airport so Zack had shrugged that thought off. It would come to him overnight.

Would she?

Of course she would. The attraction had been through the roof but by ten he'd downgraded his expectations because the speeches were surely well over with.

By eleven-thirty he'd woken from a doze and stared out to the LA night.

Not at the city but at the mountains beyond and he knew he had to ring his parents before the lines got busy. He got up and took out his cellphone and took a steadying breath before he made the call.

Zack was thirty-three and the last time he'd been home, a couple of years ago, he'd been the same age as his brother Toby had been when he had died.

Except Toby had been married and working in the family practice and his wife, Alice, had wanted to start a family.

Whereas Zack, as his parents had constantly pointed out, was a drifter.

He was a highly skilled paediatric cardiac surgeon, Zack had riposted, but that was just boasting, he was told. And what good were his skills when they were so badly needed in Kurranda, the remote outback town where he and Toby had been raised.

He could picture the phone ringing in the hall. Reception was haphazard there and the landline to the family doctor really was a lifeline for the community.

His mother answered on the third ring.

'Hey, Mum,' Zack said. 'Happy New Year.'

'I'm sure it is where you are.'

Zack closed his eyes, it was just more of the same.

'How's Nepal?'

'I'm in LA,' Zack answered.

'I thought you *had* to be in Nepal.'

'I did have to be there for Christmas,' Zack answered. 'There was an operation I wanted to do before I left but we had to wait for some equipment to arrive. I would have been home if I could.'

'Well, why aren't you now?'

'Because I've got an interview tomorrow.'

'In LA?'

'It's a top medical centre. They've got some of the most amazing equipment and facilities and I don't want to let that side of things slide…' Zack stopped even attempting to explain. He did not want to argue with his mother. Judy Carlton simply could not, would not, get it, and Zack was over trying to explain. 'Is Dad there?'

'You just missed him. He got called out for Tara. Do you remember her?'

Of course he damn well remembered, they'd been friends. What his mother didn't know was that they had been each other's first. Zack had fought to stop that getting out as Tara's father was very religious.

Zack stayed silent.

'She married Jed.'

'Yep.'

'Well, the baby's not due till the end of January but it looks as if she might deliver early and it's breech. I can't talk for long, they might need the air ambulance...'

'I get it.' Zack said. 'Will you wish Dad a happy New Year for me and could you—?'

'Zack,' his mum broke in, 'you should be here to say it to him for yourself. Even if you'd just come home on a stopover it would have been something.'

'I would have but this interview is being slotted in, they need me to start straight away. There's a very sick child—'

'Oh, I don't have time for your fancy position,' Judy said. 'I'll pass on to Tara and her husband how well you're doing, shall I?'

Zack knew that translated to, *You should be back here, scrubbing in with your father, rather than Tara having to be airlifted.* 'That was a low blow.'

'I know.' His mother didn't quite apologise. 'I'm tired, Zack, and your dad is too. He didn't get any break over Christmas and the place just seems to be getting busier. So much for retiring.'

Zack closed his eyes. Sometimes he wished he could just give up on his own dreams and give them the solution they wanted.

'By now you and Toby...' Judy swallowed and Zack then heard his mother, a very strong woman, give way to tears. New Year always did that to her and this coming year marked another difficult milestone. 'It will be ten years soon.'

'I know it will.'

At the beginning of February it would be ten years since Toby had died.

He and Zack had been on a weekend away. Both had been good horsemen but a snake had spooked Toby's horse and thrown him off.

Zack looked out of the hotel window again and out towards the dark shadows of the hills and thought of the red earth of home. Even if he didn't want to be there for ever he missed it at times and now was one of those times. As he stood there he remembered too the agony of hours spent with his brother, waiting for help to arrive while knowing there was none to be had.

At the age of thirty-one Toby had died in his younger brother's arms.

Zack knew his mother needed to talk and so he forgot about the sniping and let her.

'Things would be so different if he was still alive. He loved the clinic. Toby and your father had such plans for it. Alice is pregnant again by her new husband.'

He was hardly her new husband, Zack thought. Alice had been remarried for seven years.

'Mum, she's allowed to be happy.'

'She and Toby were so happy, though,' Judy said. 'I wanted grandchildren.'

'I know.'

'And that's not going to happen, is it?'

'No.'

'Are you seeing someone?'

She asked him the same question every time they spoke and it was always the same answer he gave. 'No one serious.'

'Zack...?'

'What?' Zack said, and when there was silence he

told her the truth. 'Mum, I won't be giving you grand-children.'

Zack was direct, yes. There was no point giving her false hope. The life his parents had planned for him wasn't the one he wanted. He never wanted to be tied down, not to one person and not to one place.

Zack wasn't cruel, though.

What he didn't tell his mother was that Toby had been far from happy with his life.

That was the reason Toby had called him up and asked if he'd join him on a weekend away. There, in the out-back, lying by a fire, looking up at the stars, Toby had told him the truth—that he felt stifled, and wanted away, not just from Kurranda and the medical practice but also from his marriage.

Zack had been stunned. He'd thought that Alice and Toby, childhood sweethearts, had been so happy but Toby had told him that, no, things hadn't been good for a very long while.

It had been a long night spent talking, sometimes seri-ously, but also they'd shared laughter, not knowing what was to come the very next day.

Toby hadn't quite taken that secret to his grave, it had been left with Zack. He'd never shared it with anyone and it weighed heavily inside.

'I really do have to go,' Judy said. 'I'd better head over there now in case your dad needs help to organ-ise the air ambulance and things...' His mother wasn't a doctor or nurse but she was a huge part of the fabric of the town. She would liaise with the air ambulance and locals and make sure the transfer was seamless. Then she'd have Tara's parents over for coffee and a meal as they awaited news.

That was who his mother was.

'Happy New Year,' Zack said.

Judy made a small huffing noise.

His parents had decided, on Toby's death and Zack's failure to settle, that there could be no more happy years.

'Happy New Year, Zack,' Judy said, but even that came out with a slight edge. Zack made sure he was happy, that he lived, that he grabbed this rare gift by the throat and got every bit of life out of it.

He'd promised his brother he would.

'Mum,' Zack suddenly said. 'I'll come home for a visit in April. Tell Dad that.'

'For how long?'

'I'm not sure, but I'll be back to see you both then.'

He ended the call and though he could not stand the thought of living back there, and being in a place where everyone knew your business, it didn't mean he didn't love nature and space and the people.

And, though things were strained, he loved his family.

Zack lay on the bed and closed his eyes but he couldn't unwind. Speaking with his parents always left him feeling like that. The plans his parents had had for him had been set in stone from the day he was born. They just hadn't thought to consult the baby they had made.

He was to study medicine in Melbourne as his father and brother had done, but even before he had left for the city Zack had known in his heart that he wasn't coming back.

Tara had known it too.

Of course he remembered Tara.

Not just the hot, sexy kisses behind a barn and sultry outback nights, more he remembered a conversation that had taken place the night before he'd left as they'd lain in each other's arms. 'You're not coming back, are you?' Tara had asked.

'You talk as if I'm leaving the country. I'm only going to Melbourne. I'll be back for the summer breaks.' Even at eighteen he'd been direct. 'But, no, I can't see myself here, Tara.'

'And I don't want to be there,' Tara said. She was a country girl and loved it and neither wanted to change or to change the other.

'Have you told your parents?' she asked.

'I've tried,' Zack said. 'They don't understand.'

He was still trying.

And all these years later they still didn't understand.

Zack went to pour a drink but the half-bottle of wine was empty and he wasn't a big fan of American beer.

He was about to ring for room service but, still churned up from the conversation with his mother, he pulled on his boots again and took the elevator down, but it only took him to the mezzanine level and he decided to take the escalator down to the bar.

There were people everywhere, all standing on the stairs, and then he found out why.

The wedding.

'You'll have to use the elevators if you want to get to the ground floor,' someone told him, and they sounded annoyed. 'The escalators and stairs are in use.'

And there was the woman from said elevator, organising the wedding party, telling people to step back or to stand a fraction more to the left.

Zack watched as a gentleman came over to her and whatever she said had him step abruptly back.

Oh, she was a snappy, bossy little thing, Zack thought.

Not with him, though.

And then she looked up.

Oh, my... Freya thought, and another of Edward's sleazy come-ons left her mind.

If Mr 2812 had been sexy before, he was sinfully so now—dishevelled and just raw male, he made her toes curl in her very painful shoes. His hair was messy, his T-shirt was all crumpled and, alongside all the suits and formal clothes, in those dark jeans and tight T-shirt he stood out, deliciously so.

Freya dragged her mind away from rude thoughts. This shot was important and the countdown had started. Beth and Neil were in position and everyone was in place and she should be able to relax soon. All she had to do was wave the happy couple off and the rest of the night was hers.

Concentrate, Freya.

She couldn't.

There was just this prickling awareness all over her as she recalled his scent and the feel of his hand on her arm.

Oh, God. She gazed up at him and hoped her eyes weren't frantic, but that was how she suddenly felt—frantic for him.

'Ten!' everybody shouted. 'Nine!'

They could not stop staring and, as the countdown drew to its conclusion, as everyone started cheering and kissing, Beth's carefully organised photos were ruined by a tall guy bursting through and dashing down the stairs.

'Auld Lang Syne' was being sung out around them as his hands took her by the upper arms. Briefly she wondered why, instead of kissing her as she badly needed him to do, he was moving her away. But then Freya found out exactly why.

This wasn't a kiss suitable for public exposure.

They were in a small booth to the side of the hotel's reception when his mouth first met hers. They came together so hard that their teeth met and his tongue was strong and thick and very indecent. Her hips were held by him, and animal passion, which had never taken up residence in Freya before, rapidly made itself right at home.

Her hands were pressing into his chest, not to push him away, just to feel him, to rub those solid muscles beneath greedy palms. Then they went up to his head and her fingers dug into his hair. She kissed him back on tiptoe, so that her heels lifted up out of her shoes in an attempt to scale him.

He pulled back and gave her an intense look and there was no mention of going up for a drink.

'I have to get back…' It was a feeble protest she made. 'I just need ten more minutes to sort the wedding party out.'

'We can't wait.'

His erection was in her groin and Freya herself was pressing hard into him.

'I have to make sure that they get off okay…'

He peered out.

'They're waving and the bride is about to throw the bouquet. Do you want to go and try to catch it?'

The question was a loaded one.

What was she looking for—an amazing night with no names, or to dash off and catch the bouquet and the dream that it might one day be her?

'God, no,' Freya said. She was more than happy with being a third-time bridesmaid and so she took his head in her hands and got back to that mouth for one more deep kiss before they hit the elevators.

Freya pressed the button for the twenty-eighth floor.

'You remembered,' he said.

'Oh, yes!'

CHAPTER THREE

SADLY FOR THEM the elevator was full.

The wedding guests were dispersing and either heading to their rooms or to the bars. There were many, many opportunities for Freya to change her mind on the long and frustrating ride to the twenty-eighth floor and say that this was a terrible idea and so not like her.

It never entered Freya's head to do so.

Her rigid, controlled life was in desperate need of fun and adventure, and he offered that and more.

He was beautiful.

Even with her back to him she could feel the energy between them, it was utter attraction and arousal at its most basic and Freya could not wait to indulge.

'What floor are you on?' he asked, running a finger over her bare shoulder as they crawled towards her floor. His touch was electric and, yes, it was terribly tempting to get off at the tenth floor, but there might be a problem as she hadn't packed her toiletry bag with a wild night in mind.

She gave a small shake of her head and then turned and looked him right in the eye as the elevator came to her floor and a couple got out.

'I haven't got...' she mouthed.

'I have,' he mouthed back. Of course he did, Freya

thought. This guy had nearly had her at five p.m. after all—no doubt he came prepared for women dropping their knickers on sight—but they were already past her floor and so they waited—oh, how they waited—for them to hit his floor.

As the crowd thinned out there was a bit more space but they didn't utilise it. She could feel his eyes on her shoulder, on her spine, and then she got the bliss of his mouth on the part of her she hated the most.

She leant back into him even as the doors opened.

'Thank God,' Zack said, and he took her hand and they just about ran the length of the corridor.

He opened up the door and they fell into the room. Their mouths locked and they didn't bother with the lights. Just hot, hard kisses as Freya kissed him with abandon up against the wall.

He more than partook because he tore that dress off and the sound of it ripping was as delicious as the feel of his hands on her bare skin.

'Oh, God,' he said as he played with her breasts and tweaked her nipples as if he'd been waiting for them all night.

He had been.

Freya had never been more grateful for ignoring the bride's plea because, unable to resist a taste, he lowered his head and took one nipple into his hungry mouth.

'She wanted me to wear sticking plasters over them.'

'We don't like the bride,' he said as he withdrew his mouth, and it made her laugh. It was just such a relief after a very long and difficult day to laugh and vent to someone who got her. He took the other breast in his mouth and sucked hard. Freya pushed him off, only because it was her turn to taste *his* salty chest. Oh, he tasted amazing, like he'd been swimming in the ocean and had then showered in ice. Salty, refreshing and so firm.

Freya dealt with his heavy leather belt as best she could with her mouth on his chest, licking him, tasting him and then moaning her frustration.

'Why button-ups…?' Freya whimpered.

'So I can picture your fingers undoing them and getting it out.' She was doing just that and Freya herself wasn't gentle. He was so thick and long and already there was a silver drizzle that trickled onto her fingers as she explored him.

'Get naked,' he told her, and he went into his pocket. He wished he'd kicked off his boots so he could do the same but there really wasn't time. As she shed her knickers he dressed his erection and Freya toppled a little as she took off her shoes.

'Come here,' he said, and she just stepped to him and he lifted her to where she'd wanted to be all along.

'Oh…' He didn't guide her on, he held her hips as her hands went behind his neck.

'Lean back,' he told her, and as he held her by the hips he rubbed her wet sex over his stomach and scented himself with her.

'I'm going to come…' Freya was, the feel of the hairs on his stomach, the rough guide of his hands, the way he was holding her, and she couldn't hold on.

'That's the intention,' Sexy Bastard said.

She had kind of got this wasn't going to be like anything she'd experienced before but she found out for certain then. As her body arched, as she let out a building moan, he took her coming. He just drove into her tight and twitching and moaned at the pleasure.

'Oh, yeah,' he said.

Oh, yes, Freya thought.

He just parted her orgasm, it was like being a virgin all over again, or not, Freya thought because that had been *such* an underwhelming encounter.

This wasn't.

She went limp for a moment and he took full advantage, grinding her down to meet his thrusts. Her hands took in his muscled shoulders and she dug her nails in, and then she just had to taste that shoulder, sucking it as her hands explored his broad upper back.

Her nails dug in again, deeper, and he took her a bit slower but with measured tension. It was an odd consent but she read it—he wanted more of the same so she scratched him hard.

'Careful,' he warned as her mouth sucked skin, but he wasn't telling her to stop, she knew that. 'You'll pay for each bruise.'

Oh, she would gladly pay.

He took her to the desk, or she guessed that's what it was, because it was cold and hard on her back. Freya went to wrap her legs around him but his hand pressed her thighs apart and he took her hard and so deep that she just about performed a sit-up as her entire lower abdomen contracted.

'Come on,' he said, and she opened her eyes to his gruff command but then her eyes met his and he smiled down at her.

'Nice,' he said, bucking into her.

'So…' Freya couldn't finish. She had never known anything like it. His face tensed and then he released into her, and she met the impact with a deep force of her own. Her orgasm just rolled through her like thunder and then lightning clapped her tight with no pause in between. It just dissolved her from the inside out, and as it left she quivered and then he collapsed onto her.

He was so heavy, and breathless, but then his mouth was an unexpected soft caress. Even as he came out of her he kissed her. Even as he unsheathed he kissed her back to earth, and as he stripped off his boots and jeans, his mouth never left her skin. Naked now, he picked her up from the hard desk and carried her to the bed.

He got in beside her and scooped her into his body. His hand stroked her breast and he kissed her shoulder as she lay feeling bewildered yet drowsy and sedated.

'Go to sleep,' he said.

He seemed to know just what she needed and yet they didn't even know each other's names.

'How...?' She attempted to gather a thought into a sentence.

'Chemistry,' he answered.

And to sleep they went.

CHAPTER FOUR

'I SHOULD HAVE paid way more attention in science class,'
Freya said a few hours later as she woke to the thought
of his last word and the feel of her loose, relaxed body
in his arms as he spooned in behind her.

'Oh, I'll make you pay attention,' he said low and deep
into her ear. 'Happy New Year.'

'And you,' Freya said.

'It already is.'

Last night he'd barely been able to get the words out
to his mother, knowing how pointless they were, but now
Zack was happy, indulging in one of his passions.

The other was work and that was so intense that he
lived for escapes like this.

'Were you going to come to my room?' he asked.
'Honest answer.'

'I was thinking about it,' Freya said. 'I wasn't having
the best night.'

'What did you say to that guy?'

Freya frowned.

'The one who walked off just before you saw me…'

'Oh, that was Edward—'

'No names,' he interrupted, and Freya lay there, feeling his fingers gently kneading her stomach.

Freya wanted to know his name, she wanted to know

more about him, and yet he'd reminded her that there would be no exchange of names. But as she lay there, enjoying the gentle massage of his fingers, and thought about it, she realised that it was actually quite freeing. There would be no *I'm Freya Rothsberg. Yes, Aubrey St Claire and Michael Rothsberg are indeed my parents.* And if he recognised the name, then he'd know about their messy divorce. And there would be no *I'm thirty-one, single, perfectionist, infertile but trying not to be, recovered anorexic.* She didn't have to say she was a big shot in PR. Or that she was stressing about taking on the charity side of her brother's medical centre. Or that, though she'd pushed James to let her, really she wanted to use her psychology degree.

No names didn't mean no past but it meant she didn't have to reveal anything that she didn't want to.

Who was she without all of that? Freya lay there and pondered.

She.

The woman in his arms, and that was enough for him.

He.

Freya understood now the bliss of no names.

'He's an ex.' Freya answered the question after a very long pause. 'And he tried it on last night. Several times.'

'I'd try it on again with you…'

'He's married.'

'Bastard,' Zack said. 'Did you know that he was when you were together?'

'He wasn't married then,' Freya said. 'From the way we broke up it would seem he wanted a wife and children. He's got what he wanted but his wife wasn't there last night. He said he wanted to bring in the New Year with me up in his room.'

'What did you say to him?'

'I told him I hadn't enjoyed sex with him the first time around and that I felt sorry for his short-suffering wife.'

He laughed.

'You're not married, are you?' Freya checked.

He could lie, she guessed, but she felt he wouldn't.

There was no point in lying.

'Oh, no,' Zack said. 'And I have no intention to ever be. This is absolutely guilt-free sex, baby...'

Freya doubted this encounter would be entirely guilt free, no doubt she'd be crawling with shame a few hours from now, but that was her.

'Do you have any New Year's resolutions?' he asked.

'Many,' Freya said. She had pored over them for hours and had them all written out.

'Such as?'

They were mostly the same as every other year—unlike other people, who seemed to swear to go on a diet or exercise, Freya's resolution was to not embark on a sudden diet or obsess over exercise. Not that she told him that.

Neither did she tell him about the baby she wanted and her dream of having her own little family.

Nor did she tell him that she was over men. Though perhaps not completely over them, given where she was.

So she just lay there, overthinking but oddly lulled by the soothing stroke of his hands and the nudge of his erection behind her. No, there was no need to tell him about the career she wanted to tackle but had been avoiding doing so.

'I made my list of resolutions yesterday after my run,' Freya said.

'Do you run a lot?' he asked, his fingers examining her slim, toned body.

'On alternate days,' Freya said.

'And what do you do on the other one?'

'I go for a walk,' Freya said, and the threat of tears was back but she held them in, although she did admit a truth she would never dare to another. 'And I try not to run.' She was more honest with a stranger than the people closest to her and his response was kind.

He gave a light kiss to her shoulder.

'It's okay.'

He could feel her near to tears and he got that.

Anonymity at times came with deep trust, for you were at your most bare.

'I ran,' Zack said. 'Well, I'm not a runner but I ran from all that was expected of me and I'm still running.'

She couldn't imagine him running from anything.

He was so confrontational to all of her senses she could not imagine there were things he might not be able to face.

'So what list of resolutions did you make?' he asked.

She smiled as he ran a lazy hand down her body and pulled her into him.

'Making more time for the things I like.'

'And me,' Zack said, and he started to kiss her neck.

'Try new things…' Freya said, and the arm under her moved and fingers came to her small breast and stroked it.

'I like that one too.'

He pinched her nipple and she properly understood what he'd meant about him picturing her undoing his button flies because in her mind's eye she could see those brown fingers squeezing her hard. Instead of slapping him away, she took a shaky breath as he squeezed it tight again and she felt like a bud bursting.

He took her hand and put it between her legs and then,

still tweaking her breasts, his other hand met hers between her legs and *they* explored her.

'Not that one,' Freya said, and he laughed into her
shoulder.

'I'm just feeling you all over,' Zack said. Working out
boundaries had never been more fun. 'I want to taste
you all over.'

'I don't like oral,' Freya said.

God, this was freeing, just to say it outright! To declare
her needs and to state what she didn't want.

'You would.'

'No, thank you.'

He took himself in his hand and aimed the head at
her fingers and moistened them as she brought herself,
with a very nice lot of help from him, right to the edge.

'Not yet…' he said.

'You don't dictate my orgasm,' Freya responded in a
brittle voice, trying to remember how *she* dictated her
world.

'Oh, but I do.'

He went against everything she believed in the bedroom but fantastically so.

He was right at her entrance and she refused to beg,
she just lay on her side, hot with anticipation. The easiest
thing to do would be to not play safe but he rolled away
from her and she heard the tear of foil. Freya loathed the
intrusion but then he was back, lifting her hair and warm-
ing up her neck again with his mouth.

'Watch my neck,' Freya warned.

'Wear your hair down.'

'Okay.'

They both smiled at the ease of the solution.

He was making a terrible mess, she was sure, and she
was doing all she could not to beg when finally he slid

in and she moaned because she was swollen from last night, and it hurt quite a bit.

His large thigh came over her and he took her very slowly, painstakingly so, and she pressed back, trying to hurry him.

'What would you have done if you'd come to my room?' he asked.

'Guess,' Freya said through gritted teeth. It was obvious to her they would have had sex, only he wasn't letting her get away with that.

'Would you have knocked?'

'I don't know…' She was frantic, wanting to close her eyes and just focus on her building orgasm—not be dragged into conversation.

'I'd left the door open,' he said.

'Faster…' she begged.

'Would you have knocked?' he persisted, taking her at a slow, leisurely pace.

'No.' He gave it to her faster as a reward for her answer and then slowed when she didn't elaborate.

'I'd have come in,' Freya said as he dragged out her fantasy, as he made her reveal her thoughts.

'I might have been asleep.'

He rolled her onto her stomach and crushed her with his weight and the angle had him stroke her to the edge of bliss but he refused to push her over.

'What if I'd been asleep?' he asked.

'I'd have woken you with my mouth,' Freya said because, though she loathed the thought of it, she wanted to be the woman who could do that. 'More…' she now begged. It was like he had unbuttoned her.

'More?' Zack checked, and pulled out of her. She let out a sob of frustration.

He knelt up, pulled up her hips and Freya told him exactly where her thoughts last night had been.

'I'd have got you hard with my mouth and climbed on.'

'Dirty girl.'

'Yes,' Freya said. 'I am.'

She could hear his ragged breathing and his hand hovering over her bare cheek before he gave her a light spank.

'Yes…' Freya whimpered, and she did not recognise her own voice, or her own requests. He spanked her harder and she just about came and as her hand shot between her legs to ensure she did just that, Zack spanked her again.

'More,' Freya said.

Oh, he would have loved to carry on with the spanking, but the sound of her moans and the sight of her meant he had to be inside her.

She asked for more but he told her to be quiet, disobeying her plea to spank her again as he took her.

He seared inside her and not gently.

God, she always held back now but she was asking for more, for rougher…

He just took over and she pressed her face into the mattress.

Freya came, choking out her sobs as she pulsed around him, but he did not relent and he did not come.

There was a slight curse from him and the condom was gone, she knew, it had to be. She had never had sex without one and this was amazing.

For Zack too.

The feel of her hot and swollen was more acute and the sound of her moaning. Her hand came back and she dug her nails into his thighs. He scooped an arm under her stomach and drove in harder.

She felt like a rag doll, limp everywhere except on the inside, where she was pulled taut by him.

Freya had never completely let go in sex, she had tried to and had thought she had in those little slivers of orgasm in days gone by, but she knew now she hadn't.

Rude words were uttered and her head felt as if it had turned red as he swelled and shot into her.

Her orgasm was so sexy, a clutch of muscle that drew him in, and his warm come felt like ice seeping over her hot, swollen tightness.

And he pushed and groaned and let go deep into her until they were spent.

She listened to his long, pleasured sigh as he pulled out and then another sigh as he slipped back in to where it was warm and then out he went.

He joined her and they lay on their stomachs, facing each other, sleepy, satisfied smiles on their faces.

Freya had never had this moment where nothing else mattered than this bliss.

Soon other things would but for now nothing did.

God, she had spent most of her life trying to stay in control, only to find in some things she didn't want to.

And for Zack, who, as fleeting as his relationships were, did his best to be considerate and hold back, now looked into the eyes of someone who didn't need him to.

'Sore?' he asked, running a hand over where he had spanked her.

'I'm still high.'

They lay there and Zack said something that he usually wouldn't. 'I wish I could be your alternate day...' But that sounded way too much like making plans for Zack so he made light of what he'd just said. 'Nope, you'd be hanging up your running shoes for good.'

And Freya too kept it light. 'I don't think I could deal with you even on alternate days.' She smiled.

Freya actually meant it.

He had changed everything in her very ordered world and had awoken a side to her that she hadn't been aware existed.

They were touching down on their real worlds, and, on a very clear day, flight-wise, it was a surprisingly bumpy landing that was to come.

Maybe paradise *was* hard to leave because, as it turned out, they did it terribly.

The buzz of her phone as a seven a.m. alarm went off was equalled by the chime of his and they both groaned.

'I have to go…' Freya said.

'We need to talk.'

They really did, Zack had realised.

No names definitely didn't mean no condoms.

'Look, you don't have anything to worry about from my end.' Zack had his doctor's voice on, not that she knew it. 'I'm always careful and I've just had some health checks.' He dealt with all this in a very practical, forthright way. He was completely in work mode now, and what Freya couldn't know was that at work Zack was a very different man.

'You don't have to worry about me getting pregnant.' Freya wasn't going to go into detail about her fertility issues so she let him assume she was on the Pill, but his expression remained serious, even as they lay on their stomachs facing each other. 'I had some blood work done this week,' Freya said. 'It was all fine.' His expression was still grim and she was starting to get annoyed. 'I can go and get my computer if you don't believe me.' Her voice was rising. 'It was a torn condom, for God's sake.'

Accidents happened!

Just never to her.

Freya made sure of it.

She sat up, not liking all she had told him.

This man knew more about her than she'd told any-one and it was getting harder and harder to look him in the eye.

Zack sat up, knowing he hadn't handled that well. He tried to improve the sudden drop in atmosphere. 'Let's get some breakfast…' He'd made her feel bad and that hadn't been his intention, but in his line of work Zack had to be sure.

The snooze alarm went off and he swiped it and then picked up the hotel phone and ordered breakfast for two.

'Coffee?' he checked.

Freya shook her head. 'I'll have a green tea.'

He ordered and then climbed from the bed. 'I'll just have a shower…' Zack said, and threw her one of the robes. 'In case breakfast arrives while I'm in there.'

He turned on the cold tap and, apart from the issue that needed to be discussed, Zack felt amazing. So much so that he was considering not just explaining that his career was the reason he needed more information but breaking their game and finding out names.

Seeing her again.

Freya.

Just as he'd predicted it would, overnight her name had come to him.

It couldn't be!

Zack turned off the shower and stepped into the bed-room, and saw that she had gone. The robe lay on the bed and her clothes and shoes were gone, and Zack let out a breath for his poor handling of things. He went into his laptop and pulled up the glossy brochure that had been sent along with the forms he'd had to fill in.

There was a photograph of the luxurious Hollywood Hills Medical Center, where he was to be interviewed this morning. He scrolled through several photographs of the doctors and nurses who practised there but Zack bypassed them and went to the section near the end.

He had already looked her up.

A few flirty emails had had him curious as to what Freya Rothsberg looked like.

Zack looked at the photo and remembered being in Nepal and checking out who the woman at the end of the emails was. It was a head shot and her long hair was blonde and straight in this image, unlike the curly brunette of last night. Here it was sleek and worn up and her make-up was neutral and she was wearing a dark grey dress with a high neck and capped sleeves.

She looked corporate and elegant and almost unrecognisable from the sultry beauty of last night.

Still, it explained better to Zack why they'd ignited on sight—for a couple of weeks up till Christmas they'd been flirting!

CHAPTER FIVE

ZACK READ THROUGH their email exchanges in the taxi on the way to The Hills.

At first it had been a semi-formal 'Dear Zackary' type of exchange.

Zack had been head-hunted by James Rothsberg and he'd had some questions about the charitable side of things so James had flicked over to Freya some of the questions that he had raised.

To: ZCarlton@ZackaryCarlton.com
From: Freya.Rothsberg@TheHollywoodHillsClinic.com
Dear Zackary,
James has passed your concerns on to me and I hope I can address them.

For some time The Hollywood Hills has been looking into a suitable charity to partner and support.

The highly regarded Bright Hope Clinic was chosen. The clinic treats underprivileged children and is situated in the south of LA, where its services are desperately needed in the densely populated area. As a result their facilities and equipment are severely stretched.

The partnership of the Bright Hope Clinic with The Hollywood Hills aims to increase the number and scope of cases that can be treated. We are lucky to have world-class facilities and can also allow for easy transfer of emergency or overseas patients using the Hills' helicopter or ambulance transport system. The Bright Hope Clinic in South LA will still run as usual, with cases requiring more complex care being referred to the Bright Hope at The Hollywood Hills.

Sincerely,

Freya Rothsberg

Public Relations Consultant

To: Freya.Rothsberg@TheHollywoodHillsClinic.com
From: ZCarlton@ZackaryCarlton.com
All good. I'll take a look into the Bright Hope Clinic and get back to you with any questions.
Zack

To: ZCarlton@ZackaryCarlton.com
From: Freya.Rothsberg@TheHollywoodHillsClinic.com
Dear Zackary,
I have attached some further information on the Bright Hope Clinic as well as the names of some contacts I have there, who would be happy to answer any of your questions.
Sincerely,
Freya Rothsberg

To: Freya.Rothsberg@TheHollywoodHillsClinic.com
From: ZCarlton@ZackaryCarlton.com
Zack!
Please can you email the forms and brochures on The Hills, the postal service is a bit slow in Nepal. Also, I note

that you have the same surname as James and wondered if The Hills is a family-led clinic?

Zack loathed the politics of work and the thought of butting up against husband and wife with their own agendas held no appeal.

To: ZCarlton@ZackaryCarlton.com
From:Freya.Rothsberg@TheHollywoodHillsClinic.com
Dear Zack!
Please find attached the brochure that will better explain the clinic structure. ·

To address your concern—James is my brother. So, no, there aren't twenty Rothsbergs or husband-and-wife teams :-)
Freya!

He grinned that she'd read between the lines and understood his concerns.

To: Freya.Rothsberg@TheHollywoodHillsClinic.com
From: ZCarlton@ZackaryCarlton.com
Good to know!
Zack!

Flicking through the brochure, he had smiled again when he'd seen who he was dealing with and on a rather long night in Nepal he'd responded again.

To: Freya.Rothsberg@TheHollywoodHillsClinic.com
From: ZCarlton@ZackaryCarlton.com
I meant good to know that there aren't hundreds of you, as opposed to your marital status.
Zack!

He'd regretted sending it, because Zack never flirted or got involved with anyone at work, but it had been such a subtle flirt that she probably hadn't got it.

Two days had passed and he'd actually forgotten when her response had come back.

Oh, she'd got it.

To: ZCarlton@ZackaryCarlton.com
From: Freya.Rothsberg@TheHollywoodHillsClinic.com
Zack!
Is there a question mark missing in the previous email?
Freya!

No he never got involved with people at work, but a quickie with the PR rep surely didn't count, Zack had thought, and there were slim pickings where he'd been that night and it was nice to dream.

To: Freya.Rothsberg@TheHollywoodHillsClinic.com
From: ZCarlton@ZackaryCarlton.com
?

Her response?
There hadn't been one.
His next email, after a long day of surgery followed by a very long night in Nepal:

To: Freya.Rothsberg@TheHollywoodHillsClinic.com
From: ZCarlton@ZackaryCarlton.com
??

To: ZCarlton@ZackaryCarlton.com
From: Freya.Rothsberg@TheHollywoodHillsClinic.com
Very single. (Don't tell James.)

To: Freya.Rothsburg@TheHollywoodHillsClinic.com
From: ZCarlton@ZackaryCarlton.com
I never kiss and tell.

He smiled as he finished reading and did a quick search on her name, and suddenly Zack wasn't smiling.

There was an article on Freya, accompanied by a picture of her collapsed and being taken out of a nightclub and he read about her drug habit. There was a quote from her mother, stating that Freya was finally getting the help she needed and was in rehab.

He thought of the woman who had slunk out of his hotel room rather than face the music.

Oh, yes, they needed to talk!

Freya wasn't proud that she had dressed and left but she hadn't wanted last night to dissolve into a terse exchange.

And neither had she liked how one minute they'd been so, so intimate and the next he had reduced it to a lab-report exchange. She'd heard the shower being turned on and had gone red in the face as she'd recalled her pleas and her demands, and what had felt fine—in fact, amazing—just a short while ago had then felt like an embarrassing mistake.

She'd pulled on her dress and slipped out of his suite, taking the walk of shame back to her own room. Once in there she had surprised herself by letting out a shocked burst of laughter.

Who knew?

Not she.

Freya showered and massaged loads of conditioner into her hair and then as she dried herself off she looked at her body, turning to see her red butt cheeks. God, she felt better for it. And, now that she thought about it more calmly, Freya liked the head-on way he had tackled the awkward subject.

She'd print off her results, Freya decided. She would cross out her name and other details and put the relevant part in an envelope and leave it at Reception to be delivered to his room.

Freya got ready and dried her hair so that it was its usual straight self, and was about to put it up when she remembered why she couldn't.

The memory of them had her wanting more. Freya did her best to quell a building want and she pulled out of her wardrobe the dress she had worn before the bridesmaid outfit.

It had been a one-off, a little sexual adventure and one that was never to be repeated again, Freya told herself.

She pulled on a neutral linen shift that she wore with flat ballet pumps and she carefully did her very neutral make-up then gave a sigh of relief when she finally recognised herself in the mirror.

Freya.

She called down to Reception and asked for her car to be brought around and decided that, given she had late check-out and Red was feeding Cleo, she would come back after the interview to pack. She took the elevator and went to one of the juice bars in the foyer and ordered her regular blend along with a nutrition bar and she was back in control.

Freya headed over to the business centre and printed the necessary form off, blacked out all details except the relevant part and lined up at Reception. The want and desire for him wasn't diminishing in the way she'd hoped.

It was building.

If anything, the thought of never seeing him again, of

it really having been just one night had her hesitate when the receptionist asked if she could help her.

'Could I check in for another night?' Freya asked.

'Sure.' The receptionist smiled. 'I'll just check that we don't have anyone incoming for your room. No, that's fine. Is there anything else I can do for you?'

'Yes,' Freya said. 'Could I have another card for my room, please?'

'Of course.'

It took just a few seconds but Freya knew what a monumental few seconds they were. The receptionist popped the card into a little wallet with Freya's room number on it, but instead of putting it in her bag Freya put it in the envelope along with her blood results.

'Could you please deliver this to room 2812?' Freya asked, determinedly not blushing, telling herself that the receptionist would not care or even guess what she was up to.

'Sure.' The receptionist smiled. 'I'll make sure that's done for you. Is there anything else I can help you with?'

'That's it, thanks.'

Oh, my!

Freya was all flustered as she drove to work and then parked in her reserved spot at The Hills.

It really was stunning. James had put everything into the place and the patient list read like a who's who of the film industry. They did a lot more than just cosmetic procedures here, though. From obstetrics to intensive care, everything was luxuriously catered for. Well, everything except eating disorders, but Freya was planning on addressing that.

Just not today.

Today she had this interview to get through, but there

was one good thing about last night, Freya thought—it had made a tiny email flirt seem pretty tame.

Yes, she'd get through the interview and then head back to the hotel and wait and see if lightning did strike twice.

Freya walked through the entrance into the foyer with its marble floor and pillars and stunning floral arrangements that were changed daily. A huge chandelier shed a calming light and Freya did her best to walk as if she hadn't been having torrid sex all night.

Sometimes the luxury of The Hills gnawed at Freya.

All her life, disparity had. She could remember tours of Africa with her famous parents. Seeing the utter poverty and then taking off in a luxury jet had felt so wrong. Being photographed with people who walked miles just for water and then watching her mother guzzling champagne for hours and bemoaning her menu selection later had made Freya furious.

Her questions to her parents had gone pretty much unanswered. 'Why are they hungry and we're not?' Freya had asked. 'I just don't get it.'

'We're doing our bit,' had been Aubrey's dismissive response, and her father, Michael, had had no time for his daughter's questions either.

'Freya, can you just, for five minutes, stop trying to change the world.'

James *had* listened, though, when Freya had approached him, and now things were finally getting under way.

'Hi, Freya.' Stephanie, the receptionist, smiled. 'James said to go straight through to his office.'

Freya nodded and promptly ignored Stephanie's instruction by heading for her own office. Yesterday evening James had finally sent Freya the bio for the cardiac paediatrician. He kept all staff files himself and there were no sneak peeks, even for his sister.

She wanted to read up on Zackary Carlton rather than explain to James that she was utterly unprepared for this interview. She was usually meticulous in preparation and her intention had been to read up on Zack over a leisurely breakfast this morning.

She opened up her laptop and accessed the file but looked over as there was a knock on her open door.

'Freya,' James said. 'I asked Stephanie to tell you to come straight though.'

'Happy New Year to you too.' Freya smiled at her brother. 'Stephanie did ask me to go straight in but I'm just having a quick read through.'

'I'll deal with all the medical stuff, you just need to explain the publicity side of things and get a decent bio, so we can get the word out he's on board.' James gestured for her to come to his office and Freya picked up her laptop and went with him.

'Is he on board, though?' she asked.

'He has to be. We need this guy,' James said as they arrived at his office.

Freya took a tentative seat and thanked the spanking gods he'd stopped when he had, and she started to scroll through the file as James spoke.

'I'll bring you up to speed—Zackary Carlton. Australian, drifter, arrogant bastard. He won't commit to more than three months anywhere but, God, he does magic with his hands...'

Indeed he did.

Freya looked at the résumé and very impressive bio. There was also a photo attached and, yes, she could concur, Zackary Carlton made magic with his hands.

It was Him!

The man she had thought was safely in one of the clinic's luxurious apartments reserved for visiting guests had been staying at the hotel all along.

Freya felt sick.

And doubly so when she thought of the daiquiri-laced emails she'd sent him.

It was the same man!

How could she possibly face him?

Quite simply, Freya couldn't.

'James,' Freya croaked.

'What?'

But Freya couldn't answer straight away. After all, how did she tell her brother that she'd had random sex last night with the cardiac surgeon he wanted to hire?

'Do you really need me here for this interview?' Freya attempted. 'I've got the worst hangover. I actually feel a bit sick.'

'You hardly drink.'

'Well, I did last night,' Freya lied. 'I really think I need to go home…'

'Freya, you couldn't even begin to match my hangover,' James said, and as the intercom buzzed and interrupted him, it would seem her nightmare had just arrived.

That sexy, somewhat scruffy man she'd met yesterday scrubbed up terribly well.

He was clean shaven and wearing a dark suit in a lightweight fabric. His hair was so thick that it was still a touch damp from the shower he had been in when Freya had run, and she wanted to run again now.

Absolutely she did. So much so that Zack watched her eyes dart to the door.

Poor thing, he thought.

Zack was also surprised, not that he showed it. He hadn't expected her to be on the interview panel and seeing her face pale, rather than redden, he did what he could to put her at ease.

'James.' He shook James's hand. 'It's good to meet you.' He turned then to her. 'Freya...'

She swallowed.

'I saw you in the brochure,' he explained as he took a seat, and her embarrassment turned into anger.

He knew who she was.

Which meant that he'd known who she was last night.

Zack's teeth gritted as he saw her eyes flash in anger and he realised that, far from putting her at ease, he'd made things worse.

James and his very real hangover were going through the mountain of forms that had come in about the man he would hopefully be recruiting.

'You said no to the apartment?' James checked as he caught up on some finer details. 'Was there a problem?'

'Not at all. I just prefer to stay in hotels,' Zack said.

'What about if you work here?'

'Same,' Zack answered.

James was one of the most in-demand cosmetic surgeons in Los Angeles and he looked over at Zack, who was highly in demand too, and he chose not to play games.

'Look, I'm not going to waste your time or mine with small talk. We want you on board. The Hills needs a cardiac surgeon specialising in paediatrics and we want it to be you.'

Zack gave an appreciative nod. He preferred people who cut to the chase.

'The only issue I have,' James continued, 'is that you're only prepared to commit to three months.'

'Then you have an issue,' Zack said, and Freya blinked

at his assertion. She had never met anyone so in command of themselves.

'We're going to be building your profile and reputation and for that we'd hope—' James started.

'Now there are two issues,' Zack interrupted. 'I don't need my profile or my reputation to be built, they already speak for themselves.'

'They do,' James said. 'But our partner, the Bright Hope Clinic, desperately needs funds. I see you're keen to do some pro bono work.'

'That's the main attraction.' Zack nodded. 'Working on these cases with top-level facilities is an enticing prospect.'

'How many charitable cases were you thinking of taking on?' James asked.

'One a week during my regular list and I'll also do a full pro bono list one Sunday a month.'

There was a lot of good that he could do in three months, Freya thought.

'I've brought Freya in to discuss the PR side of things.'

'I don't get involved with any of that.' Zack shook his head and looked at her and she recognised his voice. It was the one he had used on her that morning when they'd discussed the condom issue. He was now utterly engaged in work. Only Freya was scorching with embarrassment, because Zack was looking at her and talking to her exactly as if they'd never met. 'If I come on board I won't be doing interviews and happy smiley photos. I'm sure young Paulo won't mind. I hear no other surgeon wants to touch him.'

'Correct,' James said.

Paulo was five years old and had been brought to the Bright Hope Clinic from Mexico with his single mother, Maria. His complex cardiac problems meant that no surgeon would operate on him as it was very possible that he wouldn't survive surgery.

'It happens a lot.' Zack nodded. 'I take on high-risk patients that others refuse to go near.'

'I've explained that to Freya,' James said, 'and I've spoken with my colleagues. We're all agreed that we're not involving ourselves in charity to fudge figures just to make us look good. We want to do some necessary work and that involves risks.'

'I'd only operate if I thought there was a chance,' Zack said, and James nodded. 'I focus on the surgery,' Zack continued, and turned to Freya. 'That's it.'

He was arrogant, utterly immutable, and if Freya wasn't so angry that he'd known who she was all along, she could possibly have jumped on his lap and started purring.

She didn't know how she could simultaneously be embarrassed and cross while also being impossibly turned on.

'I work on short-term contracts and the patients benefit from that.' Zack further explained his stance. 'I might not be around to do the follow-up but they have my skill and attention in the operating theatre, or the OR, or whatever the terminology is you use here. In Nepal I was working in a field hospital so I can't wait to use the amazing facilities here. I am up to date with technology and I am also very hands on with the basics…'

Freya crossed her legs.

'Will you consider extending your contract?' James asked. 'If things are going well?'

'I'll speak with you after a month.' Zack conceded the smallest fraction. 'If I can commit for another three months, I'll let you know then. If I can't commit to more than that it will give you time to start looking. I am, though, going to Australia for a couple of weeks in April.'

'To visit family?' James asked, and Freya blinked as Zack simply didn't answer the question.

Yes, they were being told that what Zack did in his own time was his concern only.

And then Freya glimpsed again the joy of anonymity and the pain of it going wrong. Zack had told her in bed this very morning that he was running from stuff. Their gazes met briefly and then Zack flicked his away and she saw his neck stretch in slight discomfort.

Oh, she wanted to know this man.

'So, when could you start?' James asked.

'I just have to sort a couple of details out and then I can let you know.'

Freya's phone buzzed and James tensed. He loathed texts and Freya rolled her eyes at his familiar response. 'It's mine.'

She glanced in her bag and saw that it was Mila.

'Sorry about that,' Freya said.

'Do you have any questions for Freya?' Jack asked.

'I do but I'll speak with her later,' Zack said.

'I…' Freya was about to say she couldn't hang around but she knew she was just putting off the inevitable. 'Sure.'

'I'll send Zack through to you when we're done.'

'Thanks,' Freya said. 'It was nice meeting you, Zack.'

Her voice was pleasant and her lips smiled, but her eyes told him what a bastard he was.

She went into her office and her skin was crawling with embarrassment and she pressed her fingers into her eyes.

This was, very possibly, going to be the longest three months of her life.

'Freya?'

She turned at the sound of Stephanie's voice.

'Are you okay?'

'Just...' Freya took a breath. 'A bit dizzy,' she explained. 'It was a big night last night.'

'Sure,' Stephanie said and handed over some files and then left.

Great, Freya thought. Stephanie just loved to have her nose in everyones business.

No doubt, that Freya was dizzy, would soon work its way back to James.

Freya made the call she had just missed.

'How are you?' Mila asked.

'You really don't want to know,' Freya said.

'Oh, but I do.' They both laughed. 'I'll have to prise it out of you later.'

She'd better not! Freya thought.

'I just wondered if there was any news about that surgeon for Paulo? I've got Geoff, his cardiologist, here now and he's concerned.'

'He's in with James now. Let me...' Freya glanced up as James and Zack came to the door. 'I have to go,' Freya said hurriedly. 'I'll call you back.'

Zack noticed her cheeks redden and that Freya was flustered as she quickly ended the call.

'All okay?' James checked, because Freya was usually completely together, or did everything to appear to be.

She was behaving very oddly today.

'Of course it is,' Freya said. 'I thought you were giving Zack a tour.'

'We're going to do that at eleven. I've just got a patient that needs a quick review. If you can get started on the paperwork, and a head shot so that everything is in order, that would be great. We'll also need you to write up a press release and let the world know we've got Zack on board.'

'Sure.'

'Oh, and I'll ring the Bright Hope Clinic and see about getting the child looked at by Zack today,' James said.

'I can do that,' Freya offered.

'Do what?'

'Arrange his transfer.'

'Zack has to see the patient first.' James frowned. 'Since when did you start acting as a receptionist? I'll leave Zack with you.'

He walked out and Zack stood and watched as Freya picked up the phone.

'Could you give me a moment, please?' Freya asked.

'Sure,' Zack said, and stood there.

'I meant I'd like a moment of privacy, please,' she snapped, and Zack stared at her for a second before exiting her office, closing the door behind him.

God, this morning was a disaster, she thought as she frantically called Mila back.

'You haven't told James about me yet,' Mila said. 'Have you?'

'No,' Freya admitted. 'And he's just about to call the clinic.'

'It's fine,' Mila said. 'I don't generally man the phones. I'll have him put through to Geoff, but, Freya, he needs to know that the Bright Hope Clinic is mine.'

'I know he does and I am going to tell him.'

'If you can't do it face to face, just text him.'

'He hates texts.'

'Well, he's going to hate finding out that we're going to be working together a whole lot more.'

'Leave it with me.'

Freya ended the call, took a breath and opened the

door on her currently more overwhelming problem. Zack was leaning up against a wall outside and not looking very impressed to have been asked to step outside. 'Sorry about that! Come on through,' Freya said, and put on her bright corporate smile and stepped back to let him in. She waited till the door was safely closed for the smile to go and then she let him have it.

'You knew...'

'No.' He gave a small shake of his head.

'You weren't even surprised when you walked in. It was supposed to be one night, no names...'

'I thought you looked vaguely familiar but it only clicked this morning when I was in the shower,' Zack said. 'I just looked you up, and you were quite a wild child, it would seem.'

He thought of the photos of her collapsed and being carried out of a nightclub that he had seen, and he thought of the article he had read that spoke of drugs and alcohol and a lengthy stint in rehab.

'I'm not discussing this here,' Freya said. 'I don't bring my private life to work.'

'And neither do I,' Zack said. 'So go and get some blood work done and then tell me when I can start work.'

Where were the green eyes that had locked with hers last night? Oh, he was looking right at her but his expression was serious.

Grim.

'I'm a cardiac surgeon and this morning we had unprotected sex and it would appear you've had a habit. I'd like a little more than your word that you're not using.'

And she could only find a grudging admiration that he had the guts to address it directly.

'I've never done drugs.' She looked at him. 'I did have some tests last week and they all came back clear.'

'Has there been anyone since then?'

'Zack!'

'Freya, don't play coy. You've got all my lab results sitting on your desk, I haven't been with anyone since I had blood pulled, and I sure as hell haven't been in rehab. So I need to know the score.'

'I had some blood work for fertility issues and they ran the tests as routine. I was in rehab for an eating disorder. Happy now?'

'Well, *happy* isn't the word I'd use to find out the condom split with someone having fertility treatment, but, yep, glad to know we're both clean.'

'Well, you don't have to worry about the fertility issue. I haven't started treatment and I shot my ovaries.'

'Shot your ovaries?' Zack frowned and then got it.

Her eating disorder meant she couldn't have kids and he understood better now what she'd told him about running and trying not to.

'I'll let James know that I can start straight away, then.'

He gave her a nod and turned to go but Freya halted him. 'Zack, you won't—'

'Freya.' He turned around. 'I'd never say anything and, as you're about to find out, I'm a very different person at work.'

'Sure.'

'The only reason I am talking about last night in this office is because it's pertinent to work. What happened is not to be brought up or discussed, do you understand that?'

'Yes.'

It was the longest day.

All she wanted to do was go home and curl up with

her shame, yet, now that Zack was on board, her life had gotten busy.

His résumé was impressive on a professional level. He'd worked all over the globe, in both lavish and sparsely equipped hospitals. She looked up his hometown and her eyes widened when she read about the tiny population and how widely it was scattered.

Well, they could go with the country-boy angle, Freya thought, and then tried to picture herself suggesting that to Zack.

Ah…perhaps not.

What else could she find out?

It would seem that five years ago he'd been in Canada at an ice hockey match when a player had gone into cardiac arrest and Zack had successfully resuscitated him.

A couple of phone calls later and she was in touch with the player's own PA. Nothing was said, just a little touching base query to see if the player might be open to being flown to LA.

'He's on vacation but I'll get back to you at an *appropriate* time.'

God, no wonder people were tense, Freya thought as she realised that most of the world considered today not really a day for such calls, but at The Hills, though there were no scheduled operations, it was a work day as usual.

The staff up on the cardiac unit didn't say, *Oh, no, it's a holiday,* as they prepared the bed for Paulo to arrive.

And neither did the pilot of the luxury helicopter question it when, after examining Paulo and going through his tests at the Bright Hope Clinic, Zack called James.

'I've just spoken with Maria, his mother,' Zack said. 'I've told her that I'm still not sure if he's a candidate for surgery but I would like to run some more tests at The Hills. Their equipment is terrible.'

And so by three that afternoon a new little patient with black hair and eyes and a gappy smile was sitting in bed with his worried mother by his side.

And by five all Freya wanted was home and was struggling to hold it together when James knocked at her door.

'He's not very sociable, is he?' James rolled his eyes. 'I tried to schedule a meeting and he wants it to be held in a meeting room, rather than my office. Neutral territory, he said.'

Freya actually laughed.

'Three months in a hotel...' James shook his head. 'The guy's a well-dressed gypsy. I've asked him to come and get a security tag—can you please sort out his head shot?'

'I shall,' Freya said.

She'd sort it tomorrow.

All she wanted now was home.

CHAPTER SIX

So DISTRACTED WAS Freya that she forgot she'd booked in
for another night at the hotel until she was nearly home.
Freya decided to check in on Cleo and then head back,
grab her stuff and just come home and sleep away the
shame.

She really wanted to curl up and pull the covers over
her head and hibernate till the end of March when Zack
would be gone but knew that wasn't going to happen.

Freya parked and went up to her apartment, and as she
opened the door she saw that her neighbour Red was just
on his way out after feeding her little pug, Cleo.

'Hi.' Freya smiled.

'How are you, Freya?'

'I'm well! Thanks so much for this.'

'No problem. Are you back for the night?'

'I'm not sure,' Freya said, deciding she might just
crash at the hotel. 'If I'm not here, can you let her out
for me?'

'Of course.'

She had great neighbours and favours were freely
given and returned. Red told her that he'd watched a
movie last night with Cleo and had had a couple of beers.

Freya thanked him again and kept her smile on and
wide, and only when Red had gone did she sink down

onto the sofa and let her smile fade. She rested her head in her hands and just sat with the panic that had been chasing her all day since she'd worked out who Zack was.

'Oh, Cleo…'

She picked up her little, fat friend and told her all of it, well, not in specific detail, but that she'd lost her head last night to the most gorgeous of men on the promise they would never again meet.

'And now I have to work alongside him for three months. I don't know what to do.'

Cleo gave her no answers, just snuffled. The little pug was the absolute love of her life. James had bought her for Freya on her discharge from rehab and Freya had finally found a soul she could pour her heart out to.

'How can I face him?' she asked her fur baby.

Freya cuddled her for a good hour and then she carried her down for her little walk. Cleo was getting so tired and so old and Freya knew she wouldn't have her for much longer. James, because he was concerned how Freya would cope when her beloved companion died, had suggested, under the guise that it might give Cleo a new lease of life, that Freya get a puppy.

'I don't want another dog,' Freya said to Cleo as she popped her onto the sofa.

And not just because she could never love another dog as much as this one.

Freya wanted a baby. She was so over attempts at relationships and had no qualms about being a single mom.

She couldn't do a worse job than her parents had, and they'd been together till Freya was thirteen.

As she drove back to the hotel, Freya felt drained and exhausted. She'd had basically no sleep all night and the most awkward, uncomfortable of days and, joy, she had to face him again tomorrow.

She stood in the elevator and tried not to think of what had taken place such a short while ago and then she wearily swiped open her hotel door.

And there, just sitting there, drink poured, tie loose and wearing a triumphant grin, waving an envelope, was Zack. He just watched Freya groan as she remembered the room card she'd left.

'One night, no names?' Zack checked, holding up the envelope.

And when you've been truly caught, all you can really do is admit it.

'Two nights, then,' Freya said. 'I never said I didn't enjoy it.'

'Great, wasn't it?' Zack grinned. 'Well, thank you for the test results. That was actually very good of you. So good of you that I'm here to service you. Get over here.' He stamped the floor with his boot.

'I thought we were never to discuss it again.'

'At work it is never to be brought up,' Zack said. 'Out of work is a completely separate thing. So come here.'

Oh, now she understood better his stance on not answering questions.

'I can't,' Freya said. 'I'm so embarrassed.'

'Don't be.' He grinned. 'Come here.'

Freya made her way over and he pulled her onto his lap and she was just one burning blush but he was laughing.

'I really don't get involved with people I work with,' Freya said. 'Dating and—'

'Guess what,' Zack interrupted. 'I don't date.'

'Never?'

'Nope,' Zack said. 'So don't worry about awkward stuff and holding hands and all that sort of thing. Poor us, just sex.'

'Oh, no.'

'Liar, liar…' And her knickers *were* on fire because he slipped a hand up her dress.

'And you don't have to worry, no one will ever hear your secret from me.'

'Secret?' Freya frowned.

'That the uptight Freya likes a bit of no-name spanky on the down-low.'

'Zack,' she said, 'I didn't know till last night that I liked that…' She looked at him and could tell he didn't believe her. 'I'm not like that.'

'Freya, you emailed me a couple of weeks ago and said you were *very* single and not to tell James.'

'That was after a very difficult night being told by my soon-to-be-married and married friends that it would be my turn next. I'd had too much to drink and decided to live a little. Believe it or not, you're the only person I'd been with for the whole of last year.'

'Well, given we saw in the New Year downstairs, you had no one last year, Freya, so you have some catching up to do.'

'I don't think so,' Freya said, yet she was fighting not to undo the buttons on his shirt.

'I'm here for three months,' Zack said, 'and we're both as clean as whistles. Though, given we couldn't get through one night without tearing the rubber, you need to get on the Pill. I really don't want to rely on your shot ovaries, as you so fondly refer to them.'

'Zack, we can't.'

'But you know that we shall.'

Freya said nothing, he was so assured they'd be back in bed.

Sadly for her self-control, he was completely right— she was already unzipping him and taking it out.

'Don't tell James…'

CHAPTER SEVEN

ZACK REALLY WAS a master at keeping his private life separate from work.

By day he was remote, perhaps even a bit unfriendly at times. There were absolutely no shared looks, or exchanges, not even behind closed doors.

He dived straight into a very full schedule but occasionally Freya found herself back at the hotel, and, yes, the sex was amazing but they didn't talk much. She knew some stuff, but the information he shared was as generous as a waiter with the cracked pepper—there was never enough.

They lay there one morning and he was the monkey on her back, unknotting all her muscles, when he asked her something.

'Why are you avoiding James?'

'I'm not,' Freya said, and he felt her shoulders stiffen.

'Who were you speaking to on the phone the morning of my interview?'

'I can't remember.'

'You got all flustered.'

'Well, my one and only one-night stand suddenly had a name.'

'Tell me,' he said, 'were you on the phone to some guy?'

'A woman, actually,' Freya said, and he laughed.

'Do tell.'

'Nope.' The fewer people who knew about Mila and James's rocky past the better. And the fewer who knew about her and Zack's torrid present, all the better too!

'How come you stay here?' Freya asked as breakfast was served. Coffee for him, green tea and avocado smash for Freya.

'I just like it.'

'But you could have an apartment.'

'I don't want one.'

'Well, if you've got money to burn…'

'I've been sleeping under a mosquito net for six months,' Zack pointed out.

'Even so…'

Freya stayed quiet.

It wasn't money that was the issue, it was his transient existence that irked her.

Everything he had was in this room and he could check out tomorrow, Freya knew. His time in one place was only as long as his theatre list.

'Are you going to operate on Paulo?'

He didn't answer at first then he said, 'Is that PR Freya or Freya asking?'

'Freya.'

'Yes, I'm just trying to get him at optimum health first. You know his mother lost another son?'

Freya nodded.

'I don't want her losing two.'

And he watched as she cracked a very generous amount of cracked pepper on her avocado.

'My brother died nearly ten years ago. I saw what losing one kid did to my mother.'

For Freya, to hear Zack suddenly reveal such a vital

part of himself, it was like the cracker had fallen off the pepper mill.

'Zack! I'm so sorry to hear that.'

He grinned. 'Don't use your psychologist voice on me.' Then he asked her something he was curious about. She'd told him about her psychology degree and he wanted to know why she didn't use it. 'I know you're good at PR but do you really enjoy it?'

'I do,' Freya said, and she took a breath and told him her plans, wondering if he'd laugh. 'I want to start seeing clients. I wasn't ready to before.'

'Ready?'

'I just didn't know if I had any right to advise on eating disorders when I was working so hard on myself. I'm not sure I'm ready even now.'

'I'd say you're ready.' Zack smiled. 'I've spoken more to you than I have to anyone. You're very easy to talk to, Freya.'

'You're not.' She smiled back, glowing on the inside that he thought she could do it, but then she was serious. She really wanted to know more about him. 'How did your brother die?' she asked.

'How we all die,' Zack said, refusing to open up on her demand. He told only what he wanted to. 'His heart stopped beating.'

Aaagh! He was so frustrating but when he shared a part of himself it just made her want to know more.

'Head injury.' Zack relented a touch.

'Do you miss him?'

'I do,' Zack said, and he liked it that she didn't say that he must miss him. 'It's always there in the background, other times...' He shrugged, reluctant to explain it. 'My parents, though, still grieve every day.'

'That must be hard to watch.'

'Which is why I don't,' Zack said.

Subject closed.

And so she knew something but so little about him and that was proven on his second week at work as the day of Paulo's surgery neared and Freya wanted more for another press release.

'Everything you need is on my résumé,' Zack said, clearly less than impressed to be in her office.

'Well, can we go with the small-town angle?'

'It's hardly small,' Zack snapped. 'It's the size of LA.'

'I meant the population.'

'If you bring my family into this,' Zack said, 'then you'd better find a stand-in for Paulo's surgery. Oh, that's right, you won't be able to, so you can go and tell his mother why the clinic lost the only doctor prepared to operate on her son.'

'I'll take that as no!' Freya was used to difficult doctors. Putting the new brochure together had been difficult enough, but running promo on Zack took the cake. 'Can we just get a photo of you with him?'

'I don't work like that, Freya. You're not getting your cheesy photo.'

'Fine,' Freya snapped. 'What am I supposed to write?'

'That a child from the Bright Hope Clinic with a complex tetralogy of Fallot is being operated on at The Hollywood Hills Clinic and that—'

'I've already got that part, thanks.' Tough Freya wasn't working so she lodged an appeal with her eyes but he stared back coolly and dismissed her flirt. 'People like to see the human angle.'

'Then get it elsewhere,' Zack said. 'Because it's not coming from me.'

'I still need your head shot.'

'Take it, then.'

'Do you want to go and freshen up?'

'No.'

'You haven't shaved.'

'I don't shave on the week of a big operation.'

'Really?' Freya's eyes lit up. 'Zack, that's just the type of information people want to—'

'Freya,' Zack warned, 'I'm getting tired of this.'

She took out her camera. Usually she'd dab a bit of powder on the subject's face but she didn't think it would be appreciated in this case. Usually when someone was about to have their picture taken they would now be at the mirror, fixing their hair or rearranging their tie or stethoscope.

Zack just sat there and stared back.

'Can you at least smile?'

He gave her such a fake smile that Freya actually laughed. 'I'll settle for scowling.'

She got her shot and it was actually an incredibly good one.

'Can I go now?'

'Sure. Do you want to come over tonight?' she asked, but he just stood up and walked off.

Zack kept her hanging.

Oh, they'd agreed to never discuss the other side of them at work, but just some indication about where she stood might be nice.

Except she knew where she stood.

Zack had made it very clear.

He didn't come to her apartment. They played at his hotel.

Which meant she should not be sending her phone a copy of his photo and she should not be wondering, hoping, that night as she left work, if Zack was going to call.

He did.

Or rather he fired a text that night at eight to see if she wanted to meet at the bar of the hotel.

She wanted him to come to her home.

Freya fired back her answer.

Busy tonight.

She wasn't.

Well, there was always work she could catch up on but she was starting to struggle with her end of things.

No problem.

Zack's response annoyed her.

There were no questions or comment, no *I miss you*, no *Pity*. There was nothing to indicate that her response mattered to him.

It did.

Zack was actually relieved that Freya said no to coming to the hotel.

Well, not relieved in a sexual sense, just that he knew now that he would not be seeing her again socially for several days now.

They were getting too involved for his comfort. Too many times through the day he went to call her or saved something in his head to tell Freya about that night. Certainly he wasn't comfortable with the idea of going over to her home.

He didn't want a relationship.

He thought of his brother, chained till the day he'd died to a life that he hadn't wanted, and it would never happen to Zack. And yet he didn't feel chained when he was with Freya, he felt more open and honest than he ever had.

It was too much to think of now.

So, yes, he was relieved that she'd declined coming over as it meant that he didn't have to worry about his increasing feelings towards Freya for now. He would be in bed early tomorrow, preparing himself for a very long operation, and he would be living more or less between his office and Paulo's bedside for a couple of days afterwards.

If Paulo made it.

CHAPTER EIGHT

ZACK WASN'T AT work the next morning.

Freya noticed.

All night she had been fighting with herself not to change her mind and go over to his hotel but really, Freya knew, she wanted more than she was getting from Zack.

'How's it all going?' James asked as Freya dropped by.

'Very well,' Freya said. 'James, I'm just going to Bright Hope to take some posters over for them to put up.'

'Well, I don't want any posters put up here,' James said.

'I wouldn't tarnish your walls,' Freya said.

'Is everything okay?' James checked.

'Everything's fine. Why?'

'You just seem…,' James shrugged.

'I'm just busy and I'm also…' Freya knew that she had to tell him. Mila's name was on the posters she was holding in her arms. If the operation was a success it was going to be all over the press and it was time that her brother found out what had been going on behind his back. 'James, we need to talk.'

'Sit down, then.'

James had always made time for her and she could see the concern in his eyes. She wished he'd stop being so protective, so ready to assume that at any moment she might slip back into ways of old.

Freya was tired of being treated like glass and didn't get why they couldn't speak openly about things.

That time in their lives hurt too much, Freya guessed.

And what she was going to say now would hurt James, she guessed too, which was why she had been avoiding it.

'You know the Bright Hope Clinic…'

'What now?' James sighed. 'Freya, my charitable cup does not runneth over. I do have patients of my own.'

'I know that. It's not about a patient, it's about the founder.' She swallowed. 'Mila Brightman…'

She watched as her brother's face paled but he said nothing at first, just sat there, but then he spoke. 'Mila wouldn't get involved in anything that has my name on it.' James shook his head. 'No way.'

'Of course she would for the sake of her patients.'

'How long have you known that she's involved in Bright Hope?'

'I've always known,' Freya said. 'We've stayed friends.'

'You stayed friends with my ex?'

'She was my friend too,' Freya said.

'And you didn't think to tell me any of this?'

'It was very easy not to, you avoid the charity stuff…'

'And Mila's the reason why I do!'

'I know that.'

'No, you don't,' James snapped. 'I thought she was overseas and all this time you two have been colluding—'

'We've been doing what we can for the patients. Come on, James, look at the amazing stuff that's happened already. Paulo's getting a chance, you've got a burns patient next—'

'Get out,' James interrupted.

'James—'

'I mean it, Freya.'

And she looked at her brother who had always been there for her, now telling her to get out.

'James,' Freya said in her most patient voice, 'let's talk about this.'

'Are you still here?' he asked. 'I'm telling you, Freya, get the hell out.'

Freya walked out his office and straight to her car. She had known that he wouldn't be pleased, but to be told to get out had been unexpected.

James couldn't choose who she was friends with.

Mila and he had been engaged, had been about to be married. Just because he had chosen not to go through with it, it didn't have to mean that she'd turn her back on Mila.

Freya was so upset that for once she didn't notice Zack walking towards her.

'Hey,' Zack said. 'Where are you off to?'

'I'm just taking some posters to the Bright Hope Clinic. I'm hoping—'

'Enough.' Zack put up his hand. 'I shouldn't have asked. I'm trying not to think about tomorrow just yet.'

'Sorry,' Freya said, and she thought of the pressure he must be under.

'About last night—'

'Not here, Freya.'

'It's a car park.' Freya pointed out. 'Look, how about tonight? I could cook something. Come over—'

'Freya, not here,' Zack said again. 'We agreed.'

'Sure.' Freya said, and walked off. She loaded all the posters into her car but before she drove off she texted Zack her address and again asked if he wanted dinner. Yes, she knew she was pushing to move things along to more than they had agreed to.

She wanted things to move along, though, Freya thought.

She hit 'send' and then headed south for the Bright Hope Clinic.

'Hi,' Mila said when she arrived, and then saw Freya's tense features. 'You told James.'

Freya nodded. 'I did.' Though it wasn't just James and their row that she was feeling so tense about. She was still waiting for Zack to respond. 'It didn't go down too well.'

'How is he?'

'Shell-shocked,' Freya said. 'I think he thought you were still overseas. He pretty much left all the research of charities to me.'

Mila was busy working and Freya put up all the posters and then left. As she stepped through the door of her apartment she had her answer to dinner and her invitation to come over in a less than effusive text.

No thanks. Zack

He hadn't even put the little exclamation mark that they jokingly used in their exchanges. Oh, Freya knew it was a tiny detail but she could feel that they were slipping away from each other and she didn't want them to.

I could come over to you.

Freya read what she'd just typed and she loathed herself for it. She looked at Cleo, who just stared back at her and told her to please not do it.

She hit 'send'.

'Sorry,' she said to Cleo.

And, rather more rapidly this time than last, she got her response.

Not tonight.
I've got a big day tomorrow.
Zack

And it was there, in that second, Freya knew, that things had changed.

Maybe not for Zack.

But for her.

It wasn't just sex for her.

Maybe it never had been.

For Freya, it felt a whole lot more than anything she had ever known.

CHAPTER NINE

THINGS HAD, IN FACT, changed for Zack.

He'd declined her invitation for dinner, when he actually wanted a quiet night in with Freya, but it moved them into uncharted territory and Zack did not have the head space to explore that now.

Instead, he hit 'send' and then walked into his office to speak with Maria, which was a very difficult conversation to have.

'You've told me all this,' Maria said. 'Many times. I understand that he might not make it…'

'Maria,' Zack said, 'listen to me. You have to hear this.' They went through it again, not just the risks of the procedure but how they would deal with Paulo tomorrow as he went under anaesthetic.

He left her crying with Sonia, a skilled PICU nurse, who would help Maria compose herself before she went back in to be with her son.

Then he got Freya's invitation to come over and sex really was the last thing on his mind and, annoyed at her persistence, he hit 'send' on a thanks, but, no, thanks text and then felt like a bastard.

She was too much, too intense, yet he liked it. Freya was complex and changeable, fragile yet strong, and he simply could not think about her now.

He lay in his hotel room, turning up the news to drown out the sound of a couple at it in the next room.

Zack couldn't face the noise and chatter of the restaurant. Instead, he ordered room service, looked at the steak he'd ordered and washed it down with a side of pasta and a couple of bottles of sparkling water. Then it was time to start thinking about tomorrow.

He knew that there was a lot riding on this operation being a success. The Bright Hope Clinic desperately needed the donations that would start to roll in if it went well.

But it wasn't that that truly daunted him. What did, was a five-year-old with a seriously messed-up heart. That was all there was space for in his head.

Zack checked in on his ego to make sure he wasn't being cavalier, and then he phoned Cale, a mentor and friend in Australia that he'd trained under, and went through his proposed procedure with him when Zack still couldn't wind down.

Then he slept a dreamless sleep, which he had trained himself to do on the night prior to a big operation, and instead of the car he'd hired he had a taxi drive him in.

He went through things with the anaesthetist and the OR team and checked in on PICU. Paulo had been admitted there last night so he would be used to it when he came around and also to have some medications administered overnight.

'Hello, you.' He smiled at his little friend.

'Zack!'

He was groggy from light sedation but Paulo smiled at his big friend. Zack looked over at Maria and could see she was about to crumble. 'Not now,' Zack warned, and Maria nodded, remembering the long talk they'd had yesterday.

'I'll see you in pre-op,' he said to Paulo, ruffled his hair and walked off.

He made his last checks and then he was told that Paulo and his mother were there and Zack went through.

'Did you just get more handsome?' Zack asked, and Paulo grinned his gappy blue-lipped grin.

'He's my handsome man,' Maria said. 'I love you, baby,' she said to her son. *'Te amo...'*

'Te amo, Mamma,' Paulo said.

Maria gave him a kiss and Zack watched as she cuddled him tight while the anaesthetist started to give the medicines and then, as Maria had tried so hard not to do, once he was safely under she broke down.

'Well done,' Zack said, and he gave her a hug. 'I will do all I can, Maria. You were wonderful with him.'

That was the hard part over with, thought Zack as he headed off to scrub.

Now came the harder part, eight hours of surgery.

He just hoped that today he didn't get to the hardest part—telling Maria that her beautiful son was dead.

The whole clinic was on tenterhooks throughout a very long day.

The estimated operating time of eight hours became nine.

Nine became ten and as it did so Freya's phone went again. She knew, even without looking, that it would be Mila.

She was right.

'I know you said you'd call with any updates but I'm going crazy here.'

'I've heard nothing,' Freya said. 'I'll be the very last to know if Zack has his way. He doesn't consider PR a high priority.'

'I know,' Mila said.

'It's been more than ten hours now. Is that good?' Freya asked.

'I hope so,' Mila sighed, and they chatted for ten as they hung out, waiting for news on Paulo. 'How are you and James doing now?'

'We're still not talking,' Freya admitted. 'He's been in, observing the operation.' Then she heard familiar footsteps and knew it was James heading for his office and Freya put the phone down on her desk and ran out.

'James?'

'I was just coming in to tell you. Paulo's in Recovery and Zack is, basically, amazing,' James said, and the animosity between him and Freya was temporarily cast aside for a moment just to breathe in the relief. 'It's still very early days, of course. I can see why no one wanted to touch that heart.' James shook his head. 'It was a mess, yet it was like watching a miracle to see him operate. Zack must have nerves of steel.'

And then he seemed to remember that they weren't talking and James gave her a nod and Freya went back to the phone.

'James said—'

'I heard,' Mila interrupted, and Freya sat silent as Mila started to cry. She truly didn't know if Mila was crying with relief over Paulo or hearing James's voice, or both.

God, James! Freya thought.

Why did you have to do what you did?

He had caused so much pain and though she loved her brother very much, it didn't take away her anger for all the hurt that he had caused to her friend. And the worst part of all was that Freya simply didn't know why James had decided to end things with Mila on their wedding day.

Freya sat there listening as her friend tried to pull things together.

'I have to go,' Mila said. 'Sorry to cry.'

'It's an emotional time.'

'Well, you've had plenty of them and yet you never cry,' Mila snapped. She knew how closed off Freya was and she could sense something was wrong. 'Freya, is everything okay? Apart from James and things.'

'Everything's...' Freya didn't even know where to start. Zack had made it very clear that the two of them were not to be discussed and she guessed there would be plenty of time for introspection once he had gone. 'I'll bring you up to speed soon enough.'

'I'm going to keep you to that,' Mila said. 'Can you keep me up to date with any news about Paulo?'

'Of course I shall.'

'What time are you going home?'

'I don't know,' Freya admitted.

It was the oddest night.

As the clock hit ten, Abi Thompson, a reconstructive surgeon who had viewed some of the operation from the gallery, stopped by for a chat.

'Zack was awesome,' Abi said. 'There was no music, no chatter. Zack just stopped for water and half a banana a couple of times. It was so intense in there, there were a couple of near misses—not that you'd have known from watching Zack.'

Oh, Zack knew *all* about the misses.

He stood at the end of Paulo's bed and checked all the charts with Sonia, the PICU nurse. He knew exactly how close Paulo had come to death and the surgery would certainly have turned that way if he hadn't had such state-of-the-art equipment.

Maybe he should put himself out there a bit more, if it meant more funds.

'He's going to be a doctor when he grows up,' Maria said, holding her son's hand. 'You wait, he's going to make you proud.'

Zack nodded. Maria didn't need to know that those were the words he dreaded, and why he didn't have pictures of smiling children lining a regular office.

He didn't want the strain on a teenager's face as their father shook Zack's hand and said a similar thing.

Paulo owed him nothing.

Not even a good life.

It was up to Paulo.

His life was his to live.

'Shouldn't you get something to eat?' Sonia broke into his thoughts. 'I could be calling on you a lot throughout the night.'

Zack nodded. 'I just rang down and asked for a meal to be left in my office.' Sonia was right, he had done all he could, and for now Paulo was critical but stable and there was a whole team starting to take over his care. 'I'm going to try and grab an hour of sleep,' he said. 'Page me for anything. Don't wait.'

'Sure.'

He headed down and just nodded to James, who was speaking with Stephanie at Reception. Zack was thankful that James understood he wasn't in the mood to speak and just gave him an appreciative nod back.

He walked past Freya's open door and she saw that but then Zack turned around.

'I'm not ignoring you,' he said. 'I just can't talk to anyone right now.'

'Fair enough.' Freya smiled. She was prickly about last night but wasn't selfish enough to address that now.

'I've spoken with Maria and she says you can release the news that he's out of Theatre.'

'Thanks.'

Still he didn't leave.

'Sorry about last night,' Zack said. 'I wouldn't have been much company.'

'That's fine.' And they looked at each other for a long time, Freya trying to bite back from saying that it didn't all have to be about sex, but well aware he didn't need her stuff now.

'For what it's worth,' Zack said, 'I regretted it.'

And Freya said nothing. She guessed more than ten hours of surgery counted for a little lapse and that he might also later regret saying what he just had.

'I'm going to get something to eat.'

'Well, whatever you ordered was just delivered to your office and, I have to say, it smells amazing. Go and have a rest,' Freya said. She had never seen someone look so wiped out.

'I'm just going to try and grab an hour and then head back up there.'

'Do you want me to come and wake you?'

'Would you?'

'Sure.'

Zack went to go and then again changed his mind. 'Freya, could you take my pager and answer it? If it's PICU come and get me straight away but if it's anyone else...'

'Sure.'

'Were you going home?' Zack checked.

'Nope.'

The food was amazing, and he ate it and then rehy-drated with more water. Then he lay back on the plush couch and tried not to go over the surgery in his head. He just wanted to clear his mind.

Only he couldn't.

Twice during the surgery he'd thought he'd been wrong to take the procedure on. One hour in, he had considered closing but had pushed on. Five hours in he had been certain that the heart was too much of a mess, but it wasn't as if he'd had any choice by then but to carry on.

Watching that heart start beating when it had come off bypass, he'd heard the elation in the theatre but had said nothing.

Going in to speak to Maria, he had warned her that the next forty-eight hours were critical and had been guarded with his optimism. No matter how Zack had warned her that Paulo might not make it through surgery, that the little boy had survived was more of a miracle than Maria would ever know.

Since the operation started he had not been able to relax for a moment yet now he had to.

And Freya knew that too.

His pager buzzed and when she saw that it wasn't from PICU Freya rang the switchboard. 'He's not taking any calls unless it's PICU. If you can take a message I'll pass it on.'

'Sure,' the operator said, and Freya waited and then frowned when the operator came back on. 'It's his father calling from Australia, he says that it's urgent.'

'Okay,' Freya said. What choice did she have? 'I'll let him know.'

Freya knocked on the door to his office and went in. 'Zack,' Freya said. 'Zack!'

'Is it PICU?' He sat straight up on the second call.

'No…'

'Later, Freya.'

'It's your father,' Freya said. 'He says that it's urgent.' She handed his impatient hand the phone.

'What's going on?' Zack asked. 'Is it Mum?'

He saw Freya standing there and he glanced up, about to tell her, as she had once told him, that he'd like some privacy, given it was clearly a personal call. Then he saw the concern in her face and it wasn't intrusive.

Freya saw his glance and realised she was hovering, and tried to remember the rules, but as she went to go he caught her wrist and frowned as his father spoke on. 'Zack, I need some medical advice. Do you remember Tara?'

'Of course I remember Tara, Dad.' Zack's jaw gritted—did they think he had no soul just because he hadn't stayed? 'Is she okay?'

'Tara's doing well, it's the baby that's causing me some concern.'

'Tell me.'

'He was four weeks premature and breech but healthy, they kept him in for five days and he was discharged at birth weight.

'He's fourteen days old now and for the last couple of days Tara's been coming in. The baby seems to be doing well but...'

'Dad?' Zack frowned because his father sounded hesitant yet he was the best diagnostician Zack knew.

'He's eating, he's drinking and he's crying. I can't put my finger on it, Zack, but there's something not right. There's a big emergency north of here, only high-priority transfers...'

'What does Tara think?'

'Well, Jed—'

'Not her husband,' Zack said. 'What does Tara say?'

'She's distraught. She says that his cry has changed. I can't pick up a murmur...'

'Do you think that it's cardiac related?'

'I'm sure that it is,' his father said. 'That's why I'm calling you.'

Zack went through everything. There was some sweating but the temperatures were sky-high back home, and there was also a slight reduction in peripheral perfusion, his father felt, though that was more on instinct.

'I should get him seen but on all the guidelines he's non-urgent at this stage.'

'Dad, if he's got a ductal dependent lesion...' Zack didn't need to spell it out that these babies were all too often diagnosed at post-mortem. 'If you're worried then he needs to be seen straight away.'

'There's been a train crash and the air ambulances have to prioritise.'

'I don't think you called me for a chat,' Zack said.

'No.'

'He needs to be seen by Cale. I'll call him now and he'll put the baby's transfer as a priority.'

'There's not much to go on.'

'Yes, there is,' Zack said. 'You have forty years' experience, I'd take that any time. What's the baby's name?'

'Max,' his father answered. 'Zack, what if I'm wrong?'

'Then I'll be more than happy to wear it. I'll call you back when I've spoken with Cale. You tell them to send the air ambulance as a priority.'

Zack no longer felt tired now.

Freya sat on the couch as he rang his mentor and then called his father back.

'It's all sorted in Brisbane—they're expecting him. Cale's coming in and will be there when the baby arrives.'

'Thanks, Zack. We've got clearance for the air ambulance.'

Zack breathed out as he ended the call.

His head couldn't take it. The very thought of Tara going through what Maria had today brought it all too close to a personal level, which Zack did his best to avoid.

'That was my father…'

'I heard,' Freya said.

'Tara's my ex.' He shook his head. 'Too much?'

'No, I think it's nice that you care.' Freya really did, as the impression given by Zack was that he always walked away without a second glance.

'Well, my parents don't think that I do. They've both asked if I remember her, as if I've cut off the first eighteen years of my life. In fairness they never knew we were on together, but as if I'd forget a friend!' He was not going to spill it all out just because he was tired, and anyway PICU rang at that moment to alter some drug doses for Paulo.

'He's doing all the right things,' Zack said, leaning back. 'I'll go and review him at midnight, unless there's any change before then.' He glanced at his phone and Freya saw that he was looking at the time in Australia.

'What does your father think is wrong with the baby's heart?' Freya asked.

'Some defects aren't picked up at birth but when the ducts close at around a couple of weeks old… It might be nothing, it might be a small lesion that could have waited, but if my father's ringing me that means he's seriously worried because nothing would get that proud old bugger to call me otherwise.

'Hell, I still can't believe that he did.'

'Well, you are a cardiac surgeon.'

'Ah, but he'd prefer…'

Zack stopped and then handed her the phone. 'If PICU calls...'

'Sure.'

'Or are you going home?'

'I'm staying tonight.'

'You don't usually.'

'No.' Freya didn't know what to say—she was here because she wanted to be and Zack didn't know what to say because it was actually a help to him that she was.

He didn't like leaving his pagers with others, though he had to at times, of course.

He looked at Freya and he told her more about Paulo's operation. 'I thought twice I'd lost him,' he said, and for the first time he *told* another person what he usually put in his reports, though he gave Freya a far less comprehensive version.

'And if you put any of this in your press releases...'

'I never would,' Freya said. 'I'll email them to you first if you prefer.'

Zack nodded. It felt odd to be unloading thoughts that he usually kept in his head and he was grateful that Freya, when he was too tired to do so, drew a very firm line to ensure that nothing he said he could live to regret.

'I called a colleague last night to go through the surgery I planned and also to check that it wasn't my ego taking him to Theatre. He agreed that Paulo had a chance and that he'd proceed. It's actually the guy Tara's baby has gone to. I spent a year working on his team.'

'So the baby's in good hands.' Freya smiled.

'The best of hands,' Zack said, and then continued to talk about the surgery he'd performed. 'When I first opened him up I was just going to close him and then five hours in I actually wished that I had. I was just going through the motions for the last hours, repairing what I could, remembering all I'd been taught. When they took him off bypass and I saw that heart fill…' The adrenaline that had kept him going through surgery and again when his father had called was still surging through his veins.

'I can't switch off,' Zack admitted.

'When are your days off?' Freya asked.

'I'm not going to get out of this place for the next couple of days.'

'Do you want to come riding at the weekend?' It just popped into her head and then she realised that it might be open to misinterpretation. 'I meant horses.'

He grinned. 'I got that. Do you ride?'

'Not very well,' Freya said, 'but I love it when I do, it helps me to unwind… It was a part of my rehab.'

'Really?'

Zack was about to say no but then thought about it and, yep, a few hours on horseback to look forward to sounded like a good way of staying sane during these coming days.

Freya could see, though, that he was hesitant.

'No strings, Zack. I'm not asking you out on a date.'

She'd got his back-off message yesterday loud and clear.

'I know,' Zack said. 'Are we awkward?'

'A bit.' Freya shrugged slightly. 'But that's because I've never done this before.'

'Done what?'

'Not now,' Freya said, and shook her head. Now really wasn't the time to explain how she was struggling with her feelings for him and the inevitable ending of them. Maybe there would never be a suitable time to tell him all he was starting to mean to her, Freya realised. 'I'd better go.' Only that was the problem—she didn't want to go. She wanted to be here with him and she'd never stop wanting him.

The energy between them was undeniable.

How much easier would this all be if she could simply stand up and walk away, instead of looking down at him where he lay?

Zack broke his own 'nowhere near work' rule and his hand went to the back of her head to pull her down to his mouth. The long, slow kiss that evolved she wanted just as much he did. And it blew beyond proportion in a moment as her hand moved down. He put his hand over hers, though not to halt it, and then Freya moved her mouth back from the kiss and licked her lips as she had the night they had met.

She wanted to sink to her knees just as much and just as naturally as she had that first time, and he wanted ten minutes of pleasure to get out of his head.

'Do I stay or go?' She ran a finger along his erection.

'I thought you said you didn't like it?'

'A concession?' Freya smiled.

'Lock the door.'

She got up and did so and as she walked over he went to check in that she was okay with this, because he had pulled back from the two of them last night, Zack knew that. 'Freya—'

'I get it, Zack.'

They did not need a long discussion tonight so they got back to what they were supposed to be about—sex.

Yet this was different, because Zack never brought it to work and he never just lay there and did nothing except moan with want and relief.

And he could never have known that for Freya this was very different indeed; she had never done this before. She just knelt on the floor and lavished him, loving the pressure of his hand and how he held her hair tight. She took him first with her tongue and then deeper as her hand worked his base.

'More,' Zack moaned, just as she did on occasion, and she took him in as deep as she could and gave him the oblivion he craved.

He sank into bliss and she knelt up higher and her thighs were pressing together at the noises they made, and on the most hellish day and at a less than romantic coupling, they were possibly the closest they had ever been.

Feeling him start to come in her mouth, hearing his shout of relief, Freya came to the salty taste of him.

He made her dizzy.

Her cheek rested on his stomach and she gathered back her breath as Zack lay there. She took it as no insult that his hand slid from her head and he was already asleep.

There was one odd talent Freya had, from too many years hiding in the bathroom, and that was performing a quick tidy up. Freya dealt with all that, she popped it all back and retied his scrubs, then slunk out of his office and sat silent in her own.

And she admitted it properly then.

The life goals she'd had just a short while ago had all shifted.

She was thirty-one years old and, for the first time in her life, Freya was wondering if she was falling in love. Never could she imagine she'd have done what she just had. Zack had no idea that the thought had always made her feel ill.

Not now.

Was this love?

Very possibly, because the thought of him leaving, hurt enough for it to be.

CHAPTER TEN

'THE DONATIONS ARE pouring in,' Freya said to James early on the Saturday after a meeting about Paulo.

It was a reluctant meeting on both their parts.

James had been 'too busy' during the week to touch base, but given the publicity surrounding Paulo, James slotted in a brief catch-up.

Freya didn't want to be there either. It had been a very busy week with work, and Zack aside, the only place Freya now wanted to be was on the back of a horse and letting go some of the tension that she was carrying.

'Donations for the Bright Hope Clinic have started to take off,' Freya said. 'And the general feedback regarding The Hills is positive.'

'General feedback?' James checked.

'As to whether or not the charitable side will be maintained.' Freya pulled no punches. 'The Hills is high-end luxury and people are waiting to see if it's a gimmick.'

'We'd play with a five-year-old's life as a gimmick?'

'I've pretty much responded with that,' Freya said. 'Still, given that it was such a risky procedure, had it not paid off some people are asking if that would have been it for your foray into charitable work.'

'Well, they don't know me,' James said. 'Still, hopefully not every case will be as complicated. Maria has given her consent to Paulo being photographed, if you could get onto that now.'

'Sure. Will you be in one of the photos?'

'He's not my patient.'

'No, but I'm not going to get Zack to agree. I am working on another angle for him, though. I'm trying to get in touch with an older patient of his—perhaps he'll agree to that—but for now we'll just make it about what's so far been achieved and that's thanks to The Hills partnering with Bright Hope.'

Yes, Freya was tense.

In the absence of Zack, the best photo would be both Mila and James with Paulo, but Freya wasn't game to suggest that!

Things weren't great between them and she guessed now wasn't the time to be asking James about her starting to see her own clients, so instead they finished things up.

'Freya?' James said as she folded up her laptop.

'Yes?'

'I'm still angry.'

'I get that,' Freya snapped, 'but surely you can see that both sides benefit and I happen to care about both sides.'

'I'm not discussing that now,' James said. 'I'm just saying that, even though I'm angry, I'm still your brother and if there's a problem...'

'Problem?' Freya frowned.

'Stephanie said the other that day that you went dizzy.'

'And?' Freya rolled her eyes. 'I knew that she'd make a deal out of it. James, I'd been out all night for New Years Eve. I don't need your concern.'

'Well, like it or not, you've got it.'

'It's not necessary, James. I was ill a long time ago.' She had been seventeen! James still looked out for her, was still way too overprotective. 'Don't worry, if I need to see someone I'll be sure to ask for a referral.'

So much for leaving it! But that was Freya—once her mind was made up she could not just sit by.

He stared back at her and Freya wondered if he'd got the point she was making so she spelt it out.

'Why don't you have an eating disorder unit here?' Freya asked.

'We can't have everything.'

'Please!' Freya said. 'That's the whole point of The Hills, the patients have everything! Given that the majority of your clientele are in the public eye I'd say an eating disorder unit might be a necessity rather than a luxury. Yet you refer them elsewhere.'

'I'm trying to…' James started, but then he halted and it incensed Freya.

'Trying to watch out for me, trying to avoid hurts, trying to pretend it doesn't exist.'

'You're better now,' James said. 'Do you really need constant reminders?'

They were getting nowhere.

'I need to get on,' Freya said. 'I'll see you up there.' She walked out, collected her camera from her office and headed up to the cardiac unit, where Paulo was now being cared for.

He looked amazing.

The dusky colour of his skin on admission was now a gorgeous coffee colour and his lips were pink and he was sucking on an ice stick.

And then Zack came in with a colleague he was handing Paulo over to, to check on the boy before he headed off on a well-deserved weekend break.

'I thought you were off for the weekend!' Maria exclaimed.

'In an hour I shall be,' Zack said, and then looked at Paulo. 'I don't have to ask how you are, do I?' He glanced over and nodded to James and saw Freya and her damned camera. 'Is Maria okay with this?'

'Maria is,' Freya said.

'I'm delighted to have our picture taken if it will do some good.' Maria nodded. 'Will you be in it?'

'No, thanks.' Zack shook his head. 'I keep it up here, Maria.'

'Come on, Zack.' Maria was the one who pushed for him to join in the happy shot.

'Seriously.' Zack shook his head. 'Maria, I've got to go and see another patient now.' He was honest. 'They don't need my smiling thumbs up if it doesn't go well for them.'

It was who he was, Freya thought.

Private.

And she wanted in, though she was doing her best to hold back.

Zack went and wrote up his notes and his instructions for Paulo and his other patients while he was away.

He had a small baby on NICU that had already had more tests and procedures done than most people had in a lifetime but he had to go back up there now and order some more before he made a decision next week as to whether or not to operate.

'Hey,' Zack said, when Freya came out from the photo shoot. 'Are we still on for riding?'

'We're at work!' she reminded him.

'Sorry.' He rolled his eyes. 'I've got cabin fever. I've been here since Tuesday.'

'I've booked us for midday,' Freya said. 'We can meet there.' She gave him the address and Zack nodded.

She had meant what she'd said, Zack thought, about today having no strings attached.

Their paths had only crossed briefly since the other night.

For Zack it still felt like it had been a bit of a dream. Even when she had come in to wake him up when PICU had paged him a couple of hours later, Freya had made no reference to what had taken place.

He had brought them to work and the trouble for Zack was that he wasn't adequately troubled by it.

Even now he had asked her about riding, and there were people around.

He needed to reel things back, but it was very hard to do so when you were walking through stables and another person had come up with the very thing you needed.

It felt so good to get away and be doing something he probably wouldn't have made the time for today.

'I didn't know how experienced you were,' Freya said when he arrived. 'I said intermediate...'

Oh, no, he wasn't.

It didn't take long to establish that Zack knew his way around horses and he was given Bullet, who, Zack was assured, lived up to his name.

Freya had Camp, her usual horse, who was patient and steady and everything that she was not.

And they were off.

Together but separate and it suited Freya today. Half an hour in, Zack found a lovely flat length and went for a gallop as Freya just plodded along and looked at the stunning view, past the city and out to the Pacific Ocean.

Then she heard Zack coming back and he was all breathless and Bullet wasn't even sweating.

'I needed that,' Zack said, falling into pace with her.

'And I needed this,' Freya sighed.

After a while they stopped to eat the lunch Freya had made. It was nice to breathe in fresh air and eat but Freya was distracted. Her mind kept going over that morning and her conversation with James.

'You okay?' Zack checked.

'I will be,' Freya said. 'I had words with James.'

And they weren't anonymous strangers any more and this wasn't about Mila and James so she told him the part she felt she wanted to, even if it was rare that she spoke about it.

'James took on a lot when I was ill and now we can hardly talk about it.' She told him how he'd come and hauled her out of a nightclub and that she'd collapsed. How James had found a rehab place for her that was a bit alternative but which had suited her.

'How long were you there for?' Zack asked.

'Six months. Two of those were spent fighting.'

'Fighting?'

'Well, pretending I agreed with them while waiting for an opportunity to do another hundred sit-ups… And I loathed group discussions. Anyway, finally I saw the damage I was doing to myself, that I'd already done, and I decide to work on getting well. They didn't believe me at first. They thought I was just going through the motions to get out.'

'I'm not with you.'

'Well, I just made a decision without all the drama and crying and pouring out my fears. I just set a goal—to get well. So, yes, two months fighting, four months starting to get well and then a lifetime of keeping to it.'

'Is it a fight every day?' He was curious.

'Some days,' Freya said. 'James wants it cured, fixed, healed, and in many ways it is. I'll never go back to how I was.' Freya was sure of it. 'I know that. I just need healthier ways of dealing with tension. My parents said I was attention-seeking…'

'Were you?'

'Not at first,' Freya said. 'I was actually trying to get away from attention. My parents' divorce was everywhere, all their lovers were speaking out, and it was horrific. I know you think I'll go to any lengths for publicity but I'm nowhere close to them. They spoke not just about the rows and the money but about their sex lives, and their lovers did too.'

He said nothing and she was so glad.

'It was excruciating,' Freya admitted. 'I turned to food.' She told him about the reports about her being only a little younger and a whole lot larger than her father's latest girlfriend. 'I was a teenager and there were pictures of my stomach and thighs everywhere. I lost some weight and I lost it quickly, but instead of stopping I carried on, and then maybe I did get some attention from my mother...'

Freya thought back. 'Not for long, though. And so I'd go to clubs and drink and get into trouble and then sit at home and watch an interview my mother might be having about how hard it was to have a troubled teenager. And then I had my father, when I collapsed, on the one hand asking the press to respect the family's privacy while on the other getting off with some nineteen-year-old, knowing the press would erupt.' She still could not stand the memories. 'Everyone knew my business, or thought they did,' Freya said, 'but I had a bigger secret and I was on a mission by then—to get below a hundred pounds.'

'You met that goal?'

'I knocked that goal into the ground and kept going,' Freya sighed. 'James was beside himself. I think he was the only one in my family with any sense at that time.'

'You're usually close to your brother?'

'When we're not arguing.' Freya smiled.

They lay there for ages and then looked at the map. 'I'm going to take the long way back,' Zack said. 'And go fast.'

'I'll take the short way and go slowly.'

They met back at their cars, all dirty and smelly and worn out from the bliss of a day away from it all.

'Do you want to go and grab dinner?' Zack offered.

'No, I want to go home and shower and get changed,' Freya said. 'And then eat.' She deliberately didn't invite him this time but the very last place Freya wanted to be was back at the hotel.

She was tired of putting on the same clothes in the morning, tired of her hair smelling of the lemon ginger hotel shampoo.

It smelt fantastic on Zack, she just didn't want it on her.

Freya liked her own things and if he didn't want a part of them that was up to Zack.

'Sounds good,' Zack said. 'I'll see you there.'

And Freya did her very best as she got into her car, and drove off, not to look for a deeper meaning.

CHAPTER ELEVEN

FREYA LOST ZACK on the freeway and she stopped off at a store to get something more suitable for a tall, muscled male who had been riding than anything she had in her fridge, so he was already outside her place when she arrived.

Red was leaving the building as she got out of her car. 'Been riding?' he asked with a cheerful smile.

'Yes.' Freya smiled back. 'Red, this is Zack.'

'Hi, Red.'

Zack watched as Freya and Red chatted for a couple of moments. 'We're all getting together next Friday,' Red said. 'Are you in?'

'I'm in.' Freya nodded. 'I'll see you then.'

They walked up the stairs to her apartment and Zack was surprised when Freya opened the door and a small dog wagged her tail from the sofa and Freya went over and made a huge fuss of her.

'You have a dog?'

'I do,' Freya said. 'Her name is Cleo and she's a very old lady.'

It really was a home, Zack thought as he looked around. It was large, open-plan and very tidy, as he might have expected from Freya, but the dog he hadn't expected.

'Who lets her out when you stay with me?'

'Red or another of the neighbours…we all help out. Cleo's too old to go to a boarding kennel now.'

'You all get on?'

'We do,' Freya said. 'We try and get together once a month and have a barbecue or something.'

She had a life, a very, very nice life.

'I'm going first,' Freya said. 'Help yourself to a drink.'

'First?'

'I want a shower.'

And Zack got the hint that she wanted to shower alone and if he wanted a beer he'd better start liking the American stuff.

He sat out on a large balcony that looked towards the hills that they'd ridden in and it was actually nice to sit out on a balcony that didn't have one above and one below.

Freya rinsed off a whole day of riding and used her own shampoo and conditioner and soap.

She stepped out and, even with a steamy mirror, a very self-aware Freya frowned at her reflection.

She had spent way too much time examining her body but it was for different reasons that she examined it now.

Wiping her mirror with her towel, she saw the pink of her breasts and the swell of them.

She might be getting her occasional period, Freya thought, but then glanced at the packet of pills she had been taking since the second night in his hotel room.

And then she put it out of her mind.

It was nice to be able to open a drawer and pull on some yoga pants and a top rather than scrabble on the floor for last night's clothes.

And, she decided as she combed her hair and tied it

back, if she went to the hotel again, next time she was going to bring some things.

He might choose to live out of luggage.

Not she.

'Do you need a hand?' Zack called as she came into the kitchen.

'No, thanks.'

Freya grilled two steaks, one massive, one smaller, and she made a large salad. He watched her measuring everything out when he'd have just thrown it in.

Two spoons of oil, one of vinegar, a quarter of a teaspoon of salt.

And she could feel him watching her from the balcony but she wasn't going to change her routines for him.

She carried them out and he got the massive steak and she and Cleo shared the smaller one.

'I'm going to ache tomorrow,' Freya said. 'It's been ages since I rode. I should try and get around to it more often.'

'And me,' Zack said. 'It's been great. I'm so glad I didn't give it up.'

'Why would you give it up?'

'My brother was killed in a riding accident. You know how they say get back on the horse...'

'Zack!' Freya was appalled. 'This must bring up some—'

'Freya, it does and it doesn't. I love riding; I miss that part of home. I don't spend my life avoiding thinking about my brother. It's there every day, the same way your eating disorder is. Sometimes it's hard, sometimes not so much, but it's a part of your past that has to live with the you of today.'

It was always there, a part of her past that could never be erased.

The fattest pug he had ever seen looked up at him. 'Not a chance,' Zack said, but cut off a piece.

'Don't give it to her,' Freya said. 'She's already had some.'

'How old is she?'

'Thirteen,' Freya said. 'James got her for me when I came out of rehab.'

'Did it help?'

'Very much,' Freya said. 'I didn't have Red and a group of neighbours then and dogs don't forget meal-times…' She looked at Cleo and she could hear her heavy breathing. 'I don't think I'll have her for much longer. Still, the vet says that if she loses some weight it will help with her joints. I can't imagine my life without her.' And then she shook her head. 'Sorry.'

'For what?'

'We've been talking about you losing a brother…'

'Freya,' Zack said. 'Losing Cleo will hurt.'

'Yes,' she said. 'James thinks I should get another puppy before she dies.' She rolled her eyes.

'Are you going to tell me what's going on between you and James?'

'I told you.'

'You two haven't been talking since before this morning.'

She looked at Zack and Freya was confused. She was handing over more and more of her life, yet she wanted to.

Freya trusted him, she knew nothing would go further than them.

'When we were growing up, as dysfunctional as it was, my parents were involved in a lot of overseas charities. They'd take James and me along for photoshoots and things but a lot of good was done. James pours everything into The Hills and it annoyed me that there was no charitable side to it. He avoids that sort of thing.'

'A lot of people do.'

'Not James,' Freya said. 'And last year we had a discussion and he said if I found the right charity and handled all the PR side of it, he'd implement it. Anyway, I didn't have to look far. I already knew about Bright Hope. My good friend Mila runs it.'

'I met her when I saw Paulo,' Zack said. 'Actually, there's another patient she wants me to review. She seems nice. Very dedicated.'

'She's James's ex,' Freya said.

'Oh! I see.'

'Believe me, you don't. She and I have remained friends. I just told James that Mila's the founder of Bright Hope.'

'How could he not have known?'

'Because the reason he avoids anything that combines medicine and aid work is because Mila is so heavily involved in it. She works overseas but she came back and started the foundation...'

'Was it a bad break-up?'

'The worst,' Freya said. 'He jilted her on their wedding day.'

Oh, there were so many reasons Freya didn't trust people.

She loved her brother very much but still had no idea how he could have done that to Mila, or why.

'Families!' Zack said.

'We all have them.' Freya shrugged. 'Even if we choose not to deal with them.'

He heard the slight dig.

'I'm going back in April,' Zack reminded her.

'I know. How's the baby doing?' she asked.

'He collapsed in the ambulance on the way to Brisbane. Cale said that they got to him just in time. But he's doing okay. He'll need more surgery when he's older, but fairly minor.'

'What does your dad say?'

'We haven't spoken about it.'

'You haven't spoken about it?'

'Freya…' He went to get another beer. 'Do you want one?'

'No, I just keep them there for Red if he comes to keep Cleo company.'

'Do you want—?'

'Nothing,' she said. She was actually incredibly tired but curious about Zack. 'Do you help out when you go back?'

'Help out?'

'With your father's practice.'

'I don't stay there long enough for that,' Zack admitted. 'You know how you said you couldn't stand everyone knowing your business—that's what home's like,' he explained. 'Everyone knows everything and it's great for some, but not for me. I swear I could not get out of that place fast enough. I used to come back in my breaks but it just got harder and harder to after Toby died. He'd worked in the family practice so his dying left a big hole, not just for his family.'

'On the community?'

Zack nodded.

'One they think you should fill?'

'They can't get another doctor, it all falls on my dad. As well as the fact I don't want to settle down and give them grandchildren. Toby was married and Alice wanted babies, and by now…'

'So if your brother had lived?'

'He didn't, though,' Zack said. 'But, yes, they seem to think that had he lived...' Zack didn't tell her the rest. 'Anyway, it's not the life for me.'

'What is?'

'What I've got,' Zack said. 'A few weeks here, a few months there.'

'Why can't a few months be *there* to give your father a break?'

Zack didn't answer.

'I still don't get why you'd choose a hotel over an apartment.'

'It suits me.' Zack said.

'Company on tap,' Freya said, and was cross with herself for the jealous note to her voice. She couldn't knock it as that was how they'd met after all.

Zack said nothing and Freya got up and sorted out the plates, which had Cleo wake up, suddenly interested. Freya knew why—he had saved some steak and thought she didn't notice when he sneaked it to Cleo.

'I'm going to take her for her little walk,' Freya said.

'I'll clear up.'

She was suddenly unsettled.

Freya carried Cleo down the stairs and took her for her little nightly outing and was, despite a wonderful day and one of the nicest evenings, very, very close to tears.

He didn't deny that his life was the life for him.

Zack didn't make excuses about his ways with women.

She wished, in some ways, that it had stayed at one night.

One amazing night instead of a very intense glimpse of a future that Freya now wanted but could never have.

She'd been snarky.

It had been but a few weeks and already she was counting down the days left to her, or biting her tongue to stop herself from suggesting he ditch the hotel and stay with her instead.

He'd decline, Freya knew.

And that was just as well because imagine having three months of bliss and...

Two months.

January would be over soon.

'I'm going to be without both of you soon, aren't I?' In the darkness all she could see was Cleo's pink tongue and her fur baby was out of breath from the shortest walk. 'You'd better be here when he goes,' Freya warned Cleo. 'I'm going to need you so much.' And then she picked Cleo up and buried her face in her fur. 'I'm so selfish...' Freya said, but she had to tell her friend. 'Cleo, I think I'm pregnant.'

Cleo just carried on breathing. Just kissed her face and cuddled in till Freya's panic subsided.

'I can't be,' Freya said to Cleo, who really didn't care if she was or not.

She just loved her back.

Freya carried Cleo back up the stairs and put her on the sofa with her toy. The kitchen was tidy and Freya could hear Zack in the shower and it hurt that it felt so nice to turn off the lights and get into bed and know that he'd join her.

Zack wasn't sure that he would.

Here was everything he had always avoided and possibly with good reason because it made him want more.

He should get dressed and go, Zack thought.

Cleo had got off the sofa and was crying at the bedroom door, and Zack grinned when he came out.

'I'm sleeping in her bed.'

'Yes, and she'll hate you for it, even if you did sneak her some steak. Did you have pets?'

'A few,' Zack said, and got into bed and tried not to think of home.

'I'm going to start seeing clients,' Freya said. 'I haven't told James yet, but I'm going to.'

'Good.'

'I was thinking about it while we were riding.'

'I was thinking too,' Zack said.

'About?'

He didn't answer. Zack just lay there thinking about plans that had been made and might be broken. He was tired, not physically, though. For the first time he was tired of hotels and starting over, of borrowing a horse, leasing a car, starting out, over and over again...

He wanted this but did not want it, just as he wanted home but not to be there.

Life was easier with no names.

Except *she* had one and, lying in the dark, he told Freya what he hadn't been able to over dinner.

'I stay away because I'm worried that I might end up telling them that Toby wasn't happy when he died,' Zack said.

He'd told no one.

Ever.

'We'd gone camping for a weekend,' Zack said. 'I was surprised when he suggested it but we just went out into the bush. It was great...'

Actually, no, it hadn't been. It had been revealing.

'He told me how unhappy he was,' Zack said, and Freya looked at him.

'He'd been going out with Alice since they were teenagers and she'd stuck by him while he'd gone off and studied medicine. He said that he'd had enough and wanted to move to the city. So when I am home I get to hear how happy Toby was, what a great son, husband, doctor, and how happy he'd been there and how he'd hate how I've let them down. I dread that one day I'll tell the truth: that he was planning on getting out...'

'He was going to leave his wife?'

Zack nodded.

What a terrible secret to carry, Freya thought, to be the only one to know and be able to say nothing.

'That was why he'd asked me to go camping with him. He wanted my take on things.'

'And that was?'

'I had lots of takes on it,' Zack said, and he told her about that last night. 'Never knowing that the next day he'd be dead.'

'Was he killed outright?'

'No. At first I didn't think it was that serious,' Zack said, but then he shook his head. 'Actually, I think I did know because I activated the locator beacon and you only do that if things are dire. And then it was a matter of waiting.' The longest wait ever. 'I love the outback,' Zack said. 'You have never seen anywhere more beautiful and the remoteness is hard to comprehend, but it's a long wait if someone you love is dying.'

'How long?'

'Four hours,' Zack said. 'Well, three spent dying, one hour with him dead. I told him I'd live for both of us...'

And he had.

Zack crammed everything in.

Then he corrected himself in his head.

He had crammed everything in bar a relationship.

CHAPTER TWELVE

FREYA SLEPT WITH the windows open.

For everything Zack liked about hotels, windows that didn't open were one of the things that he didn't like. It was a cool night and the sound of rain was lulling.

Not for Freya.

She lay listening to the sound of night-time from her bed but with Zack by her side, and all in her world was shaken.

Beautifully so but scarily so.

And how could you let yourself simply enjoy something when you'd been told it couldn't last?

And what if what she had discussed earlier with Cleo turned out to be right?

'What's wrong?' Zack asked, as Freya turned to get comfortable again.

'Nothing,' she said.

'Liar.' He gave her a kiss. 'But that's okay.'

Side on they faced each other and Freya found that she was smiling. 'You smell of my soap.'

'I taste of your soap,' Zack said. 'If you need to check.' His leg hooked her in closer and he made her feel all shivery as his hand played with one tender breast. 'For someone who doesn't like it...'

'I didn't like the idea of it,' Freya said. 'I'd never done it.'

Zack frowned.

'So in my office…'

'It was my first time.'

They'd never spoken about it. Sometimes, for Zack, it almost felt like a dream, only he knew that it hadn't been. It had been the night they'd moved their relationship into work. They'd shifted the lines but in ways he hadn't even known at the time.

That should daunt him. No doubt it would soon—that something that was clearly an issue for her wasn't when she was with him. Zack had thought oral the least intimate of sex, but not now.

He slipped his hand between her legs and got the clamp of her thighs.

'I don't think I'd like it.'

'Do you want to try?'

Freya nodded.

Her mind was going at a hundred miles an hour. She wanted everything while she had him. Always she stopped him, beneath the belly button a no-go zone for that beautiful mouth and she didn't really know why.

'I'm messed up, aren't I?' Freya said.

'I told you the day I met you, that's how I want you.'

It hadn't been what he'd meant then but it made her smile now. He kissed her long and deep until her thighs were loose to his hand. And then he moved down and her breasts were so tender, and Freya was starting to know why.

Zack was oblivious, blissfully so. He just heard her fevered moans as he tasted and sucked and licked till she rolled from her side to her back.

He slid down and paid the same attention to her stomach and then he moved lower and kissed her right up her thighs, nibbling at the top inner part that she had once hated so much.

Zack made her body feel beautiful, every part of it. She had worked on herself for ever and had got to like herself enough, but he made her in love with it.

'I don't like it,' Freya said when his mouth took possession, and he ignored her and probed at the tension, tasting her deep, and then back to her clitoris. Freya closed her thighs on his head and he burrowed in deeper and her hips lifted from the bed. She resisted the pleasure, she stayed tight to his tongue, and then Zack moaned into her.

She felt the vibration, the sensual moan of his want and his turn-on. His focus was intent now and she succumbed. It was the most bliss she had known, to come to the most intimate kiss his mouth could give, to be tasted and adored.

There was no triumphant smile as his mouth lifted, Zack was the one crossing his own lines now. He came up the bed and kissed her mouth as deeply as he had her sex. He had Freya taste herself on his lips, his cheeks, and then he moaned again as he slid in. The same moan he had given earlier, and they stopped holding back because this wasn't just sex.

'I'm going to come,' Zack said, almost with regret, because he was loving her, he knew.

Freya was frantic, coming, while making this strange attempt to climb out of arms that would one day let her go. They were saying each other's names, breathing, kissing, coming and so close, so completely besotted and not fighting it now.

'Zack…' She pressed her lips together because she was going to say the wrong thing and lay there afterwards, with something else building—tears. The utter release to her body, the clearing of her mind and she was as close to crying as she dared to be.

He held her so hard afterwards. 'You can cry,' Zack said.

But she wouldn't.

He'd had everything, all of her, he had taken her right to the edge. She would not give him that.

CHAPTER THIRTEEN

'WHY DON'T YOU ditch the hotel?' Freya said.

She shouldn't have.

It was six a.m. and they lay chatting in the dark, talking about, of all things, his suits.

'How much can you get into a backpack?' Freya had asked. And then she'd found out he bought suits and that, when he moved on, he donated them.

'It's an expensive wardrobe.'

'Yeah, well, it's an up-to-date one.'

And then he'd admitted that living out of a backpack was tiring at times, and had been about to say he was actually looking forward to going home for a few weeks, when someone, namely Freya, who had to fix everything this very minute, suggested he move in.

'Freya,' he half groaned in frustration.

'I'm not asking you to move in as in live together, just...' She could have kicked herself.

Zack just lay there.

'Forget it,' Freya said. 'I was just thinking out loud.'

She simply could not stop thinking.

About them.

'I'm going to take Cleo out.'

Freya stood in her dressing gown and she was too

embarrassed to even admit to Cleo what she'd just said to Zack.

'It's not such a stupid idea,' Freya said hopefully to her friend, but then gave in.

Oh, it was such a stupid idea and, of all things, to say it on the first night that he'd come back to her apartment.

Freya was worried, though.

The clock was ticking on them and not only couldn't she imagine him gone, Freya was rather worried that there might be a more permanent reason for them to keep in touch.

She felt sick.

Not a nervous sick feeling, more there was a taste in her mouth as she came back into the apartment.

Cleo waddled into the bedroom and Zack lay there with his hands behind his head as she jumped up onto the bed.

He *was* leaving LA at the end of his three months.

He looked around the bedroom and he knew that he needed to head back to the hotel.

'Hi.' Freya came in, trying desperately to detract from the prior conversation. 'I just got an email…' Zack blinked, he was just waking up but Freya was in busy mode. 'Do you remember when you were in Canada a few years back and that hockey player went into cardiac arrest…'

Zack nodded. 'Why?'

'Well, I was just trying for a new angle. I get that you don't want to be photographed with kids, but he's here in LA and I thought we could get the two of you together.'

'Freya,' Zack said, sitting up, 'how many ways can I say it? I don't want to be a part of your publicity stunts. I'll do the surgery—'

'It's just such a great opportunity.'

'I don't get involved, Freya, they don't owe me any-thing. I do my best for them in Theatre, without obliga-tion. I don't want to be making small talk with some guy who had the misfortune to go into cardiac arrest in front of ten thousand people and now has to feel he needs to publicly thank me for doing my job.'

Freya gave a tight shrug. 'Just trying to do mine.'

'It's Sunday,' he pointed out. 'And I only get one off a month.'

'Sure.' Freya nodded. 'Do you want some breakfast? I'm just making some.'

'A coffee would be great.'

He lay back on the bed again. She'd be in soon with a needle and thread to try and hem him in.

Cleo waddled up to his chest and stared at him with her big pug eyes and he stroked her head and thought, What the hell am I doing?

He'd told her stuff last night that he could never have envisaged telling another, he had made love, and Zack had not lied with his mouth, he'd adored her.

It was all too close, and that was the very thing he avoided.

He didn't want to be tied down like his brother had been, or chained to a town as his father was. They were getting far too close and another couple of months of this and, Zack wasn't stupid, his leaving was going to hurt her.

And no hurt had ever been intended.

It was time to call it now, Zack knew, before they got in any deeper than they were.

Cleo bared her teeth.

She just stared him down and bared her teeth and it was as if she warned him, in or out?

'Cleo!' Freya threatened from the kitchen when she

heard her growl. She went to make coffee but found she had none. Coffee wasn't something she drank but she generally kept some in case of company.

She added it to the list she kept on her phone and divided the drink she'd blended into two glasses as the toast popped up. For the first time in the kitchen she was distracted. Freya had bigger problems on her mind than food for once, and instead of preparing just one plate she made two plates and smeared on some avocado she'd mashed and added a shake of black pepper.

She would go and get a pregnancy kit today and get this over and done with. Maybe when she'd found out it was a false alarm she could relax. Freya carried the tray into the bedroom. 'I was thinking, maybe today we...' And then she stopped because Zack was sitting on the edge of the bed with his jeans and boots on and he was pulling on his T-shirt.

'I need to get back to the hotel,' Zack said. 'There's some work I need—'

'It's Sunday,' Freya pointed out, just as he had.

'Yep.'

'Have some breakfast.'

'I don't generally eat breakfast, and definitely not green ones.' He was direct, he was honest and, yes, it hurt a lot. 'It's all too much, Freya.'

'Zack—'

'Freya, I made it clear. I don't want a relationship, I don't want someone making plans for my day off, I don't want to have to account—'

'You're annoyed because I suggested you move out of the hotel.'

'A bit,' Zack said. 'Do you know why I like it there, Freya?' He looked at the tray she'd prepared. 'If I ask for coffee, I get coffee. When I put the "Do not disturb" sign on the door, guess what? They don't disturb…'

They weren't talking about coffee or signs on the door, Freya knew.

Zack didn't want more than sex. He'd been upfront from the start and she had been more than willing to go along with it.

It was Freya whose wants had changed.

And he told himself that on the drive back to the hotel.

Last night had been amazing—dinner, conversation and the sex had been amazing.

More than amazing.

He wanted to turn the hired car around and go back there. He wanted to have a decent row with Freya and tell her to get out of fixing and sorting mode and get back to bed.

Zack got back to the hotel, went up in the elevator and then passed the maid with her trolley, doling out the toiletries so that five hundred guests smelt the same.

Then he stepped into the room that had been beautifully serviced and he thought about heading out for the day. Just driving into the hills, or taking a walk along the beach.

He needed a shower, he smelt of sex, or rather he smelt of Freya.

Zack did everything on his to-do list. He showered, changed and then headed for the hills, and that evening, instead of the hotel bar, he took a walk on the beach and told himself that this was the life he had chosen. And he had chosen it carefully. He never wanted to be tied down, or have people reliant on or beholden to him.

Not his patients—he fixed what he could and let them get on with their lives.

Not his family—they all knew how that had worked out.

And certainly he did not need someone who decided what he might want to eat for breakfast!

Damned cheek, Zack decided, and headed back to the hotel.

He went to the bar because it really was *that* easy, only it wasn't so easy tonight because he didn't want company.

Only his own.

Back up to his room he went and the bed had been turned down, the towels and soaps all replaced, and Zack found himself kicking his backpack across the room.

CHAPTER FOURTEEN

IT HURT.

Far, far more than the end of any other relationship ever had.

Even though Zack would insist that it hadn't been a relationship because he didn't do that type of thing.

'Men!' Freya said to Cleo as they stood in the little patch of garden early one morning, more than a week after their row.

She carried her back up the stairs and, instead of driving to work, Freya decided that she would run. She hadn't run all week, she'd been huddled on the sofa at night with Cleo and busy with work by day.

It was time to get back on track with her schedules. She had a change of clothes at work so she pulled on her running gear and put in her earphones and did what she loved to do. She arrived at work all hot and sweaty and stood bent over in the stunning foyer.

'James will have you using the side entrance,' Zack said as he went past, and Freya actually laughed.

She wasn't the prettiest sight for such expensive surroundings but she felt better for a run and glad that she and Zack were almost at the point they could acknowledge each other in passing.

There was a meeting with James this morning and

Zack would be there so Freya wasn't looking forward to it one bit.

She walked into the changing rooms and they were like a luxury spa. There was soft music and fluffy towels and Freya stepped under the delicious jets of water, and then everything shifted.

Her legs started to shake and Freya went dizzy. She didn't even turn off the taps, she just stepped out and grabbed at a towel then sat on the bench with her head down.

'Freya?'

She could hear Stephanie's voice and it seemed to be coming from a long way off, except her face was right next to her ear.

'I'm okay,' Freya said.

'You're ever so white.'

'I just need a moment,' Freya said. 'Could you get me some tea?'

The waiting rooms all had oolong tea, kept warm by a candle, and little glasses and so it was just a couple of moments before Stephanie returned.

By then Freya had put on a robe and was a bit more together. 'Sorry about that,' she said.

'It's fine.' Stephanie smiled. 'I saw that you ran in. Maybe you overdid it.'

'Maybe,' Freya said, and she felt a twist of indignation because she knew the implication behind Stephanie's words. She had, in fact, underdone things this week but it was always there, the feeling that everyone was waiting for her to slide back into ways of old.

Even James, Freya thought.

They made no mention of her past, it was a subject he avoided, but she could always see the concern in his eyes.

She didn't need it.

And it was one of the things she had loved about Zack. He hadn't raised his eyes at her ways, he had let her be, and she missed him so much.

So much.

Over and over she tried to tell herself it had just been a few weeks, that you couldn't fall in love in that time, and certainly it wasn't love if it was unrequited.

'I'm fine now,' Freya said, and put down the little cup but she knew she was going to throw up. 'Honestly.'

Please, go now, she thought.

Freya walked to the toilet and closed the door and she wished Stephanie would leave as she threw up the tea as quietly as she could.

No, Freya thought, she hadn't overdone her run—the nausea and dizzy spells were for different reasons altogether.

How the hell could she ever tell Zack that she was pregnant?

Freya put on her grey dress with capped sleeves and did her hair and make-up and then she had another glass of tea and that one was nice.

Feeling a whole lot better, she arrived at the meeting room.

'Where's Zack?'

'He's talking to your good friend Mila about another patient.'

Freya ignored the dig and James got down to business and said he would, as of today, be starting to put out the feelers for a new cardiac surgeon to replace Zack. 'Already?'

'Well, if they have to give notice. I just asked Zack if he'd go on a month-to-month contract but he said no, he's out of here at the end of March.

'And it's February today.' James said.

So it was.

'Morning.' Zack came into the meeting room with no apologies for being late and she and James shared a small smile.

He was such an arrogant bastard.

Even down to the fact they were having this meeting in a meeting room when usually they'd be in James's office for such things.

Zack played second fiddle to no one.

'I can't stay long,' Zack said. 'I've got a patient that's not doing well on NICU.'

'I heard,' James said. 'Are you going to operate?'

'I don't know. I've just spoken with Mila and we're trying to schedule Bright Hope patients. I want to squeeze an ablation onto the end of the Sunday list on the fourteenth.'

'That's Valentine's Day.' James raised an eyebrow. 'Won't you want to be finishing up early?'

'Same as any other day to me,' Zack responded. 'I'm an incurable unromantic.'

James took a call and it would seem that it was a personal one because he excused himself and took it outside the office, leaving Freya bristling beside Zack.

'Can you not do that?'

'What?'

'Consistently point out...' She was so incensed. 'I get you don't do romance but your little digs are unnecessary.'

'I wasn't digging, Freya.' Zack gave a bored eye-roll at her drama. 'I've used the same line for ten years. I'm not changing *anything* for your benefit.'

That was a dig at the breakfast she'd made him.

Oh, yes, it was because there was a small smirk on his lips as she opened her mouth to argue.

Then she closed it and then, to hell with it, she said it. 'I'd run out of coffee.'

'What on earth are you talking about?' Zack asked.

He knew full well!

'You overthink everything,' he said.

'No, I don't.'

They were sulking and turned on and now staring ahead as they sniped, and both wanted to be down on the floor.

He had told James with absolute certainty that he would not be staying on after March, but the certainty had been in his voice only.

'Freya.' James came back into the meeting room and his voice had them both turn around. 'That was Red.'

'Red?' Freya frowned. 'Why would he call you?'

'Because he can't get through on your phone.'

Red had James's number in case Freya was away and there was an emergency.

'He thinks you ought to go home. Cleo's not well,' James told her. 'I'll drive you.'

'I don't need you to drive me,' Freya snapped, and got up. 'I can drive myself.'

But she'd run to work this morning.

'What's going on?' Zack asked James when Freya had left, as if he didn't know, as if just last week a fat pug hadn't been asleep on his feet and then stood on his chest, baring her teeth at him.

'Her dog's not well,' James said. 'She's a vicious little thing.'

Freya or Cleo? Zack nearly said, but stopped himself. It was getting harder and harder to separate things, and he was glad when James gave up on the meeting.

'Can we do this tomorrow?' James asked.

'I'm in Theatre all day tomorrow.'

'Well, I've got a list this evening.' James was distracted and so too was Zack. 'We'll work out a time later.'

'Will she be okay?' Zack asked.

'Cleo?' James said, and Zack frowned as if he had no idea who James was talking about. 'Oh, you mean Freya. I think so, though you never really know with Freya. She always says that she's fine.'

Zack found her coming out of the changing room, where Freya had left her phone.

'You haven't got your car,' Zack said. 'Do you want me to drive you?'

'No, thank you,' Freya said. 'You're busy today. I'll get Stephanie to call for a car.'

Stephanie did so. 'Are you still not feeling well?' she enquired, and Freya wished she was more like Zack and simply didn't answer questions that she didn't want to.

'I'm much better. Thanks for all your help this morning,' Freya said. 'I just got a call and my dog's sick.'

'Cleo?'

'Yes.'

Freya knew that Red wouldn't call without good reason and she was right.

The vet was there and Cleo lay on the sofa and her little tail thumped when she saw Freya.

'She got all breathless,' Red said, and then the vet told her things weren't going to get better.

'She's comfortable. We can take her back to the clinic and put her on some diuretics...'

'No.' Freya shook her head. 'She hates being away from here.' It was why she didn't put her in boarding kennels and why she'd be grateful forever to Red because in the last year of an old dog's life she'd stayed home every night.

It was time, but not for Freya.

'Can I have a day with her?' Freya asked. 'Can you do it here?'

'I'll come by with Kathy at the end of surgery,' he said, and Freya nodded. Kathy was her favourite nurse at the vet's.

She thanked the vet and she thanked Red and saw them all out, and then she sat on the sofa with her best friend who'd seen her so far on her journey.

'I'm not getting another puppy,' Freya told her. 'I could never love it as much as you.' She buried her face in Cleo's black fur. 'And I don't think it would be very fair on the baby.' She looked into loving black eyes. 'Shall we find out?'

Poor Cleo had been listening to her rabbit on about it for days now and it didn't seem very fair that she died not knowing for sure.

And so she peed on the stick and came out a few moments later.

'I am,' she said to Cleo, and she accepted her lick and gave Cleo a kiss as the news sank in.

She was pregnant by a man who had hauled on his boots at the first sniff of commitment.

A man she was seriously head over heels about.

But more than that.

She was pregnant.

But more than that...

Freya wanted to be.

Zack knew that James had an evening theatre list and he actually drove past Freya's and wondered if he should go up.

It was odd, but when James had said that Cleo was vicious, Zack had wanted to laugh. That morning, back in her bed, he'd thought Cleo had been warning him to be nice to her mistress. Instead, it had just been a demented dog.

It was her demented dog, though, who had been with her through all the hard times. He saw Freya come down the stairs, carrying Cleo and chatting to her as she did her business and then back up the stairs they went.

And a little while later he saw a couple come down carrying a bundle in a blanket and he knew it was the vet and assistant and that Cleo had just been euthanised.

Zack, who never got close to anyone, was tearing up over a dog, or was it over Freya and how devastated she must feel right now?

This would not end up in bed, Zack told himself as he got out of the car. He was knocking on a door as a friend.

Or maybe it would end in bed, he amended, but only if she so chose.

Yet the woman who answered it didn't just surprise him—Freya shocked him.

'Yes?'

She was pale and rather angry looking but what floored Zack was that she was absolutely dry-eyed.

'I heard that your dog wasn't well…'

'And?'

'Freya?'

'What do you want, Zack?' Freya asked. 'Do you think sex is going to help?' She looked at him. 'You do, don't you?'

'I get what works for me might not for you. I'm just checking if you're okay.'

'Well, as you can see, I am.'

She slammed the door on him.

Screw you, Freya thought.

Oh, she wanted him but, more than that, she wanted Cleo tonight.

Her phone buzzed and it was a text from Mila.

James told me about Cleo.

Then it buzzed again and it was James.

Do you want me to stop by?

No, thanks, I'm fine.

How many ways could she say it?

Red came and drank all her beer and he cried and then he did all the stuff with the bowls and leads and things for her.

And finally a teary Red headed off and it left Freya alone in her apartment minus Cleo, and that had never happened before.

She'd done everything right by her, Freya told herself. Cleo had had the best possible last day.

There was only one thing about this day Freya regretted.

That Zack wasn't there.

Not for the sex, or the possible progression of them, and not because she had found out she was pregnant...

It would have helped to have him here tonight.

Just that.

CHAPTER FIFTEEN

IT WAS THE oddest week.

No Cleo to chat to.

All her routines felt shot and she didn't know how to tell Zack the news.

Beth had returned from her honeymoon and they had a girls' night in to go through the photos and videos.

The tamest girls' night in—they were all pregnant now, not that Freya let on.

She was detoxing too, she told them!

'The photos are amazing,' Beth said. 'Except these ones.'

There was Zack striding down the stairs and people turning and frowning in annoyance as he messed up the shot.

And Freya found herself laughing quietly and said that she wanted a copy.

'I can have the crowd edited out,' Beth offered.

The crowd being her friends!

'No, no,' Freya said. 'I like it.'

So much so that when they were all talking husbands she snapped a photo of it onto her phone.

After that it was a weekend for thinking. Freya knew that she had to tell Zack and she went by his office on the Monday morning but got cold feet.

'What I can do for you, Freya?' Zack said.

There were so many possible answers to that question that they even shared a smile, and Freya made up something about the Canadian hockey player. It served its purpose and diverted them back to work, and Zack got cross but it was clear the lust remained.

Freya was now swiping oolong tea every time she went past one of the waiting rooms just to keep hydrated as she was throwing up so often.

'How are you?' James stopped by her office.

Lately he seemed to be doing that a lot.

'I'm fine.'

'That doesn't mean anything with you,' James said, and finally he told her what was on his mind. 'You've lost weight.'

'James...' Freya took a breath. 'Every time I drop a couple of pounds it doesn't have to mean that I'm back to sticking my fingers down my throat.'

'I didn't say that. I asked if you were okay.'

'Well, I am.'

'Good.'

'And while we're discussing the great white elephant of my eating disorder,' Freya said, 'I'm going to start taking clients. I'm having some cards made up. If you want me to see them elsewhere...'

'Are you sure you're not taking on too much?'

'Do I ever ask you that?'

'Actually, yes,' James said. 'I've got to go. I've got interviews but I'll let the others know that you're taking on clients and if they have anyone who might benefit from a referral.' He gave a roll of his eyes. 'That's half my patient list, actually. I don't think you'll ever need to advertise.' He turned at the sound of Zack's footsteps coming down the corridor. 'I'm just about to start interviewing for your replacement.'

'Not now,' Zack clipped. 'I've got a patient to see.'

He was dreading it.

It was the last-chance saloon for this little mite and his parents knew it.

All night he had been up late, speaking with colleagues, going over and over the ultrasounds with the best brains he knew, and the response had been the same. Zack would take on more than most, which was why his stats came in low, but in this...

Zack sat with the twenty-year-old mother and the twenty-two-year-old father and he told them as best as he could that their son would die.

'Please,' Rachael begged. 'Can you at least try...?'

And he went through it all over again, how the damage was too much and that his system was collapsing.

'He'd very likely die on the operating table, or shortly post-operatively,' Zack said. 'Or he can die in your arms.'

Zack could have gone then but he stayed and spoke with them extensively and made sure they understood he wasn't simply giving up on their son.

Sometimes you didn't get a choice.

Like ten years to this day when his brother had died.

It was not a good day at the office!

Freya tried not to notice Stephanie's raised eyebrows as she came out of one of the patients' very luxurious restrooms. She hadn't been able to make it to the staff one.

Oh, no. If Stephanie mentioned to James that she'd seen Freya dash off to vomit, he'd have her back in rehab by the end of the week.

And there was Zack, handing over his pagers.

'I'm not on call tonight,' Zack said to Stephanie.

'I'll call if there's anything urgent with one of your patients—'

'I said that I'm not on call tonight.' Zack made things clear to Stephanie. 'I'm going to get blind.'

'Oh.'

He was as grey as she'd seen him and they didn't bother with small talk as they walked out to their cars.

'Freya…' he called her over as she climbed into her car.

'Yes?'

She turned and looked up at him and Zack stared back and he honestly didn't know what to say, he hadn't even meant to call out to her.

He needed her tonight.

Sex, yes, but he wanted all the rest tonight too. Hell, he'd even take the green smoothie.

Just because he didn't want to move in it didn't mean he had wanted it to end, and he was kicking himself for doing what he did best—put on his boots and get out.

'How have you been since Cleo?'

He didn't get to know that, Freya decided. 'It happens.' She went to walk off and then remembered what she'd heard. 'I heard that you lost a patient today. I'm sorry.'

'It happens,' Zack said, but it nearly killed him when it did, especially one so tiny.

Especially today.

And she looked at his eyes and he said not a word of that but she knew him, and she could feel the want between them.

And that was why she cried each night. She was crazy about this guy.

'You've lost weight,' Zack said.

'Oh, here we go. Have you been talking to James?'

'No,' Zack said. 'Is he worried?'

'James is always worried.'

'Does he have reason to be?'

'No.'

'Freya, I know I didn't end things very well.'

'There was nothing to end, Zack. It was sex, we both agreed to that and no more, and as good as it was…'

Their eyes met at the memory and Zack looked very deep into her eyes. She could not believe his gall.

Yes, his eyes were asking her for that.

'You are kidding me,' Freya said. Did he really think they were going to have sex?

She wanted to so much.

To just ignore that she was completely incapable of *not* wanting a relationship with this man and to take the good they had.

It would be too much for her heart to bear, though. She had to tell him about the baby, but she could see his anguish today so Freya chose not to now. She abruptly pulled back from telling him and got angry instead.

"You know what, Zack? We should have kept it at one night. Life was so much easier when I didn't know your name.'

Freya climbed into her car and reversed out angrily.

She wanted him—oh, my, she wanted him.

But even if they had kept it at one night, she'd still be in trouble.

Freya drove towards home and hoped she wasn't too late to let Cleo out and then she remembered that Cleo wasn't there any more.

And so instead of knowing that patient black eyes awaited her, Freya had the joy of chatting with herself on the drive home.

She had to tell Zack.

Or not.

He'd be gone in a few weeks.

And she'd been considering donor eggs and donor sperm after all.

But the donors *chose* anonymity and it would be her baby's right to know, and Zack had the right to know too.

He'd find out anyway soon.

Stephanie was gossiping, Freya knew, and she trusted Zack wouldn't just assume her eating disorder was back.

They had both messed up that first night but it wasn't a disaster. Freya had it all under control.

She was thirty-one, she'd planned to be a single mom.

Zack deserved to know and he also deserved to know that she neither needed nor expected nothing from him.

Freya took the exit and then joined the traffic heading into the city.

She left her car with the valet and walked into the hotel and went straight to the elevators. Down a familiar corridor she walked, but with a different type of anticipation knotting her stomach now as she tried to guess his reaction.

There was a 'Do not disturb' sign on the door and Freya ignored it and knocked.

'Read the sign,' came his deep, surly voice in response to her knock on the door.

'Zack, it's…' Freya started, and then she had the appalling thought that he might be in there with someone he might have met in the elevator or bar and was banging his brains out, as was clearly his chosen stress response. But then the door opened and he had on only a towel, and then she glanced over his wet, naked shoulder and saw that, no, there was no one else in his suite.

'I'm just in the middle of a phone call,' Zack said.

'Do you want me to wait outside?' Freya offered.

'No, no,' he said, and as she walked into his suite he

caught her off guard and pulled her in. 'Thank God,' Zack breathed into her ear, and then his mouth was on hers in a hungry kiss and she got a slab of wet muscle pressed into her. It took Freya a second to register that he had assumed she was taking him up on his earlier offer.

'Zack…'

'I won't be long,' Zack mouthed, and put his finger to his lips and then walked over to the bed and picked up the phone he had left there. 'Sorry, Mum, it was just the maid.'

He gave her a wink and took her right back to their first conversation and straight back to when all they had been was sex. Freya stood there, her dress damp from his freshly showered body, and she tasted him as she licked her lips. She was unsure what to do as Zack carried on the conversation and she could actually see the tension in his back as he tried to keep his patience as he spoke with his mum.

'Alice has a right to have a life…it's been ten years,' Zack said. 'She's allowed to go out on his anniversary. We don't have to sit behind the curtains to grieve.'

Oh, God, it was the anniversary of his brother's death, Freya realised as he spoke on.

On top of it all he was dealing with that today.

He went over and got out another glass and went to pour her some wine from an open bottle.

Freya shook her head and he held up some water and she nodded.

'Why don't we at least try it tomorrow?' Zack said. 'It's all set up and we can speak face to face wherever I am in the world.'

He gave Freya a smile that said, thank God he wasn't video chatting with his parents today, because the towel was lifting and Freya, who hadn't properly smiled in a long time, found that she was.

He put ice and lemon in her water and then, while dealing with this very difficult conversation, he came over and placed it down on the desk. And there was one little problem, Freya realised.

Well, there were many, many problems, but he thought she was there for sex and the sight of him naked and a taste of his tongue, and, as his hand slid around her waist, she was turned on.

Okay, sex tonight, and she'd tell him tomorrow, Freya thought, and she stood.

Or, should she just write 'I'M PREGNANT' on the little hotel pad now and pass him a note?

Zack was just finishing up the conversation as his fingers worked her breasts. Her thick nipples told him she was just on the edge of getting her period and he loved the intensity of a woman's orgasm then.

He turned off the phone and was just so relieved that call was over and especially that she was here and his response told her so.

This kiss was as fierce as their first. It was actually more so because it toppled her back onto the bed.

'Freya.' He said it like a moan. He was kissing her face, her mouth, her ears and just pressing her into the bed. Her legs were over the edge and he was roughly parting them and just tearing at her knickers but Freya was hungrily kissing him back.

She was holding his face just to keep it still enough for her mouth and then she gave in and held onto his shoulders as Zack seared inside.

His feet were on the floor and his elbows were each side of her head.

He thrust in hard and the friction they generated meant

neither would last. Her legs wrapped around him as all the hurts of past weeks were gathered into an intense peak.

Freya came, a beat before he did, and it was a come so deep that it demanded him now and Zack spilled into her.

'God, but I needed you tonight.' He really did, so much so that he had been planning to head to Freya's because living like this wasn't working. 'What made you change your mind and come over?'

He saw her rapid blink.

'Freya?'

'I came here to talk to you…'

'What?'

He replayed the events and Zack pulled out and got up and whipped a towel around his hips and looked at her as she pulled down her dress.

'I didn't force you?'

'Zack,' Freya said, 'I might not have come with the intention of sex but I was a very willing participant.'

'But you came here to talk?'

'Yes.'

He was still going over it in his head. 'For a moment there I thought…'

'Thought what?'

'It doesn't matter,' Zack said. 'What did you want to talk about?'

'I'm pregnant.' It came out faster than she'd intended. It just came out.

He hadn't had even a hint that she was and there was no lead in, no warning, she just hit him right with it.

'You choose your moments, don't you?' Zack said.

'I thought I'd tell you when you weren't working…'

'I lost a six-week-old today, I've got my parents on the phone, crying about St Toby and all the grandchildren they haven't got. Should I ring them back and tell them I'm going to be a father?' He went on, 'But do you know what, Freya? I wouldn't do that to them on a day like today!'

'I didn't know it was the anniversary of your brother,' Freya said. 'We don't know enough about each other to do specific dates.'

'I lost a six-week-old today!' Zack said. 'How's that for a specific day because his parents will remember it for ever!'

'Zack?'

'You know for a moment there, I thought...'

'What?'

He shook his head. He had honestly, for a moment there, thought that Freya had got him.

That the woman he had first met had come to his room and that they were back to the beginning but with history and understanding now.

That maybe, just maybe he'd met someone who things might work out with, but he had only just been starting to think like that and now Freya had her voice on.

'Now, I know it's a lot to take in, Zack, but—'

'Don't do your psychologist voice with me,' he warned. 'Don't tell me it's a major life-changing event, but that soon I'll—'

'It doesn't have to mean a major life change.'

He looked at her.

'Er...do I have a say here?' Zack checked, but there was still a warning note to his voice. Was she popping by to tell him she was on her way to get a termination?

'That's why I'm here, Zack.'

'Stop calling me Zack in that voice,' he hissed. Freya was using her patient and reasonable and very together voice and it was driving him insane.

'I'm not having a termination.'

Zack looked at her as she told him how things would be, as Freya, because it was Freya, dealt with all the current things on her to-do list.

'I was already looking into fertility treatments and donors—'

'Oh, so I've done my job, then.'

'You're being petulant.'

'I feel petulant,' Zack said.

'I'm just saying that I've thought this through and there's no need for you to get worked up. I can more than cope with single motherhood.'

'That's good to know,' Zack said, but with an edge. 'And do I get to see my child in this plan you've made?'

'If you choose to, then I'm sure we can sort that out.'

'You've really thought this through.'

'I have,' Freya said. 'So when I have your thoughts we can make plans or not.'

'Are you worried, upset?' Zack checked. 'You were just getting back into psychology.'

'I don't see that one has to exclude the other.'

'Are you—?'

'Zack, I'm thirty-one,' Freya interrupted his questions. 'I was already planning on single parenthood. I'm not going to fall in a heap.'

'You don't like it when the tables are turned, do you?' Zack said. 'You want my thoughts, yet you refuse to give yours.'

'Ask away,' Freya said.

'Okay, what about us?'

'You've made it clear that it's just sex you want from me.' Freya put her nose in the air as if she disapproved.

'You don't want sex?' Zack asked, and she didn't answer. 'Well,' he said.

Freya pressed her lips together. She didn't know this mood. He was arrogant and angry yet there was this twist of a smile on his face that she didn't get.

Zack carried on. 'With all this sexual attraction do Mommy and Daddy do it when you drop the baby off?'

'I don't know where this is leading, Zack.'

Oh, my God, Zack thought, she'd just used that voice again.

'Well, you've been so busy sorting it out I just wondered if that was covered already. Curious…' Freya could see that black smile was there and it wasn't the news he seemed annoyed with but her.

Freya.

The woman, Freya knew, that he didn't want to have a relationship with.

'What about the two of us?'

'No,' Freya said. 'I lived through my parents' unhappy marriage. I'm not inflicting it on my child.'

'You jump straight to marriage.' His grin was incredulous now!

'I'm saying that I don't want a marriage, I want to do this on my own. Of course you'll be entitled to access.'

'Do you know what I like about you, Freya?' Zack said. 'You've got it all worked out.'

Freya looked at him.

'Do you know what I don't like about you, Freya? That you've got it all worked out without me.'

'I don't understand.'

'That's okay.' Zack shrugged. 'I'm not in the mood for explaining. Well, thank you for dropping by.'

He stood and went to the door.

'Are you asking me to leave?'

'Yes.' Zack said. 'Pay attention to the sign next time. If it says don't disturb, don't disturb.'

'But we need to talk.'

'We already have.'

'I need your thoughts.'

'Well, you can't have them yet.'

He didn't have a clue what they were.

CHAPTER SIXTEEN

HIS HANGOVER WAS impressive and instead of going to The Hills, where no doubt Freya would be tapping her feet, waiting for him to snap to her snappy tune, he took the morning off and in the afternoon he drove into South LA and to the Bright Hope Clinic.

'Mila's not here today,' Geoff said.

'I know. I'm just dropping by to see how things are going.'

'Well, we're taking delivery of an MRI machine tomorrow,' Geoff told him, 'and I've just ordered a state-of-the-art ultrasound that might mean we can have intelligent conversations...'

It had been frustrating. Knowing that The Hill's equipment would give clearer answers, there had been a lot of doubling up. Zack wanted state of the art, so nearly every test Geoff had done had been repeated.

'It's great news about Paulo.'

'I think he'll be going home soon,' Zack said.

They went through the patients and Geoff said he'd like to come and watch the scheduled ablation.

'On a Sunday?' Zack checked. 'And it's Valentine's Day.'

'My wife is very understanding.'

Zack saw a few patients and then drove back to the

hotel and lay on the bed with his hands behind his head and tried to make some sense of his thoughts.

He took out his laptop and typed in a few things, and found out that their baby, assuming it had been conceived on the first night, was due on September twenty-fourth.

He stared at that date for ages and then he texted Freya.

Are you okay?

She took less than a minute to respond.

I've told you I'm fine with it.

He fired back another text.

Such a well thought-out response!

Then he deleted it, unsent, and wrote another.

Let me know if you need anything.

She wouldn't.

That much Zack knew.

He still couldn't get over how she'd been the night Cleo had died. Even he had teared up but not Freya. It was like she kept all her emotions inside and yet he had glimpsed them.

The things she'd told him, Zack knew, only he knew.

And it worked both ways. Freya knew stuff he would never discuss with anyone else.

She had pushed too hard and too soon, though, Zack thought, but then he smiled as he did so because that was Freya.

They were so good together and she had wanted more,

and he could see now that she'd probably known she was pregnant and starting to stress.

His head was a mess and there was no one he could talk to, or was it that there was no one he would talk to?

His alarm went off and Zack remembered that his mother had reluctantly agreed to try video-chatting.

Zack sat up and picked up the laptop.

This should be fun!

Not.

After a few goes, there was his mum and she had make-up on, when she only wore it at Christmas or on birthdays.

'How are you?' Zack smiled when he saw her.

'Sorry about yesterday.'

It had been a very tense phone call, which was why Zack could not have been more relieved when Freya had arrived.

'It's fine,' Zack said. 'Yesterday was a tough one.'

'You're right,' Judy said. 'Alice deserves to be happy.'

'So do you guys,' Zack said. 'Where's Dad?'

'He's in with a patient. Max is here for a check-up.'

'How is he doing?'

'Very well,' Judy said. 'I was thinking when you come home in April...'

And that was the trouble with communicating like this. Judy saw Zack close his eyes.

'You've changed your mind?'

'No,' Zack said, but how did he tell his mother that things here in LA had suddenly got very complicated? They didn't speak about such things.

Could they?

'I've got some stuff going on at the moment...'

'Another patient who needs you?'

'Isn't Dad the same?' Zack challenged, and Judy smiled.

'I guess.'

'Anyway, it isn't work that's complicated,' Zack said. 'I like someone.'

His mother said nothing.

'A lot.'

'You can tell me, Zack.'

'I'm trying to.'

'Times are changing.' Judy sat very composed and Zack looked at her, and then his face went right up to the screen.

'Do you think I'm gay?'

He could not believe it.

'You've never had a lady friend,' Judy said. 'Tara had a thing for you and you never did anything about it…'

He'd been trying to keep Tara's dad from knowing! 'Mum, just because I don't discuss my sex life with you it doesn't mean that I don't have one.'

'I'm talking about relationships. You've never spoken about anyone special and I was worried that you felt you couldn't tell me.'

'There hasn't really been anyone special,' Zack said. 'Till now.'

'And you said that there would never be grandchildren.'

'Because I could never see myself as a parent or tied down.' And he sat there in silence, with his mum doing the same, and it wasn't a strained silence this time. He didn't feel tied down with Freya. That morning when she'd suggested he move in had jolted the hell out of him but he could laugh about that now. That was Freya. It was who she was.

'I need to work a few things out,' he said.

'Well, I think that's a very good reason not to come home,' Judy said. 'Does *she* have a name?'

He was about to say 'Fred' but realised his mum maybe wouldn't get his joke. 'Freya.'

And he named her.

He named the woman who, wherever they were headed, was in his life.

Freya and Zack.

'I might have a glass of sherry tonight,' Judy said, and Zack laughed.

'I am coming home soon,' he told her, and he thought about what Freya had said. 'Maybe for two or three months. I could help out properly and give you and Dad a break.'

'That would be wonderful.' Judy smiled. 'But sort yourself out first and while you're at it, get a haircut.'

And the relationship that had always been difficult was being worked on and it felt good that it was.

'There's your dad. I'll let him say bye to Tara and then go and fetch him.'

'Can I see Max?'

He wanted to see the little guy.

After a little bit of drama getting them all on the sofa and the computer in place, there was Tara and they shared a smile.

'Thank you,' Tara said.

He looked at his ex and the feelings were only of friendship, both knew that, but all these years on and, without talking, this friendship remained a good one.

It wouldn't have.

Both knew that had they stayed together and made promises that the other could not keep, they would have been fighting and, yep, a divorce statistic now. And he thought of Toby and Alice. It had been such a hard secret to carry but Freya knew it now and that helped.

'This is Max,' Tara said. 'The cause of all this drama.'

'He looks fantastic. Cale told me that the surgery went really well.'

'It did,' Tara said. 'But apparently we got there just in time. He collapsed in the air ambulance.'

Jed, Tara's husband, spoke then. 'We're very grateful to the surgeon and to you and Dr Carlton. You made a great team.'

Even if they'd only managed to work as a team that once, it was a great result. Max was healthy and starting to cry and Tara tried to quiet him with her finger as Jed spoke on. 'I was saying to Tara it's hard to imagine now but in a few years he'll be bringing in the cows...'

And Zack looked at a very little infant that would probably be as strapping as his father one day and there were all the assumptions there, but then Tara spoke.

'Max gets a chance to be anything he wants to be now.'

It was a little message between her and Zack.

'He does,' Zack agreed.

'Thanks, Zack.' Tara smiled. 'You'll be sure to stop by when you're home?'

'I shall.'

They stood and walked off and left Zack with his dad. No doubt his mum was leading them through to the kitchen where she would have some cake ready. It was never just a visit for some patients.

Zack could remember most days getting in from school and the lounge would be full with patients, or families of patients.

'I've been tough on you, Zack,' his father said.

'And I get why you have been,' Zack said. 'I hate that

it all falls down to you. And I do worry about you retiring and what's going to happen but—'

'You've got your life.' His father said it without malice now.

'I'm good at what I do,' Zack said. 'I need to stick with it. In the same way you stuck with general practice when it was tempting to go to the city.'

He was about to tell his dad his plans to come back, maybe at Christmas so that he and his mother could have a break, maybe take a holiday, but then Zack smiled to himself. If things worked out, and he hoped that they would, there was no way his parents would be heading off on a holiday the next time their son came home.

Whatever happened between him and Freya there would, God willing, be a grandchild for them to get to know.

Now he just had to sort things out with the person who thought she had it all sorted out—Miss Freya.

CHAPTER SEVENTEEN

HE WAS OVER at Bright Hope the next day and made no effort to contact her. His lack of response to the issue drove Freya insane.

And then, when he finally did rock up at The Hills, at ten the next day, he gave absolutely no indication as to his thoughts or feelings.

He kept her on the boil all week and she made an excuse to have to be there on Saturday afternoon, just because she knew he was passing through.

Zack had brought cake.

A great big white chocolate cake piled with fresh raspberries and the staff all oohed and ahhed and Freya sat there in the staffroom, trying to fathom its meaning.

For a clue.

And she was still searching for the secret sign when he came down and sat opposite her, having cut a large slice. He crossed his long legs and gave her a smile.

'How are you, Freya?'

'I'm very well, thank you.'

'I don't usually see you here at the weekends.'

'I've got a consulting room for my future clients that I'm setting up,' Freya said, which was true, but she was hardly grappling with an Allen key. This was The Hills after all. Her consulting room was gorgeous. It was attached to her office and Freya had chosen the artwork and rugs to ensure that it was an oasis of calm.

'Did James mention that I might have a client for you?' Zack checked, and Freya shook her head.

'I haven't seen James today.'

'Her name's Emily, she's nineteen years old. I'm seeing her sister. Her mother mentioned some of the issues that she was having with her daughter. I gave her your card to give to Emily if the time was right.'

'Thank you.'

Stephanie stood up. 'Thanks for the cake, Zack, it was a lovely gesture.'

'No problem.'

She walked off and Freya sat there facing him.

'Cake?' Freya asked.

'Do you want some?' Zack pretended that he didn't know what she meant.

'No!' She wanted to know what the hell he was thinking. The only change in him she could see was that he'd brought in a cake and was sitting there with almost a smile on his face.

'Why cake?'

'Because I was pretty off the other day, with Stephanie and a couple of others, when the baby died, and I thought I'd apologise to the staff.' He stood. 'It's not all about you, Freya.'

'We need to talk.'

'When I'm ready,' Zack said. 'Anyway, what's the rush? You've already got it all worked out.'

She closed her eyes in frustration.

'And we've got months to sort things out,' Zack reminded her, and Freya shushed him.

'I want this sorted. I want to know what your plans are.'

'When I've decided I'll be sure to let you know.'

'You're the most annoying—'

'Why?' Zack said. 'I only jump into bed, Freya, not to your tune, and *my* thoughts are measured.'

'Meaning?'

'Just that,' Zack said. 'No deeper meaning. Do you want to go out for dinner tonight?'

She stared at him and she hated that, yes, she tried to search for a deeper meaning to his offer.

'Yes.'

'I'll pick you up at six.'

'Six?' Freya said. 'Are we going to check out the children's menu for future reference?'

He resisted laughing. 'I'm operating early tomorrow, I need to be in bed at a reasonable hour.'

And he still had that smile and she was still, still searching for deeper meaning in every word he said.

He set her on fire.

Just that.

She was squirming on the inside and wondering if it was dinner and bed together, or bed alone, if it was talking or what the hell went on in that beautiful head.

He gave her no clue.

Zack cut himself another slice of cake and walked out.

CHAPTER EIGHTEEN

'HI...'

Freya had just put the final touches to the consulting room and was about to dash home for a quick shower and change before her very early dinner with Zack when the phone in her office rang.

She was about to let it go to the machine but at the last minute changed her mind and was very glad she had when she heard the nervous young voice.

'My name's Emily...' the young woman said, and then she started to cry. 'I've just done it again.'

'It's okay,' Freya said. Whatever Emily had done, it wasn't the point right now, but that she'd called was so, so important that Freya wasn't going to waste time questioning her for details. 'It's okay,' Freya said, and gradually the sobbing stopped.

Freya just listened as Emily told her that she'd had a massive binge and purge and her mother, who was already worried sick about her sister, had found her and was now upstairs, crying.

'She doesn't need this,' Emily sobbed.

And Freya thought of James, who had tried so hard to be a parent for her, and the anguish she had caused him, and how relieved he'd been when she had accepted help.

'Are you going to tell her that you've called me?'

'Yes.'

'Well, I think she'll be very relieved to know that you're talking to someone about it. So that might be something you can tell her when we've finished chatting.' They spoke for a few moments until Emily had calmed down. 'Why don't you go to bed now?' Freya said, knowing how drained Emily would be. 'Tell your mom that you're coming in to see me tomorrow at nine. Would that be okay?'

'It's a Sunday.'

'That's okay,' Freya said.

They spoke a little more, but Emily really was exhausted and Freya was glad that her plan for her to tell her mom and meet tomorrow seemed to have given her some measure of relief.

'I'll see you in the morning, Emily,' Freya said, and then the oddest smile came to her lips as she realised Zack was right and she had her *voice,* as he called it, on. 'I'm looking forward to meeting you,' Freya said, more normally. 'Go and speak to your mom and then get some rest.'

Of course Freya did some major overthinking on the drive to her apartment, wondering if she should have seen Emily straight away, but there was no real point speaking at length with Emily tonight.

And she wasn't going to be available every time her clients had a binge.

Emily needed to rest and recover and get some fluid into her...

Tomorrow.

They would start this journey tomorrow. She just hoped that Emily didn't cancel, because that first reaching out was the hardest, Freya knew.

She had fifteen minutes to get ready when she had

hoped to have thirty and Freya quickly peeled off her clothes as she turned on the shower, and then everything stopped.

There was a flash of blood in her knickers and when she saw it, Freya was convinced she was losing her baby.

Everything in her world just stopped and the panic that hit had her frantic. She felt like a cat with its tail on fire and yet she was crouched, kneeling on the bathroom floor, and, she was sure, losing her baby.

'No...'

And it was all her fault, for not eating, for running, for riding and for believing for a second that she could be a mother. She felt as if she was back to being seventeen and being told her bones would one day crumble and she'd never be able to have babies. Freya was sobbing so violently she couldn't breathe.

She could hear someone knocking at the door and then they started to knock louder.

Realising that it must be Zack, Freya pulled a towel from the rail and, barely covered, wrenched open the door. Zack saw her red face and angry eyes and this time there *were* tears streaming down, and because she was scared she hit out with words.

'Panic over!'

She never cried, never, ever, but they were pouring out now. 'I've lost it,' she shouted to him, 'so panic over.'

'Freya...' He was so calm that it angered her further. 'I'm not panicking.'

'Because you don't care!' she screamed. 'You didn't want it anyway.'

'Tell me what's happened.' His voice was normal and it made hers sound all the more mad. 'Are you bleeding?'

She was holding up a towel and Zack looked down at her legs and there was no blood that he could see.

'Yes, I'm bleeding!'

'Come on.' He led her to the bedroom.

'I knew I'd never be able to have children, after all I've done to myself, I don't deserve them, you don't want them…'

And he remembered her 'I shot my ovaries' comment and knew that all the loathing was aimed at herself.

'How much are you bleeding?'

He was still so completely calm, like a doctor, only he wasn't the doctor, he was the father, and she hit out at him but he caught her wrist.

'Freya.'

She'd lost her towel on the way to the bedroom and Zack sat her on the bed. 'How much bleeding is there?'

He looked at her and she seemed fine and he heard the shower and went in and the relief that hit when he saw the tiny amount in her knickers was something he kept to himself.

She was a mess.

He looked out towards the bedroom where Freya was sobbing and curled up in a ball on the bed. Whatever he had intended to say over dinner would just have to wait now. He turned off the taps in the shower and went back into the bedroom.

'Have you got any cramping?'

'No.'

'Everything might well be fine…'

She couldn't believe it.

He tried to unfold her tight body but she wouldn't relax and he got onto the bed beside her and brought her cold body against his warm one. 'Match my breathing,' he said. It was like he was breathing for her, and she tried to get hers as slow and as deep, and then he spoke.

'Freya, a lot of women get bleeding. You're eight weeks pregnant—'

'Six.'

'Eight,' he corrected her, and smiled because sometimes he forgot she had studied brains, not bodies. 'You add two weeks.'

How was he smiling and talking, all calm and normally? It wasn't because he didn't care, she knew that because he was lying on the bed beside her and she was curled into him.

'Did you lose anything in the shower?'

'I didn't get into the shower,' Freya said. 'I just saw the blood and I freaked…'

'I know,' Zack said. 'Well, I don't exactly.'

How was she, Freya wondered, breathing and calming and starting to believe that it might be okay? And then she remembered how she had lashed out before. She had utterly lost it and it was something she had fought all her life not to do.

'Turn over,' Zack said.

'I can't,' Freya admitted. She had screamed, she had hit at him, she had shown her worst self and all her fears, so how could she turn around?

'We can go now and do an ultrasound,' Zack said.

'No.' Freya shook her head. 'I don't want anyone at The Hills knowing.'

'They won't. I can—'

'No.'

'Have you got an OB?'

Freya nodded. 'I'm seeing someone for fertility so I already had an appointment for next week.'

'Do you want to call her and see if I can drive you in?'

'On a Saturday night?'

'Yes,' Zack said, and then he realised she might be stalling. 'Do you want to see someone?'

'I don't want to find out,' Freya said. 'I just want one more night where I might be pregnant. I don't want to know yet if I've lost it. Zack, I've wanted a baby for years, I honestly thought I couldn't have one. I wasn't using you.'

'I know that.' Zack said. 'Who told you that you couldn't have children?'

'In rehab,' Freya said. 'I had stopped menstruating and they said I was a shoe-in for infertility, osteoporosis...'

'Whoever said what they did was trying to scare you into eating.' He could only guess the damage of knowing for years that you'd blown your chances. 'They were clearly talking rubbish.'

She turned around in his arms and he gave her such a nice smile.

'Do you really think that I might still be pregnant?'

'Well, I haven't been anywhere near that field for many years but, yes, a little show, no cramping. I think it happens a lot.'

And from hell she entered calmer waters.

'I'm sorry you saw me like that.'

'I'm very glad that I saw you like that,' Zack said, and Freya closed her eyes.

She knew she'd blown any chance for them now.

They lay for a while, Freya becoming calmer, Zack thinking.

'You've got surgery tomorrow,' Freya said, remembering he'd said he needed an early night.

'I do.' Zack nodded. 'I'll go and make something to eat.'

Zack got out of bed and went into the kitchen. He bypassed all the little measuring cups and returned to the room with two bowls of lovely creamy pasta.

'We'll go and get you checked tomorrow. I'll call work and have them reschedule.'

'No.' Freya shook her head. It was his Sunday list and there were so many people relying on him. 'Unless things get worse, you ought to go in. I've got to go in as well—I've got that young girl coming in. It would be awful for her if I cancelled.'

'Okay.'

His calm control seeped into her.

They ate pasta and she found out he could cook and they lay in bed and watched a movie. Zack noticed something on the bedside table and asked what it was.

'Cleo's ashes.'

'No way!' Zack said, and he wasn't Mr Nice now. He took them straight out to the lounge room. 'I can't sleep with them next to me.'

'Are you staying?'

'Freya?' Zack checked. 'You really think I'd leave you now?'

'You want an early night.'

'And you need one!'

He got into bed.

'You're not keeping the ashes, are you?'

'I don't know.' She looked at him. 'Are they freaking you?'

'A bit.'

'I didn't think anything freaked you.'

'I'm a mystery,' Zack said.

He turned out the light and he was back in her bed when she had never thought he would be.

'I really am a mystery,' Zack said. 'It turns out that my mother thought I was gay.'

Freya laughed and she told him about the hotel events coordinator checking him out when he'd checked in.

It was nice to lie in the dark, talking and then falling quiet.

'So, is this what parenthood looks like?' Zack said when she was feeling a little calmer. 'Knot in your chest and no sex?'

'I think so.'

He rolled over and put his hand on her stomach and then he said the nicest thing.

'I want you to be pregnant,' he said. 'I want the baby.'

And, because it was Zack, she knew he meant it.

'So hang in there, little one.'

CHAPTER NINETEEN

ZACK WOKE TO the mechanical sound of a blender.

Get used to it, Zack, he told himself, because he might well be waking to it for the rest of his life.

And so, as Freya pulped broccoli and blueberries and did what she had to do to keep her place on this planet in order, she watched as a dishevelled, barely dressed, sexy Australian came out of the bedroom and walked out of her apartment.

And there was no feeling of dread when he left this time.

A few moments later he walked back in with a tin of coffee, which kept his part of the planet in better order, and they shared a smile.

'Why do you have coffee in your car?' Freya asked.

'Because I like coffee in the morning and I know you don't have any.'

'Oh, so were you intending on staying last night.'

'Yep,' Zack said. 'Well, I was hoping to.'

And she opened a cupboard and showed him that she had indeed bought some coffee since he'd walked out.

He wrapped his arms around her and Freya let herself be wrapped in them.

'Any bleeding?' he asked.

'None.'

'How do you feel?'

'Better,' Freya said.

She couldn't give a completely honest answer—that the world felt safer just for the fact that he was next to her now. Freya knew she pushed too hard, pressed for too much, and so she held it back.

Last night he had taken such precious care of her and she let herself be grateful for that.

And so, getting into separate cars, they both waved to Red and then headed into work.

Today would be a day that Freya found out how strong she was. Maybe pregnant, maybe not, and with her love life in shreds because Zack was probably thinking what hell was he going to have to co-parent with after her outburst last night.

And yet she could put it aside.

Not too far aside, because her issues came with her, and they were needed today.

For a long time Freya had doubted if she was the right person for this role, whether she had healed herself enough to offer advice to someone going through what once she had.

Now, though, she knew it was a lifelong journey and she had learned so much on this path.

'Thank you for seeing me,' Emily said.

They sat in her new consulting room and Freya told Emily she was her first client and then she told her a bit about herself. Emily said nothing at first, but when Freya mentioned her food diaries Emily got out her phone and Freya looked through it.

It was like looking back on her own life.

The exercise, the obsessions with food, the waiting till someone left the room so you could do a hundred more sit-ups. The agony of a cruel disease. Emily wasn't dangerously thin but, Freya knew, the real battle was in her mind.

They went way over time and Emily laughed at the end when Freya said, 'You're far more honest than I was.'

'There's no point lying any more,' Emily said. 'I just want to get well.'

Emily would do well, Freya was sure.

They made another appointment for Thursday.

'Just to let you know,' Freya said, 'that I might be having a small procedure during the week, so if I have to reschedule, that's why.'

'I'm sorry to have messed up your Sunday.'

'You didn't,' Freya answered. 'It's good to get things under way.'

Emily left and Freya knew that she felt better and so too did she. It had been right to come in today and it was time to get something else under way. Freya was ready to know now if she was pregnant or not so she called Hilary.

'Hi, Freya.'

'Sorry to call on a Sunday,' Freya said.

'I doubt you would without reason,' Hilary said. 'What's happening?'

'I got a positive pregnancy test, I think I'm eight weeks,' Freya said, 'but then last night I bled.'

'Are you still bleeding?'

'No.'

'Any pain?'

'No.'

And Hilary asked some more questions just as calmly as Zack had. 'Do you want to come in today?' she offered.

'On a Sunday?'

'Babies keep their own schedules,' Hilary said. 'I tend

to write off uninterrupted weekends, that's why my vacations are taken overseas.'

As Freya walked out she stopped at James's office. He was a complete workaholic and catching up on some files.

'Hi,' Freya said.

'Freya.' He gave her a nod. 'How was your first client?'

'It went well,' Freya said. 'It was helpful to me too. Thank you, James, for all you did for me back then.'

'I'm your brother,' James said. 'Freya, are you okay?'

'I am,' Freya said.

She was.

However it all unfolded, Freya knew now she would be okay.

'Are we talking?' Freya checked.

'Not really,' James said.

But he was still her brother.

He gave her a smile and Freya headed off, alone, to find out about the baby.

She loved Zack and however he felt about her, or them, she could handle it. That he wanted the baby meant the world. If they got the chance to be, they would be good parents. Possibly unconventional ones, with a father who drifted, but when he was there, Freya knew that he'd be the best dad in the world.

Freya sat in her car for a moment before going in and when tears came she shed them.

She just let them happen for the first time as she acknowledged she wanted *this* baby so much.

This father.

This miracle.

This life and this world.

And so in she went.

Hilary didn't care a jot about Freya's leaking eyes, she was more than used to them.

And then, just as Freya thought she had everything a little more under control, the most appalling thing happened, and she found out she *really* had no control.

'I feel sick,' Freya admitted, as her green breakfast rose in her stomach, and her eyes scanned the room for an exit, because, in her head, no one could see her do that.

'Are you going to throw up?' Hilary asked.

Absolutely she was.

In front of another person!

And there was no chance of being tidy and hidden any more.

'Feel better now?' Hilary asked a few minutes later as she calmly took away the little dish she kept for these moments.

Freya did.

She had cried, she had thrown up, she'd had a cuddle from Zack and had seen her first client, and she was being open and honest and vulnerable.

It was the oddest of days, the scariest of days, but it felt like the nicest too.

'I'm nervous to find out.'

'I know,' Hilary said. 'Have you had a lot of vomiting?'

'Loads,' Freya said. 'And I got dizzy after my run. Should I have run?'

'Do you run regularly?'

'Yes.'

'Then that's fine. Just keep hydrated. You know your body.'

'Sex?' Freya asked.

'Well, that's how babies get there in the first place!'

They talked. Hilary knew already about Freya's past

medical history and after answering some of Freya's
questions Hilary had a few of her own.

'I admit that I'm confused. I'm looking at your notes
and we were talking sperm and egg donors the last time
I saw you.'

That seemed like such a long time ago.

'Do you know who the father is?' Hilary asked, and
Freya laughed at the directness of the question.

'I nearly didn't,' she admitted. 'It was supposed to be
no-name sex.'

'Ha-ha.'

Oh, and the world was so much better when you were
honest.

'He's amazing,' Freya admitted.

'Does he know about the pregnancy?'

'Yes,' Freya said. 'He knows and we both want the
baby. It's just a bit too soon to know if we want the
other...' Then she looked at Hilary and a doctor's office doubled as a very nice confessional. 'Well, it's not
too soon for me to know but I'm trying not to push and
crowd him and just see where we go...'

And it was time to see where this pregnancy was
going.

She lay on an examination table and Hilary had a feel
of her flat stomach and squirted some jelly onto it.

'I guess you might not see much,' Freya said, 'given
it's so early and...' She chatted to keep herself busy. 'I
haven't got a full bladder, so you probably can't—'

'Freya,' Hilary asked, 'how often do you menstruate?'

'Every six months or so.'

'Okay.'

And she was going to be told, no, Freya knew, that
maybe in six months or so's time that she could try again.

'Well, when your ovaries zap, they really zap,' Hilary said, and she turned the screen. 'What do you see?'

A map of the moon, Freya thought, and then she looked again and there was a tiny person, a little bean with a head and a flicker that was a heart.

'Oh...' Freya said, because she was still pregnant.

'And over here,' Hilary said, and Freya's eyes wandered to another little bean and another tiny flicker that was a heart.

'Beautiful embryos,' Hilary said. 'Their position is perfect and their heartbeats are strong and a very good rate...'

'Their?' Freya checked.

'Twins,' Hilary said. 'So get used to throwing up for a few more weeks. Double everything, including the fun.'

'What about the bleeding?'

'It happens,' Hilary said.

'Do I have to be careful?'

'I tend to find they stay put or not whatever a woman does,' Hilary said, 'and these two look to me like they're staying put.'

It was overwhelming, completely, and then she thought about telling Zack that they were having twins and she blew out a breath.

Oh!

Drifter Zack the father of twins.

Freya had blood taken and then thanked Hilary and walked out to her car. She sat there for ages and then drove home and collected Cleo's ashes, feeling so glad she'd told her about the baby before she had died.

Babies!

'Thank you,' Freya said, as she scattered her friend's ashes into the huge ocean that separated the US and Australia. It was a place Cleo had loved in younger days and she was so glad of the gift James had given her at a time she had been so fragile.

Not any more.

Oh, it was a sad and happy day and she watched the sun go down and thought of Cleo. Her phone rang and when she saw it was Zack she answered it.

'Hi,' Freya said.

'You've been crying?'

'Yes, I scattered Cleo's ashes. And don't you dare suggest I get another dog.'

'How was your client?'

'It went well,' Freya said. 'How was surgery?'

'Long,' Zack said. 'Have you had any more bleeding?'

'No.'

'That's good.'

'It is,' Freya said. She didn't want to tell him the news over the phone and decided she'd wait till a more suitable time than the last time she'd dropped a bombshell on him.

'Freya, can I ask a favour? I'm going to be here all night and I'm supposed to be speaking to my parents. They're driving me mad with video chats. Can you stop by the hotel and bring my adaptor?'

'Adaptor?'

'I don't have US appliances and I need to charge my laptop.'

'Oh.'

Well, what chance did they have? Freya thought as she let herself into his hotel room. Even their plugs were wired differently.

Freya lay on the bed in a room that had seen an awful lot of their goings-on and she smiled and decided to pinch a shirt of Zack's while she was there.

And if he found out, so what?

It wasn't a crime to be in lust, she would tell him, and just leave the love part out.

She drove to The Hills and there was Stephanie and her beady eyes at Reception, mentally weighing Freya as she walked in.

'Hi, Freya.'

'Hi.' Freya smiled but didn't stop for conversation. Thanks to Stephanie, rumours were flying but because of her past everyone was assuming her eating disorder was back with a vengeance, rather than that she had a baby on board.

Two babies.

Yikes!

She knocked on his office door and waited.

'Come in,' Zack called, and as she stepped in it dawned on Freya the possible real reason she was here.

The room was in darkness and, as memory served, Zack liked to unwind after Theatre.

'Did you get me here to give you…?' And then she stopped because there was a table and two places laid and it was lit by a candle.

'Valentine's Day,' Zack said.

Oh, so it was.

'What did you get me?' Zack asked.

'You don't do Valentine's Day,' Freya said. She had truly forgotten. 'Actually, I've never done Valentine's Day either.'

She sat at the table and as lovely as it all was it was dark.

'I can't see you,' Freya said, and he laughed and put the lights on.

'Better?' Zack said, and now that she could see him it was. 'I got you a present.'

'Are you trying to make me feel extra-awkward for forgetting?'

'I am.' Zack nodded.

'And then I'd have been accused of being over the top,' Freya said.

'You are over the top, Freya,' Zack said, and he went behind his desk and very carefully carried over a very large box.

Oh, no, Freya thought as he gingerly put it down, and she watched for movement and saw all the little holes punched in the box so it could breathe.

He'd got her a puppy.

And she didn't want one.

'Zack…'

'Just open it.'

'I don't want it.'

'You might when you see it.'

Twins and a dog, Freya thought. Well, there goes any chance of freedom for the next two decades. And what about dog jealousy? And yet of course she was going to love her new puppy, it had come from Zack after all and it beat stealing a shirt from his wardrobe.

Freya pulled back the lid, waiting for a wet nose to peek out, but it didn't.

The box was empty, except for one thing.

A ring.

'Where's my puppy?' Freya croaked.

'A puppy is a big commitment and you have to be very sure,' Zack said. 'Pretty much the same with this. Freya, marry me.'

'Oh, Zack.' Freya shook her head. 'It's way too soon…'

'Not for me.'

'You're marrying me because I'm pregnant.'

'Freya! One, we don't even know if you're pregnant.

Two, I don't marry women because they're pregnant. In fact, usually I'd be running out of the door the same way you did the morning after we met.'

'Really?'

'I'd have had morning sickness just at the thought,' Zack said, 'but I don't feel like that with you. I am in love with you. You're the most difficult, grating person I have ever had the fortune to get to know, and I want to get to know more of you, every day.'

He gave her a smile, a self-satisfied one. 'You'll never be able to top that,' Zack said. 'Even with all your PR skills, you have to concede that I have organised the best Valentine's Day and you, Freya, didn't even get me a card.'

'Of course I did,' Freya said, and she went into her bag and handed him a card, well, a photo of her ultrasound.

'Top that,' Freya said, and she watched his mouth open as he realised that, yes, Freya was pregnant and, because he could read ultrasounds far more easily than Freya, he saw straight away that it was twins.

He laughed.

He had everything he'd dreaded having for so long, but everything had changed—he wanted it all now. With Her.

They had arms and legs and heads and they were so much more than hers or his, they were theirs.

Then Freya watched as his laughter died and tears pooled in his complex eyes.

He wanted his brother to have had this moment.

Zack wanted his brother to this day and for ever he would.

'If we have a boy, can we call him Toby?'

'Yes.'

'He was so unhappy…'

'Not all of him was unhappy and he had someone

he could speak to,' Freya said. 'His last night was spent under the stars, drinking and being honest with you. That's a very nice last night to have had on this earth. I know that I'd take it.'

She turned his world around.

The last night of his brother's life had always been an agonising memory.

Not now.

Zack could now, without reservations, remember their laughter and two brothers talking and just a night where you put the world to rights.

Now they had put their worlds to rights.

'I don't want to tell people yet,' Freya said. 'I am the happiest ever but I want some time to get used to the idea and—' she rolled her eyes '—don't get me started on my parents.'

'Okay, we shan't tell anyone, though you'll start to show fairly soon.'

'No.' Freya shook her head. 'I meant all of it. I meant I need to get used to the idea of us.'

'The idea?' Zack checked.

'That you love me.'

'Get used to it,' Zack said. 'But I get it.'

It was like being handed a prized package and being told to sign for it, the start of a life he had never imagined.

'I'm such a difficult person,' Freya said. 'Don't say I didn't warn you.'

'Freya, I'm so glad I saw you raw the other night. I don't care how much you try to change, or control me, or rush me with my thoughts. You can't.' He smiled. 'You can keep on being you and I'm just going to keep on being me.'

'You're sure?'

'Completely.'

Zack took on the hardest hearts. Ones that others shied away from. But the hardest hearts gave the sweetest rewards and ones that were just so unexpected, because, for all she wanted to keep them quiet for now, on a night that should be just about them, Freya offered to share the happiness around.

'Tell your parents,' Freya said, 'when you video with them.'

'I'm not speaking to them tonight. That was just a ruse to get you here.'

'Tell them,' Freya said.

'Now?' Zack raised an eyebrow. 'I set up a romantic dinner and you want me to speak to my parents?'

Life changes.

Zack rang them and told them to get on the computer and they did.

'Here's the reason I didn't think I could come home in April,' Zack said, and he pulled Freya onto his knee.

'Hi, Freya!' they both shouted.

'They know about me?'

'I told them that there was someone special in my life,' Zack said.

That he had told them about her told Freya that this was real.

'Freya and I shall be home for Christmas, and hopefully with twins.'

'Zack!'

Oh, there was an exclamation mark at the end of his name for a reason.

Freya held up the ultrasound and watched his father put his glasses on, and it was such a precious moment.

'He's having twins,' Zack's father said to his wife and then recovered. 'I mean you are, Freya. I just don't know what to say.'

'We thought he was gay,' Judy confessed.

'Well, I'm pleased to say he's not.' Freya laughed and realised that must have been his mother's reaction when he'd told them about her.

It was a very nice meet-the-parents and after a few moments Zack told them that, unlike in Australia, it was still Valentine's Day in LA, and he was getting back to his.

'Thanks for that,' Zack said, and as he closed the laptop she remained on his knee. 'Well, I guess we've both made it a special Valentine's Day, even if you forgot.'

'I didn't,' Freya lied. 'And I do have something for you.'

She opened up her phone and found a photo and they both smiled as they looked upon the night their world had changed.

A perfect shot.

Almost.

Save a man coming down the stairs and walking over everyone just to be by her side.

'I'm going to love you for ever,' Zack said, and it wasn't a revelation.

They knew.

'I'm going to be busy doing the same,' Freya said.

This was love.

* * * * *

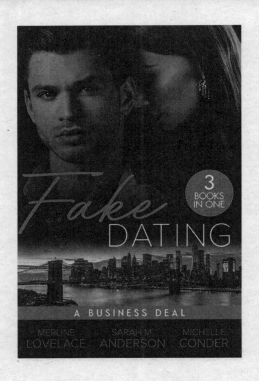

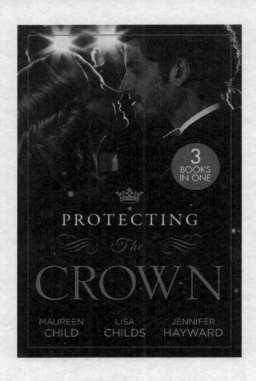

LET'S TALK
Romance

For exclusive extracts, competitions and special offers, find us online:

f MillsandBoon

𝕏 @MillsandBoon

◉ @MillsandBoonUK

♪ @MillsandBoonUK

Get in touch on 01413 063 232

MILLS & BOON

THE HEART OF ROMANCE

A ROMANCE FOR EVERY READER

MODERN

Prepare to be swept off your feet by sophisticated, sexy and seductive heroes, in some of the world's most glamourous and romantic locations, where power and passion collide.

HISTORICAL

Escape with historical heroes from time gone by. Whether your passion is for wicked Regency Rakes, muscled Vikings or rugged Highlanders, awaken the romance of the past.

MEDICAL

Set your pulse racing with dedicated, delectable doctors in the high-pressure world of medicine, where emotions run high and passion, comfort and love are the best medicine.

True Love

Celebrate true love with tender stories of heartfelt romance, from the rush of falling in love to the joy a new baby can bring, and a focus on the emotional heart of a relationship.

Desire

Indulge in secrets and scandal, intense drama and sizzling hot action with heroes who have it all: wealth, status, good looks…everything but the right woman.

HEROES

The excitement of a gripping thriller, with intense romance at its heart. Resourceful, true-to-life women and strong, fearless men face danger and desire - a killer combination!

To see which titles are coming soon, please visit

millsandboon.co.uk/nextmonth

JOIN US ON SOCIAL MEDIA!

Stay up to date with our latest releases, author news and gossip, special offers and discounts, and all the behind-the-scenes action from Mills & Boon...

 @millsandboon

 @millsandboonuk

 facebook.com/millsandboon

 @millsandboonuk

It might just be true love...